CHRISTINA JAMES

FAIR OF FACE

SALT

LONDON

PUBLISHED BY SALT PUBLISHING 2017

2 4 6 8 10 9 7 5 3 1

First published in Great Britain in 2017 by
Salt Publishing Ltd
International House, 24 Holborn Viaduct, London EC1A 2BN United Kingdom

www.saltpublishing.com

Salt Publishing Limited Reg. No. 5293401

A CIP catalogue record for this book is available from the British Library

ISBN 978 1 78463 108 6 (Paperback edition)
ISBN 978 1 78463 109 3 (Electronic edition)

Typeset in Neacademia by Salt Publishing

Printed and bound in Great Britain by Clays Ltd, St Ives plc

For Pamela and Robert, Madelaine and James,
who have devoted their lives to helping children
achieve full potential in a safe environment

Chapter 1

H E SAT IN his prison cell drafting a letter to the Home Secretary. He'd worked assiduously to prove his reliability from the first day he'd started to serve his sentence and it had paid off. He was respected by the other prisoners because he'd devoted a lot of energy to setting up a new literacy programme and he'd long since graduated from building cardboard boxes to working in the library. This job was crucial because among its associated privileges was access to a workstation, which meant he could carry out his research during periods when the library was quiet. His spare time was spent drafting letters that set out in detail why he was innocent, backed up by what he was pleased to call forensic evidence.

So far, he hadn't managed to elicit a reply from the several politicians that he'd contacted, but he did have a large and growing group of supporters whom he had managed to persuade that his conviction was a miscarriage of justice. One of them, a journalist, had even set up a website for him.

He knew that he'd be able to write only part of the letter today: he was still awaiting the results of some tests that he'd asked a ballistics expert who'd joined his 'friends' on the website to carry out for him, but it was worth making a start on it. He took immense trouble over these letters and wanted the words that he chose for this one to be both precise and perfect. It would probably be the first of many drafts, but he could think of no task on which he'd rather be engaged.

He sucked his pen thoughtfully as he mulled over the paragraph he'd just composed. At present, it seemed to him to be incapable of improvement, but he would sleep on it. No natural wordsmith, he'd had to learn by painstaking practice how to capture *le mot juste*. Tomorrow he might not perceive the same degree of elegance in his prose that he believed he saw now. Complacency was not one of his weaknesses.

He ran quickly through the incomplete draft again and decided to call it an evening. He was quite tired and had a busy day ahead of him tomorrow, as a new consignment of books would be arriving and would need to be unpacked and checked in to the library, bringing a small surge of excitement into his monochrome life. Nevertheless, he would watch the news. He never missed it. Apart from keeping him in touch with what was going on in the outside world, there was always the chance that something would crop up that he could add to his portfolio: some point of law or appeal to the Court of European Rights that he could use as a precedent to aid his case. He'd have to get out of here before 'Brexit' kicked in. And he would do it. He would get out.

Chapter 2

JENNIFER DOVE HAD not always been a bookseller. She'd started her working career as a city analyst, and made a substantial but not dazzling amount of money before she'd hit the 'glass ceiling' that she'd always known would defeat her when she reached a certain age. She wasn't bitter about this: she'd used her looks and easy attitude to get herself as far and as fast as she could before the men who'd ruled the companies she'd worked in turned their attention to younger women as nubile and malleable as she had been in her twenties.

Switching to an earlier, more modest, ambition, she'd explored her native Yorkshire for a promising town with no bookshop and finally settled on the city of Wakefield. She'd discovered that once it had boasted two bookshops, one run by a chain, one independent, but both had now closed. Ms Dove had decided to rise to the challenge: she'd refused to believe that the people of Wakefield were so benighted that they would not support a single enterprising bookseller and so it had turned out, though not without the exercise of a considerable amount of ingenuity and hard work. Now coming up to its fifth birthday, her shop sold a judicious selection of children's toys and fancy goods as well as books and cards and she'd built up a solid clientele of account-based customers. She could now include a number of local schools and businesses among her regular patrons.

She hadn't needed to borrow from the bank in order to

establish the business and she'd made it into a success: turn-over was steady throughout the year and her profits were sufficient to fund the modest lifestyle she'd now chosen to lead.

It was the library at the prison that had proved to be the jewel in her crown. HMP Wakefield was a maximum-security jail; many of its inmates were dangerous men serving long or indefinite sentences and the amount of money allocated to their well-being was correspondingly generous. Ms Dove, who had researched local business opportunities as diligently as she'd once delved into the structure and promise of stocks and shares, had in the first months of her bookselling career read a home office report on prison budgets and been pleasantly surprised by Wakefield's expenditure on books. The prison already had a long-standing relationship with a book supplier, but this did not faze her in the least. She embarked upon a professionally-conducted but systematic campaign to oust her rival, playing her hand close to her chest until she finally trumped the other supplier with the 'support local businesses' card. The prison had been her star customer for almost four years now, its spending on books increasing handsomely each new financial period.

For Jennifer Dove, the fact that the prison library account supplied her, if not with her bread and butter, then with many of life's luxuries, was a major but not her only reason for liking it so much. Her life in West Yorkshire was undoubtedly more congenial and less fraught than when she'd worked in The Square Mile, but it lacked the frisson, the edginess, that had made the former so exciting. As a city colleague had said, it had been "like living in a thriller every day of your life". Ms Dove knew the books she was selling to the prison were destined to be read by some of the most evil men in the country and was stimulated by it.

She was immensely intrigued by having discovered the identity of the prison librarian some time ago. An avid reader both of crime fiction and true crime, when she'd received a docket with the words 'T. Arkwright, Librarian' inscribed on it in small, neat letters, she recognised the name of the Brocklesby Farm killer. To make doubly sure, she'd looked Arkwright up on a 'notorious criminals' website and established that he'd been incarcerated at HMP Wakefield. It was next to impossible that the jail held two prisoners who shared such a singular name.

She had not spent more than fifteen years succeeding in the macho, cut-throat world of high finance without negotiating with more psychopaths than most people encountered in a lifetime. She'd been attracted to such men and had enjoyed pitting her wits against theirs. Most of her lovers were forged in the psychopathic mould. She'd both flirted and gone much further than flirting with them, protecting herself from danger by choosing married men she knew would be too hard-headed to jeopardise their fortunes by divorcing wives who were themselves only too happy to turn a blind eye to an indiscretion in return for their share of the fat annual bonus.

It had been fun while it lasted and she'd got out when she could. The problem was that in Wakefield she'd not been able to replace those dangerous, often sadistic lovers with anything approaching a satisfactory sex life. She'd been out with a few local businessmen, but they'd quickly alienated her with their honest intentions and humdrum goals; even the married ones assumed she shared their values and tried to woo her with promises of eventual white weddings and refurbished manor houses. Few had enough conversation to sustain her through a single evening and none showed prowess as lovers. Bored and frustrated, Jennifer Dove had of her own volition been celibate for the whole of the past two years.

This didn't mean that in her own way she wasn't a romantic. She could think of nothing that would appeal to her more than to inveigle herself into the affections of a convicted murderer. She'd made it her business to find out as much about Tristram Arkwright as she could. She knew him to be a good-looking, well-educated man from quite a polished background; an urbane man who liked books; a ruthless man who would stop at nothing to get what he wanted.

Tristram Arkwright was, in short, precisely the type of man that most attracted her.

Chapter 3

THE BLUE TRANSIT van trundled slowly out of the prison courtyard. The warder who had helped to unload it escorted the driver to the inner gates, having hitched a short ride perched in the passenger seat. He told the guards to open the gates and then jumped out and stood to one side. The driver edged the van over the security grid. As soon as its tail was clear of the gates, they glided smoothly together again.

No prisoner was allowed in the courtyard when vehicles were there, but he could watch the departing van from the library window. He knew that Jack Rose, a warder whom he liked, would soon escort a couple of his fellow prisoners to the library. They'd be dragging along a flatbed trolley laden with several cartons of books. Normally this was the high spot of his week: he loved unpacking the books and secretly delighted in the fact that they'd just come in from the outside world; he fancied they smelt of everyday life. He'd take each one carefully out of the box, scrutinising it for faults before stamping it with the prison stamp and sticking in the borrower's date label. Then he'd take meticulous pains to shelve it correctly. The bulk of the delivery would be fiction, but he drew particular pleasure from putting in order the non-fiction that had been requested by those prisoners who were studying. He'd mastered the Dewey Decimal system to make sure the library's small stock of books for study was properly classified.

A faulty volume gave him especial joy, because it meant

he could draft a note to the bookseller and request a replacement. This had happened on two occasions during the past year, once when the book had been bound upside down and once when a sheaf of photographs that formed the centre-piece of a book fell out because they hadn't been tipped in properly. Both times, the notes he'd written had been vetted by a warder, but on both occasions before he'd parcelled up the book. The second time, he'd taken advantage of this small lapse in security to strike up a relationship with the bookseller. The outcome had been more successful than he could ever have hoped.

As he'd predicted, after about ten minutes Jack appeared in the doorway with two of the younger lads. They steered the flatbed trolley awkwardly through the double doors, bashing both as they went, and eventually brought it to a halt by his desk. This month's order had been a big one: there were four large cartons on the trolley. The lads lifted the cartons off one by one and lined them up beside his desk.

"You want me to open those up for you?" said Jack.

"Yes please." Naturally, he wasn't allowed a Stanley knife, so Jack always did the honours. Jack was quite a small bloke and bandy-legged as well, a man he could easily have over-powered and deprived of the Stanley knife and then thrust and thrust and thrust it into him many times and watched the blood run before he brandished it to slash his way out of the prison to freedom. But he wouldn't do that, because he liked Jack and also because it was too fanciful a vision ever to succeed: he'd be most unlikely to escape this super-secure flea-pit and even if he did he'd be on the run for evermore, not a prospect that appealed. He was a cautious man: much better to stick to his plan, bide his time and continue to persuade the Home Secretary of his innocence, even if it was driving him fucking crazy being incarcerated here.

"You all right?" said Jack, looking up from the last of the four boxes as he slit the tape holding the flaps of the lid down. "You're scowling away there. I thought you liked getting a delivery."

"Yeah, I'm fine. Just got a bit of a headache, that's all. You're right: I do like deliveries."

"That's sod's law," said Jack. "You want one of these to help you?" He pointed at the two lads, both of whom were hovering. Library work was preferable to almost anything else the prison had to offer.

"Nah, thanks. Wouldn't give either of them the time of day."

"Watch it, you!" said one of them.

"You watch it, too," he snarled.

"No need for that," said Jack evenly. "We'll leave you to it." He shepherded the two kids out of the library.

That was why he liked Jack: he was a born peacemaker. Easy-going, rather than cowardly. All of the prisoners liked Jack. He'd been like Jack himself once. Could be like him again.

He removed the books from the boxes methodically, in short piles of three or four, and inspected them. His heart wasn't really in it today, but still the unpacking gave him an opportunity to think, helped him to focus. He knew he needed to be careful, too. Jack had deflected his display of bad temper just now, but a different warder might have let him get into a fight and then he'd have lost privileges for days, maybe weeks. Worse, he would have spoiled his pristine record of good behaviour.

9

He checked the books against the invoice. Every item on the order was correct; all the ISBNs matched the list on the flimsy slips of paper he held in his hand. None of the books was damaged, either. It was just as well, he reflected, because he didn't have time to make use of that kind of opportunity at the moment. He'd bide his time where that was concerned.

Chapter 4

JENNIFER DOVE HAD sat at her kitchen table thinking very carefully about what to do next. She knew that sending Tristram Arkwright more than brief notes about the books he bought for the prison would be not only risky, but probably also futile. She wondered if there were some aspect of his personality or interests she could tap into to contact him in a more secure way. She'd researched the man exhaustively, knew everything that had been published about him, even on the most obscure websites. She was a cyberstalker, if there was such a thing. She smiled at the idea. She doubted if Tristram would object to her obsession, if he found out about it. When he found out about it, she corrected herself.

Chapter 5

H E WAS THINKING of her now and feeling excited, but not because he was engaged in playing mind games - if luck was on his side, he knew he might now have found a way of reaching her for real.

Some time ago, the bookshop had provided a replacement for a faulty copy of a novel he'd returned. The book had been sent by post, in a jiffy bag. Jack Rose had brought the bag to him and asked him to open it in his presence. When he tore open the package, he saw immediately that the same copy of the book had fallen out: the shop had obviously packed up the damaged volume again in error.

"That'll have to go back again," he said to Jack. "It's the same one I sent them."

"Bloody typical!" said Jack. "Do it up again straight away, will you, and I'll make sure it catches today's post."

"I'll need to make up an address label."

"Right, you do that. I'll be back in a minute: I just need to check on that light in the corridor. The bulb seems to have gone. I mean, literally gone! Some bastard's removed it."

He watched Jack go out into the corridor. The warder had only half-closed the door, but he couldn't get a view of the librarian's desk from the passageway. There was no-one else in the library: the other prisoners were still at work. He'd have to take a chance on Jack's not opening up the parcel to check on it. The stakes were high: if he forfeited Jack's trust, he'd lose all sorts of other freedoms as well.

He'd have to be quick, now. Fortunately, he'd rehearsed the letter he was about to write many times in his head. He could write it down from memory, without having to waste time on whether the words conveyed exactly what he intended. He debated whether to type it: not only would it look more professional, but if it were subsequently discovered he would have an outside chance of getting away with denying that he was its author. He decided against this because he didn't know enough about computers to know what kind of trace it might leave, even if he didn't save the file. Instead, he set up the printer to print the largest, blackest letters that he could squeeze onto the biggest label the jiffy bag would take while he wrote the note. It was an ancient printer, and he knew it would chunter away at the task for some time.

As it clattered on laboriously, he wrote his note quickly on the back of the returns slip, tucked it into the book and rammed the book back into the same jiffy bag, which he secured with brown tape. He stuck the label over the address of the prison and for good measure taped round that as well. He crossed out the address of the shop that had been written on the back of the parcel and was just writing 'HMP WAKEFIELD' in small neat capitals when Jack returned.

"Beats me why anyone would want to take that light bulb," said Jack. "I've put a new one in, anyway. Let me know if you see someone trying to fiddle about with it."

"Sure I will. Thanks for taking this for us." He handed Jack the parcel.

"Christ, do you think you've put enough tape on that? And look at the size of the label! They'd have to be blind not to be able to read that!"

"I had to put a big label on it to cover the first address," he said smoothly.

"I suppose you did. By rights I should have asked you to leave it open until I'd checked it, but you can't have slipped much in there while I've been gone, can you?" Jack grinned.

"Nah, only a nail bomb and an exploding letter."

"You shouldn't make jokes like that. Someone might take them seriously. But I can tell this weighs the same as it did when I brought it in. I'll trust you."

"Thanks, Jack. I'll trust you, too."

"Less of the cheek. You need to show me some respect," said Jack cheerfully. He went off with the parcel in the crook of his elbow.

He was taking a gamble, but he'd been a cautious gambler all his life, if there was such a thing. In his mind's eye he envisaged the bookseller - Jennifer Dove, her name was, a gentle and gullible-sounding name if ever there was one - opening up the envelope. She'd probably be a county sort of lady wearing a nice skirt and jumper, good quality, hard-wearing clothes not unlike the ones his 'mother' would have chosen. She'd quickly realise her mistake, be embarrassed to have the book sent back again. Then she'd find his note. He'd sent her a couple of notes before, just short little matter-of-fact messages. She'd responded equally curtly, but at least they'd established a relationship now, however tenuous. That and making up for her silly error might prompt her to look on his request favourably. As in the previous communications, he'd signed the

14

letter 'T. Arkwright, Librarian'; he hadn't otherwise identified himself.

It was a gamble. On the whole, he liked gambles; and there was precious little opportunity for them in this place.

Chapter 6

WHEN TRISTRAM ARKWRIGHT had first written directly to Jennifer Dove, she felt very pleased with herself. Her clever ruse had worked: she'd guessed that someone as driven as she understood Tristram Arkwright to be (at his trial, his defence counsel had said that he suffered from Obsessive-Compulsive Disorder) would not let it pass if she 'mistakenly' sent back a faulty book. They had since used the same tactic several times to communicate. Then she had another brainwave: she decided to apply to be Arkwright's official prison visitor. There was quite a lot of red tape to work through, but she knew she would eventually succeed. She would be, she was certain, meeting Arkwright for the first time very shortly. Anticipation of what they would say to each other filled her waking hours. She guessed he'd be both civilised and courteous in manner, but that small glimpses of his depravity would be apparent to someone as perceptive and well-versed in his past as she was.

Chapter 7

"POLICE IN SPALDING *have closed Fulney Lane, following the discovery earlier today in a house in Lady Margaret Dymoke Street of two bodies. No further official details have been released. Local residents say the victims are a mother and her infant daughter.*"

Amy Winter was driving home to Brocklesby Farm as she listened to the news on the radio. The short bulletin made her shudder. She reasoned that it would have had the same effect on anyone, but, for Amy, it also immediately triggered an unbearable rush of conscience.

Chapter 8

IT'S A RUN-DOWN house in one of the roughest streets in town. The council denies that it designates 'sink streets' to house the rowdiest and most unreliable of its tenants, but I'd be willing to bet that more than half the residents of Lady Margaret Dymoke Street are 'known to the police'.

Tim is sitting outside in his car, waiting for me. There is already a gaggle of reporters loitering nearby. They've been herded across to the other side of the road by PCs Giash Chakrabati and Verity Tandy. They're standing a little apart from a motley gathering of residents. Giash acknowledges my arrival with a curt nod. Verity's face is blotchy and she looks flustered. She barely registers me. It's obvious they're both very upset.

I get out of my car as Tim comes to join me. We both cross the police barrier as quickly as we can, but it's impossible to avoid being caught in the flashlights of half a dozen cameras as we enter the house. A couple of the reporters call out to us, but their tone is half-hearted, much less raucous and intrusive than usual: the death of a small child is distressing to even the most hardened of hacks. The neighbours mostly look downcast, too, though I notice a few of them are gaping curiously. It's unlikely there'll be universal observation of decorum in Lady Dymoke Street.

Tim grabs my elbow and leads me inside the house; we stop at the foot of the stairs.

"Are you ok?" he asks.

"I've no reason not to be, yet," I say, managing a smile. "Thanks for asking, though. I admit I'm not looking forward to going up those stairs."

"No, it's a distressing sight. I shan't forget it in a hurry. Nothing horrific to see, although I know that's scant comfort. The baby looks as if it's sleeping."

"And the mother?"

"I think she woke up, but only just. She's got a startled expression, as far as I can tell. But rigor mortis is well advanced and it may have distorted her features."

"Any idea when it happened?"

"No. I don't think it was today. Perhaps yesterday, or even longer ago. Professor Salkeld's on his way. I'm hoping he'll be able to give us some idea, but I'm certain he'll say that he can't give a precise time of death."

"Should I wait until he's here before I go up there?"

"Your decision. He'll start moving them around, once he's got some photos, so you might like to take a look now. One of Patti's team has already been photographing for Forensics. She sent some white suits; they're in the kitchen."

"Who found them?"

"Giash and Verity. The local postie called the station. He saw that the front door was wide open very early this morning and thought it strange that it was still like it when he passed by later, but he says he didn't come into the house."

"You'd think one of the neighbours would have noticed."

"Some of them must have done. You know the rule around here: you mind your own business, and you certainly don't involve us in anything."

"Even so, that means that someone besides the killer could

19

have been in the house since. Local kids, for example. There are dozens of kids living in the Lady Dymokes, some of them half wild."

"You're right. But surely even these kids would report a murder?"

"Who knows? Besides, they may have come into the house without going upstairs."

"I'm sure Patti's lot will find evidence of that, if there is some. You ready now?"

I nod and let Tim lead the way up the steep, narrow flight of stairs, which are covered in the old- fashioned way with a strip of carpet up the middle secured with heavy brown stair-rods, the legacy, perhaps, of a previous tenant. The surround on either side has been inexpertly varnished. The carpet itself is dangerously worn in places and speckled with thick drifts of fluff. Its colour is indeterminate.

The woman's body is lying on the bed in the larger of the two bedrooms. It is skewed sideways, her legs still entangled in the bedclothes, as if she died in the act of trying to get up. She is . . . was . . . a small woman with a round face and rather bulbous features. Her brown stringy hair is shoulder-length, greasy and greying. Her head is turned towards me. As Tim says, she looks surprised, as if she couldn't believe what was happening to her.

There's not much furniture in the room besides the double bed and a small old wardrobe with an oval mirror set in the door. Otherwise, just a chair with a rounded back that might have started life in a pub. It's heaped with clothes.

I move closer to the bed and see the pressure marks on her neck. There can be little doubt that she was strangled, but I know Professor Salkeld will want to find other evidence beside the bruising. There's an unpleasant odour coming from the bed. It could be caused by putrefaction, but I think it's a bit early for that. It's more likely that the bedclothes haven't been washed recently. The room is dark and Tim doesn't want us to touch the light switch even with gloves on, but the sheets look grubby and the bedspread bears stains in several places.

I crouch down to look under the bed.

"There's a cardboard box pushed into the corner on the far side of the headboard," I say.

"I saw that, too," says Tim. "Probably best to leave it for now. We'll ask Forensics to get it out when they come."

"Have you looked inside the wardrobe?"

"Yes. Nothing much in there. Mainly clothes, as you would expect, and a few other items: Christmas tree decorations and that sort of thing."

Tim moves into the other bedroom. I go after him reluctantly, dreading the shock of seeing a dead child. He stands aside and I peer into the cot. Tim's right – the baby almost looks as if she's asleep, though her skin is waxy and her face has a bluish tinge. She's wearing a yellow towelling suit. The fastener at the neck has been unbuttoned to reveal some bruising there.

There's suddenly a huge lump in my throat. It's threatening to choke me. I pass the back of my hand across my eyes as the room swims before them. Involuntarily, I grasp the side of the cot to balance.

"Steady!" Tim says. He puts out his hand to take my elbow again.

"Sorry! I'm all right, really I am. It's the sense of waste. It's so sad."

"I know. Child deaths are always the worst."

21

Pulling myself together, I look into the cot again.

"It's all very clean," I say. "The baby was well looked after, even if the rest of the house seems neglected. Do we know what she was called?"

"According to the next-door neighbour, the baby's name was Bluebelle. The mother's name was Tina. Tina Brackenbury."

"I wonder whose the single bed is?"

"I assume it's a spare bed."

"You may be right, but it's been slept in and not made properly."

"The neighbour didn't say there was anyone else living here. She mentioned a bloke, but said he left some time ago. According to her, he was violent."

"I'll check to see if we have any records of domestic call-outs to this address. Though I doubt if the partner did it, if that's what he was. Strangling isn't typical of abusive men. They're more likely to lose it and batter the woman and the kids. Or knife them."

"It's unlikely that he'd have been sleeping in the baby's room if he did show up again. But we do need to find out who last slept in that bed."

"What's the neighbour's name?"

"Mrs Wolansky. If you want to visit her while we're waiting for Professor Salkeld, the two back yards are joined. There's a privet hedge between them, but it's more or less dead."

Chapter 9

H E FLICKED ON the television, lolling back on his bed, and was annoyed to see he'd missed the first few minutes. However, the main story was about cutting public spending on defence and therefore of no interest to him.

The next item electrified him. He sat bolt upright and turned up the sound.

"Earlier today, police in Spalding were called to a house in Lady Margaret Dymoke Street and discovered two bodies there. It is understood that the victims are related and that one is a woman in her thirties, the other an infant. A few minutes ago, Detective Inspector Tim Yates, of South Lincolnshire Police, said that police were carrying out formal identification procedures and would release the names of the victims as soon as possible. Neighbours say that the family was well-known in the area and kept themselves to themselves. Fulney Lane, the through road leading to the Dymoke estate, has been temporarily closed. Drivers are advised to follow diversions . . ."

He switched off the rest of the news. He needed to spend the time doing some quality thinking.

Chapter 10

MRS WOLANSKY IS a large-boned, spare-framed woman in her early sixties. Her long, doleful face is almost as grey as her hair, the skin pitted and deeply wrinkled. She wears a short-sleeved blue cotton garment with large patch pockets, a cross between a wrap-around apron and what the French call a 'house dress'.

"Come in," she says, opening the door as soon as I knock to announce myself, as if she is expecting me. She points towards the kitchen. It turns out to be painted in cheerful shades of yellow and is clean and tidy. A middle-aged man, possibly older, is sitting at the square table; he looks up as I enter, but appears to stare straight through me.

"That's Marek," Mrs Wolansky says, her English heavily inflected. "Do not trouble about him. He is a little bit . . ." She puts her forefinger to her temple and twists it.

"Is he your son?"

"Yes. I care for him ever since he was born. He is a good boy. He repays me."

I look at Marek, whose head is now lolling forwards, and wonder what he can possibly give his mother in return for her care.

"Does anyone else live here?"

She thrusts her hands into the patch pockets. The cotton's flimsy, and I see her fingers twitching nervously.

"No. Marek's father left. He could not cope."

I nod and decide to get to the point.

"Mrs Wolansky, I think you've already spoken briefly with my colleague, DI Yates?"

"Yes. He asked about Tina and her family. I told him the baby's name is Bluebelle."

"You know that they have both died?"

She nods without speaking.

"Was there anyone else in the family?"

"Tina's man left her before the baby was born. His name is Frank. There's Opal, too, her other daughter."

"Does Opal live with her mother?"

"No, she lives in the South somewhere. With a soldier. She has her own baby now."

"Has she been here recently?"

"I do not think so. She doesn't often come."

"There's a bed in the baby's room. It looks as if someone's slept in it recently. Do you have any idea who that might have been?"

"Of course. It is Grace."

"Who's Grace?"

"She's from the social. Tina was fostering her."

"Why didn't you mention her before?"

Mrs Wolansky shrugs.

"You asked about family. Grace isn't family."

"But she usually lives next door?"

"Yes. I've said. She is being fostered."

"Mrs Wolansky, if Grace was in the house when her foster mother and sister died and she's missing now, we need to find her. Her life may be in danger."

Unexpectedly, the old woman lets out a throaty cackle.

"Not her. She will be with Chloe Hebblewhite, her friend.

She spends most of her time round at Chloe's. Tina said she's been sleeping there."

"I urgently need to find Grace and speak to her. And Chloe, too. Do you have Chloe's address?"

Serious and reserved again, Mrs Wolansky shakes her head.

"But I can tell you where she lives. I don't know the number, but is the first house you come to in Lady Margaret Dymoke Crescent."

"Thank you. And you haven't seen Grace during the past couple of days?"

She shakes her head again.

"Or anyone else entering or leaving Mrs Brackenbury's house?"

"No."

"Did you notice that the front door had been left open?"

"I don't go out much." She's defensive now. "It is not possible for me to leave Marek, except when he is at the day centre."

"When is that?"

"Sometimes Tuesdays, always Thursdays. And sometimes on Fridays, too."

I look across at Marek. The mention of his name has caused him to stir and raise his head again. His dull eyes peer out from an unhealthy casing of flesh. I can find no spark of intelligence there and involuntarily turn away from him.

"Thank you, Mrs Wolansky. You've been very helpful. One more thing: you'll have seen the reporters outside. We'd be extremely grateful if you wouldn't talk to them for the moment."

"I will not do that. I don't want no-one snooping here. Marek must be left in peace."

Chapter 11

TIM DECIDED TO wait in the kitchen of Tina Brackenbury's house for Professor Salkeld. It was a dingy room with fly- and grease-spattered paintwork, in considerable need of modernisation. The gas cooker was old, its cobalt-coloured enamel chipped. The radiants were black and greasy. A work surface ran along one wall, forming the top of a row of cupboards fixed to the floor. Higher cupboards were fastened to the wall and there was a larder to the left of the back door, which opened straight into the room. Two pans had been left to steep in a bowl full of water in the sink, but the washing-up rack was stacked with clean plates and cups. A cardboard pizza box was wedged behind the bin. There was a small table on which cereal boxes, newspapers and an open bag of sugar rubbed shoulders untidily with each other. An assortment of shoes had been heaped by the door, on the back of which were several coat-hooks bearing a woman's and a girl's anorak, a hand towel and two or three tea towels. The red-tiled floor was grubby. Two small plastic bowls on a spread sheet of newspaper appeared to have been used for cat food.

There was nothing remarkable about this room at all; Tim guessed that it looked like the kitchens of many houses in the area. He noted that the back door was locked. The key had been removed. They'd have to look for it, but he doubted that its being missing was a matter of significance, particularly as the front door had been left wide open. There were no signs of forced entry at either door. It looked as if the perpetrator had just walked in off the street. At what time, though? Tina Brackenbury had been in bed, which suggested that she and the baby had died between late evening and the following morning, either yesterday or the day before, but this was just surmise. Tina could have gone to bed early or slept late, or felt unwell or simply been tired out and needed to sleep during the day. Katrin had often snatched a couple of hours' sleep when Sophia had been the same age as Bluebelle. Thinking of Sophia made him feel unbearably sad for the child who had died. Harsh that many of Bluebelle's contemporaries would see out the century, while her short life was already over.

Tim was startled from his reverie by a tapping at the back door.

"DI Yates?" He recognised Giash Chakrabati's voice. "Can you open this door, sir?"

Tim looked out of the fly-spotted window. By craning his neck, he could just see Giash standing close to the door-step. His figure was partly obscured by the two young girls who were accompanying him. Tim thought they looked about twelve years old.

Tim, who was still wearing latex gloves, tapped on the window. One of the girls stared straight at him. She met his eye and giggled.

"PC Chakrabati," said Tim, as Giash stepped sideways so that he was properly in view, "The door's locked and we haven't found the key yet. If those girls have something to tell us, can you and PC Tandy interview them in one of the cars? I don't want to let anyone else into the house."

"I've got a key," said the girl who'd giggled.

28

Her simple statement filled Tim with unease. He was at a disadvantage, talking through the glass to an unidentified child. What did Giash mean by bringing the girl round to the back of the house like this? And who was she?

As if he'd read Tim's thoughts, PC Chakrabati immediately answered both questions.

"This girl's name is Grace, sir. She says she's Mrs Brackenbury's daughter. I've brought her to the back of the house because the reporters were trying to talk to her."

Tim had to think quickly. If the girl really was Tina Brackenbury's daughter, did she know that her mother and sister were dead? It seemed impossible she could be unaware of the murders unless she'd just arrived from somewhere well outside the neighbourhood, yet her behaviour showed no distress. And where had she been for the past couple of days? One thing was certain, Giash was right about the reporters. If the girl was genuine, to let her into their clutches would spell disaster, especially if she didn't yet know about the deaths. Histrionics in the street were the last thing they needed.

"All right, PC Chakrabati, if she has a key let her use it to open the door and come into the kitchen. Who's the other girl?"

"Her friend, sir. Grace says she's been staying with her. Her name's Chloe."

Tim sighed. He wished Juliet would come back quickly.

"You'd better let them both come in. But only into the kitchen."

The door was unlocked smoothly and the girl who had caught Tim's eye entered the kitchen, closely followed by Giash Chakrabati. The other girl seemed to hesitate. Grace turned and shouted at her.

"Come in, Chloe, don't be nesh."

The second girl shuffled through the door and stood next to the first. She looked terrified.

"PC Chakrabati, would you close the door, please? Use a cloth so that you don't touch it."

Giash Chakrabati was in the act of removing a handkerchief from his pocket when Juliet appeared in the doorway.

"DI Yates, according to Mrs Wolansky, there's another girl living here. She's a fos . . ."

Juliet halted mid-sentence as she entered and saw the two girls. One of them was huddled into a corner, her shoulders hunched, as if she was trying to make herself as small as possible. The other girl smiled at her. It was a smile that lit up her whole face. Tim saw that she was jarringly pretty.

"DS Armstrong," Tim said, "This is Grace, and her friend Chloe. I think Grace is the person you mean."

To both Tim's and Juliet's astonishment, Grace held out her hand to Juliet.

"Pleased to meet you," she said.

Chapter 12

TIM ASKS IF he can speak to me outside for a minute. We leave Giash Chakrabati with the two girls and stand in the back garden a little way from the house, talking in whispers.

"I'm not sure if Grace Brackenbury knows about her mother and sister. From the way she's behaving, I doubt it."

"I'm inclined to agree with you, but I don't see how she could fail to have found out. The Dymokes are buzzing with the news, not to mention that she's been approached by one of those reporters out there, although Giash did stop him from speaking to her."

"Even so, we're going to have to tell her formally, to make sure she knows exactly what's happened. We'll have to contact social services, as well. Obviously she can't stay here tonight. And she needs to be placed in the care of an adult."

"Apparently she's been staying at the other girl's house for a few days, which could explain why she might not know anything, although it's only a couple of streets away. I imagine she may be able to go back there, but you're right: social services will have to make the arrangements."

"We need to know where she's been for the last few days and when she last saw her mother alive. Also, what she knows about visitors to the house, or anything unusual she can tell us – whether her mother seemed worried or depressed about anything, for example. She has to be interviewed."

"You want me to do it, don't you?"

"Yes, but you'll have to tell her they're dead first. I guess that that means bringing a social worker here before you can do anything."

"What about the friend?"

"She's a damned nuisance, but we don't want the reporters to get hold of her. If she lives as close as you say, we could send Verity to fetch her mother and take them both home in the car."

"That's a good idea, as long as it doesn't upset Grace. And wouldn't it be handy for the mother to stay to meet the social worker as well, in case she is willing to look after Grace for the time being? They're certain to want to meet the mother before they agree to it."

"I suppose you're right. Who do you know? Can you get hold of someone quickly?"

"I saw Marie Krakowska yesterday. She said she'd be on call this week and next. She's very experienced."

"I'm not too keen on her. She's a bit of a pantomime dame . . . and always a hundred and ten per cent on the kid's side, which often doesn't help."

"We're not talking about a young offender here. Grace is a primary school kid who's just lost her mother."

"Sorry, I was forgetting. Is she really just a primary school kid? She seems older, somehow."

"According to Mrs Wolansky, both Grace and Chloe are about to go into the last year at Lady Margaret Dymoke First School."

"Ok. See if you can get hold of Marie. If she can come, she can help you break the news to Grace."

"I'll have to let her decide whether Grace is fit for

questioning afterwards. My guess is that Marie'll say we have to wait at least another day."

"Well, do your best to persuade her, unless the kid gets really hysterical, of course. I'd better go back in now. Will you call Marie while you're still out here?"

"Probably the best idea, isn't it? Then I'll come and ask Chloe for her address. I know where she lives, but not the number."

Chapter 13

TIM WAS FILLED with dread as he walked back into the kitchen. He hated scenes. He'd known he was being cowardly when he'd asked Juliet to break the news to Grace, but at the same time he felt deeply for this kid who'd just been bereaved in the most horrific way possible. Did she have any inkling of what she was about to be confronted with? It dawned on him that Grace had not asked where her mother was nor why her house and street were crawling with policemen and reporters. Kids often got caught up in the excitement of the moment and didn't think about the implications of injury, crime or death until much later, but Grace seemed mature for her age . . . no, mature was the wrong word. *Knowing*, that was what he meant.

She was still standing in the kitchen, talking to Giash Chakrabati. With the flick of an eye, she showed she was aware that Tim had come back into the house, but she didn't pause or acknowledge him. For the first time, Tim looked at her properly. She was very fair – her hair was almost silver – and extremely . . . again, he groped for the right word, which wasn't 'pretty'. This girl was beautiful, dramatically so. There was nothing of the softness of prettiness about her: hers was a disturbing sort of beauty. She had a long face with fine bone structure and her green eyes were huge, but also both watchful and bold. Her lips were full and fell into a pout when she wasn't speaking. She was talking animatedly to Giash, making a strenuous effort to command his attention. The other girl, Chloe, stood by silently, shrinking into herself. The difference between her and Grace was striking: it was as if Chloe, not Grace, had been swept into a catastrophe.

Grace had evidently been telling Giash about how she and Chloe had been spending their time together over the past few days. Occasionally she glanced at Chloe for endorsement of her words. "And today we went for a bike ride, didn't we, Chloe? We got as far as Crowland, didn't we?" Chloe nodded miserably. Tim was struck by Grace's voice. It wasn't musical – it was too flat for that – but, for want of a better word, it was almost 'posh'. Grace had no trace of a Lincolnshire accent; nor did she speak like someone from the Lady Dymokes.

Juliet came into the kitchen again.

"Marie Krakowska says she'll be here in twenty minutes," she said, addressing Tim. Grace stopped talking immediately. She stared at Juliet, sizing her up.

"Thanks," said Tim. "I think we need to get rid of the Press now. PC Chakrabati, can you go and tell the reporters we'll be giving a statement from the station later? Say that we won't be issuing any information from this address."

Giash nodded. Tim guessed he was only too keen to be given a task that took him out of the house. Grace Brackenbury seemed to be annoyed at his departure, as if he'd insulted her by not continuing to focus on what she had been saying. She stuck out her lower lip for a moment, frowning in concentration. Then she spoke.

"Can we see them?" she said.

"See them?" Tim echoed, doubting his ears.

"Yes, see the bodies. Me and Chloe would like to see the bodies. If that's all right."

Chloe put her hands over her eyes.

"No," she shrilled, almost beside herself. "No, I don't want to see them. I don't! I don't! I want me mam!"

I feel as horrified as Tim looks. Neither of us knows how to treat hysterical ten-year-olds. None of us has had first-hand experience of children of that age except Giash; perhaps Tim shouldn't have sent him out to talk to the reporters, but he's the only one wearing uniform and they're more likely to take notice of him. It's going to be a long twenty minutes before Marie Krakowska gets here.

I put my arm round Chloe. She's an unprepossessing child. She has none of Grace's poise or good looks: she's skinny and raw-boned, with rats' tails of brown hair in need of a wash. She leans her head into my jacket, burying her face. As Chloe clings yet harder to me, a sudden impulse makes me glance at Grace. She's stopped talking and her face has hardened. Her expression is disturbing: unmistakably it shows naked contempt for Chloe, but there's something else there, too: a kind of gloating, an attempt to cover up some other emotion? I can't read her, but I'm certain I've never seen such a look on a child's face before.

Then Tim is speaking to her gently and the look vanishes. She recomposes her face, and is now concentrating on his words, grave and attentive. Tim's words to her surprise me: I thought we'd agreed we couldn't interview the girls, however sensitively, without professional help. But I can see that Grace herself has precipitated this, made the question inevitable, in fact.

"Grace," he says, crouching so that his face is level with hers, "how did you know about the bodies? Did someone tell you?"

She shrugs, flashes him a quick, bold, challenging look and shrugs again.

"I don't know. I suppose they must have."

"Who was it, Grace? This is important. It's important that we know who told you, and when."

She tosses her head and smiles a little, as if he's given her an idea.

"I expect it was one of those men outside. Did you say they were reporters? I expect one of them told me. Me and Chloe were just coming round to get a few things."

Tim hasn't asked her why she is there. She volunteers the information as if he's likely to require it, even though she had been returning to her own home.

"Which man, Grace? Would you be able to point to him if you saw him again?"

"I don't know. You've sent them away, haven't you?"

"Yes. Now, Grace, can you tell me when you last saw your Mum and Bluebelle?"

"Just before I went to Chloe's. It was Saturday morning."

I'm aware that Chloe has stopped snivelling and turned her head sideways so that she can listen. Grace doesn't look at her.

There's a slight commotion outside. Giash Chakrabati comes back into the kitchen with a tall, spare man in his wake.

"Professor Salkeld!" Tim says. "Thank you for getting here so quickly. I wasn't expecting you for another hour or so."

"Aye," says the Professor laconically. "Ye're lucky, aren't ye?"

Grace immediately transfers her attention to the newcomer. She gives him a bright smile.

37

"Who's this young lady, now?" he says. He looks at Tim questioningly. It's clear what he's thinking: why are there children here and how are they involved?

"It's my Mum up there," Grace explains. Her tone is chatty, informative. "She's dead. And my baby sister, too."

I've seen Stuart Salkeld at work a few times, and know that it takes a lot to faze him, but he blanches visibly at her words.

"Is that so?" he says at length. He grimaces desperately over Grace's head, imploring Tim to rescue him.

"This is Professor Salkeld," Tim says awkwardly. "He's a Home Office pathologist. That's a kind of scientist."

She nods and continues to smile at Stuart Salkeld, staring into his face in a way that I can see unnerves him.

"Well, best get on," he says, then, addressing Tim, "Can you show me the way?"

"I can show you if you like," says Grace. I feel Chloe clutching at me harder.

"It's better you stay here with DS Armstrong," says Tim quietly. "Professor Salkeld can come with me."

Grace puts on a sulky look, but she doesn't try to follow them as they leave the kitchen via the door that leads into the hall.

"Can we have a drink?" she says, addressing me.

"Yes. I've got a bottle of water in my bag. You can share it."

"But there's probably some Coke in the fridge," says Grace, evidently prepared to argue.

"We mustn't touch the fridge at the moment, Grace. I'm sorry. Would you like some water?"

"No," she says, "and Chloe wouldn't, either."

I'm casting around desperately to think of what to do with the two girls until Verity comes back with Chloe's mother, when Tim returns. It's impossible to leave them on their own, so we have to talk about what to do next in front of them.

"We've got two options," I say. "Either we use one of the rooms here, or we take them to the station."

"You asked Marie to come here, didn't you?"

"Yes, but perhaps I should have thought more carefully about it. If we stay here, we're running the risk of contaminating evidence."

"But if we take them to the station, we'll still have to wait until Marie comes and you can bet she won't like that idea. She'll say we'll be frightening them unnecessarily by taking them there unaccompanied, when they're probably already traumatised."

I'm acutely aware that once again Grace is listening intently, although I doubt if she can understand the point that Tim's making.

"I suppose their prints and DNA are on everything here, anyway," I say slowly. "As long as we don't let them go upstairs, our best bet is probably to use one of the rooms here, at least for a preliminary conversation."

Tim nods. Grace is still watching him.

Chapter 14

TIM AND JULIET moved Grace and Chloe to the dining-room which led off the kitchen and set out two dining chairs in the middle of the floor. Juliet told them to sit down while she stayed with them until Chloe's mum came, herself remaining standing. Grace was more subdued now, sitting silently beside Chloe, her hands folded demurely in her lap. Chloe herself had become yet more withdrawn following her outburst. Tim returned briefly to see if Stuart Salkeld needed him, but he was back in the dining-room with them when Marie Krakowska arrived.

Tim never thought he'd be so pleased to see Marie as he was when he watched her draw up in her flamboyant red Astra. She was a professional child psychologist who combined zealous support for every child who came within her care with a somewhat equivocal attitude towards the police. Originally, she'd worked independently of South Holland Social Services, but she'd been seconded to so many of the cases in which they'd been involved that she was now a full-time employee. There was no denying that Marie could be effective, and she had her champions among the social workers, including Tom Tarrant, a man whom Tim held in considerable esteem.

Tim was a bit surprised when Marie turned up with Tom in tow, but on the whole he thought this was a positive development. Tom would be able to moderate Marie's behaviour if she became too overbearing. He was curious to know why she'd invited him, though.

Tom himself explained this when Tim and Juliet left the girls alone for a short time to go outside to greet them.

"I've come because I'm supporting Chloe Hebblewhite's family at present," he said. "Her mother has seven children to look after, and no partner. Quite frankly, she struggles. The two oldest boys can be very unruly. Chloe's one of the middle ones. She's not doing well at school. She's quite a withdrawn child."

"Do you know Grace Brackenbury as well?"

"Not personally. We do have a file on her, but it doesn't tell us very much. She's a foster-child. There is a North Lincolnshire social worker we can contact if we think Grace is having problems."

Tim let this sink in for a moment.

"Are you saying that Tina Brackenbury isn't Grace's real mother?"

"That's precisely what I'm saying. Why? Does it make any difference?"

"No. No, it doesn't. It's just that she referred quite clearly to her 'mother and baby sister'.

"Preconceived ideas, DI Yates! How often have I warned you about them?" Marie tutted, but in a good-natured way. She was paler than usual and her normally robustly rotund body seemed to be sagging a little. Tim supposed that, like himself and his colleagues, she was profoundly shocked by the murder of an infant. "We encourage foster children to identify with their foster parents. It helps to assimilate them into the family and we hope that sometimes the family will want to keep them for good. Adopt them, in other words."

41

"So Brackenbury isn't Grace's real surname?"

"No," said Tom. "Her name is Winter. Grace Winter. That's one thing the file does tell us."

"Can you trace her birth parents?"

"We should be able to trace the mother, at least. Usually we'd have details of her identity and other basic information about her in the file, though, so it may be that she doesn't want to be traced. We'd have to get in touch with North Lincs social services to find out more. Grace's file is unusually thin; there could be a reason for that."

"What sort of reason?"

"It could be any number of things, but often it's because there's something in the child's background that social services feel it's in her interest to keep concealed. It could be something as simple as that both parents have abandoned her."

"That doesn't sound very 'simple' to me," said Tim. "But go on. What other reasons might there be?"

"One of the parents might be notorious – have a criminal record, for example; or, less sensationally, a history of mental illness. Either of those two things could put potential foster carers off. Or perhaps the child herself has done something anti-social in the past."

"But surely if that were the case, any prospective foster-parents should have the right to know?"

"That's correct, normally they would. And no child would be put out to foster if they were considered a possible danger, either to others or to themselves."

Tim looked at Tom sharply, wondering if he had any particular reason to say this, but his expression betrayed nothing except a desire to help.

"We're going to need to find out more about Grace's

background," he said. "And probably Chloe's, too. Her mother's on her way."

"We're well-acquainted with Mrs Hebblewhite," said Marie. Tim couldn't fail to pick up the irony that had crept into her tone. "It would be useful if we could have at least a brief conversation with the two girls before she gets here. Is there anything that you'd like to tell us before we see them? DS Armstrong said they'd just turned up here when she called me. She said Grace had been staying with the Hebblewhites. How much do either of them know about what's happened?"

"They certainly know that Tina Brackenbury and the baby are dead," said Juliet. "Grace asked if they could see the bodies."

"Really?" said Marie. There was a long pause. "What did you tell her?"

"We didn't answer her," said Tim. "We didn't know what to say. She didn't ask again."

"It's not unusual for children to display what to adults seems like morbid curiosity," Marie said when she finally spoke, but Tim noticed that her pallor had turned ashen. Tom made no comment.

Tim opened the dining-room door. The two girls sprang apart, but not before he noticed that Grace had been holding Chloe's arm behind her back. Chloe was looking scared out of her wits.

Grace lowered her hands into her lap and looked up meekly. She clocked the newcomers immediately and smiled at them in the same way that she'd smiled at Stuart Salkeld. Tim thought he saw a flicker of recognition when she spotted Tom Tarrant, but he couldn't be sure. Chloe obviously knew who he was.

She squirmed as if embarrassed, trying to lean back behind Grace so that Tom couldn't see her face.

"Hello, Chloe," he said quietly. "It's all right, you're not in any trouble. I've just come here to help you, that's all."

"Are you going to help me as well?" demanded Grace pertly.

"Yes, Grace, if you need me to. Do you remember me? We met when you came to live here."

"Yes," said Grace. "You work for the social." The term sounded strange coming from her lips. Tim guessed it was an expression she'd learned from Chloe Hebblewhite.

"That's right," said Tom gently. He crouched down on his haunches. "And this is Ms Krakowska. I think Chloe's met her before. She's come to help you both, too."

Marie Krakowska plumped herself down on the floor, wafting the scent of patchouli released by a flurry of cotton skirt which she proceeded to draw circumspectly over her knees.

"That's better," she said. "Are you girls quite comfortable?"

Chloe nodded obligingly. She'd perked up quite a bit since Tom Tarrant had come into the room. Grace continued to fix both Marie and Tom with her smile.

"Good," Marie continued brightly. "Now I'm going to ask you a few questions. Nothing to worry about. We must try hard to help DS Armstrong. And DI Yates, too."

"We were just dropping by," said Grace quickly.

"I know you were," said Marie sympathetically. "Where did you come from?"

"From Chloe's. We left our bikes there."

"So you walked here?"

"Yes."

"And you came to see your Mum, I suppose?"

44

Tim tried not to sigh. Marie wouldn't be helping him if she was going to ask them leading questions.

"Yes. And we'd still like to see her."

Chloe stood up, balling her fists and rubbing them into her eyes.

"I don't want to see her!" She started crying again, making a high-pitched whining noise, reminding Tim of a trapped animal. At first, she edged backwards, colliding with the table that stood behind the chairs, but when Tom Tarrant held out his hand to her she ran forwards and flung herself at him so fiercely that it knocked him off balance. He managed to catch her with his outstretched arm so that she didn't fall and himself quickly dropped to a kneeling position so that he could hold her steady. Chloe clung to him, sobbing. She was trying to say something, but the words came tumbling out incoherently.

The door opened and a tall, slender woman with hair cut in an immaculate glossy bob entered, closely followed by PC Tandy. The woman was well dressed: she was wearing a black and gold tunic over black trousers, and ankle boots with spiky black heels. Her face was expertly made up, her gold jewellery tasteful rather than obvious. On closer inspection, she wasn't as attractive as the first impression she gave: the woman had over-sharp, rather shifty features and darting black eyes that didn't inspire confidence. Despite her polished veneer, her resemblance to Chloe was striking.

It was to Chloe the woman addressed herself, ignoring everyone else in the room.

"What have you been up to now?" she demanded.

"Nothing," snivelled Chloe, clinging tighter to Tom.

"Don't you 'nothing' me, my lady. I want a straight answer!"

"Mavis . . ." Tom began.

"It was my idea," said Grace, turning her pellucid green eyes on Chloe's mother. "I thought it would be nice to nip in and see Mum."

To Tim's astonishment, her words seemed to mollify Mavis Hebblewhite.

"Well, anyway," she continued, most of the energy departing from her voice but still talking exclusively to Chloe, "if you didn't tell so many lies I wouldn't have blamed you this time. And I still want to know what you were doing, coming here without telling me."

"Mrs Hebblewhite," said Tim, "I'm DI Yates, South Lincs Police. I'm assuming you know what's happened here?"

"I've given Mrs Hebblewhite some brief details," said Verity.

"We're going to need to question both Chloe and Grace," said Tim. "That's why we've asked you here. Now that you've come, it would be better if we could all go to the station and leave this house to our forensics team. Is that ok with you?"

"I suppose so. The kids at home will have to fend for theirselves. I won't hold myself responsible for Donovan and Jagger, though. Donovan's got an ASBO and Jagger's up for twocking next week. If they do something while I'm out you can't blame me."

"We can send a police officer to stay with your other children if that will put your mind at rest."

Mavis Hebblewhite barked a short mirthless laugh.

"Ha! Do you think they'd get out alive?" She halted suddenly once the words were out, belatedly mindful that they were in poor taste in the present circumstances.

Tim raised an eyebrow but made no further comment. He

was mystified by the reactions that he'd received from this woman and two girls, all of them resident in the Dymokes, to the knowledge that a woman and baby from their community had been murdered. A woman and baby well-known to them, too. Only Chloe was distressed, and this apparently for some convoluted reason unrelated to any feelings of empathy. He wondered if their behaviour would change when the facts sank in properly.

"We've got three cars between us, so we should manage easily," he said. "You obviously know Tom Tarrant, from Social Services, and this is Marie Krakowska . . ."

"Yes, I know both of them," said Mavis shortly, waving her hand. "Doesn't surprise me that you want them to come. They've both got a nose for trouble when it comes to dealing with kids."

Chapter 15

IT'S WELL INTO the evening when I eventually get home to my flat. At the station, the interviews with Grace Winter and Chloe Hebblewhite didn't last long, partly because Marie wouldn't let us continue after Chloe began to cry again, partly because Mavis Hebblewhite's presence seemed to have such an inhibiting effect that Grace became increasingly reticent, whilst Chloe herself was rendered speechless. We managed to establish nothing new: Grace, speaking for her friend as well, repeated her previous story word for word. They'd been on a bike ride this morning; they'd left their bikes at Chloe's; they'd decided to drop round to Grace's house on a visit; one of the reporters had told them that Tina and Bluebelle were dead. Grace couldn't describe the reporter, but she thought she'd recognise him again. She hadn't seen her foster-mother or the baby since Saturday.

Tim had begun to ask Grace why she had requested to see the bodies when Chloe started sobbing and the interviews were adjourned until the following day. After some consultation with Marie and Tim, Tom agreed that Grace should be entrusted to Mavis Hebblewhite's care overnight. Mavis had shortly afterwards left in a taxi with both girls.

"I'm surprised you let Grace go with them," I'd said to Tom. "You gave me the impression that the Hebblewhite household is far from ideal. And Mavis is a piece of work. I hope she's going to be kind to Chloe this evening."

"Far from ideal is right, but I couldn't think of a better alternative," said Tom. "If Grace is traumatised, placing her with a strange new foster-parent isn't going to help, and in any case I'm unlikely to find someone who can take her today." He looked at his watch. "I've just about got time to nip back to my office to look at Grace's file again and contact North Lincs Social Services, if that's all right with you. When we've got a handle on her background we can make more permanent arrangements for her. I doubt if Mavis would be approved as a foster-mother, but mainly because those two oldest lads of hers are tearaways. Mavis herself isn't too bad: her bark's worse than her bite."

"I'll take your word for it."

"Well, I won't," Marie had said. "I can't stand the woman. But I think you're right: going home with Chloe is the best we can do for Grace today. Tomorrow it will be a different story."

She and Tom had left quite quickly after that and I'd helped Tim set up a rota for door-to-door enquiries, starting with the Dymokes and widening out in a fan across the whole town. It took us about four hours, after which Tim had said I should get some rest. He was going to return to Lady Dymoke Street to see Professor Salkeld again.

*

I notice that my flat is dusty and untidy. A bunch of sweet peas I'd put in a jar on the table a couple of days ago have dropped, their shrivelled petals lying in an arc across the table. I open the fridge door and inspect the shelves: there's a ready meal (a shepherd's pie), half a dozen eggs and a packet of mixed leaves. Nothing to inspire, but I feel shivery with hunger, even though it's a warm night, and decide that the pie will have to do. There's a convenience store a couple of streets away, but I don't have the energy to walk there and I can't be bothered to take the car. I turn on the oven and pour out the dregs from the bottle of red wine I opened yesterday while I wait for the pie to heat up. There's just about enough wine to fill the glass. I don't have a second bottle; if I want another drink after this, I'll have to resort to one of the two cans of lager I have left.

I lean against one of my kitchen cupboards, sipping the wine. I know that sleep tonight is unlikely, perhaps impossible. I'm haunted by the dead baby. Her face floats up before my eyes, looking quite peaceful, but her neck disfigured by that shameful bruise. The expression on Tina Brackenbury's face returns to haunt me, too: it's not predominantly a look of fear, but one of astonishment, even incredulity. What did Tina see in those last few seconds of her life?

Most of all, I'm troubled by the memory of Grace Winter's lovely face. I can recall in detail how it changes as different emotions flit across it. I hear her 'educated' voice; I see the power she has over the witless Chloe Hebblewhite. Tim says he's certain he saw her giving Chloe's arm a twist. I wonder why Chloe is so distraught when forced to contemplate the deaths of Tina and Bluebelle: she doesn't strike me as being a particularly sensitive child and they weren't related to her. Much stranger is Grace's attitude: even though we know she isn't a blood relative of the two victims, she's been living in the same house as them – in Bluebelle's case perhaps since she was born – but she seems completely lacking in any kind of pity for them. On the contrary, she's clearly both excited and curious about the deaths, yet she wanted us to believe that she really was Tina's daughter. Perhaps Marie is right when she says that Grace is behaving oddly because what's happened hasn't sunk in yet, but I know that even she blenched when I told her Grace had asked to see the bodies. I wonder with some dread what Tom found when he opened her file and whether he managed to contact North Yorkshire Social Services before they closed their office for the day. It may have no direct bearing on this case, but I'm very curious to find out who Grace Winter really is.

Chapter 16

HE WAS OBSESSED by what he'd heard on the news. He was certain she'd done it. Now he must seize the opportunity, by the means he had so carefully contrived, to contact her.

Chapter 17

TIM AWOKE EARLY the following morning. He got up quickly, managing to avoid waking Katrin as he showered and dressed, and tiptoed from the bedroom and out of the house. Outside, it was a typical late summer's day. There was a nip in the air, but the rising sun, low in the sky, shone red and glowing and the birds were singing, even though the swallows and martins were already gathering in small groups on the telegraph wires before their big push south.

He drove to the station and was surprised to see Juliet's car already parked outside. He ran up the stairs two at a time, wondering if something was wrong. Since he and Superintendent Thornton had promoted Juliet to Detective Sergeant the previous autumn – there had been several rounds of interviews with both internal and external candidates and (especially after their whim candidate had dropped out) frankly over-protracted deliberation before they finally decided to give Juliet the job – Tim had been aware that their relationship had changed. Juliet had shown she was no longer willing to accept the unofficial role of Girl Friday, always on hand, always covering for him when he was over-hasty or neglectful, always putting him before herself. To Tim this wasn't a puzzle: in the past, he'd suffered the odd glimmering of guilt as he'd allowed Juliet to be the last to leave when someone had to be at the station or taken the credit for some action in which she'd played at least an equal part, but it was only now that he fully realised how lucky he'd been to enjoy those years of devotion. He knew Juliet would still support him one hundred per cent when the chips were down, provided he understood she'd become much more her own woman; or, as Katrin had put it, uncharacteristically tartly for her, "You've lost your doormat, Tim. Now you'll have to work hard at building a good relationship with Juliet." Tim didn't mind putting the work in; what really spooked him was the prospect of losing Juliet altogether. He knew, because she'd told him, that, before her promotion, she'd applied for at least one other job and then withdrawn the application. He hoped she would be happier as DS, feel she was getting somewhere, sort out her personal life, perhaps, put down some roots. He'd tried to tell her this, but she'd thrown him an arch look and said, "You weren't too concerned about that when you were considering giving half the force this job, were you?" Tim had blustered and tried to blame Superintendent Thornton and police protocols for making her go through the full selection procedure, but Juliet had merely smiled. Tim had stopped in mid-sentence, realising that he was making a fool of himself.

When he reached the open-plan office area, Juliet was sitting serenely at her desk, talking to Superintendent Thornton and Professor Salkeld, who were both standing.

"Ah, Yates," said the Superintendent, looking at his watch. "I was wondering when you were going to appear."

"It isn't seven o'clock yet, sir," said Tim, with a grimace.

"Correct, Yates, correct, but we have a double murder on our hands, don't we? Professor Salkeld has been up all night. He's just dropped in to give us his report before he goes home for a well-earned rest."

"I haven't actually . . ." began the Professor, but Superintendent Thornton carried on speaking, raising his voice a little louder, forcing the pathologist to abandon his protestations.

"Now, perhaps you'd like to tell DI Yates what your conclusions are?"

"Of course, though I have little more to report than when I spoke to DI Yates yesterday evening. I can confirm that the woman was strangled. Some attempt may have been made to strangle the baby, too, but death was by suffocation, almost certainly while she was sleeping. The woman may have woken up during the attack, but my guess is that if she did it was only momentarily, too late to defend herself. There are no defence wounds on her hands or arms, no other wounds or bruises at all, in fact, either on her or on the child, except for the marks on their necks. Despite that, it's my opinion that the woman took some time to die, almost as if her assailant was only just strong enough to complete the deed."

"That's odd," said Tim. "Are you saying that she wasn't killed by a man?"

It always irked Professor Salkeld when the police tried to attribute hypotheses to him.

"No, I'm not saying that at all. I've no idea whether she was killed by man, woman or child; just that whoever it was didn't have a particularly strong grip," he said with some asperity.

"Quite so," said Superintendent Thornton, glaring at Tim. Tim ignored him.

"Thank you. Sorry, I wasn't taking in what you were saying properly. What about the time of death? I know you can't be specific, but how close can you get to a realistic estimate?"

"They didn't die yesterday, I can tell you that. My best

guess is they died on Sunday, and had probably been dead at least twenty-four hours when I first examined them."

"Most likely during the day?"

"Yes, but that's just a best guess. It could have been as long ago as Saturday afternoon or evening. Certainly not before then, I'd say."

"So we shouldn't rule out a night-time intruder?"

"Not rule it out, no, but the forensic evidence isn't going to help you very much, either way. Both their stomachs were empty, but that of itself doesn't prove anything. I'd say the circumstantial evidence will be of more use in this case. You say the front door was left wide open. How long for?"

"We're trying to establish that," said Juliet quietly, "but we have to bear in mind that it wasn't necessarily the killer who left the door open. It would be a strange thing for a killer to do, to draw attention to the crime so that it'd be discovered earlier. It's possible that a neighbour or some local children opened the door afterwards."

"And didn't report finding the bodies?" said Superintendent Thornton testily. "That takes some believing!"

"They may not have found the bodies. Perhaps someone knocked on the door and opened it when there was no answer. They may have gone into the house to wait, or even looked round to see if there was anything worth stealing, but without going upstairs. They may actually have stolen something and then left."

"If that's what happened, it would explain why they haven't come forward," said Tim.

"Ha!" said the Superintendent. "Today, I expect you to make better progress than dreaming up a lot of conjecture. This is a murder investigation."

"I know that, sir," said Tim to the Superintendent's retreating back. He turned back to Professor Salkeld.

"Thank you. I'll look forward to reading your report when it comes. Are we waiting on anything else from you?"

"There'll be a toxicology report, too. It'll take a few days to get the results from the samples I've sent. But I'll be very surprised if it turns anything up. In my view, strangulation and suffocation were the respective causes of death, with no other contributory factors."

"I've called a meeting at eight-thirty of everyone who's doing the house-to-house enquiries," Tim said to Juliet after the Professor had gone. "I want you to be there, so you know what their instructions are."

"You don't want them to report back to me throughout the day?"

"You can probably help later. First, I want you to brief Marie and then have her sit in on your interviews with Grace Winter and Chloe Hebblewhite. If Mrs Hebblewhite wants to come we'll have to let her. You'd better ask Marie if Grace should have her own 'responsible adult', though I'm hoping she'll say that her own presence will be enough. I don't want too many people to be in on it if we can avoid it."

"Ok. Are you thinking what I'm thinking?"

Tim paused.

"If you mean, do I think those two girls are more mixed up in this than they say, the answer is 'yes'. I think they probably went into the house after the murders took place, perhaps even saw the bodies, before running away and then coming back again later, all innocence. It could have been them who left the door open, though that would imply they knew of the deaths long before the bodies were discovered, which seems far-fetched. It's more likely that someone else left the door open and they found it like that. Is that what you think?"

"Sort of," said Juliet. "It's not like me to dream up Gothic theories: I usually leave that to you. But I couldn't help feeling struck by Stuart Salkeld's words: that he had 'no idea whether she was killed by man, woman or child'. I know he didn't intend us to read anything specific into what he said. But it did indicate that he wouldn't rule out the murders' being committed by a child."

"God, that *is* Gothic," said Tim. "I see what you mean, especially as he said that whoever killed Tina had quite a weak grip. But I certainly wouldn't tell Marie. It's going to be tricky enough, anyway, having her there saying the kids are traumatised or being bullied every time you try to get the truth out of them. And they'll learn to play on that."

"Chloe doesn't seem to be the sort of child who could play psychological games."

"Maybe, but I'd put money on it that Grace Winter can. When this morning meeting's over I'm going to see Tom Tarrant. He said he'd ring North Lincs Social Services to find out more about Grace's background. It seems a ridiculous thing to say about a child, but everything suggests that there's something murky in her past."

"Good luck with that," said Juliet.

"You're the one who needs the luck. All I'm facing is the possibility of having to circumnavigate some red tape."

Chapter 18

H E BARELY SLEPT that night. Though he might tell Jack Rose he had a headache to cover up his snotty behaviour, at the end of this day a genuine migraine had mangled his brain. Unable to eat his supper, he'd lain prone in his cell until lights out, waiting for the Mogadon that eventually he'd been given to kick in.

As the night wore on, the drug brought some relief from the immediate pain, but his head filled with nightmare images, a succession of terrifying scenes that until now he'd managed to exile from his conscious memory for four whole years. He'd been forced to haul himself off the narrow bed so that he could vomit into the toilet. Alerted by the noise, the night warder came by to check on him.

"Sick bay tomorrow if you're no better," the warder said gruffly.

"I'll be ok tomorrow," he'd answered shakily. "It's just a migraine." He needed to be able to listen to the news and he knew he'd have no chance of that in the hospital wing.

"We'll see," said the warder suspiciously. Most prisoners jumped at the chance of a few days 'off sick'. The cell would have to be searched in the morning: a stash of smuggled-in drugs was the most likely explanation, both for the vomiting and the attempt to trivialise it.

He got up as soon as the lights went up and forced himself to shave, wincing as he burned his flesh with his blunt single-blade disposable razor. To be allowed to shave unsupervised was another concession that he'd won through painstaking months of 'good behaviour': at first, he'd been allowed no razor blades, no shoe-laces and nothing with a drawstring. He washed his face and flicked some water on his hair, combing it back while it was still wet. Then he cleaned his teeth. He hadn't changed out of the clothes he'd been wearing yesterday, but believed he made a passable impression of being fit and tidy. The headache had gone, leaving the familiar dull and empty sensation that always followed a migraine.

He turned on the television, keeping the sound as low as possible. Anxious not to miss the early news, he was ready, seated on his bed, by the time it was broadcast. He had to watch crap for several long minutes before the story he was waiting for was announced. It was unsatisfyingly short: "Police in South Lincolnshire were carrying out door-to-door enquiries late into the evening yesterday after the discovery of the bodies of a woman and her infant daughter in Lady Margaret Dymoke Street, Spalding. Foul play is suspected. Superintendent Dennis Thornton said that the names of the two victims will be released later today, after formal identification has taken place."

Someone was banging on his wall. "Turn that fucking thing off!" shouted a furious voice. "Do you know what fucking time it is?"

"Sorry," he said. He turned off the TV. He'd have to work out ways of picking up other news bulletins later in the day. He wondered if he'd be able to wangle a day in the cell, convince them he was too ill to work but not ill enough to be sent to the sick bay.

Chapter 19

MARIE ARRIVES EARLY, as I have asked her to. I see straight away that she's feeling less subdued than she was yesterday and correspondingly more combative. The wobble in confidence brought on by the shock of the murders is troubling her no longer: she's back full fig in her *all children are innocent, if they do wrong they're the victims of adults* mode. I sigh inwardly. I'm apprehensive enough about the interviews ahead, which I know will have to be delicately handled, without having to contend with Marie's aggressive brand of altruism. I'll have to work hard to get her onside.

I offer her tea, settle her into the interview room, which she inspects critically. She notes with approval the jug of orange squash and the plate of biscuits set out on the table alongside the teapot, and the cushions I've placed on two of the chairs. She's wearing a mid-calf dirndl skirt and a broderie anglaise blouse with huge puffed sleeves. Her thick blonde hair has been tied back with a piece of embroidered ribbon. She could pass for a very generously-proportioned Coppélia. Even her face is doll-like: her cheeks are smothered in pale powder, the lids above her cornflower-coloured eyes a vibrant blue, her mouth painted into a vermilion bow. You'd think her strange enough to frighten the average child, and yet kids always seem to trust her.

"Did Grace go home with Chloe last night?" I ask, mainly

because I want to begin the conversation on safely neutral ground.

"Yes, I believe so. Tom organised it. He doesn't think that Mavis Hebblewhite's a suitable foster-mother for her, even if she wanted to take Grace on permanently, so he'll have to find someone else quite soon. But it was the best we could do last night. They're coming at ten, are they?"

"Yes. Mavis is going to bring them. We offered to send a car for them, but she said she'd rather walk."

"Not surprising. There aren't many people in the Dymokes who'd like to be seen getting into a police car."

"I'll ask Mrs Hebblewhite to be the responsible adult accompanying Chloe. Can she do the job for Grace, too, or will you do it?"

Marie regards me suspiciously.

"They're not being accused of a crime, are they?"

"No, we just want to question them. We want to know why they showed up when they did and when Grace last saw her foster-mother, what she said to her, etcetera; also, exactly when they went on their bike rides, who saw them, that sort of thing."

"It sounds to me as if you do suspect them of something. You're not suggesting that they're killers, are you?"

Marie tosses back her head and gives a short harsh laugh at the ridiculousness of such an idea.

"No, but we do think they might have been in the house earlier, after the murders took place, but before they were reported. That could explain why Chloe seemed so distressed yesterday, and even account for Grace's strange request to see the bodies."

Marie lets her guard drop for a second.

"I must admit that *was* strange, although I wasn't there myself, so I can only form an impression out of context." She skewers me with a challenging look. "To answer your question, Mavis Hebblewhite and I will be quite adequate support for the girls today – as long as you are just asking for information, I could actually do it on my own. But if eventually you try to charge them with anything, or even accuse them of some misdemeanour, then both will need a responsible adult present and both will need a solicitor. At present, I'm here both to safeguard their interests and yours: to make sure they aren't frightened and that you don't overstep the mark. I could choose one role or the other if future circumstances dictate."

"With friends like these . . ." I think, but aloud I thank her somewhat meekly. I decide not to mention my and Tim's suspicions. They seem outlandish when viewed through the lens of Marie's robust 'common sense' and I'm sure if voiced will cause her to postpone the interviews while she assembles a formidable bunch of professional supporters for Grace and Chloe.

Marie sips her tea warily. I'm not sure if I've been successful in brokering peace.

Mavis Hebblewhite arrives punctually on the hour with both girls in tow. Her outfit today is similar to yesterday's: she's wearing another tunic – this one is scarlet – still over black trousers with the killer-heeled ankle boots. Grace and Chloe have been spruced up. Both have silky clean hair and although both seem to be wearing the same clothes as yesterday – Chloe a yellow little-girl dress with a Peter Pan collar that sits uneasily on her gawky frame and Grace, who is much slighter, a striped T-shirt with denim jeans – they are so clean and neatly-pressed that Mavis has undoubtedly been busy laundering. Chloe is deathly pale; her cheeks bear smudges of tears. Grace is very self-possessed, as if she knows the meeting is important; beneath her calm confidence, I sense suppressed excitement.

Marie fusses a little over the girls, getting them settled in their chairs and pouring out glasses of squash for them, while I offer Mavis tea. She accepts it and sits down, placing the cup of tea on the table in front of her, but she makes no attempt to drink it.

"How long are you going to be?" she says. "We haven't got all day."

"That depends on Grace and Chloe. Some children need more breaks than others when they're being interviewed."

"I'll make sure they get on with it." She gives Chloe a fierce look.

"To be fair to the children, we have to give them as much time as they need," says Marie in measured tones. "It isn't strictly necessary for you to be here while I'm present. You may leave, if you wish, and come back later."

"I'm not leaving Chloe here on her own. Not Grace, neither." Mavis looks at the four walls surrounding her and then up at the ceiling, as if it might come crashing down.

"We're very grateful to you for looking after Grace last night, especially at such short notice," Marie says soothingly.

"Yeah, well, she was staying anyway, wasn't she? Besides, she's a good kid." Mavis nods at Grace and smiles. "Got a level head on her shoulders, that one."

Grace sits up straight in her chair and smiles back. Chloe sinks deeper into dejection.

"Shall we start?" I say brightly.

64

No-one speaks. I look to Marie for approval but she doesn't meet my eye. She's ostentatiously engaged in pushing Chloe's beaker further on to the table.

"For the tape," I say. "It's five minutes past ten a.m. on Tuesday 23rd August. Present in the room are Ms Marie Krakowska, child psychologist, Mrs Mavis Hebblewhite, her daughter Chloe Hebblewhite and Grace Winter, Chloe's friend. Chloe and Grace are minors. Each is ten years of age. Mrs Hebblewhite, I'd like to start with you."

"Me? I haven't done owt."

"I'm not accusing you of anything, Mrs Hebblewhite. I'd just like a few details about the past few days. Did you invite Grace to stay with Chloe at your house?"

"Chloe invited her. I didn't mind. Chloe was bored and her brothers don't play with her."

"When did she come?"

"Some time on Sat'day morning. I don't remember exactly."

"So she was at your house most of the day on Saturday and Sunday and stayed both nights?"

"Yes."

"And she was with Chloe all of the time?"

"As far as I know. They was in and out. I don't think they left the street over the weekend."

"And yesterday?"

"You know she stayed here yesterday. Your lot asked if she could."

"Yes, I do know, and we're grateful. But what about during the day? What did Grace and Chloe do yesterday morning, for example?"

"They said they went on a bike ride. Grace borrowed our Jagger's bike. They reckoned they got as far as Crowland."

"We did," said Grace. "We went into the Abbey and everything."

I write a quick note.

"How long did it take you to get there?"

"I don't know. About two hours, wasn't it, Chloe?"

Chloe nods, tongue-tied. Marie gives her hand a little squeeze.

"What time did you leave?"

"After they'd had their breakfast," says Mavis. "I didn't know they was going that far. I thought they was going for a ride along the Cut."

"What time was breakfast?"

Mavis shrugs. "Nobody got up very early. I couldn't say, really." She looks up at the ceiling again.

I turn back to Grace.

"If you took two hours to get there and two hours to ride back, and you spent some time there as well, you must have been gone for more than four hours."

Grace just looks at me.

"Do you know what time you got back?"

"No."

"It was after the boys had had their dinner," Mavis puts in. "I was getting a bit worried."

"So what time would that be?"

"I was clearing up. About two, I suppose. I made them some sandwiches."

"I expect they were hungry after cycling all that way."

"Grace was. Chloe can be funny about food."

Chloe has been following the conversation, apparently too cowed to contribute anything. I see an opportunity to draw her in.

"You're very quiet, Chloe. Did you enjoy the bike ride?"

She nods.

"Why didn't you want your dinner?"

"I just didn't. I was upset."

I see Grace give Chloe a surreptitious but vicious jab with her elbow. Chloe fights back the tears.

"We'd had a row," she says. "Grace and me fell out."

"What did you fall out about?"

"Nothing much."

"It was just about some sweets," Grace says.

"Did anyone see you while you were in Crowland?"

"Oh, yes, lots of people."

"Did you speak to anyone?"

"No."

"Not even when you went into the Abbey?"

"No."

"Did you speak to anyone, Chloe?"

"No."

"Did you see anyone you knew when you were coming back? When you were getting closer to Spalding, perhaps?"

"Not that I remember."

"Grace?"

"No. I don't know that many people round here."

I hesitate. Grace's past is not something I want to explore until we know more about it. She sees my hesitation. Once again, she's watching me intently.

"So you biked back to Chloe's without seeing anyone either of you knew and ate a sandwich. What did you do then?"

"I said to Chloe let's go and see my Mum and she says we'll take the bikes, but Jagger says you can't have my bike any longer. I want it."

"So you both walked. Didn't Chloe want to take her bike?"

"No. She said she'd walk, too."

"Is that right, Chloe?"

Chloe nods again. She's behaving like a totally lost soul, responding as she thinks she's expected to, as if by rote. Mavis Hebblewhite looks at her and sighs impatiently.

"Why did you want to see your 'Mum', Grace?"

"I hadn't been round since I left on Saturday. I wanted to see her. I wanted Chloe to see Bluebelle."

"So was that when I first met you, when you came to the house past all the reporters?"

"Yes."

"Had you been home before that? In between when you left for Chloe's on Saturday morning and when you came back yesterday afternoon?"

"No. I told you: we biked to Crowland."

"She did say that," says Mavis Hebblewhite, as if I'm a bit slow on the uptake.

"Chloe, did you go to Grace's house between Sunday morning and yesterday afternoon?"

"No," says Chloe tremulously.

"What is this?" exclaims Mavis. "Why do you keep on asking them the same things over and over again?"

"You're quite sure of that, Chloe?"

"Yes."

I get up and walk to where Grace is sitting, crouching down so that our faces are on the same level. I'm between her and Chloe.

"Grace," I say, "I know this is probably going to be difficult. Do you remember when you were talking to me and DI Yates?"

"Yes." She's looking grave but steadfast.

"You told us about the bike ride. Then you asked us for something. Do you remember what it was?"

"Yes." She gives Chloe a sidelong glance. "We asked if we could see them."

"Who do you mean by 'them', Grace?"

"The bodies. We asked to see the bodies."

"Whose bodies, Grace? Whose bodies do you mean?"

"Mum's. And Bluebelle's." Her voice is steady. On my other side, I'm aware that Chloe is fidgeting and I hear Marie get up. I know that Marie's fussing round her and I make a huge effort to keep focused on Grace. I'm acutely aware that Marie might call a halt to the interview at any moment now.

"Grace," I say gently. "How did you know that there were bodies? How did you know that your – Mum and Bluebelle had . . . come to harm?"

Her seriousness turns flinty; her pale cheeks flush a hectic red.

"Like I said, I think one of the reporters must have told me."

"Would you know him again? Could you pick out his picture?"

"I don't know. P'raps."

"And . . . Grace . . . why did you and Chloe want to see the bodies?" I've introduced Chloe's name to avoid making it seem as if I'm victimising Grace, but immediately I realise it's a mistake.

"I didn't want to see them! I didn't! I didn't! I didn't!" Chloe shrieks, breaking into loud sobs. Marie enfolds her in her arms.

"Shut up, you silly little bitch!" says Mavis unexpectedly

69

to Chloe. Then, turning to me, "See what you've done now. I'm taking the two kids out of this madhouse!"

"DS Armstrong," Marie says firmly, "I think we'll have to continue with this on another occasion, don't you?"

Chapter 20

Tom Tarrant had agreed to meet Tim in his own office about mid-morning. Tim, who had kept the briefing with the officers engaged in the door-to-door enquiries short, was sitting at his desk trying to make sense of the photos taken at the crime scene when Tom was shown in. Tom always looked dishevelled and his trademark windswept look had been heightened by the fact that he'd obviously been running. A large man, untidily built rather than overweight but clearly not very fit, he was gasping for air, painfully out of breath.

"Tom!" said Tim, standing up. "Are you all right? Sit down, for goodness' sake."

Tarrant collapsed gratefully into the chair Tim pulled out for him.

"What's the matter? Has something happened?"

Tom smiled wanly.

"You could say that. Can I have a glass of water?"

"Sure. Or would you rather have tea?"

"Water's fine, thanks. I've come to talk to you about Grace Winter. I've been on to North Lincs this morning – I didn't catch them last night. There's more they haven't told me yet – I'm going to have to go and see them – but I thought you ought to know what I've found out straight away."

"Steady on, Tom. You can spare a couple of minutes to get your breath back. And tell me about it slowly when you

71

do start. It'll save time in the long run. I'm just going for the water – I'll be back in a minute."

When he returned, Tom was sitting straighter in the chair and had smoothed down his tangled hair. He took the flimsy beaker of water that Tim held out to him.

"Thanks. I'm sorry if I freaked you out, but I've had a bit of a shock. And I'm not particularly impressed by my colleagues in North Lincs, either. I understand about confidentiality, but we should have been given a lot more information about Grace Winter before we took her on, for her own sake as well as everyone else's."

"Start at the beginning, Tom," Tim said. "And take it slowly. Have a drink first."

Tom took a few sips of the water.

"Sorry," he said again. "As you know, Grace Winter was being fostered by Tina Brackenbury. But Winter isn't her real name, either, or at least wasn't her name at birth. She was born Grace Arkwright. Does that mean anything to you?"

"No," said Tim, mystified. "Should it?"

"Not Grace Arkwright's name, perhaps. What about Tristram Arkwright?"

"You might as well ask me if I know who Ian Brady is! Unless there's another Tristram Arkwright, you're talking about the guy who turned a gun on his family three or four years ago. You're not going to tell me that he's Grace's dad?"

"Not her father, no, and in fact not a blood relative at all. But he *is* her uncle – by adoption."

"I remember now that Arkwright was adopted. The parents were quite well off, weren't they? Arkwright killed them so that he could get his hands on their money. He murdered his sister, too, and both of her kids. Did she have other children? Is Grace the sister's daughter?"

"You got it in one! Except that both the sister's children who were staying at the farm weren't murdered. Grace was spared, or she managed to escape. When police finally got into the house, they found her hiding in a cupboard."

"Christ! I don't remember that. I could have sworn both the children died."

"That's what the police thought at first and even after Grace had been found she was reported dead in error. They did correct their statement eventually, but they didn't make a deal of it. They didn't give the media her name. Grace was only six and between them and social services they managed to shield her from the publicity."

"She must have been badly traumatised."

"She was given extensive psychiatric care. All sorts of tests were carried out on her. It was eventually established she was ok."

"Do you mean that she'd recovered?"

"In one sense. The main psychiatrist in charge of her care concluded she hadn't been severely damaged in the first place. Perhaps because she was too young."

"What happened to her then? Who looked after her?"

"The Arkwrights owned a lot of property, which they let out. Mrs Arkwright had turned the letting into a business and took on other people's properties as well. She had an assistant, Amy Winter. Mrs Winter adopted Grace."

"You mean, properly adopted her? She didn't just act as a foster-parent?"

"No, she was officially adopted. Grace's name really is Grace Winter now."

73

"But in that case why was she being fostered by Tina Brackenbury? It doesn't make sense."

"I don't know the answer to that, but I'm sure there is one. I've told you everything that North Lincs would tell me over the phone. There's more stuff they have on file about Grace, but they wouldn't give me any more information. They've said I'll have to go and see them."

"Can you go today?"

"Later on, possibly. They're going to ask Grace's psychologist if they can release the information."

"Do they know why you want it?"

"I've had to give them a few details, so they'll probably be putting two and two together. It'll be obvious to them as soon as you release Tina's name to the Press."

"It will, you're right. We'll have to make sure they don't talk to any reporters."

"Huh!" Tom let out a short, sarcastic laugh. "There's not much chance of that. It's taken me all my time to get what bit I have out of them and I'm a fellow professional with an interest in the client."

"Even so, we'll need to give them more than they'll get from the press notice. Would you like someone from the force to come with you?"

"I'd better ask first. I don't want to intimidate them. On the other hand, you or one of your colleagues will know better than me what sort of questions to ask and what other information you need to take away with you."

"We can take out a warrant to get the information if they don't co-operate."

"They know that, without a doubt. But I'd prefer not to antagonise them. That way we'll get better support from them in the long run, and we may need it. I'll give you a call when they've called me back, let you know if they'll see me today and if so whether they'd rather I was alone or accompanied."

Chapter 21

TIM WAS ABOUT to check on the door-to-door teams again when he caught sight of Juliet and Marie Krakowska deep in conversation in the open-plan area. He went out to meet them.

"That was a quick interview," he said. "Did you get anywhere?"

"No," said Juliet. "I'm no wiser than I was yesterday. Grace is being helpful, at least on the face of it, but I'm convinced she's holding back something. And Chloe's an emotional wreck. She's the reason we've had to stop the interview. I don't think having her mother there is helping."

"It's going to be hard for you to get rid of Mavis unless you can find someone else she agrees is suitable to support Chloe," said Marie.

"I don't suppose the father's a possibility?"

"Not a snowball in hell's chance. Mavis has been 'known' to social services for a long time, since before her first child was born, and there's never been a man in evidence for very long. According to Mavis, all the children have different fathers and none of them has any kind of paternal support, at least not that Mavis admits to."

"Benefit fraud?" said Tim.

"It's a possibility, but I think unlikely. I believe Mavis really is bringing the kids up on her own."

"Do you think it would work better if we interviewed

Grace and Chloe separately?" said Juliet.

"Probably. That would solve part of the problem. Separating Mavis and Chloe will be a tougher nut to crack."

"When are you going to interview them again?" asked Tim.

"Not until tomorrow. Mavis has agreed to have Grace to stay for another night. Then we really must take her away from there. Tom Tarrant's looking into possible foster homes today."

"Tom was here a bit earlier," said Tim. "He's found out more about Grace, but he needs to visit his colleagues in North Lincolnshire to get the whole picture. It turns out that Grace's story's quite complicated. I don't suppose he's had time to tell you about it?"

Marie looked self-conscious.

"I haven't seen Tom today," she said evasively.

"Or spoken to him?"

"No. But I know what you're going to say."

"Really?" Tim stared keenly at Marie, who dropped her eyes. "Don't tell me you already knew about Grace's identity?"

"Grace's *identity*?" said Juliet. "Do you mean she's not using her real name?"

"Grace Winter *is* her real name," said Marie quietly. "She was legally adopted by a woman called Amy Winter about three years ago. Before that her name was Grace Arkwright."

"Oh, God!" said Juliet. "Do you mean the kid who survived the family massacre at Brocklesby Farm?"

"Do you remember that?" said Tim. "I'd forgotten that one of the children survived."

"I don't think the press made much of it. They were put under pressure to leave the child alone. I remember reading the police reports at the time. They contained more details

77

than were disclosed to the papers. And the name Arkwright sticks in your mind, like Nilsen or Shipman."

"I suppose so," said Tim. "Why didn't you tell us this yesterday, Marie? You obviously knew exactly who Grace was – or is, I should say."

"Client confidentiality," said Marie glibly. "Tom doesn't know that I know. I didn't tell him, because North Lincs Social Services undertook to provide Grace with as much anonymity as possible. It was up to them to decide how much he should know. They've been very protective of Grace's interests, and rightly so. Tom must have done a good job on gaining their confidence for them to have told him as much as they have. I'm not surprised they want to get official permission before they tell him any more."

Tim sighed. It was impossible to challenge Marie on whether she had acted correctly, but nevertheless her behaviour was intensely irritating. She could have saved them a lot of time if she'd been prepared to have an off-the-record conversation with Juliet when she first got involved in the case.

"That wasn't my only reason for not telling you what I know about Grace," Marie added, as if reading Tim's thoughts. "I wanted Juliet to have at least a stab of talking to her before she found out about her background. From now on, however hard Juliet tries, she'll always be thinking that it's Grace Arkwright that she's really talking to, the damaged survivor of a murder spree."

"I suppose that's fair enough," said Tim grudgingly. "How is it you know so much about it, anyway? You weren't working for North Lincs then, were you?"

"You know I wasn't: I've been working here for ten years

now. But Grace's psychologist called on me for a second opinion."

"Why was that? Was she suffering from some specific disorder?"

"On the contrary, she couldn't find anything wrong with her. She'd have expected her to be deeply traumatised by what happened at Brocklesby Farm, but she discovered no evidence at all that Grace was disturbed. She wanted me to confirm her findings."

"And did you?"

"The interviews with Grace were taped. I listened to the tapes and also looked at the results of some tests she was given. I came to the same conclusion: Grace appeared to be a perfectly normal six-year-old."

"So you didn't actually meet her at that time?"

"No. The responsible adult with her decided it would be unfair to subject her to any more interviews and social services agreed. With good reason, I might add."

"Who was the responsible adult?"

"Amy Winter. The woman who eventually adopted her."

"Why do you think North Lincs Social Services have insisted on seeing Tom in person? What more is there for us to find out about Grace?"

Marie became pensive again.

"I don't know the answer to that, and believe me, I'm being entirely on the level with you now. It may just be that they're going through the formalities of getting permission before they show you the results of the tests I've mentioned. If so, you won't find much there of interest. But my guess is that they have extra information relating to the period after Grace was adopted. Unless Amy Winter is ill, it seems odd to me that Grace was subsequently put into the care of a foster-mother. It's certainly something I'd want to know the answer to, if I were you. But I honestly don't have that information myself. I wasn't consulted by either her psychologist or North Lincs again."

Verity Tandy appeared at the top of the stairs.

"Excuse me, sir. Opal Smith is here. She's in a bit of a state."

"Who's Opal Smith?"

"She's Tina Brackenbury's oldest daughter. She's come to identify the bodies. She's brought her partner and her baby with her."

"Has she been to the morgue yet?"

"No. She came straight here. Essex police provided a car."

"Bring her up to my office. I'll go to the morgue with her myself."

"And her partner and the baby, sir? Do you want them to come upstairs, too?"

Tim sighed.

"I suppose so. It'll be better than letting them loose on the press pack. I want to make sure that no-one talks to the newspapers yet."

"Only a couple of reporters outside," said Verity. "I expect there'll be more later. According to one of them, Superintendent Thornton said there'll be an announcement at 4 p.m. today."

"Did he?" said Tim. "It's the first I've heard about it. Let's hope we have something to tell them, then."

Chapter 22

OPAL SMITH WAS recognisably her mother's daughter. Blobby-featured and plump, she seemed doll-like, but it was soon apparent that this was underpinned by a certain steeliness. Tim felt immediately that, although distressed, she would not be averse to turning the situation to her own advantage.

She was dressed in black leggings that clung more tightly to her generous legs than they were intended to and an oversize white jumper made of some pilled synthetic material. She was carrying a fat, vacant-faced baby whose chubby fingers were kneading the jumper. She entered Tim's office in a sort of rush, her face set and important. It was an expression that Tim was familiar with: it displayed the sense of entitlement conferred by grief. She was followed more slowly by a very young soldier.

Tim went to greet her with outstretched hand.

"Mrs Smith," he said, "thank you for coming so quickly. I'm very sorry for your loss. Is this your husband?"

"Yes," she said, as she took his hand briefly, not shaking it.

"No," said the soldier, a little behind her. "Not exactly."

"I'm sorry?"

"I said, not exactly. Me and Opal isn't married."

"But we will be, though," said Opal, giving him a furious look. "His name's Pete."

Tim gave Pete Smith a nod which was barely returned. He

did, however, come to stand protectively behind Opal's chair once she was seated.

"You don't know that it is my loss yet, do you?" Opal continued.

"I'm not sure that I follow . . ."

"We don't know that they're dead yet, do we? Isn't that why I'm here, so you can find out?"

"Technically you're right, of course, but for your own sake you should know there isn't much doubt. Your mother and sister were both found in their beds."

Opal's brows knitted furiously. She seemed to be outraged rather than grieving.

"I told her to keep away from that Frankie," she said. "Nothing but trouble, that one. It'll be him that's done this."

"You don't know that," said Pete soothingly, rubbing her back. Tim found the gesture irritating: it was a stock response, picked up from the news, like the expressions 'come forward' and 'get closure' that all crime victims seemed to trot out these days. He realised he was being uncharitable.

"Who is Frankie?" he asked gently.

Opal shrugged. Tim saw the shutters go down and understood that she was either afraid of Frankie or disliked the idea of shopping him to the police more than she disliked the man himself. Even if he'd killed her mother?

"Ms Smith," he said more firmly, "the more you co-operate with us, the more likely we are to find the person who did this. You may be right about this Frankie, but it's even more likely that we just need to eliminate him from our enquiries. Now, could you tell me who he is?"

Opal's mouth drooped into an ugly sulk.

"Pete knows him," she said. "Why don't you ask him?"

"He's one of my mates' dads," said Pete in a conciliatory way. "I haven't seen him in an age, though. Course, I don't live here no more."

"What's his full name?"

"Frank Roberts. I'm mates with Oscar Roberts."

The name Frank Roberts didn't mean anything to Tim, but it was quite a common one. He'd be more likely to remember someone called Oscar, but this didn't ring a bell, either. Perhaps the Roberts family was straighter than Opal believed.

"Thank you. And what's his relationship to Opal's mother?"

Pete Smith hesitated.

"He's Bluebelle's dad, that's what!" Opal flung out. "Not that dad's exactly the right word for his attitude towards her. If he goes round twice a year, Mam thinks she's lucky."

"Ms Smith, you're not making much sense. Why do you think that Frank Roberts might have harmed your mother and sister, if mostly he neglected them?"

"Went round when he wanted some cash, didn't he? She was fool enough to give it him, usually. She told me that next time she'd say no."

"Was she afraid of him?"

"She's afraid of everybody, my mam. Wouldn't say boo to a goose."

"Now, Opal, don't go saying . . ."

"Get *off* me, Pete! You're enough to drive anyone mad, the way you horm around." Opal raised her face so that her dull eyes met Tim's. "Didn't have much going for her, my mam. Rotten judge of blokes, never any money, trying hard to make ends meet. You could say she was too honest in some ways, but truth be told she was more of a doormat. But she *was* my mam." Opal scrubbed at her eyes with a tissue. Pete

83

started rubbing her back again. The child in her arms stirred and flung himself backwards, startling in his sleep. Opal gathered him into the crook of her arm and he settled down again.

"Do you know his address?"

"What?"

"This Frank Roberts. Do you know where he lives?"

"He's got a caravan down Spalding Common," said Pete.

"Yes," agreed Opal, "but more often than not he's at his mam's."

"Where does she live?"

"Down our road. A few doors down, on the other side."

"By 'down our road', you mean Lady Dymoke Street?"

"Well, there isn't anywhere else, is there?"

"And his mother's name is Roberts, too?"

"I suppose so. I've always called her Fan. Isn't it time I was getting on with it - what I came for, I mean?"

"You've been very helpful and yes, we'll leave for the morgue shortly. I'd just like to ask you one more thing before we go."

"Ok," said Opal doubtfully.

"Your mother was looking after a little girl - fostering her. Did you know that?"

"Oh, Christ, yes - Grace. I'd forgotten about her."

"Do you know Grace well?"

"What do you think? I was living there when she first came, wasn't I?"

"Do you like her?"

"That's a funny question. She isn't the first foster kid Mam's had. She does it for the money, or so she says - I reckon she spends more on them than they bring in. I thought

Grace was all right, as far as I took any interest in her. Not as gormless as some of them. Could twist Mam round her little finger, but then so could most people. Grace wasn't there, then, when they . . ."

"No, she was staying with a friend. Chloe Hebblewhite. Do you know her?"

"I don't know Chloe in particular, but I do know Mavis Hebblewhite. Got a whole brood of kids. I take it she's one of them?"

Tim nodded.

"What'll happen to Grace now? I suppose she'll go back to the social?"

"Probably. Would you like to see her before you go home?"

"I suppose so. If she wants to see me. Is she upset, like?"

"It's difficult to say. She's been behaving quite calmly, but shock's a funny thing. It shows itself in different ways and can sometimes be delayed."

"I should think the biggest shock for her will be getting packed off back to the social. She'd settled in well with Mam. Good with Bluebelle, too, Mam said."

"Yes," said Tim. "You're probably right. Are you ready to go, now? What are you going to do with the baby? Do you want to leave him here with Pete?"

Opal clutched the baby tighter, as if it had suddenly dawned on her what she was expected to do. She threw Pete a look of pure anguish. Tim saw him blench.

"Tell you what," said Pete in a husky voice, "Why don't I do it?"

"Do what?"

"Come with you to identify the . . . come to the morgue with you."

"You're not next of kin," said Opal, but there was hope in her voice.

"I'm as good as."

"Did you know Mrs Brackenbury?"

"Course I did. Since I was a little kid."

"What about Bluebelle?"

"Her, too. We've visited a few times since she was born. I've seen her as often as Opal has."

"All right," said Tim. "Thank you. Ms Smith can stay here with the baby. I'll ask the canteen to send in some sandwiches."

Chapter 23

TIM HAS SENT me with Tom Tarrant to visit North Lincs Social Services. Their offices are in Lincoln, which is a good hour's drive from Spalding. Tim's told me to play it by ear: Tom seems to be of the view that they might ask me to leave and if he's right Tim doesn't want me to push it. We can demand that a police officer is present, of course, but we're more likely to get the information we need quicker if we don't upset them. For once, Tim wants to play the situation the way I always would, even if I do have to bite my tongue when he suggests I might otherwise have taken a more impetuous approach.

I'm delighted to be getting out of the police station for a while, a reprieve made the sweeter by my previous assumption that I'd be spending most of the day conducting child-sized interviews with Grace Winter and Chloe Hebblewhite. Marie's vetoed that: she thinks they're overwrought and we should give them more time to recover. She also wants to move Grace from the Hebblewhite household before the day is out, and needs time to liaise with Tom and some of his colleagues to find another foster-carer. She feels this is a priority and in our interests as well as Grace's. Having had Mavis Hebblewhite sit in on the first interview, it's hard to disagree: at least we'll then be able to interview Grace without Mavis, but she'll still be there when we talk to Chloe. Even so, I've a hunch that Chloe will be less hysterical without Grace.

I've offered to pick Tom up, but he insists on taking me in his own car, claiming that although he knows the way he's a hopeless navigator. His car is an ancient rust bucket – some kind of collector's marque, I have no doubt, but whatever it is, it's magic is lost on me. I get in apprehensively, but find it's surprisingly comfortable inside.

We chat away quite easily on the journey. Tom must surely remember me from the Claudia McRae case, but he doesn't allude to it. This is understandable, given that we were certain his wife was more mixed up in it than either of them admitted; I know Tim believed that she was having an affair with one of the suspects at the time, though it didn't come out in court.

It's perhaps because we respected his privacy then that, although he's clearly bursting with questions, Tom doesn't probe too directly for information today. I know that he's really desperate to find out whether I think Grace knows more than she's admitted to us, but I can't answer that question. Despite what I said to Tim, I doubt Grace is a murderer, but I think it's possible that she and Chloe went into the house before the open door was reported and perhaps saw the bodies before running away. Why they won't admit to this if it's true is a mystery, but it's probably too much to expect ten-year-olds to behave logically. Chloe, in particular, has the hangdog air of someone who's perpetually being blamed for others' wrongdoing. They're probably assuming they'll get into trouble if they admit they were there. But there's still something deeply disturbing about Grace . . .

"Strange child, isn't she?" says Tom, as if tapping into my thoughts.

"Do you mean Grace or Chloe?"

"I could say both, but Chloe isn't really strange – not in the sense of out-of-the-ordinary, even if she does struggle intellectually. No, I mean Grace: I don't think I've ever met a child like her. I find her mixture of reserve and chattiness quite uncanny."

"I understand what you're talking about, but maybe it isn't so surprising. She's a child who's been passed from one family to another at least three times. I'd say that making herself agreeable while not actually letting anyone get near is a pretty effective coping strategy."

"Perhaps you ought to be the child psychologist!" Tom laughs.

"And perhaps I've just spent too much time with Marie today." I laugh, too. Then I remember that we're going to see another child psychologist this afternoon. How many has Grace met in her short life? Can she second-guess their analyses in the same way that I appear to be doing?

"Just be nice to Lenka," Tom is saying. "She's not at all like Marie, but she does have a very fragile ego. You'll need to massage it a little bit. If she lets you in, that is."

"I'm always nice," I say. "Or polite, at any rate. But what is it about that profession? Why can't they just be normal?"

"I won't answer your question with the obvious comment," Tom laughs again. "More seriously, the best analogy I can think of is with acting: actors are said to play so many roles that ultimately they don't know who they 'really' are. I'd say that the same goes for psychologists: they see so many strange cases, they're no longer sure where the parameters of the 'norm' lie. It makes them touchy when their judgement is challenged."

"You're going in a bit deep for me there. How do you get on with this Lenka?"

"Ok. I've known her quite a while. She practised in London when I worked there."

"Presumably she moved to Lincolnshire for an easier case load?"

"You'd think so, wouldn't you? But she'd hardly been here a year when along came Tristram Arkwright. She isn't just a *child* psychologist: she told me when I spoke to her earlier that she saw Arkwright as well as Grace."

"So you knew her at that time?"

"Yes, but she didn't discuss the case with me; as I've said, I had no inkling that Grace was Grace Arkwright."

"She discussed it with Marie, though?"

"As we've now both found out." Tom is smiling more wryly now. "She consulted Marie professionally, for a second opinion, as she was entitled, perhaps wise, to do. Hence Marie's failure to tell us: it would have been a breach of professional trust."

"Yeah, right. I'd be more inclined to sympathise with her if I didn't know she was delighted to have had the upper hand."

Chapter 24

VISITS TO THE morgue always made Tim uneasy. He knew he wasn't alone: only ghouls liked mortuaries and most people merely saw the dead when they'd died from natural causes, lying in repose after reaching a fine old age. One of the worst things about being a copper was that you regularly had to view the corpses of murder victims or those who'd suffered catastrophic accidents – and they were rarely old and seldom looked peaceful. Usually you were accompanied by a relative of the deceased, which meant you couldn't show your true feelings while somehow having to gauge theirs and respond appropriately. It might be all in the day's work for a policeman, but he'd never got used to it; neither, for that matter, had any of his colleagues. That he'd first seen Tina and Bluebelle Brackenbury dead in their own beds didn't ease the anguish: he knew he'd find it harsher observing them laid out on a mortuary slab. Far from numbing his emotions, the cold, sterile environment accentuated yet more savagely the fragility of their hold on life and with it that same woeful sense of waste that had struck him when gazing down at Bluebelle lying dead in her cot.

At least he could be grateful that it was Pete Smith he was accompanying and not Opal. He'd found Opal hard to read – she'd seemed to be sometimes on the verge of hysteria, sometimes calm to the point of callousness – but he had no doubt that if she'd been obliged to stare into these two dead faces her reaction would have been extreme. Pete Smith, on the other hand, whilst noticeably scared, was one of the most understated people Tim had ever met; added to which, he wasn't a blood relative.

Tim had driven him to the morgue and taken him into the ante-room where those required to identify their deceased always waited. Pete's face was ashen; he didn't sit down when Tim gestured towards a chair. Instead, he paced aimlessly, a few steps forward and then back again, before asking Tim whether he could smoke.

"Not in here, I'm afraid. You'll be able to light up as soon as we get outside again." Tim gripped Smith's forearm and gave it a squeeze. "I know this is a bit of an ordeal, but it'll soon be over. It was good of you to do it for Opal."

"Never have heard the last of it if I hadn't," Smith muttered, destroying at a stroke the graciousness that Tim had attributed to him. "She'd of gone on about it for weeks."

Tim gave him what he hoped was a sympathetic smile. "I'll just go and see if they're ready for us. I'll be back in a minute. Why don't you sit down?"

"Because I don't feel like it," said Smith sullenly. "I'm on leave this week, too. Nice holiday this is turning out to be."

Tim didn't reply. He passed through the double doors into the morgue where the mortuary manager was waiting. Tim didn't like Charlie Onson all that much: a gloomy Yorkshireman, he seemed to delight in the discomfort of his visitors. Superintendent Thornton privately called him 'Charon' – one of those rare instances when Thornton's humour resonated with Tim.

"That the next of kin you've got out there?" he said.

"Not quite – the woman's other daughter's partner. But he knows them both. He'll do. Are you ready for him?"

"Aye. Not much patching up to do on these two, was there? Apart from Professor Salkeld's depradations, that is. But he didn't touch the faces and there wasn't hardly a mark on either of them. I'd best warn you that the baby's no longer a good colour, though. The woman doesn't look too bad."

"I suppose I'd better take a look at them first."

"Help yourself. You don't need me to do the honours. They're over there, on the same gurney. I didn't see the need to lay them out separately."

None of the other gurneys appeared to be in use. Tim moved across to where Onson had indicated. There was a single full-size olive green body bag lying there, with a very small bundle beside it, wrapped in white plastic.

"I didn't have a body bag for the child," Morris explained. "We can get them, but not usually as small as that. I've improvised. You should be able to bare the face without exposing the rest of it."

Tim unzipped the body bag first. Tina Brackenbury's eyes had been closed now, thus concealing the astonished expression that he'd noted previously. Her hair had been combed and arranged neatly over her shoulders. She looked like any corpse that had been laid out ready for placing in its coffin – unless, that is, you spotted the bruising on her neck, which had now turned a livid purplish black. He wondered if Smith would notice it. He zipped her up again and turned more hesitantly towards the child. Bluebelle's body had been wrapped around with the plastic as if she'd been swaddled, but her face was covered only by a white towel. Tim lifted the towel and saw what Morris meant. Bluebelle was lying in the same position that she'd been found in, but already her skin had become discoloured and mottled. It was as if death had claimed her the more quickly because her hold on life had been so tender. The light in the mortuary was subdued; Tim hoped that Smith wouldn't notice the extent of her decay. Bluebelle's Babygro had been fastened up to her neck, so he'd be spared sight of her bruise, at any rate.

"That do you?" asked Onson brusquely. "I'm afraid I can't improve on them much, so the sooner the lad sees them, the better."

"You've done a good job; I can see that. I'll bring him in."

Tim went to fetch Smith, who was still wandering round the waiting-room. When he heard Tim enter, he pretended to be reading something on the notice-board.

"We're ready for you now," Tim said. "Don't worry: they don't look too bad."

"Yeah, yeah, you're going to tell me next that they look as if they're sleeping, aren't you?"

"No," said Tim. "I don't want to make it any worse for you than it has to be, but I won't tell you any lies. Let's get it over with, shall we?"

Smith nodded and passed Tim, grim-faced, while he held open the door of the mortuary. Tim saw that Charlie Onson had made himself scarce. Despite his gruff matter-of-factness, he hated watching identifications almost as much as Tim himself.

Smith made for the gurney with a purposefulness that suggested to Tim that he'd done this before. The man was a soldier, of course: if he'd been on active service, he'd probably already encountered death.

"Do you want me to uncover her?"

He nodded curtly. Tim unzipped the body bag again, trying to expose Tina's face while leaving her neck covered. Smith barely glanced at it.

"That's her," he said. "Can you just undo it a bit more?"

"Are you sure you want me to? She's . . ."

"I said, undo it a bit more. She'll be wearing a silver locket. I said I'd take it for Opal."

Tim unzipped the bag an extra few inches so that the bruise was exposed. Smith seemed not to register it.

"Where's the locket?" he demanded. "I can't see it."

"The pathologist may have removed it. I'll ask the mortuary manager in a minute. Would you mind identifying the baby first." He lifted the towel.

"Yeah, that's Bluebelle," said Smith indifferently, before adding, "poor little kid", as if for the sake of appearances. "Now, what about the locket? Tina always wore it. It must be here."

As Tim zipped up the body bag and covered the baby's face again, Charlie Onson appeared at the far end of the room. Tim beckoned him over.

"Did Professor Salkeld register any possessions for Mrs Brackenbury?"

"A T-shirt and bra, and knickers, but that's all. She's wearing a wedding ring, but we've left that on her finger. Do you want it?" he said, addressing Smith.

"Nah," he said, "but there was a locket. A silver locket. Opal – that's her daughter – asked me to fetch it back for her."

"She wasn't wearing a locket when she was brought in here," said Onson. "I can ask Professor Salkeld for you, just to make sure."

"Please do," said Tim, worried that Smith would get

belligerent. "Don't worry, we'll check," he said, turning to Smith himself. He thought back desperately to the scene in the bedroom, trying to visualise every detail. Had Tina Brackenbury been wearing a locket when they'd found her? He'd scrutinised her neck to look at the bruising, and although this had been his first concern, he was sure he would have noticed the locket if It had been there. He'd have to ask Juliet. If neither of them remembered a locket, Tina probably hadn't been wearing it when they'd found her. The photographs taken by the SOCOs would confirm it one way or the other. And if it was true that she always wore it, and had been wearing it when she died, where was it now – or, more to the point, in whose possession?

Chapter 25

DR LENKA ASTANI is as unlike Marie as possible, except in one respect: both are of Eastern European descent. Why is it that of the few psychologists employed by social services in Lincolnshire, two come from such similar, not to say exotic, backgrounds? Briefly I ponder the significance of this, before deciding that there probably isn't any, except maybe that it's possible for those from a different culture to gain unusually incisive insights into the one they're working in. More likely, however, is that Marie and Lenka are just part of the huge influx of people from many different nationalities who currently prop up the NHS and social services in the UK.

Lenka is tall and angular, with olive-coloured skin. In repose, her elongated features fall into a morose expression. Her hair is raven black and cut quite short at the back; at the front, she wears it in an asymmetrical fringe which flops over her forehead like the glossy wing of a bird. Although she has quite a musical voice, it is tinged with anxiety: instead of ending on a rising note, her sentences have a tendency to dip as she finishes speaking.

According to Tom Tarrant when he he has reappeared from his initial sortie into her office to sound her out, Lenka doesn't object to my accompanying him to sit in on the interview with her; however, when I enter she welcomes me with such elaborate courtesy that I feel uncomfortable, as if I've committed a breach of etiquette that she can smooth over only by making an extra effort.

She offers tea, which we both accept. She makes it herself: there is a small counter in the corner of her office bearing an electric kettle and a portable fridge. She sets two cups down on the low table beside the chairs where she has seated us, but does not join us. Instead, she retreats behind her desk, which is large and imposing. I wonder if she keeps her clients at a similar distance.

There are several fat folders on the desk, piled in a neat stack. She lifts the top one and opens it.

"You have come to see me about Grace Winter?" she says. Her voice is inflected, but not as heavily as Marie's.

"Yes," Tom replies. "Or Grace Arkwright. Is that the name that you knew her by?"

"It was when she was first put into my care," Lenka replies severely, "but she is Grace Winter now. That is her legal name. As I have already told you."

"Yes, you have. Very kindly: it's helped us a great deal. We'd still like a bit more detail, if you can manage it," Tom says. "When we spoke earlier, you also said she'd been adopted by the woman who used to work as the secretary at Brocklesby Farm."

"That is correct. Mrs Amy Winter. She took Grace to live with her immediately after the shootings. Amy and her husband adopted Grace about a year afterwards."

"Did you continue to see Grace after she was adopted?"

"Not after the actual adoption, no. As I've already told you, Grace showed astonishing resilience after the shootings. I could find no evidence of trauma. That's why I asked Marie Krakowska to provide a second opinion. She concurred with my diagnosis completely: Grace seemed unusually – you could almost say, unnaturally – well-adjusted, given the circumstances. Even so, I saw her every two months for the year that Amy Winter fostered her, just to make sure there was no delayed shock or other signs that she was disturbed. On the contrary, she always seemed very happy. She was particularly happy when the Winters offered to adopt her. Amy and I agreed that I wouldn't need to see her again after that."

"So you haven't seen her for the past three years? Not since she was seven?"

Lenka steeples her fingers and looks at Tom defensively.

"Well, yes, I have seen her since then, because some time ago Amy contacted us at social services to ask if Grace could be fostered for a while. We decided that I should see Amy and Grace separately, to try to find out what had gone wrong."

"And what conclusion did you come to?"

"This is very confidential, you understand. Amy is extremely sensitive about it all. I strongly advise you not to talk to her about it."

It's on the tip of my tongue to say that we can't make any such guarantees if Amy's help is required in a murder investigation, but Tom cuts in.

"We've come to hear your account, Lenka. I'm sure it will be more accurate and objective than anything that Mrs Winter can tell us."

"All right, as long as you understand my position. I do blame myself, as well, for what happened. We were so preoccupied with worrying about Grace that we didn't think to check that Amy herself was coping. Mentally speaking, she turned out to be much more fragile than Grace was. It was Amy who finally had the breakdown, not Grace."

"Was Mrs Winter present at the shootings?"

"No, but she was very close to all the Arkwright family – including Tristram Arkwright, incidentally. She'd been working as a farm secretary for Norman Arkwright since she left school – for getting on for twenty years, I think; and later for Jane Arkwright's letting business. I believe Norman was actually her husband's uncle. Suddenly the enormity of it all hit her and she could no longer bear to live under the same roof as Grace. She said that Grace was a perpetual reminder, that Grace's presence in the house gave her nightmares. But she did hope to have Grace back one day – still does. She still regards herself as Grace's adoptive mother."

"How did Grace react to being passed on to someone else again?"

"Remarkably well. Emotionally speaking, she seems to be made of rubber."

"Does she have any contact at all with Mrs Winter?"

"There were supervised visits once a month at first. These have stopped since the baby was born. Amy's hoping to start them again when the baby's older, as a first step to taking Grace back again permanently."

I'm confused for a moment and think Lenka must mean Bluebelle Brackenbury, before realising that this doesn't make sense.

"Which baby are you talking about?"

"Amy had a baby about six months ago. Her first. She thinks it best that Grace doesn't see her with the baby until it is older, in case it reminds her of Laura."

"Laura was the name of Grace's little sister? The child who died at the farm?"

"Yes. And Grace spoke of her a lot. That was the only thing

that was striking about all the sessions I had with Grace. She hardly spoke of her mother and the grandparents who died at the farm, but she would talk a lot about Laura, sometimes at great length."

"Is that unusual, when a child has been bereaved?"

"No. Nor is it unusual for a child of that age not to be able to grasp the concept of death. The strange thing about Grace, though, was that although she clearly understood that the adults who'd been in the house were all dead, she spoke of Laura's death as though it was temporary."

I have remained silent so far, but there's a question I want to ask that's unlikely to occur to Tom.

"Lenka, thank you for telling us all of this. We're very grateful. There is something that's puzzling me, though. Why was Grace fostered so far from her original home? Spalding's almost fifty miles away from Lincoln, and comes under a different social services department. And – it's difficult to find a way of saying this without sounding snobbish – why was she sent to be fostered with a woman from Tina Brackenbury's background? The Arkwrights were what you might call county people, and I understand that Amy Winter's husband is also a farmer. Why send Grace to be fostered with a single mother living in a run-down part of Spalding?"

"I can't answer that, except to say that it was Amy's own idea. She knew Tina Brackenbury, who wasn't new to fostering. She was vetted and found to be suitable. As for the distance involved, I think that Amy thought that would make it easier for both herself and Grace. It cut down the opportunities for frequent meetings, even if Amy had wanted them."

"I see," I say, although I don't see at all. The more Lenka tells us of Grace's background, the more questions she raises.

I can see that she is growing warier of me by the minute. I can't gauge why this might be, unless she feels her professional integrity is being compromised in some way. But although I don't expect to get any further with her today, there is one final question that I must ask.

"I understand that you were one of the people who prepared the initial psychological reports on Tristram Arkwright?"

She fixes my eye stonily.

"DS Armstrong, I agreed to see you today to talk about Grace Winter. If you wish to obtain information about Tristram Arkwright, you will need to contact the governor of the prison where he's being held, and quite possibly also the Home Office. As I am sure you are already aware."

Chapter 26

TIM HAD TAKEN Pete Smith back to the police station. Opal was still sitting in the interview room. The baby had woken up and was perched docilely on her lap while she fed it something from a jar. There was a plate of sandwiches on the table in front of her, but they'd barely been touched. Verity Tandy was sitting with her. There didn't appear to have been much conversation between them.

"Are those going begging?" said Pete, eyeing them covetously.

"Help yourself," said Opal. "They aren't very nice, but I haven't got no appetite, in any case."

"Would you like some more tea?" said Verity.

"Yes, please," said Pete. "I'm bushed now."

Opal met his eye. "It was them, then?"

"Yeah," said Pete. "You knew it would be, didn't you, let's be honest."

Opal nodded silently. Tim thought she might be going to cry, but instead she said suddenly,

"You get the locket all right?"

"No. It wasn't on her. They're trying to find out what's happened to it."

"But it must have been on her. She always wore it. You know she did. Someone must have taken it," she added darkly, glowering at Tim.

"Ms Smith, as your partner says, we're trying to find out

what's happened to the locket. It's just possible that a scene of crime officer removed it and put it in an evidence bag, but unless it had been broken in some way, I think that's unlikely. If you're certain your mother would have been wearing it and we can't find it at the scene, the likeliest explanation is that the murderer's taken it. That would make finding it very important to our investigation."

"Yes, well if I was you, I'd start at Frankie's," said Opal with some energy. "He isn't particular about who owns what when he takes a fancy to something."

"Careful, love, think about what you're saying," said Pete indistinctly, his mouth full of sandwich.

"Well, you know it's true. It wouldn't be the first time he'd lifted something off Mam."

"Ms Smith, we're going to need a very accurate description of the locket. Do you think you could describe it - or perhaps draw it for us?"

"You could draw it, Ope. You're good at drawing."

"I'll have a go," said Opal doubtfully. "You take Alfie. Have you got some paper?"

Tim produced a sheet of paper from the cantilevered desk tidy that stood on a wall shelf in the interview room. He handed it to Opal, together with his own ballpoint pen.

"It's an antique," she explained, as she carefully outlined an oval. "It belonged to Mam's grandma. Quite heavy, it is, and kind of scored on the surface with a fern pattern."

"Do you mean 'chased'?"

"I don't know. I suppose so. I can remember the pattern quite well: it's like this."

She sketched an elaborate fern pattern, separately on the sheet of paper from the oval she'd drawn.

"And the chain is heavy, too. It's not really a chain: it's more like a necklace made of little silver beads."

"It's obviously very unusual. Would there be any photographs of your mother wearing it?"

"She wasn't one for having her photo taken very much, but she did wear it all the time, so probably, if she wasn't in her outdoor clothes."

"Did she use it as a locket? Was there anything inside it?"

"There used to be pictures of me and my Dad in it at one time. I don't know about now. She might have put that bastard Frankie in it, I s'pose." Opal scowled. "Or Bluebelle, maybe. I just don't know."

"Thank you. We'll look for photographs at your mother's house and of course we'll carry on looking for the locket itself. Do you have some of your own photos of her?"

"She might be on a few I took last Christmas," said Pete.

"Yeah, she might. We'll look when we get home."

"How long are you planning to stay in Spalding?" Tim asked.

"I don't know. We haven't thought much about it, have we, Pete?"

"I've only got leave until Thursday, though I might be able to get compassionate. I don't know how long it takes to . . . I've never had to organise a funeral. How soon will it be?"

"I'm afraid it's unlikely that we'll be able to release the bodies for some time yet," said Tim. "The coroner may ask for further tests. We'll arrange for you to stay in Spalding if you want to: we can book you into a hotel. Or we can take you home now. We'll certainly need to talk to you again, so if you go home, you'll have to let us know if you make any plans to go away."

"I think we should go home," said Pete quickly.

"Yeah, let's go home. We'll only get gawped at here."

"I'm afraid that's almost certainly going to be the case," said Tim. "Superintendent Thornton has agreed to talk to the Press in about an hour's time and now that we have positive identification we'll be releasing the names."

"Why'd you do that, then?" said Pete.

"Partly because it might help us with our inquiries; partly because if we don't tell reporters the truth, they're liable to jump to wild conclusions."

"Can't get much wilder than murder, can you?" said Pete in a reasonable voice.

"I must warn you not to talk to the Press for now and on no account to agree to sell them your story. If you get some offers later on and choose to accept one of them, we can't stop you, but at this stage it will harm the inquiry if you speculate in public."

Tim noted the flicker of interest in Pete's eyes.

"If we *what*?" said Opal.

"If you make suggestions about who you think might have killed your mother and sister, for example, or otherwise give the papers information that might damage the work we're doing."

"You mean, tell them about that bastard Frankie," said Opal.

"That sort of thing. And I should also warn you that if you make unfounded allegations about anyone, anyone at all, that is slander, and the person concerned is entitled to sue you. It could even prevent us from prosecuting the person we believe to be guilty. I'm sorry to have to speak like this when you're obviously very upset about what's happened."

"Yeah, understood," said Pete.

"When did you last talk to your Mum, Opal?"

"Sat'day morning. She usually calls me Sat'days."

"Was she alone? And did she seem quite normal?"

"Well, Bluebelle was there. I don't know about Grace. And, yeah, she seemed fine."

"Thank you. That's helpful. PC Tandy will order a car to take you home now. Could you give her your address and contact phone numbers before you leave?"

"Yeah," said Opal. "Will you keep on telling us what's going on?"

"We'll inform you of any new developments. We won't be able to name names, but we'll let you know if we've arrested any suspects. I know you think that Frankie Roberts may have harmed your mother. Is there anyone else you can think of? Anyone she might have made an enemy of?"

"No. Everyone loved Mam."

Pete shifted uneasily.

"What about your Dad?" he said. "No love lost there, was there?"

"My Dad wouldn't've done a thing like that," said Opal. "Besides, no-one knows where he is now. He might of gone back on the boats."

Tim had intended to save this type of questioning until Opal was in a calmer frame of mind. He'd already thought that Opal's father might offer a possible line of enquiry, though it was a long shot.

"How long is it since your parents separated?"

"About four years, I think. Yeah, it must have been four years."

"Did they keep in touch?"

"On and off, but mostly off, and I don't think she'd seen him in a while. Dad was in the right, see? He left because Frankie come sniffing round. And although Dad tried to come back a few times, she never got rid of that fucker."

"What about you? Do you still have any contact with your father?"

Pete unexpectedly blew a raspberry.

"I did keep up with him for a while – phone calls and that, I didn't know where he was living. But he didn't like Pete. When I told him me and Pete was getting together, he lost his rag. I haven't heard from him since. Like I said, he'd been thinking of going back on the boats, if that's any help."

"Is he a sailor?"

"Yes and no. He used to work as a steward on the ferries, before he met Mam. He always said he had a hankering to go back. Well, there was nothing stopping him then, was there?"

"Do you know which ferry company?"

"I think he'd worked for several. North Sea crossings mostly. But I s'pose he could have taken a job with any of them."

"Can you give me his full name?"

"Yes. It's Roderick Jonathan Brackenbury."

"And his mobile number? Do you still have it?"

"I've got it on my phone. I'll find it for you."

Opal and Pete Smith had been gone for some minutes when Tim remembered that he'd forgotten to arrange for them to meet Grace. It had slipped their minds, as well: either that, or they weren't too keen on the idea.

Chapter 27

IT HAD BEEN a long and tedious day. Not that he was complaining: he knew how lucky he was that Jack Rose had come back on duty that morning.

"You all right, mate?" Jack had asked sympathetically. "Barry Griggs told me you'd been sick in the night."

"Yes, just one of the usual headaches. It's a lot better now. I wouldn't mind staying in here today, though, if you can swing it."

"You don't seem bad enough for the sick bay. What makes you think you aren't up to working?"

"I don't want to throw up on the books. You know the vomiting comes on suddenly sometimes."

Jack shrugged.

"It's all right by me if you stay in here. You'll have to go to breakfast, though. Barry's put in a report saying you might have taken something. 'Banned substances', he means. He's asked for a cell search."

"Bastard!" He tried to grin while he said it, but it turned into a grimace. He could murder the officious little twat. Jack picked up something in his tone and looked alarmed. He cursed himself: he'd have to be more on his guard; he'd be lost without Jack's support.

"Yes, well, Griggsy's a stickler for detail. And rightly so, too. You aren't meant to be on holiday here. Not everyone's as soft as I am; and a good thing, too. You're lucky I trust you. Most in here would get short shrift from me."

"Sorry, Jack. I've had a rough night. I didn't mean to sound so nowty. You can search all you like: be my guest. You won't find anything."

He'd thought that Jack might say he believed him, not to worry, but evidently he'd triggered a spark of suspicion.

"Get down to breakfast, then. You don't have to eat owt, but if you want to come back here, make sure you aren't sick down there. Otherwise you'll be straight off to the quack and there's nothing I can do about that. You do just want to stay in here because you're feeling off it, don't you?"

"What other reason would I have? You know I like it in the library."

Jack nodded as if satisfied.

He'd quietly joined the queue for breakfast and managed to force down some bread and jam.

Jack and another warder were in his cell when he got back. His bed had been stripped and all his possessions gone through. They'd been left in a heap on the floor, together with his bedclothes. He tried not to look disgusted.

"You're right, we didn't find owt," Jack said cheerfully. "You can put this lot back together again now. We'll let you stay in here this morning. You'll probably be fit for work this afternoon, won't you?"

He carefully sorted through his things to make sure none of them was damaged. Jack had probably read the draft of the letter, but there was nothing incriminating in it. He set about making the bed and lay down on it.

Throughout the morning, every hour on the hour, he'd turned on the television to pick up the news bulletin, keeping the sound right down. There had been nothing more about the murders in Spalding.

Jack Rose had looked in on him twice, fortunately on occasions when the TV was switched off. Each time he'd been lying listlessly on his bed with his eyes closed. Jack wasn't to be fobbed off, though. At lunchtime, he returned. He spoke more sharply than usual.

"Time to get up now, Arkwright. Either you go back to work or I'm sending you to the quack."

He'd opened his eyes and sat up slowly.

"The rest of the day in here would set me up."

"I daresay, but as I said it isn't a 'oliday camp. You've not been sick again today, have you? A bit of pen-pushing isn't going to do you any harm. Do you want lunch or not?"

"I won't bother."

He knew he'd still be able to look at news bulletins on the PC in the library, but he'd have to be a lot more careful. Once before he'd clicked on a news clip with a commentary: the reporter's voice had come suddenly booming out at him and disturbed the screws on duty, sending them charging in to find out what was going on. He mustn't give them a reason to take away his internet access.

He got on with classifying the previous day's books, looking at the BBC website every so often and minimising it the rest of the time. It was just past 4 p.m. when the item he'd been waiting for finally came through on 'breaking news'.

"Police in South Lincolnshire have released the identities of the woman and baby found dead in Lady Margaret Dymoke Street yesterday. Speaking at a press conference, Superintendent Thornton of South Lincs police confirmed the names of the victims as Tina Brackenbury, aged 36, and her daughter Bluebelle, who was just one year old. Superintendent Thornton refused to comment on rumours that the mother and her child had both been strangled, saying that the police were still awaiting pathologists' reports to ascertain the causes of death. He did confirm that foul play was suspected, and that both deaths are currently being treated as murders."

He smiled grimly.

That would certainly put the cat among the pigeons. He could look forward to a productive evening doing more work on his case. Or perhaps it would be more sensible to hold off for a while until he knew the lie of the land.

Chapter 28

TOM TARRANT HAD been strangely rattled by Lenka Astani's limited willingness to co-operate. He'd known that she had a reputation for being reserved, some would say aloof, but he didn't understand what she hoped to achieve by stalling DS Armstrong.

Juliet herself didn't seem to be too perturbed by it. She appeared to be satisfied with the information she'd gathered about Grace Winter and admitted she'd been pushing her luck when she'd tried to pump Lenka about Tristram Arkwright, too.

"What next?" Tom asked. "Lenka will have to tell you what she knows about him eventually, won't she?"

"Perhaps. But, as she says, I'll need to contact the appropriate authorities first; and he may have seen a psychiatrist that specialises in psychopathic disorders both before and after he was convicted, so there could be more precise professional evidence available than she's able to give. On balance, she was right to turn me down. She was probably wary of misleading me and may even have thought I was being lazy. I admit I saw her as a possible short-cut. Permissible in a murder enquiry, but I'm going to have to read more on the Arkwright case this evening."

"I remember it quite well," said Tom. "I read all the newspaper accounts at the time; though I never put two and two together and linked Amy Winter to Grace Arkwright."

"I read the police reports on it, but of course I haven't remembered all the details. It's often the small points that are most telling, which is why I'll have to read them again. I'd forgotten all about Amy Winter, for example. She was more than just a secretary, wasn't she? Didn't she and her husband move into Brocklesby Farm quite soon after the shootings?"

"Yes, it was all over the papers. As Lenka said, Amy's husband was Norman Arkwright's nephew. As Tristram Arkwright had murdered his entire family and by law couldn't benefit financially from his crimes, the nephew inherited the farm. I don't remember his name, but Amy's stuck in my mind. She was interviewed on television, saying that she and the husband were not at all worried about living in the farm where so many of their relatives had died. She said that apart from the deaths they had only happy memories there and that over the centuries many people must have died there besides the Arkwrights."

"I don't think I saw that; quite ghoulish, really, wasn't it? I suppose that's why the reporters were so interested. Anyway, from what Lenka says it turned out that Amy Winter wasn't as unimaginative as she believed herself to be. The deaths came back to haunt her afterwards."

"Or Grace Arkwright did," said Tom thoughtfully. "If Lenka's correct, and she's a stickler for getting things right, it was Grace's presence in the house that gave her the abdabs, rather than knowledge of the actual murders."

"We've all noticed something unsettling about Grace. She's a very beautiful child, but there's an air about her – a kind of prescience or perhaps I mean precociousness – that makes me feel uncomfortable. Maybe that was what worried Amy Winter."

"Maybe, although I would have thought the actual deaths, and the fact that Tristram Arkwright's still alive, would be a lot more disturbing than the presence of a pretty child, even if she is old beyond her years. It's hardly surprising, given what she's been through, is it?"

"You're right. Do you think you'll soon be able to find a suitable foster home for Grace?"

"Some of my colleagues are making enquiries. I'll be working on it as soon as we get back to Spalding. If we can't find a foster home, we can certainly put her into care temporarily, though I'd rather not do that unless it's unavoidable. I think she needs the security of a family around her at the moment."

"You mean, send her to a children's home?"

"Yes. The one in Spalding is quite good. It's not too big, and the kids who stay there long term seem to do all right. It would be better than leaving her with the Hebblewhites."

"That's probably a non-starter. DI Yates is very keen to separate her from Chloe Hebblewhite, partly because he wants to be able to interview Grace and Chloe separately. I assume that either a foster parent or someone from the children's home would be willing to take on the responsible adult role?"

"Almost undoubtedly. If not, I could do it."

"That would be great, but Marie said . . ."

"Marie said she could do it if you stopped using her as a police adviser, but it could be tricky. She's been involved in Grace's previous psychological analysis, although without direct contact. The same doesn't apply to me: I was as ignorant as you were about Grace's past history until yesterday. Anyway, let's see what else I can come up with first, shall we?"

Chapter 29

"EVERYTHING ALL RIGHT?" Katrin said to Tim. He'd eaten his supper almost without a word and was now immersed in reading something on his laptop.

"Uh? Yes, sorry, I'm not being very good company, am I?"

"I know you're upset about the Brackenbury case."

"I'm always upset by murder cases, even though solving them's what I do – or am meant to do. But child murders are something else. Who would want to kill a baby?"

"I don't know. I guess one way of finding out is to look at other murders of babies, and try to understand the killers' motives."

"I'm inclined to think they must all be psychopaths, but you may be right. I've got my work cut out working through this lot, though."

"What lot?"

"I'm reading up on the murders at Brocklesby Farm. I told you the little girl who was being fostered by Tina Brackenbury was Grace Arkwright, now Grace Winter, the only survivor except Tristram Arkwright, the perpetrator."

"I remember the Brocklesby Farm killings."

"I think most people do; what I'm trying to do now is rediscover the detail. It seems too much of a coincidence that this child has been involved in two multiple murders."

"But she's not really been involved in the Brackenbury murders, has she? She wasn't there: otherwise she'd almost certainly be dead as well, now. Besides, Tristram Arkwright's in jail. You're not suggesting they got the wrong person for the Arkwright killings?"

"Certainly not: the evidence against Tristram Arkwright was overwhelming, even though he continues to protest his innocence. But I can't help feeling there must be some link between the two, and that Grace is the key to it."

"Have you interviewed her?"

"Juliet's made a start. Grace was staying with another kid at the time and the other kid's been quite hysterical."

"It sounds as if you need a child psychologist to help. What about Marie Krakowska? I know she can be irritating, but she's good at her job."

"Believe me, she's in this up to the hilt already; and is being just as irritating as usual. But we have to have an expert present at the interviews and Juliet gets on with her as well as anyone can. What are you working on, anyway?"

"You don't have to pretend to be interested in my work if you want to get on with your reading."

Tim smiled. He realised several times each day how lucky he was to be married to Katrin. This was one such occasion.

"I'm afraid I'm being even more devious than that. If you haven't got much on, could you do some research into murdered children for me?"

Katrin cocked her head to one side.

"I've just finished a piece of work for Superintendent Thornton on burglary statistics. As far as I know, he hasn't lined up anything else for me yet. Do you want me to ask him if I can spend a couple of days working for you?"

"It would be great if you could help, if you don't mind. But I'd better ask Thornton."

"Otherwise he might think you're being devious?"

Tim grinned before settling down again with his laptop.

Chapter 30

I'M FEELING A bit flat when I reach home. I'd returned to the station in time to attend Superintendent Thornton's press conference, which I thought he handled quite well (or, rather, he was allowed to be gracious because the reporters didn't press him too hard – that same subdued reverence when there's a dead child involved that I'd noticed earlier), but even the few snippets of information that he threw to them got me thinking again about the sight of Bluebelle Brackenbury's tiny corpse. I could visualise it lying there in that dingy little back bedroom; and Grace Winter, that beautiful, uncannily poised young girl, hovering nearby, in spirit if not in fact.

Not something I could confide to Tim or Superintendent Thornton; neither of them ever has any truck with 'funny feelings' or the supernatural, an attitude that I can sympathise with because in the past it's been hardened by offers of help with murder cases from bogus mediums seeking the limelight. But, though I know Tim would scoff at any hint of a premonition, the sentiments behind it might impress him more. We've pussy-footed round it a bit, but I think we're both convinced that Grace Winter is somehow mixed up in the deaths at Lady Margaret Dymoke Street and we both think that focusing on the detail of the four-year-old murders at Brocklesby Farm may provide the key.

I've downloaded the police reports about the murders as well as the official account of Tristram Arkwright's trial. I know there are many archived newspaper reports of the trial if I look for them, as well as books by various 'true life' crime authors, some of them convinced of his guilt and others equally staunch defenders of his innocence. Eventually, I may read some of these, but for now I want to study as plain and unvarnished a set of the facts as possible. I understand that even the official documents can't be taken at their face value, however: I'm aware that Mortimer Bayles was Arkwright's defending counsel and I seem to remember that the prosecuting QC was more of an establishment figure, but equally persuasive. Then there's Arkwright's website: I'm full of curiosity about it; it seems to beckon like some evil mantra. But I'll leave it for the moment. I know it's bound to cloud my views.

It's dismal sitting here alone, knowing I'll be spending the evening poring over grisly accounts of four violent deaths and the even more graphic photographs taken by the scene-of-crime officers afterwards. I look at my watch: it's seven-thirty and though it's not dark yet, there's an autumnal nip in the air. I can hear children playing in the street outside; an adult yells and the shrieks and laughter stop. They've been called in to the safety of their homes. How terrible for a child to believe it's safe and then be brutally killed in its bed.

I'm not hungry and decide not to bother with supper. I pour myself a vodka and tomato juice, open a packet of crisps and settle down to read.

The first document is the transcript of a 999 call. The time is given as 02.53 a.m., the date as 18th August 2012. I note with a jolt that it was my birthday: I'm surprised I didn't pick that up at the time. That means the murders happened almost exactly four years ago. I wonder if the date is significant? Did the anniversary trigger some sleeping demon? I return to the transcript.

"Please help me."

"Caller, can you identify yourself? Which service do you require? Police, fire or ambulance?"

"Police. I think there's been a murder. I called my father and I heard gunshots and . . ."

"Take it slowly. Please identify yourself and give your location."

"I'm calling from outside Brocklesby Farm. It's on Brocklesby Road, about five miles from Lincoln. My name is Tristram Arkwright. My parents live at the farm. I called my father on my mobile and I thought I heard gunshots."

"Where are you?"

"I'm standing outside the farmhouse – some distance away from it, in fact. I daren't go in. I think my father's gone berserk with his shotgun. Or it may be my sister. Yes, I think it's probably my sister."

"Mr Arkwright, please stay where you are. Repeat, stay where you are. Keep out of range of the windows of the house and wait at a safe distance. Do not go into the house. We'll be sending a police car to investigate. Stay where you are until it arrives."

"Thank you. I . . . I'm scared. I'm so worried. Thank you."

The second document is a statement by Larry Bates, one of two police officers called out to the farm following the 999 call from Tristram Arkwright.

PC Gibson and I arrived at the farm at 03.23 a.m. The house was in darkness. A man came out of the shadows and approached the car. I got out to talk to him. He said his name was Tristram Arkwright and that he'd made the 999 call earlier. He appeared to be very distressed. He was almost incoherent, and shivering, although it was a warm night and he was wearing a jacket. We told him to get into the back of the police car and asked him what he knew. He said he'd called his father earlier and hadn't been able to get much sense from him. His father had sounded angry, but it wasn't clear why. Then he'd heard a gun going off, then there was silence. Originally he'd called his father from his mobile, but now he tried the landline. He couldn't get through. He'd come to the farm and tried all the numbers he could in succession: the landline, his father's mobile and his mother's and sister's mobiles. He was afraid that something terrible had happened.

PC Gibson and I relayed this information back to the station and were told to wait for an armed response team to arrive. We were told to wait outside the house and not to approach it unless anyone came out to ask for help. Anyone who did come out should be treated with extreme caution, even if they appeared to be distressed.

We told Mr Arkwright what our instructions were and asked him to wait with us in our car. He seemed to be suffering from shock. We wrapped him in a foil exposure blanket and tried to make him drink some water. He didn't take the water at first, but after twenty minutes or so he had to leave the car quickly and was violently sick outside. Then he accepted the water.

The armed response team took almost two hours to arrive: their vehicle drew up alongside ours at 5 a.m. precisely. There were four of them, including Sergeant Wilkins, their leader. Sergeant Wilkins instructed us to get out of the car and take refuge behind a barn, so that we would not be within firing range of the house. Mr Arkwright began to shake violently when he heard this instruction. He said, "You won't hurt any of them, will you? There are two children in there."

Sergeant Wilkins came and joined us by the barn. He asked Mr Arkwright to draw a sketch of the interior of the house and indicate in which rooms the occupants usually slept. He asked for information about the occupants. Mr Arkwright said they were his parents, Norman and Jane Arkwright, his sister Jacqueline and her two children, Grace and Laura. Sergeant Wilkins asked how he could be sure all these people and no others were in residence. Mr Arkwright said he couldn't be absolutely sure, but that he'd called in on them that evening and all were there then. His sister and her children were staying there. It was unlikely any of them had left the farmhouse after his departure and equally unlikely that anyone else had joined them there, as it had been quite late in the evening when he'd gone home.

Sergeant Wilkins asked whether he'd forgotten to mention Jacqueline's husband. Was he also staying at the farm? Mr Arkwright said his sister didn't have a husband; he added that the children had different fathers, but no-one knew who they were.

Sergeant Wilkins asked which of the people in the house had access to a gun. Mr Arkwright said that in theory all the adults did; his father's gun cabinet was locked, but his mother and sister both knew where the key was kept.

Sergeant Wilkins asked what types of gun were kept in the cabinet.

Mr Arkwright said that his father owned two shotguns and an air rifle. There was also a handgun that had belonged to his grandmother, who had worked as an undercover agent in the second world war. Sergeant Wilkins raised his eyebrows at this.

('Far-fetched?' has been written in the margin.)

Sergeant Wilkins asked which of the adults knew how to use the guns. Mr Arkwright said that his father was a good shot, and his sister also knew how to shoot. He didn't know about his mother. He'd been told that she'd shot game in the past, but he couldn't remember ever having seen her fire a gun.

Sergeant Wilkins said he now had enough information, and that we should remain concealed behind the barn as he'd told us to. Taking shelter behind his own vehicle, he used a loud hailer to call out to the family in the farmhouse.

"Mr and Mrs Arkwright! Are you in there? This is a police armed response team. If you're in the house and can hear us, please open the door now, and show yourselves. Turn the lights on first."

There was no answer. The house stayed dark.

After a few minutes, Sergeant Wilkins tried again.

"Mr and Mrs Arkwright! My name is Sergeant Wilkins. I'm with a police armed response team. I'm going to count slowly to five. If you haven't opened the door when I've finished, we're coming in. If anyone in there is armed, please put down your arms now. No-one will get hurt unless we're threatened first. Turn on the lights if you are able."

Still no-one answered. The house remained in darkness.

Our vehicles were parked at the front of the house, a few yards away from the garden, which was short and broad. The barn was to one side of the garden, facing the track that led up to it. Sergeant Wilkins and his team edged round the front of the house. They made for the kitchen door, which Mr Arkwright had told us would be easier to break into than the front door. We could hear them issue one more warning, then proceed to ram the door. Mr Arkwright became very agitated at this point. He said, "Oh, God, oh, God, I just know that something terrible has happened." We heard no further noises once the response team had entered the house.

Sergeant Wilkins came back to us after approximately fifteen minutes. It was 05.35 a.m.

He said, "I think they're all dead. You need to call for ambulances and a doctor. I'm sorry, sir." (Talking to Tristram Arkwright.)

Mr Arkwright seemed to have trouble understanding.

"All of them?" he said. "The children as well?"

Sergeant Wilkins said they'd found three adults, a middle-aged man and woman and a younger woman, and a baby. In the heat of the moment, he'd forgotten that Mr Arkwright had said there was another child there as well. Was it possible that this child was no longer in the house when the shootings took place?

Mr Arkwright said he didn't think it was likely. Where could a six-year-old child have gone at that time of night? He asked Sergeant Wilkins if he would look for the child again. He said he thought it was possible she'd escaped the murderer: perhaps she was hiding somewhere.

Sergeant Wilkins: "Did you say her name was Grace?"

Mr Arkwright: "Yes."

Sergeant Wilkins: "Would you like to come into the house with us and help us to search for her, sir?"

Mr Arkwright: "I don't think I could do that. I'm very squeamish, you see. I can't stand the sight of blood."

Sergeant Wilkins went back into the house. PC Gibson and myself called for ambulances and a doctor as he requested. He returned at 06.03 a.m., carrying a small child.

Mr Arkwright got out of the car. He said "Oh, my God, is she dead?"

Sergeant Wilkins said that as far as he could see, there was nothing wrong with her. He asked Mr Arkwright if he'd like to hold the child. Mr Arkwright took her from him and held her in his arms. He said, "It's all right, Grace; it's all right, now."

The doctor and the ambulances arrived at 06.10 a.m. Grace Arkwright was taken to hospital in one of the ambulances, to be checked over. Mr Arkwright accompanied her.

Several things leap out at me, but I haven't read the transcripts of the trial yet, so I just make a few notes:

Is Arkwright's behaviour normal under the circumstances or bizarre / indicative of guilt?

Although guns were mentioned several times before the armed response team went in, and Arkwright claimed to have heard a shot during the telephone call to his father, according to the statement no-one actually told him that the occupants of the house had been shot. He jumps to this conclusion. Does he already know they're dead? How does he know there is going to be a lot of blood? (Is there in fact a lot of blood?)

Do his comments about the children indicate that he knows all along that Grace is still alive?

Did Grace say anything when she was rescued by Sergeant Wilkins or after he passed her to Arkwright? Is so, did anyone write down what she said?

Where did Sergeant Wilkins find Grace?

I look at my watch. It's getting late now. I know that the next file contains photographs of Arkwright's victims. If I open it now, I probably won't sleep. I pour myself another vodka and tomato juice and shut down the computer.

Chapter 31

HAVING READ A synopsis of Tristram Arkwright's trial, which consisted mainly of an abbreviated account of the judge's summing up, Tim had accessed the file of photographs. He'd wanted to know what the judge's conclusions were, but otherwise he'd decided to approach the Arkwright murders as if they were cold case crimes that had yet to be solved. He'd worked on a number of cold cases and always turned to the pictorial evidence first if there was any, as it enabled him to form opinions unbiased by anyone else's judgement. He knew the police had made several blunders when dealing with the Arkwright case and that the judge had particularly praised the high standards of the photographs taken by the SOCO photographer, which had preserved a record of evidence unfortunately later destroyed by some slipshod scene-of-crime procedures.

The first photographs in the series were the most shocking. Norman Arkwight's face was a bloody mess, his jaw half shot away. His body was lying sprawled at the foot of the staircase, as if he'd pitched down it headlong. He was wearing old-fashioned striped pyjamas. From the awkward position in which he was lying, it looked as if his neck might have been broken in the fall. The photographer had taken pictures from several angles of the body, from above and from either side, and three more close-ups of the head.

Jane Arkwright's body was lying in a doorway. It was

nowhere near as mutilated as her husband's. It was clad in a dressing-gown, which gaped open to reveal a matronly all-in-one undergarment. There was little blood on her: the first photograph, which captured the whole figure, revealed no discernible injuries. A second photo, of the torso only, showed a small wound above her left breast. The third was of the wound in close-up: a small round hole that had torn into a slit on one side, from which had leaked a modest trickle of blood. Tim guessed that she'd been shot through the heart at close range and died more or less instantly.

Tim had expected the next picture to be of Jacqueline Arkwright's body. It came as a shock when the tiny corpse of a baby flashed up on the screen. His first thought was that somehow a photograph of Bluebelle Brackenbury had got mixed up in the deck, but closer scrutiny showed him this child was younger than Bluebelle, and very fair-haired: Laura Arkwright. She was dressed in a towelling Babygro not unlike the one that Bluebelle had been wearing when she died, but this one had embroidery around the neck and cuffs. There were no visible injuries on Laura's clothed body: like Bluebelle, she looked as if she was sleeping. Tim forced himself to inspect the photograph closely, zooming in on it to magnify every detail as much as possible. From memory, he thought that all of the victims at Brocklesby Farm had died of gunshot wounds, but now he doubted that Laura could have been shot: a bullet would surely have inflicted catastrophic damage on a body so small.

Slumped on the floor between the bed and the empty cot, with both arms outstretched, as if she had made a vain attempt to stop the killer entering the room, lay Jacqueline Arkwright's body. She was lying on her stomach and spread-eagled.

Neither this first photograph of her nor the second, which was a close-up of her face, gave any indication of how she'd died. A third, which homed in on the top half of her torso, revealed bloodstains on her nightdress. Cause of death in the pathologist's report was given as wounds to vital organs caused by handgun fire.

Tim turned to the coroner's report. It stated that Norman and Jane Arkwright had died as a result of 'unlawful killing, by person or persons unknown'. It was more equivocal about who was responsible for Jacqueline's death. The pathologist's report, which including a statement from a forensics expert, concluded that it was unlikely but not impossible that Jacqueline had taken her own life. Laura had suffocated, trapped under her mother's body, but by whose hand was unclear. It was just possible her death had been an accident, but the coroner's verdict was that she had also been murdered.

Tim couldn't face reading the whole of the account of Tristram Arkwright's trial that night and instead turned to the summary of the argument put forward by his defence. Arkwright's own testimony, which he used very convincingly and with which he had initially managed to persuade the police of his innocence, was that his sister had gone berserk and shot her parents before killing herself. Forensically, this would have been difficult but not impossible.

Laura was barely mentioned. Cause of death was given as suffocation by 'person or persons unknown', but there was no speculation about who those persons might have been. Even more strangely, Tristram Arkwright's defence lawyer didn't dwell much on the baby and neither did the prosecution. Doubtless to protect her identity, no-one mentioned the six-year-old survivor of the massacre.

Chapter 32

TOM TARRANT HAD been calling registered foster parents who might be prepared to take Grace Winter at short notice, but he hadn't had much success. He hadn't revealed that his charge was the former Grace Arkwright, but he'd had to disclose her present name, and that she was the foster daughter, rather than the biological daughter, of the woman who'd just been murdered. It seemed to be mostly owing to superstition that they all refused Grace: they believed she was jinxed, or would bring them bad luck. Only one woman expressed her doubt about being able to care for a child who could be deeply disturbed by the trauma of the murders. Tom wondered what she would have said if she'd known this was the second series of murders that had touched Grace's young life. As a last resort, he'd called Lenka Astani to ask her whether Grace could return to live with Amy Winter, but she'd said it would be out of the question: Amy was still far too fragile to be able to cope.

Tom sighed. He agreed with the police that Grace shouldn't be left with Mavis Hebblewhite, but if he couldn't find a fosterer the only alternative would be to place her in the children's home. Tom didn't want to do this: he knew Grace wouldn't receive the close attention she'd get from living with a family, meaning that any mental problems she might be experiencing could go unnoticed. There was also the danger that she'd become an object of either fascination or derision to the other children in care, which would increase the pressure on her. Not for the first time in his career, he wished he could take the child home and look after her himself. Deep down, he knew this would be a mistake and that he was lucky that Alex, his wife, was made of sterner stuff. She believed in leaving work behind at the office door; it was out of the question she would admit one of Tom's 'waifs and strays' into her home.

He sighed again. He wondered if DS Armstrong could give him some advice. He'd known her for some years now, ever since Alex had got mixed up in the disappearance of a female archaeologist, and he had considerable respect for her opinion. His hand was moving to pick up his phone when it began to ring.

"Tom? It's Juliet Armstrong."

"What a coincidence! I was about to call you."

"Any luck with foster parents?"

"Unfortunately not. I think we may have to put Grace into care. Just temporarily."

"When you've heard what I've got to say you may decide that's a good thing. Mavis Hebblewhite's just called me again."

"If it's an offer for Grace to stay there longer, I thought you and DI Yates . . ."

"No, it's not that. The opposite, in fact. Apparently, Grace opened up to Mavis last night and said she thought she'd seen the killer. Mavis was completely spooked by it: even though she likes Grace, she can't wait to get her out of the house now, in case the killer comes after her."

"Is that likely?"

"Not very likely, but it's a possibility, if he realised that she'd seen him."

"So what do you think we should do with her now?"

"She needs to be kept securely somewhere: a place where we can protect her with a police guard. And we'll want to interview her again as soon as we possibly can."

"There's a flat at the children's home. It's mainly used for new arrivals who are particularly disturbed. Sometimes they stay there for a couple of days with their case workers."

"How secure is it?"

"It's in a self-contained annexe, up a flight of stairs. If you put a guard on the staircase it'll be pretty secure."

"Is it being used at present?"

"I don't know. I can check."

"I'd be grateful if you would. If it's free, it sounds as if it's just what we need."

"Grace can't stay in the flat on her own. Someone would have to be inside it with her, as well as whoever you send to guard it. There are two bedrooms."

"I thought I might stay with her myself."

"You? But . . ."

"But what?" said Juliet sharply. The warmth in her tone evaporated. Tom thought for a moment. Why not? He couldn't think of a logical reason why Juliet shouldn't become Grace's temporary carer, except that Grace might be intimidated by the fact that she was a policewoman. But Grace hadn't seemed to mind that earlier.

"Nothing. I wasn't thinking. It's a great idea, if you can spare the time."

"I'm one of the detectives on the case. It's part of my job," said Juliet stiffly.

"As I said, it's a great idea," Tom was trying to sound conciliatory without being condescending. Infusing more energy into his voice, he added "What about Chloe? Is she in danger, too?"

"According to Mrs Hebblewhite, it was only Grace who saw the suspect. I say suspect, because I don't think she's claiming actually to have seen him commit murder, just a man leaving the house. That's all I know until we talk to her, but Mrs Hebblewhite isn't worried about Chloe. Based on what was said, she's just desperate to be rid of Grace, even though she has a soft spot for her."

"I wonder why she's so sure Chloe isn't involved."

"We'll have to find out. As I said, we need to interview Grace again, and quickly. Is Marie Krakowska willing to act as her responsible adult?"

"I'll have to ask her, but probably, if you're ok with that. There are drawbacks, as I said to you before. She'll want to look after Grace, but it will cramp her style a bit. She'll have to be an observer and supporter rather than a participant in the interview, even though she's already had professional contact with Grace."

"I'll call her as soon as we've finished talking."

"Dress it up, will you, so that she can't refuse? Tell her that Grace really needs someone on her side and no-one else is willing to help."

"I don't need to dress it up to say that. It's the truth."

"Good. Will you get back to me as soon as you know about Marie and the flat? I want to interview Grace today if we can manage it."

"Sure, I'll get on to it now. But I'm still worried about Chloe. She's part of my case load, don't forget: it's my job to keep her out of danger."

"We'll visit Chloe and Mavis again soon and of course

Chloe'll be offered protection if we think she's in danger. Right now, I have to find out all Grace can tell us before she forgets or changes her mind. I don't have time for Chloe's tongue-tied hysterics or her pushy mother."

"Ouch!" said Tom.

He put the phone down. If DS Armstrong was shamed by his final comment, that was exactly what he intended.

Chapter 33

I CAN SEE Tim's not in a good mood as soon as I enter his office.

"Juliet?" he says, looking up only after he has continued reading for a protracted minute. "What can I do for you?"

He can still intimidate me when he behaves like this. It's his way of reminding me that, however much we may appear to be friends, he is still the boss.

"Grace Winter has remembered that she saw someone who looked suspicious when she went back to the house. I want to interview her here as soon as I can. I've asked Tom Tarrant to ask Marie Krakowska to be her responsible adult."

"Fine, thanks for letting me know." Tim turns back to his document, then looks up sharply as he takes in what I've just said.

"Christ! This could be the breakthrough we need. But why didn't she tell us about this before? And what about the other girl?"

"I can't answer those questions, sir. Apparently, Grace confided in Mavis Hebblewhite last night. Mavis seems to think that Chloe isn't involved, but at the moment I don't know why. Mavis can't wait to get Grace out of her house now, in case the supposed killer comes after her."

"Does she have any reason for thinking that? And doesn't that suit us? We want to get Grace away from her, don't we?"

"I don't know. And yes, we do want Grace out of there.

Tom Tarrant can't find a foster home for her at short notice, but it's essential now for her to stay in the flat at the children's home, if it's available, for security. She'll need someone to be there with her, and a police guard as well, if her story makes sense."

"Who's going to stay with her? We can't ask Marie to do that."

"I thought I'd do it. Grace seems not to mind me and she certainly likes you. I'd be grateful if you'd come with me to fetch her from the Hebblewhites', if you have time, sir."

"Can't you take Verity Tandy or Giash with you?"

"I don't think Mavis Hebblewhite would like a uniform turning up on her doorstep. We need to keep her onside while this is going on and we don't want to intimidate Grace. She isn't under arrest."

"OK, I'll come, but I buy your second argument more than the first: I don't think we owe Mavis Hebblewhite much consideration. Her sons are evil little tearaways: they're likely to end up inside as soon as they're old enough. And Mavis's past doesn't bear too much scrutiny, either."

Tim stands up and reaches for his jacket.

"Let's go then, shall we?" As he reaches the door, he adds, "You aren't serious about staying in the children's home, are you?"

"Perfectly serious, if it's necessary."

Tim shrugs.

"Your decision," he says. "I won't try to stop you. But I'd have thought you'd got enough on your plate already."

✿

Mavis Hebblewhite lets us into her house and hurriedly closes the door behind us. As always, she's immaculately turned out, today in a long, loose white shirt and skinny jeans. She leads us into her front room. It's a smallish square room, quite neat and tidy, if in some need of redecoration, but the giant cream leather sofa that dominates it looks almost new. Grace is perched demurely on a matching cream leather pouffe set in front of it. Today she's wearing a dress. It's black, with a white lace collar. Two glossy dress-shop carrier bags have been placed at her side. She catches Tim's eye as soon as he enters the room and holds his gaze.

"Hello," she says.

"Hello," Tim replies. I can see he finds her calm self-assurance disarming. He hesitates.

"Mavis says you need to speak to me again."

"It's because of what you told me last night, Grace," Mavis says in a rush. "I told you I'd have to tell the police, lovey."

"Yes," Grace agrees. "And I can't stay here now, can I?" Her voice is toneless: she doesn't sound upset or accusing, but as if she's simply stating a fact. Mavis is embarrassed.

"It's for the best, darling," she finally manages, in a wheedling tone.

Grace nods. There is a prolonged silence.

"You'll be all right, Grace," I say. "We'll find somewhere nice for you to stay for a while. Eventually you'll be able to go home."

"Where's that?" she asks, still tonelessly. She could be enquiring about the 'nice place', but I don't think so. I can't find an answer.

"I've put her things in them carrier bags," Mavis says

virtuously. "And a few bits and pieces to tide her over, until she can have the rest of her own stuff back."

Grace gives her a bright smile.

"Can I see Chloe to say goodbye?"

"Perhaps best not. Chloe's not very well, is she?"

Grace seems to accept this. Tim picks up the two carrier bags and takes them out into the hall. Grace follows him.

"Thank you for looking after Grace, Mrs Hebblewhite," I say, "and for calling us this morning. We'll need to talk to you again, and Chloe, too, quite soon."

"She isn't well. Didn't you hear me?" Mavis hisses, dropping her front-room manners.

"I'm sorry about that. If it's ok, we'll get a doctor to look at her and advise us of when she's fit to speak to us. We won't need to keep her for very long."

Mavis shrugs angrily.

"You're not really offering me a choice, are you? And why do you want to speak to me again? I've told you all that I know."

"You've been very helpful, but what you told me over the phone wasn't recorded. We need a proper statement. And you might remember something else Grace said that you didn't mention to me. Or that Chloe said, for that matter."

"Chloe hasn't said owt, and she's not likely to."

"Well, let us know if she does. And it would help if you could write down your conversation with Grace as exactly as you can remember it. You can bring it with you when we take your statement."

Tim has opened the front door again and gestures to Grace to precede him. Mavis Hebblewhite moves swiftly into the hall and I follow.

"Is that all?" she demands. "Because I don't want a crowd of people gawping over my hedge, if you don't mind, once she's out in the street."

"Yes, that's all for now, Mrs Hebblewhite, thank you. As I said, we'll be in touch. And you contact us immediately if anything happens to worry you."

She looks alarmed.

"He won't come after us if Grace isn't here, will he? There wouldn't be any point."

"I think it's unlikely that you or your family are in any danger, but as I've said, call us if anything happens to cause concern. Anything at all."

"All right, I will."

She's propelled me through the door, now, and half-closed it. She gives a curt nod and the door bangs shut. I'm about to turn towards the gate when I hear a faint tapping sound. I look up and see Chloe's face pressed against one of the upstairs windows. She's staring beyond me, into the street. I follow her gaze.

Tim has his back to me. He's opened the nearside rear door of the car and is moving something off the back seat. Grace also has her back to me and has herself almost reached the car, but now she spins round and looks up at the window. For a few seconds, her lovely face is transformed: she's scowling and mouths something that I can't interpret. I quickly switch back to Chloe, but she's gone. When I turn round again, Grace is talking to Tim and smiling as she climbs into the car.

Chapter 34

TOM TARRANT HAD evidently done a good job of persuading Marie Krakowska to act as Grace Winter's responsible adult. As Tim drove into the police station car park, he saw them both approaching. They were talking amicably. Marie was wearing a floor-length red cotton tartan skirt and a jacket with a nipped-in waist (insofar as it was possible to nip in Marie's waist) in a clashing tartan of purple and blue. Shades of Vivienne Westwood.

Tim took his time parking the car so that Marie and Tom could catch up. When it was stationary, Juliet emerged and opened the rear door for Grace. As Grace slid out and stood up, she stared at Tom intently. He caught her eye and she gave him a radiant smile. Tom smiled back. Marie fluttered her fingers at Grace, an intimate little gesture which made Grace transfer the full force of the smile to her. For an alarming moment, Tim thought Marie was going to hug Grace. However, if this had been her intention she thought better of it.

"Good morning, Grace," said Marie breezily. "How are you?"

"I'm all right, Miss," said Grace. She looked at Tom.

"Hello," she said.

"Hello, Grace. Has DI Yates explained that he wants to ask you a few more questions? Ms Krakowska is here because she's . . ."

"Let's talk when we get inside," said Tim. Grace and Marie followed Juliet, who had already started to walk towards the police station. Tim dropped back to talk to Tom.

"Thank you for sorting this out so quickly," he said.

"Don't thank me: thank Marie. She's the one who's really had to put herself out. Did DS Armstrong talk to you about the flat at the children's home, by the way? I've checked with the acting warden there. It's empty just now and he's happy to let us use it."

"Thanks. Juliet says she'll stay there with Grace. Do you think that's a good idea?"

"I must admit I was surprised when she suggested it, but now I've thought about it, I can't think of anyone better. She mentioned you might decide to put a police guard outside as well."

"That depends on what Grace tells us. I'll have to be pretty convinced that she's in danger before I do that."

"Do you think she may not be telling the truth?"

Tim paused to give Tom a searching look.

"I'm keeping an open mind," he said. "But you've intrigued me now. Do you think she's a liar?"

"I don't know her well enough to be able to judge. All I can say is that there's something about her that's . . . well, not disturbing, exactly, but not . . . straightforward."

"You can say that again. She's the most self-possessed child I've ever met. And unless she's hiding it very well, she seems untouched by grief for these two deaths."

Tom reflected on this for a moment, but didn't comment.

"Do you want me to stay? You don't really need me now that Marie's here, do you?"

"If you can spare the time, I'd appreciate it. I'd like you to watch Grace closely and tell me afterwards what you make of her behaviour."

"Ok, but Marie's the psychologist."

Tim didn't answer. He suspected that Tom knew as well as he did that Marie's brand of psychology was rooted more in the heart than the head.

"I'll ask for some tea. Would you like something besides tea to drink?" Juliet asked Grace after they had all sat down at a table in one of the interview rooms. "Some water or juice, maybe?"

"Yes. I'd like some Coke, please."

"I'm not sure . . ."

"Ask the canteen to bring us some from the machine," said Tim. "We'll pay for it."

"Thank you," Grace said sweetly. Did Tim imagine it, or had she at the same time flicked Juliet a quick smirk of triumph?

"Let's make a start," said Tim. "Grace, Ms Krakowska is here as a responsible adult. Do you know what that means?"

"That she'll look after me?"

"Yes, she'll look after you. In particular, she'll make sure that we treat you fairly, by asking you questions that you can understand, making sure that you get breaks when you're tired, and not upsetting you more than we can help. Is that all right?"

"Yes." Grace gave Marie a quick smile.

"DS Armstrong will ask the questions. If you don't understand something she says, you may ask her to explain, or you may ask Mr Tarrant or myself. Ms Krakowska is just here to observe. She will only intervene if she thinks you need the kind of support I've just mentioned. Is that all right, too?"

"Yes."

"And we'll be taping the conversation as soon as DS Armstrong starts the formal interview."

"Why's that?" For the first time, Grace seemed a little ruffled, her voice shriller than usual.

"Just so that we have a proper record of what you say. It's nothing to worry about. You know that a very serious crime has been committed – in fact, murder, the most serious of all crimes. What you have to tell us may be very important. It may help us to catch the person who's responsible. So you see we need to capture every word, so that we can play the tape afterwards as many times as we need to. Do you understand?"

"Yes." Grace's voice had returned to its normal flat tone.

"I'm going to turn on the tape now," said Juliet. "For the benefit of the tape, it's 10.58 a.m. on Wednesday 24th August 2016. Present are Grace Winter, a minor, from whom a witness statement is being taken, Marie Krakowska, the child psychologist who is acting as responsible adult on behalf of Grace, Tom Tarrant, social worker, South Lincolnshire local authority, DI Tim Yates, South Lincs police and DS Juliet Armstrong, myself. I shall be conducting the interview."

Grace giggled.

"Funny," she said, "talking to it as if it's alive."

"I know, but you've heard me do this before, Grace – I won't be talking to it again until I switch it off. Now, first I'd like you to explain why you didn't tell us you saw someone when we spoke to you yesterday. You said then that you hadn't

143

been anywhere near your house until you and Chloe came in the afternoon when the reporters were outside. Are you saying something different now?"

"I couldn't tell you before because it would have upset Chloe. She thought we'd get into trouble, see, for taking Jagger's bike."

"You said you took Jagger's bike to go to Crowland. Did you take it before that?"

"Yes, on Saturday afternoon. Jagger didn't know. It was Mavis who said I could take it when we went to Crowland. Jagger had to let me."

"Where did you take the bikes on Saturday?"

"We went to my house. The door was open."

"Did you go in?"

"Yes. We went into the hall. I called out to Mum, but nothing happened. I wanted to go upstairs, but Chloe got scared. She's afraid of her brothers and I wasn't supposed to have Jagger's bike. We'd left the bikes against the wall. She said if we kept on hanging around one of her brothers would probably see us and thump us."

"So what *did* you do?"

"Chloe ran out and got back on her bike and went home. She took Jagger's bike as well, pulling it along by the handlebars. I was still thinking of going upstairs when a man came running down. He looked cross. He pushed me against the wall and then he ran out."

"What did you do then?"

"He'd spooked me. I ran out and went back to Chloe's."

"Weren't you worried about what the man might have done?"

Grace looked down at her hands and fiddled with her

fingers. When she raised her head again, there were tears glistening in her green eyes.

"I'm sorry, DS Armstrong, but I don't think that's a fitting question. Could you stick to talking about the facts, please, and not probe Grace about her feelings?"

Juliet looked at Tim, who nodded his agreement with what Marie was saying. There was a tap at the door. Juliet opened it to take from one of the canteen staff a tray bearing a teapot and cups and a can of Coke. Tom Tarrant helped her pass around the cups and the awkward moment passed. Grace's resilience seemed to spring back as soon as she saw the Coke.

"Did you get a close look at the man?"

Grace nodded.

"Was it someone you know?"

"I'm not sure. I may have seen him around."

"Do you think you could help us build a photo-fit picture of him?"

"What's that?" Grace sounded intrigued.

"It's a bit like a jigsaw. You choose bits of face that most look like the man's that you saw and fit them together."

"I'd like to do that."

"Thank you. We'll give it a go later, then. Did you touch the wall or anything else in the house while you were there?"

"I don't know. I might have done. I live there anyway, don't I?"

"What about Chloe?"

"No. She ran out almost as soon as we went in." Grace paused as if deliberating. "Come to think of it, she might have done. She might just have brushed against the wall. I'm not sure."

145

"You say the man pushed you. How did he push you? Did he hurt you?"

"He just put out his arm and his hand was on my chest and he gave me a shove."

"What were you wearing?"

"Same dress as I've got on now. Mavis has washed it since."

"So after he shoved you, you just walked out of the house and back to Chloe's house."

"I ran, more like."

"Did anyone see you?"

"I don't know. There's always someone about, isn't there? I didn't notice anyone in particular."

"And when you got back to Chloe's house, where was she?"

"She was waiting in the garden for me. She'd taken the bikes round the back. We went in together."

"Chloe's brothers weren't hanging around?"

"No."

"So you went in. What did you do next?"

"We had our tea and watched telly for the rest of the evening. That was all."

"But you didn't tell Mrs Hebblewhite what had happened?"

"No. Donny and Jagger had come in by then. We thought it best not to say anything."

Juliet paused. Because she had hesitated, each of the three other adults in the room was looking at her expectantly. Grace alone had not fixed her eyes on Juliet's; instead, her glance flitted in turn from Tim to Marie and from Marie to Tom. Juliet cleared her throat.

"Grace, do you remember that yesterday, when we were talking with you and Mrs Hebblewhite and Chloe, Mrs

Hebblewhite said that Chloe hadn't wanted her lunch? Was that because she was upset?"

"I suppose so."

"Why was she upset?"

"I told you before, we'd had an argument. It wasn't anything much."

"It wasn't anything to do with going to your house?"

"No. Why would it be?"

"And even after you came back to the house with Chloe and met me and DI Yates there, you didn't think to tell us anyone about the man?"

"I did. I told Mavis last night. I didn't want Chloe to get upset again, that's why I didn't say anything before."

Marie Krakowska was nodding. She patted Grace's hand.

"That's quite understandable," she said. "DS Armstrong, I think we should take a break now. I'm afraid Grace is getting tired, and she won't be any help to us if we confuse her by muddling up two lots of events, will she?"

Juliet looked first at Tom Tarrant, then at Tim. It was clear they didn't want to challenge Marie. Tom was already squaring up the papers he'd put on the table in front of him and Tim was pushing back his chair. Juliet gave Marie a taut smile.

"I'm sure you're right," she said. "For the benefit of the tape, this interview is concluding at 11.39 a.m. on Wednesday 24th August 2016,"

Grace Winter giggled again.

Chapter 35

HE TOLD HIMSELF he didn't really believe in telepathy, yet he knew that semi-buried in his subconscious was a deep-rooted superstition that it might be possible to get into someone else's mind from a distance, take over their thoughts. He'd tried to influence her on many occasions since he'd been in prison by thinking of her intensely, by trying to push into her mind; once or twice, he thought he'd received a glimmer of a response, an inkling that she was obeying him. Now the Dymoke murders had half-convinced him that he might have the power to tap into and harness her thoughts.

Chapter 36

GRACE HAS BEEN allowed to rest and been taken to the canteen for lunch: beans and sausages, a reassuringly childlike choice. However, she only picks at the food, and doesn't want dessert, even though she's offered an ice cream. She prefers to fill herself up on Coke: she seems to have an endless capacity for the stuff.

Tom Tarrant has returned to his office, but Marie Krakowska is still with Grace, looking after her every need, encouraging the consumption of Coke with no apparent worries that it might make her hyper. Grace accepts these attentions without fuss, as if to the manner born.

Tim also has gone back to his office, to check up on the team carrying out door-to-door questioning in the Dymokes and beyond. I'm waiting with growing impatience for Marie to say it's fine to continue with the interview. I catch her eye. I can see that she knows very well what I'm thinking, but still she spins out the lunch break for a few more minutes. Grace is getting bored, and begins to kick at the empty chair opposite the one she's sitting on. I decide not to humour Marie any longer.

"Grace," I say, "do you think you're ready to try the photo-fit now? Every minute we lose means we have less chance of catching the man you saw."

"You don't have to say yes if you don't feel up to it." Marie jumps in immediately.

Grace's eyes are luminous. She's torn between capitalising on Marie's solicitude and succumbing to her fascination with the photo-fit.

"I'm ready," she says solemnly. "I want to help."

"Good girl," says Marie.

I take them back to the interview room. It's better if Grace works on the photo-fit unobserved. I know that Andy and Ricky will be in the office this afternoon and she's bound to be distracted by them. Or perhaps I mean that Grace is bound to try to distract them.

"I'll be back in a few seconds," I say. "I just need to fetch my laptop."

South Lincs police has only recently invested in its photo-fit software. We used to rely on employing an artist to sketch witness's impressions of suspects and a lot of people think this is still the most accurate way of obtaining a good likeness. The problem for us, as for most police forces, is that good local artists are not easy to find and expensive if we do manage to get hold of one. The software has the virtue of being both readily available and consistent. I've often helped witnesses to use it since we bought it. Its accuracy improves as we get more experienced.

When I return with the laptop, Marie is reading something on her iPhone and Grace is busy sketching. I try to look over her shoulder, more out of friendliness than because I'm really interested. Straight away she covers her drawing with her hands. The action is abrupt; she inhales with a hissing sound, which attracts Marie's attention. Marie gives me a stern look. No doubt I'm invading Grace's space or curtailing her opportunity to let out her grief by expressing herself, or some such. I turn away to plug in the laptop on the other side of the table, taking my time to set up the program.

"I'm ready now, Grace," I say. "Will you come and sit next to me?"

She rips off the sheet of paper and turns it over, wedging it under the pad so that it won't flutter to the floor; she drags the chair next to mine a little closer. Marie stays where she is.

I explain to Grace how it works, using Tim as a subject. We try out a few outlandish features: a massive domed bald head, rabbit teeth. Grace giggles.

"These aren't like DI Yates at all, are they? Now see if you can put together a picture that looks a bit like him. It doesn't have to be perfect: just get the main things right, so that someone could recognise him from it if they saw him in the street. I'll help you if you get stuck."

Grace swivels the cursor expertly round the screen: it's clear that she's well-practised in using a mouse. She selects a chin, puts it in place and pushes her chair back to get a better view. She eyes it critically, then swaps it for another. She's working competently, and she isn't rushing. She's taking the time, to be sure to be as accurate as possible. I think she's enjoying the challenge: even more, I suspect she wants the praise she'll get if she does the job well.

In less than half an hour, we have a very good likeness of Tim's face. Grace is having trouble with the hair, but to be honest there's nothing in the kit that quite resembles his curly thatch. She pushes her chair back again, her expression sulky.

"The hair's not right."

"No, but hair's always difficult and DI Yates's is unusual. I think you've done brilliantly!"

Grace looks up and beams.

"Really? But I wish I'd got the hair better."

"Don't worry about it. Shall we try to make a picture of the man you saw, now that you've got the hang of it?"

"What will happen to the picture of DI Yates?"

"We can save it if you like. Or we can print it out and show it to him."

"No, no, I don't want to save it. I don't want him to see it. It's not good enough!"

Grace is becoming agitated. Marie moves across to her, puts an arm around her shoulder.

"It's all right, Grace. You're doing really well. DS Armstrong won't save the picture if you don't want her to. Do you need a break now?"

My hearts sinks. I'd already guessed that Marie would do this. If Grace becomes more agitated, Marie'll probably say the proper photo-fit has to wait until tomorrow. I look at her. She stares calmly back at me and gives me one of her smiles.

"It would be a shame to give up on it now, when you've just mastered it," I say. "The next picture is the important one. It's the one we need."

"I know," she says bravely. "I'll try my best."

"Good girl," says Marie. "Just remember, you can stop at any time. No one's forcing you to do anything." She sits down again, this time close to Grace, so that we are seated in a row. Marie's patchouli is permeating the atmosphere. Squashed up against the wall, I find the situation claustrophobic, but Grace seems to like being sandwiched between the two of us.

She's concentrating now. She builds up the picture more rapidly than the one of Tim. She's three quarters of the way through when I begin to recognise the face I see emerging.

Grace suddenly looks round at me and grins, as if she can read my mind. I do my best to look non-committal.

"Keep going, Grace. You've almost finished now."

She turns back to the screen and continues working on the forehead. She's frowning with the effort. She tries five or six different foreheads before she's satisfied.

"There!" she says.

"Well done," I say in a voice that I hope sounds encouraging. "Now there's just the hair."

"He hasn't got any hair. That's just how he looks."

"And he's the man you saw coming out of your foster mother's house?"

Grace nods.

"You're absolutely sure?"

"Yes, I'm sure. Why are you asking? Do you think I got it wrong?"

"No, of course not. You said earlier you might have seen the man before, but you didn't know his name. Can you remember his name now?"

She shakes her head.

"No. I need to go to the toilet now."

"Shall I come with you?" says Marie.

"I know where it is, thank you." Marie looks at me.

"It's fine for her to go on her own."

Grace leaves the room.

"I take it you think you recognise the man in the photo-fit?" says Marie.

"I'm certain I do. It's Marek Wolansky, the son of her next-door neighbour."

"Wow! But why doesn't she know his name?"

"If she really doesn't know his name, I wouldn't be all that surprised. I don't think he's capable of leaving the house alone. He's very severely retarded."

"But . . . that doesn't make sense . . . does it?"

"We'll have to check it out. We'll certainly have to try and question him. But I think it's highly unlikely that he's capable of committing those two murders. He's strong enough, no doubt, but it beggars belief that he'd have the wit to go into that house, kill Tina Brackenbury and the baby without waking them up and leave again before anyone discovered him. The man that I saw being cared for by his mother would have been incapable of passing Grace and purposefully making his way home."

"Unless he's pretending."

"Or unless she is."

As I'm speaking, my eye falls on the notepad that Grace had been using for her sketch.

"Could you turn that over? I want to see if she's drawn the same person."

"I'm not sure that we . . ."

"Oh, come on, Marie, don't start talking to me about Grace's rights. We're hardly harming her by looking at her scribbles, are we?"

Marie dithers, so I walk round the table and snatch up the sheet of paper. I lay it on the desk where Marie can see it. It's competently drawn and there's not the remotest chance that it's supposed to be another depiction of Marek Wolansky. Staring up at us with a half-smile on his face is a portrait of a man in his mid-thirties. He's quite good-looking, with smoothed-back hair and even features. He's wearing round spectacles and has a scholarly air.

"Fuck!" says Marie.

"Are you going to tell me you know who this is now?" I say.

"I can't be sure, because it's a long time since I saw him, and then it was only from a distance. But his photograph was published in the papers at the time. You must have seen it, too."

I peer more closely at the sketch.

"I see what you mean. You think that Grace's drawing is meant to be of Tristram Arkwright."

Chapter 37

KATRIN WAS WORKING from home. The tiny office that she shared with Tim was one of the slope-ceilinged rooms set in the eaves of their dormer bungalow. It was sometimes uncomfortably hot in summer and always cold in winter, but she could concentrate better there, away from the noise and bustle of the house. Floating up the stairs came sounds of Sophia's and Rosie's tumultuous giggles and Margery Pocklington's more restrained laughter as they played a toddlers' version of catch-me-if-you-can.

Every day Katrin blessed the arrangement she'd reached with Margery, along with Sian, one of her neighbours. Margery looked after Sophia and Rosie, Sian's daughter, three days each week, in one or other of their houses. On the remaining two days, the two little girls attended a nursery, but if one of them was ill Margery could be relied on, regardless of the day of the week, to look after her. Katrin and Sian together paid Margery the going rate for a professional nanny for all the days on which she worked. Margery, who the previous year had almost been murdered by organised people traffickers Jas Khan and his brothers, had been awarded £50,000 victim compensation by the judge at the Khans' trial. She was saving as much of the money as she could to put herself through university, but the award, together with her nanny's wages, meant that she was financially independent and did not need to live with Katrin and Tim, an alternative they had at first considered. Instead, she shared a house with three other girls who worked in local shops and businesses. Margery spent all the free time she had studying. Despite her appalling home background, she had achieved a respectable if not stellar set of 'A' level results; she knew that she was capable of better and was planning to re-sit her exams, her sights set on the best university that would take her.

Once she'd recovered physically, Margery had turned into a well-adjusted, very attractive young woman. Her doctors were amazed at how few psychological scars she appeared to have suffered following her ordeal at the hands of the Khans. Privately, Katrin believed that this was because Margery had led such a deprived existence prior to her capture that she was more resilient to suffering than another girl would have been, but unobtrusively she kept alert, looking out for any warning signals that might show themselves. Katrin and, to a lesser extent, Sian, were proxy big sisters to Margery and now the only 'family' she had: her mother had been committed to a psychiatric institution and, after a brief show of concern when his daughter had been 'famous' and in the news, her father had moved away from the area, accompanied by his latest girlfriend. Margery had said that it was she who had finally cut the ties, but Katrin suspected he had left without giving her his new address.

The giggles and chatter suddenly grew louder: Margery had opened the door into the hall.

"Are you all ok down there?" Katrin called out.

"Yes, we're fine. We're just going out for a while, if that's all right."

"Where are you going?"

"Just to the swings."

"All right." Katrin looked at her watch. It was almost 3.30 p.m. "Can you make sure you're back by 4.30? Sian wants to take Rosie somewhere when she gets home from work."

"Sure thing!" Margery called back. There were more muted sounds as she helped the two children put on their shoes and then another explosion of chatter as they erupted into the street. The house fell blissfully silent. Katrin smiled and returned to her work.

The task she was engaged on was every bit as grim as she'd expected. She was examining the statistics of children murdered in the UK over the past ten years. The average annual figure during that period for the deaths of children aged under sixteen definitively categorised as murders was around seventy-five, but certain children's charities had gone on record as saying they believed the actual number to be double that or even higher. Most of these children had been killed by people they knew and the overwhelming majority had suffered either protracted periods of neglect or physical abuse at the hands of their parents or carers. This was particularly the case with murdered babies, who made up roughly a third of all child homicides. Some older children also died by suicide, sometimes because the home situation had become intolerable, but more often because they'd been bullied at school or online. Lastly, and much more rarely, were the cases of children who'd been killed by other children.

When murdered children didn't know their killers, they'd most frequently died at the hands of dangerous or drunken drivers or child sex killers. Katrin was horrified to discover that even babies were sexually abused, often fatally. Older children also died from substance abuse; sometimes the coroner ruled that these deaths constituted murder or manslaughter, if the children had been supplied with the substances by adults.

Bluebelle Brackenbury's murder didn't seem to fit into any of the categories. Both Tim and Juliet had said she was clearly a well-cared-for child, that her room and bedding were cleaner and smarter than the rest of the things in Tina Brackenbury's house. The pathology report showed no evidence of either physical or sexual abuse. The most plausible conclusion Katrin could arrive at was that the baby hadn't been the murderer's primary target, that Bluebelle had been killed because someone wanted her mother dead. Katrin wondered what could prompt a murderer to kill a child incapable of retaliation and too young to be able to identify him. Perhaps the motive had been superstition, like that shown by killers who shot out their victims' eyes so their images weren't reflected after death. Perhaps, after all, it was someone who'd taken a violent dislike to babies.

Chapter 38

I LEAVE GRACE with Marie. She's playing a game on Marie's iPhone while Marie drinks more tea. I go to find Tim. At Marie's insistence, I've asked Grace's permission to show Tim the sketch as well as the photo-fit. She seems to have forgotten about the subject of the drawing and is indifferent to what happens to it.

"They're not in the slightest bit alike," Tim says. "Is she now claiming to have seen two strange men?"

"She didn't say she'd seen the man in the sketch at the scene, just the man in the photo-fit."

"Did she identify either of them?"

"No. She maintains she doesn't know the photo-fit character. The sketch was just a doodle – we didn't ask her to do it and therefore have no right to ask her to explain it."

"Oh? Why is that?"

"That's according to Marie."

"I see," Tim says grimly. "I don't agree, but we'll go along with Marie for now. We may have to adopt a different approach later."

"You're probably right, but the man in the sketch can't be the murderer – at least, if I'm right about who he is."

"Who do you think he is?" Tim peers more closely. "The kid's good at drawing, isn't she?"

"Yes, very; and I'm pretty sure she intends that to be a portrait of her uncle."

"You mean Tristram Arkwright?"

"Yep. And I assume he hasn't been busted out of Wakefield over the past few days?"

"We'd know about it if he had! Perhaps we're reading too much into all of this. Grace is only a child, after all. The links may be more tenuous than we're assuming. It may just be that the more recent traumatic event reminds her of the earlier one. Poor kid!"

"That's certainly a possible interpretation, although I think we'd need a psychologist's opinion to validate it. What's probably more important is that I think I recognise the bloke in the photo-fit picture, too."

"You mean the person Grace thought was the killer?"

"She says it's a picture of the person she saw leaving the Brackenbury house after Chloe Hebblewhite had gone home: by implication, the killer. Though she claims she doesn't know who it is, I think it's an excellent likeness of her foster-mother's next-door neighbour's son, Marek Wolansky."

Tim's ears prick up. Suddenly he's energised.

"Bring him in for questioning right away. Presumably we've got a door-to-door statement from him already? Can you find it, see if you think he's lying?"

"I think it's unlikely that he could have been the person Grace saw and even more unlikely that he's provided us with a statement. Marek Wolansky is profoundly retarded. He needs his mother to do even the simplest things for him. And he never leaves the house except when he attends a day centre a few times a week, to give her a bit of a rest."

Tim's shoulders droop. I sympathise: it would have been a great lead, if not for the obvious flaws.

"Well, we'll still need to speak to him. I assume it means faffing about with all this responsible adult stuff again?"

"Yes, although the mother's very protective and may insist on being here, which would solve the issue. I suspect he'd become agitated without her, in any case."

"If you're right and it couldn't have been him, what possible reason could Grace have had for trying to implicate him?"

"That's the question that's been puzzling me, particularly as there seems to be some link in her mind between Wolansky and Tristram Arkwright."

"Do you think it's worth questioning Arkwright?"

"We may have to do that eventually, but like most long-term prisoners he'll probably be a time-waster. Even if he knows something about Grace that we don't, he's likely to lead us a merry dance before he tells us what it is. If he ever does. And we'll need Home Office permission. We've already put through a request to the Home Office to question Lenka Astani about him; it's not a good idea to ask them for too many favours."

"You're right. We should stick with Grace first, until we're convinced she's told us everything we can. Where is she?"

"She's still with Marie. She'll have to stay here for an hour or so longer, while I go to my flat for an overnight bag. Then I'll take her to the children's home. She'll be too late for their supper – they eat early in that place – but we won't want her to mix with the other children yet, anyway. I'll probably pick up a pizza on my way back here."

"Is there time enough for another interview with her? I'd like to be in on it myself."

"I don't think Marie will hear of her being interviewed again today, but I'll bring her straight back tomorrow and I'll ask Marie to get here early."

"What about Marek Wolansky?"

"We need to talk to his mother first and it'll have to be handled delicately. Again, tomorrow's probably a better bet. But don't worry, he isn't going anywhere."

"You're sure of that?"

"Quite sure."

"We don't have enough evidence yet to scale down the investigation, do we?"

"In my opinion, we don't have any evidence at all. We just have pictures of two men produced by the same ten-year-old girl within an hour or so of each other. For all we know, they're simply the result of a pretty exceptional artistic talent, combined with an overworked imagination, and have no bearing on the murders whatsoever."

"Except that they seem clearly to represent two living men. What possible reason could Grace Winter have for implicating her uncle, whom we know to be serving time in a maximum security jail, and the idiot son of her next door neighbour, in a double murder? As you've pointed out, logic defies that either of them is the killer."

"I think if we knew the answer to that, we might have solved the crime. Not all children are straightforward, particularly intelligent ones, and I'm convinced that Grace is fiendishly intelligent. She may just be leading us a dance for the sake of it, particularly if her imagination is more lurid or her mind more disturbed than we think. Or she may have something to hide. That's what we have to find out."

Chapter 39

As I unlock my flat, I feel worn and deflated. I'm not nearly as keen as Tim and Marie think on spending the night in the flat at the children's home; I just don't see a way round it. Grace Winter frightens me, but I'm not sure whether it's because she's an endangered child or a dangerous one. I'm certain we need both to protect her and to understand her better, though whether that will solve the murders gives me cause for doubt.

There's a letter that's been thrust only three quarters of the way through the letter-box. As I push open the door, it drops to the mat. I pick it up and turn it over. I recognise the bold, forward-sloping handwriting immediately: it's from DC Nancy Chappell, a detective in the Met with whom I worked briefly on the Ayesha Verma case. I know it's her writing because I've seen it on police statements – it's very distinctive – but I'm surprised to get a letter from her: in my experience, Nancy is wedded to technology and doesn't put pen to paper if she can help it. Briefly, I puzzle about how she has my home address before I remember that I posted some things back to her that she left at the station.

I tear open the envelope, feeling apprehensive. Inside, there's an official form and a short note from Nancy. I read the note quickly. It's a request for a testimonial: Nancy wants to apply for a job that involves working outside the Met and needs references to prove she's good at liaison work with her peers in other forces. I smile a little grimly as I read: working with Nancy hadn't been my choice, but unwelcome aid foisted on me by Tim. However, I must admit that Nancy handled the situation tactfully; given different circumstances, we might have become friends. I also have a sneaking suspicion Tim and Superintendent Thornton tried to persuade her to apply for my DS job and she refused, perhaps because she didn't want to leave the Met, but more likely because she thought they were treating me shabbily. If the latter, I owe Nancy and providing her with the testimonial is the least I can do for her. I resolve to make a good job of it and prop the form prominently on my mantelpiece so that I won't forget it.

I change into jeans and a sweatshirt and bundle a few spare clothes and some toiletries into a rucksack. It occurs to me that Grace should change, too: that black dress is very formal. If she does meet some of the other cared-for children, they're likely to tease her about it.

As I'm driving back to the station, I see Marie and Grace crossing the road. Marie gives me one of her little waves. I lower the car window as I draw level with her.

"We'll be with you in a minute. Grace was getting bored, so I've just been taking her for a little walk and a hot chocolate."

"You'd better get in," I say, as lightly as I can. "Grace is supposed to be under guard until we know whether she's in any danger." I look at Grace, who appears not to be listening.

"God, I hadn't thought of that," Marie says. "Grace, we'd better hitch a lift with DS Armstrong."

"No harm done," I say. "Unless you need to come back to the station, I can look after Grace now. Will you be able to join us again early tomorrow? We'd like another interview with Grace, just a short one with DI Yates present."

"Grace is my priority at the moment," Marie says. "I'll be there. You won't try asking her any questions this evening, will you? She's had enough for one day."

"Don't worry, I won't." I try not to let Marie see how infuriating I find her bossiness.

Marie opens the nearside rear door for Grace, who climbs in obediently and fastens the seat belt.

"Goodbye, Marie," I say. "Have a nice evening. See you tomorrow."

She waves again.

Before we set off, I meet Grace's eye in the mirror. She's staring at me intently.

"Are you all right, Grace?"

"Where are you taking me?"

"Back to the station to collect your clothes. Then we're going to spend the night in a flat together. There's to be a policeman on guard as well, so you don't need to worry."

"You mean *you're* going to spend the night with me?"

"Yes, Grace. I hope that's ok? We need to look after you."

"I suppose I can't go back to Mavis's. She doesn't want me any more, does she?"

"It's not that she doesn't want you. She thinks you'll be safer with us."

Grace is silent.

"Do you have some jeans or trousers you can change into?"

"I'm not sure. I don't know what Mavis packed for me. You could buy me some new ones."

"Let's see what you have first."

I catch her eye again. She's looking back at me boldly, as if I've presented her with a challenge she's determined to win.

Tim is hovering by my desk when I arrive with Grace. He gives her a quick grin, which she returns with one of her sunburst smiles.

"DS Armstrong, could I have a word with you?"

"Grace, here are the clothes Mrs Hebblewhite gave me for you. Will you see if there are some jeans or trousers in there? If there are, you know where the ladies' toilet is, don't you, for you to change? I won't be long."

Grace is still watching Tim, but he's unaware of it: he's already turned to go back to his office. I follow him, but not before I see a flash of intense dislike flit across Grace's face. It's gone in an instant. It's not the first time I've seen her beautiful features twisted into a scowl.

"Do you still think you'll need a police guard tonight?" Tim asks.

"Your guess is as good as mine. If you want my honest opinion, I think it's far-fetched to believe that Grace is in danger, but we can't be too careful."

"I thought you'd say that. I've asked Giash Chakrabati to come with you. He'll travel in a separate car, because someone else will be sent to relieve him at around 2 a.m. I'll ask them to text you on your mobile when they arrive so they can introduce themselves. I'm not sure who it will be yet."

"Thanks, Tim," I say. He misses the irony in my voice. Just what I want, a strange copper waking me up in the middle of the night.

"That's all right," he says airily.

Chapter 40

GRACE HAS CHANGED into the jeans she was wearing when I first met her. I notice they are expensive ones, but a little too small for her. She's also wearing a pale pink jumper, the colour matching the embroidery on their pockets.

"You look nice," I say.

"Mrs Winter bought these for me. I could do with some bigger ones now."

I note that she calls her adoptive mother 'Mrs Winter', although she referred to Tina as 'Mum'.

"Are you hungry? I've bought a pizza for us to share."

She shrugs. "I probably will be, later. When are we going?"

"Now, if you like. I just need to check that PC Chakrabati has arrived."

Grace's eyes become luminous. It's as if I've just mentioned a particular friend of hers.

"He was at our house the other day, wasn't he? He was the one who was dealing with the reporters."

"That's right."

"I think he quite liked me." She smiles.

"He probably did. He doesn't have any reason not to . . . and he's got daughters of his own."

She loses interest.

"Wait here for me. I won't be a minute."

I go out into the office area. Ricky MacFadyen is just packing up his stuff for the day.

"No peace for the wicked," he says. "I'm back on the door-to-doors now."

"Good luck! Have you seen Giash?"

"Yes, he's gone for a cuppa. He'll be back soon, I should think."

Ricky disappears down the stairs just as Giash turns the corner.

"Sorry to keep you waiting. I've been doing door-to-doors all afternoon. I just needed something to keep me going." He waves a plastic packet of sandwiches.

"I've got a pizza for Grace and myself for later. You're welcome to share it."

"Love to, but I've got strict instructions to stay outside."

"Thanks for doing it. It's a thankless job, I know."

"It's worth doing if the girl really is in danger. Besides, I didn't exactly volunteer." Giash grins. "Ready when you are."

"I'll go and get her. She believes you like her, by the way. It seems to be important to her."

"She probably thinks she needs all the friends she can get, poor kid. She doesn't keep hers very long, does she?"

He's added a new perspective for me. I realise that I've been thinking of Grace as a superhuman creature. Not helpful. She's just a little girl, after all.

We're back with Giash in a couple of minutes, Grace and I each carrying one of the large dress-shop bags in which Mavis Hebblewhite put her things.

"Do you want me to look after those?" says Giash. Grace has suddenly become withdrawn and shrinks away from him,

169

but I pass over the larger of the bags. "Great if you can take this one. I'll have the pizza and my own stuff to carry when we arrive."

"I suppose we'd better travel in convoy," says Giash. "Don't want you getting hi-jacked on the way!" He winks at Grace, who gives him a stony look. "Just wait while I bring the car round," he adds to me. "Yours is out at the front, isn't it?"

Grace climbs into my car and sits beside me in silence. It's a warm late summer's evening and there are several people out walking in the Sheep Market. She looks across at them mistrustfully.

"What if I see him now?" she asks.

"Who do you mean?"

"The man. The man I saw at our house."

"I think it's unlikely, Grace, don't you?" I say with meaning. It's an off-chance attempt at making her admit she knows the man in her drawing is Marek Wolansky, but I don't expect for a moment that she'll let me trap her. She stares at me sulkily.

"I don't see why. DI Yates says he's probably local. It's local here, isn't it?"

"Yes, it's local, but I doubt if he'd come anywhere near the police station," I say, to pacify her. "Here comes PC Chakrabati, so we can go now."

Giash halts his car at the entrance to the car park and waves me on. I set off towards Winsover Road, with him following close on my tail. The children's home is just beyond the town boundaries, down one of the little lanes that lead off from the Pode Hole pumping station. There are virtually no other cars on the road and our journey takes less than ten minutes.

It's past their supper hour and some of the children are playing outside. They ignore me and Grace, but are fascinated by Giash's police vehicle. I open my door in time to see one of them jump forward and hear him say, "Are you a real copper?" He's only about six years old. The older kids hang back; I see they've already been taught not to trust 'coppers'.

"'Course I am," says Giash. "Do you want to have a go with my radio?" The boy nods and the other children decide to gather round, too. Giash nods at me and then over his shoulder at the main building.

"Let's go inside quickly," I say to Grace. "You'll probably be able to meet some of the other children on another day."

"I don't want to meet them," she says. "You told me I wouldn't be staying long."

"I don't think you will, but I'm not sure what will happen exactly when just yet."

Grace falls silent. I pick up the box containing the pizza and my overnight bag.

"Come on, now. This'll be a bit of an adventure, for both of us. We're staying in a flat they have for visitors, not the home itself. It's a bit special."

"It's a bit special!" she sneers in a sing-song voice. "Special! Special! Like me!"

I wait until we're in the foyer and check there's no-one in earshot before I lay into her.

"Just stop it, Grace, will you? I'm trying to help you here. Do you think I want to traipse about the countryside with a kid who can't be bothered to speak to me nicely? You'll wake your ideas up if you know what's good for you."

I know that I'm not being very PC in the light of her situation – Marie would probably want to prosecute me – but

I decide that being firm with Grace is the only way if I'm going to have to spend hours alone with her. She backs down immediately.

"Sorry," she says, "the last few days haven't been easy."

I'm taken aback by her adult tone, until I remember that she's parroting almost word for word something Marie had said earlier.

"That's all right, Grace," I say quietly. My attention's been diverted by the footsteps I can hear approaching. A man comes through the double doors into the foyer. He's very tall and quite untidy-looking, with a thick mop of unruly black hair that is just tipped with grey. He's wearing a brown jacket with leather elbow patches over a bright green rugby shirt and jeans. He holds out his hand.

"DS Armstrong? I'm Jake Fidler. I'm the acting warden here."

"Oh, I was expecting . . ."

"Mr Dawson, I know. He's been taken ill, unfortunately. We're not sure what the problem is, but it looks as if it might be a long job. He's in hospital having some tests done."

"I'm sorry to hear that."

"Yes, so am I. I'll have my work cut out: the children love him." He suddenly becomes aware of Grace, who is fixing him with one of her mesmeric stares. Gravely, he holds out his hand to her, just as he had to me, and she takes it, irradiating an instant smile.

"Are you Grace?" he says.

"Yes." She speaks in a strong, firm voice. "I'm going to stay here. But just for the night."

Jake Fidler looks at me. I nod briefly.

"Well, you're very welcome. You and DS Armstrong will

be staying in the flat. I'll show you both where it is. Do you have some things with you? If not, we can . . ."

"My colleague has Grace's stuff. He'll bring it in in just a minute," I say quickly. I suspect Grace will take offence and show it if she's offered some of the children's home cast-offs. "He's talking to some of your . . ."

"Our residents," he cuts in, equally swiftly. "We've eaten already, I'm afraid, but I've put some things in the fridge. Salad and stuff. And there's bread and milk and cereal for breakfast. You're welcome to join us for breakfast, if you want to, but Tom said he thought it was best if you had it in the flat."

"Thank you. It's better that Grace doesn't meet the other residents at present. Perhaps if we stay here tomorrow . . ."

"I'm only staying one night," says Grace.

"You're very welcome," Jake Fidler repeats.

Giash comes through the door with the small boy in attendance. The other children have stayed outside. A cat shoots into the room at the same time.

"Hello, Finn," says Jake. "Have you been talking to the policeman?"

Finn nods shyly and picks up the cat. It's a small black cat with a white face.

"Put Sasha down, now, Finn," says Jake. He looks at his watch. "You can play outside for another ten minutes. Then it's time for you to come in."

Finn drops the cat suddenly. It lands on all four paws, then streaks away.

"Gently, Finn," says Jake. "I've told you before, you have to be gentle with Sasha."

Finn looks terrified. He turns away and tugs at the door handle in a panic.

173

"It's ok," says Jake. "I'm not cross with you. I just want you to remember not to hurt Sasha." He moves across to open the door for Finn, who disappears through it.

Jake has a perplexed look on his face when he returns to us. I'm certain he is about to tell us something about Finn, but then he remembers that Grace is watching him.

"He's a nice kid," says Giash. "He'll learn to treat animals better."

"I'm spending quite a lot of time with him just now. Being kind to Sasha is one of the things I'm trying to teach him."

I look at Grace, who instantly appears not to be listening. She hangs her head and fiddles with the cable-stitching on her jumper.

"Anyway, let's go and look at the flat, shall we? I'm afraid there are only two bedrooms. I suppose someone could sleep on the sofa."

"I won't be going to bed," says Giash. "I'll be keeping guard outside."

Jake is clearly very alarmed at this.

"She needs a guard?"

"It's just a formality," I say. "Grace is a potential witness. It's usual for the police to want to safeguard child witnesses."

"I see."

Silent now, Jake leads us down a long corridor and through a side door. We've entered an enclosed courtyard with a flight of steps to one side of it. He gestures upwards.

"The flat's up there," he says. "Do you want me to come in with you?"

"Not if you're busy," I say.

"I am quite busy. I think I'll leave you to it if you don't need me." He removes two keys from a large set of carabiner clips and hands them to me. "Here are the keys to the flat and this side door. If you should want me, my extension number on the internal phone is 001, and my mobile number's on this card." His manner is terse now, quite different from when we first arrived. I know he thinks he shouldn't have agreed to have Grace here, that he's afraid her presence will put the other children in jeopardy.

Giash takes the key from me and runs up the steps. I follow with Grace. The flat has a small vestibule that contains a chair and telephone table. Beyond is quite a smart kitchen-cum-living room with a table and four chairs and a two-seater settee. Leading off it are three doors: two smallish identical bedrooms, each with single beds, and a shower room which also contains a toilet. Grace is obviously taken with the place. She chooses the bedroom nearest the bathroom and takes her two bags of clothes in there, shutting the door behind her. It's fair enough if she wants a bit of privacy: she's had to talk to adults for almost the whole day.

"That lobby area's ideal for me," says Giash. "I'd expected to have to sit right outside. I can just stay in there with the door open."

"Do you want to come into the flat for some tea first?"

"No, I'm fine; I've got my sandwiches and a bottle of water. If you don't mind bringing a tea out to me when you make yours, that would be great."

"Any idea who your relief will be?"

"No. It could be someone from Boston or Peterborough. Superintendent Thornton has drafted outside help for the door-to-doors."

"How will whoever it is get in? They'll need someone to meet them at the main entrance."

"Good point. I'll call the station, ask them to tell the relief to call me when they set out; then I can let them in when they get here. I'll have to ask you for that side door key Mr Fidler gave you and check with him that I'll be able to open the main door from the inside at night. There may be security in place to stop the kids letting themselves out."

"Here's the key. I'll bring some tea later. Can you give me a knock when you know the relief's coming? Then I won't have to stay awake until they get here!"

"All right for some!" Giash grins. "Though I'm not sure I'd swap jobs at the moment."

"What do you mean?"

Giash glances at Grace's closed bedroom door and lowers his voice.

"That kid gives me the creeps. I do feel sorry for her and all that, but she's the weirdest kid I've ever met."

Chapter 41

M Y EVENING WITH Grace passes pleasantly enough. I prepare a salad from the ingredients Jake Fidler's left in the fridge and heat up the pizza. We eat together, Grace chattering cheerfully about school. She keeps up a stream of anodyne conversation throughout the meal, as if to steer me away from weightier topics. She needn't worry: the more time I spend with this child, the more I realise I'm not equipped to fathom her. I'll leave that to the professionals. Besides, I've promised Marie I won't question her again today.

There's a television in the flat. I've let Grace turn it on and she watches it in a desultory way while I wash the dishes and check my e-mails. I make sure that what she's watching is 'suitable', if inane: the evening's programmes on every channel seem to consist of a stream of soap operas and gameshows, punctuated by brief news bulletins.

At intervals, she tires of this fare and disappears into her room, which she's adamant I shouldn't enter. I'm a little suspicious of what she might be doing in there, but I know there's no other television in the flat and Grace doesn't own a mobile, so she can't be coming to any harm. Like most girls of her age she seems to regard her bedroom as sacred territory, though this one is so temporary that I'm surprised she's quite so territorial. I wonder briefly why she has no mobile. I must ask her, or ask Marie to ask her. Most kids of her age have mobiles and I wouldn't mind betting all the kids over five who live in the Dymokes are able to brandish one. My guess is that Amy Winter disapproved and Tina Brackenbury wouldn't or couldn't pay for one.

During one of Grace's retreats, I think I hear some squeaking and other muffled sounds coming from her room and am about to insist that she lets me in when she emerges. I think she's looking paler than when she went in, but she's so fair anyway that I know I'm probably imagining it.

"What have you been doing, Grace?"

"Nothing much."

"I thought I heard a noise coming from your room."

"I was just laughing at a comic."

"What time do you usually go to bed?"

"About ten o'clock. Not before."

This strikes me as a very late bedtime for her age, but it's difficult to know whether she's trying it on or telling the truth. I don't know about Tina Brackenbury's regime, but I can believe that there's little routine imposed on Mavis Hebblewhite's household. I decide not to challenge her.

"Ok, you can stay until the Ten o'Clock News starts. Then I want you to take a shower and go to bed."

She nods and again sits down quietly in front of the television. She needs a bit of a nudge when the theme music to the News starts up, but I have only to remind her once that it's bedtime.

"Can I have my shower in the morning?"

"Yes, if you get up early enough. We need to be ready to leave at eight. DI Yates wants to see us first thing, and the traffic could be heavy. Do you want me to give you a knock at seven?"

She nods. "Good night, then."

"Goodnight, Grace." I wonder if I should offer to settle her down - kiss her goodnight, even - but she's behaving in such a remote and impersonal way that I feel she's sure to shake me off. Still wanting to reassure her, I say: "You can sleep soundly here. This place is like a fortress and PC Chakrabati's outside, looking after us."

"I thought he said he was going in the middle of the night," she says sharply.

"He is, but someone will come to take his place. I may have to go to meet them, but I won't be away more than a few minutes. I'll lock you in. You'll be quite safe."

She grins at me. It's definitely a grin, not a smile. Unnerving. Then she disappears into her room.

An hour or so later, I pay Giash a quick visit before turning in myself. I can see that he's half asleep, though he rouses himself quickly when I open the door.

"I've brought you some more tea."

"Thanks. I could do with it. I didn't realise how tired I was."

"Did you manage to track down Jake Fidler to find out how to open the front door?"

"Yes. You'll have to come with me. It's quite a complicated procedure."

"Ok, but I don't want to leave Grace alone for very long."

"It shouldn't take more than ten minutes or so. Bill Gilby's coming as my relief. He'll text me when he's outside. Then you'll have to let me out and close the door before you let him in. It's to do with the security protocols at night: I think it's so that the CCTV catches both Bill and me on film quite clearly."

"All right. He's coming at 2 a.m., isn't he? Can you call me about ten minutes before, so that I can get dressed?"

"Sure. And thanks again for the tea."

"Do you want me to stay and talk to you for a while, wake you up a bit?"

"No need. The tea'll do that. I think you should get as much sleep as you can. It's going to be tough looking after her."

I smile and think of asserting that really she's quite easy to deal with, but Giash has girls of his own and will know I'm not telling the truth. It's not as if Grace is violent or even overtly unruly, but the psychological pressure she exerts so effortlessly is wearing. I wonder if Giash experiences the same kind of fatigue when dealing with his daughters, but suspect they're not in Grace's league.

As I get into bed, I think I hear sounds coming from Grace's room again. I listen carefully: she's singing in a very low voice, crooning softly.

I tap gently on the wall.

"Grace? Are you ok?" I say. It's only a stud wall: I know she can hear me. She stops singing, but doesn't reply.

"Grace? Do you want me to come in to see you?" Her response is immediate.

"No, thank you. I'm fine. Good night."

"Good night, Grace," I say, for the second time. Again, I'm perplexed by her behaviour, but, like Giash, I'm knackered and I don't have the strength to work through another panorama of the moods she's exhibited since Tim and I picked her up from Mavis Hebblewhite's this morning. I drop rapidly into a black and dreamless pit of sleep.

Ever reliable, Giash calls me at 01.50 a.m. The noise of the ringtone crashes into my brain, astonishingly loud. I grope around and swat at the phone. It must surely have woken Grace, but I listen for a few seconds and hear no other sound.

"Hello?" Giash is saying. "Bill's almost here."

"I'll be with you in a minute," I say. I'd decided not to undress last night, so I just drag a comb through my hair and put on some shoes. I open the bedroom door as quietly as I can and glance across at Grace's room. Her door is firmly closed and I can see no light shining beneath it. I tiptoe through the main room. Giash has already opened the vestibule door. I cross the threshold and he closes the door behind me. He opens the outer door so we are both standing at the top of the outside staircase. The evening is warm and clear. The courtyard is lit by two lamps on wall brackets and a million shining stars.

"Lovely!"

"Is it?" says Giash. "I'm afraid all I can think about is getting to bed. Is Grace all right?"

"As far as I know. I haven't seen her since I brought out your tea. I assume she's asleep. I told her I might have to leave the flat for a few minutes, just in case she wakes up. I don't want her to think she's been abandoned! It is safe to leave her, isn't it?"

"No-one can get to here without coming through the front door first and the security there is something else."

Giash checks that the Yale lock on the door of the flat is secure and gives me the key. I follow him down the staircase and back into the main building. The door to the long corridor closes behind us and he hands over the key to this as well. The corridor is dimly lit; there are just a few low-watt bulbs set in the ceiling at intervals. We're about halfway down it when I hear a scuffling sound.

"What's that?" I say, grabbing Giash's arm.

He laughs. "Probably a rat," he says. I was bitten by a rat a few years ago and contracted Weil's disease. I'm terrified of them now. Giash knows this.

"You're just teasing me."

"Got it in one," he says. "I doubt if there are rats here. The building's too new. It may have been a cat. We saw a cat earlier, didn't we?"

"Yes, that little kid was playing with it. Finn, wasn't it?"

"Dunno. You were probably listening more carefully than I was."

Giash shows me the exit procedure. We each have to stand on a marked spot on the floor and stare at the cameras before we can pass through the barrier to the main door. It's very like the security system at an airport. Then Giash types a code into the panel on the lock. "It's 2 - 4 - 6 - 8," he says. "Not very original! But I think Jake Fidler may have changed it to make it easier for us. He'll probably change it again tomorrow. I'm going out now. The door will close behind me. You'll need to key in the number again to let Bill in. The system depends on only one person crossing the threshold, so don't come out. If he's not here yet I'll text you."

"Thanks!" I say. "I'll see you tomorrow."

Giash taps his watch.

"Today, you mean," he says. "See you!"

I wait for a couple of minutes, staring at the screen on my phone. No message from Giash. I punch the numbers into the keypad and open the door. A tall, bulky copper enters, not someone I know.

"PC Gilby?"

"Bill," he says. "Hi, DS Armstrong."

"Hello, good to meet you. Thanks for helping with this – though I know it probably wasn't your first choice," I add, remembering Giash's earlier comment.

"True enough, but it's an ok job: better than picking up drunks, at any rate."

"I'm afraid we need to work our way through the security system before we're properly inside the building. It's a bit of a pain, I know. You have to stand . . ."

"It's all right, I'm used to these. I've been detailed to jobs in children's homes before. They might be a bit of a faff, but they're a good idea in principle."

I go through the barrier first; Bill Gilby follows.

"Where's the kid? Aren't we supposed to be with her all the time?"

"She's in the visitor's flat. I had to leave her to let you in. Don't worry, we'll be back with her in no time. I did tell her I'd be coming down here for a few minutes, just in case she wakes up."

"Do you think she's really in danger?"

I shrug.

"Hard to say. The woman who was looking after her was almost hysterically convinced that her foster mother's killer would come after her. She certainly sowed the idea in our heads, but my guess is that we'd have been pretty careful to protect her in any case. Has Superintendent Thornton told you who she is? About her past, I mean, not just her connection to the Brackenbury murders?"

"He told me that she was originally called Grace Arkwright and to keep quiet about it and not to mention it to her or anyone else. To be honest, the name didn't mean much to me, so I looked it up . . . What was that?"

The sepulchral quietness of the corridor is being ripped apart by a series of high-pitched, penetrating shrieks. The wailing is almost inhuman. A child's voice is yelling something incoherent.

"My God! I hope that isn't Grace!" Even as I say it, panicked as I feel, I am certain it isn't Grace's voice we're hearing.

"It's coming from that direction. Where does the corridor lead?"

"To an outside courtyard. There's a door. I have the key to it, but it can be opened without the key from the inside."

Bill Gilby hurtles down the corridor, surprisingly fast and nimble for a man of his size. I follow close on his heels.

He almost trips on something as he reaches the door. He kicks it to one side and flings the door wide. The stars are shining brightly and there is almost a full moon. It is light in the courtyard; I can see much more clearly than in the dark corridor from which I've just emerged.

A small boy is kneeling on the ground, clutching a bundle. The great shuddering sobs wracking his diminutive form are almost manic in their intensity.

Bill Gilby walks over to him. He treads softly, without making any sudden or threatening movements.

"What's the matter, mate?" he says. He pats the boy's arm, but the child shrinks from his touch. As he does so, he releases his grip on the bundle and it slides slowly to the ground. I see that it is the cat, Sasha; and an instant afterwards, I realise that it is dead, its black and white head lolling lifeless, its legs straight and stiff.

"Sasha! Sasha!" the child cries again. I recognise Finn, the boy who had earlier got into trouble with Jeff Fidler for handling the cat too roughly. His hysteria subsides. He looks up at me with huge fearful eyes, his cheeks streaked pitifully where the tears have run down them. He puts out a hand, grabs my ankle.

"I didn't do it, Miss, I didn't, it wasn't me!" He is craven with fear now. "I'll get into trouble, won't I, but it wasn't me." Then his grief overcomes him again. "Sasha! Sasha!" He says. He takes his hand off my ankle and stretches it out to reach for the cat again.

"Don't, Finn," I say gently. "Let's get Mr Fidler to come, shall we? You can explain that it was an accident."

"It wasn't no accident, I didn't do it," the boy shrieks, engulfed by another paroxysm of tears.

"Do you know how to get hold of Fidler?" Bill Gilby asks.

"He gave me his number."

"If you call him and explain, I'll wait here with the kid until he comes. I think you should go back to Grace. She's likely to have been woken up by all this noise. If so, she's probably frightened."

"Thanks," I say. "You're right."

The call is made quickly: Jake Fidler doesn't even sound as if he's been sleeping. I pass the phone over briefly to introduce Bill Gilby, then head up the stairs to the flat. I'm halfway there when I think I hear a slight click. I look across to the windows and am just in time to see a light being extinguished.

Chapter 42

TIM WANTED TO read more about the Arkwright murders than just the synopsis of the trial and the coroner's reports. He'd absorbed plenty about the nature of the injuries inflicted and he certainly didn't need to examine any more of the photographs of the carnage at Brocklesby Farm taken by the North Lincs forensics team. What interested him now was Tristram Arkwright's defence. He knew that Arkwright had always protested his innocence; there was nothing extraordinary about that – every second old lag claimed not to have done the deed he'd been convicted of – but Arkwright had been particularly persuasive: so convincing, in fact, that the members of the jury had not been unanimous in finding him guilty, despite the overwhelming circumstantial evidence against him. They'd taken almost two days to arrive at the majority verdict which the judge had reluctantly accepted. (Most judges were uneasy about sentencing someone to life unless the jury returned a unanimous guilty verdict.)

It was evident that Arkwright was not without charisma. What Tim wanted to know was how he was viewed by the rest of his family. Did he have some kind of hold over them? Were they intimidated by him? Or did they all get on brilliantly together until Tristram had unexpectedly turned guns on the others? If Tim could work out the answers to these questions, he might begin to understand Grace's relationship with her uncle a bit better. He must have made quite an impression on her: it was extraordinary that a ten-year-old child could recall in such detail the features of a man she hadn't seen for four years and capture them so exactly in a doodle.

Arkwright's defence lawyer had been Mortimer Bayles, an eminent, still relatively young silk whose clients were usually acquitted, sometimes against improbable odds. Bayles had argued that Arkwright had no case to answer; that it was clear that his adoptive sister was mentally ill and had shot her parents after a row about her medication. She'd then killed her baby before committing suicide. Bayles suggested that Jacqueline decided the baby had to die because there would be no-one left to care for her if her mother was either dead or in prison.

For the crown, Sir Ernest Arbuthnot, a crusty old QC who had since died, pointed out that if she'd trusted Tristram, Jacqueline Arkwright could have confidently expected him to arrange for the baby to be cared for. Indeed, she had other living relatives who might be prepared to look after the infant, including her adoptive cousins, to whom she was apparently quite close. There was also the indisputable fact that her older child had been spared. Was it not possible, indeed, likely, that Jacqueline had hidden the other girl or told her to hide in a desperate attempt to save her from the killer which had paid off?

"My lord," Bayles had addressed the judge, "*my learned friend is asking the jury to speculate on the thought processes of a woman who had been mentally unstable for much of her adult life. We say that he is inviting them to indulge in conjecture, not producing evidence for them to examine, and that therefore this mode of reasoning is inadmissible.*"

The judge had asked Sir Ernest to explain where his

deliberations were leading. He'd replied that he'd been trying to establish what kind of relationship Tristram Arkwright had enjoyed with his sister and parents. Tim was reading avidly now, his concentration fixed. That was precisely what he wanted to know.

The judge had observed that Sir Ernest was using a very roundabout approach to elicit information which could probably be more effectively obtained by means of some direct questions. Sir Ernest tried again.

"Mr Arkwright," he said, "how would you describe your relationship with your parents – your deceased adoptive parents, that is?"

"I owe them everything. I have tried to be a dutiful son to them."

Tim thought it was a pretty bloodless reply under the circumstances. Sir Ernest himself seemed dissatisfied with the response.

"Did you love your parents, Mr Arkwright? Once more, I stress that I am referring to your deceased adoptive parents."

"Of course I loved them. I was particularly close to my father."

"And your mother?"

"I loved my mother."

"You seemed to hesitate, Mr Arkwright. Why is that?"

"I loved my mother," Arkwright said again. The court clerk had typed 'aggressively' in brackets beside the recorded speech.

"What about your adoptive sister? What kind of feelings did you have for her? She was a bit of a black sheep, wasn't she? Did it annoy you that your parents gave her financial help while you had to work for your money?"

"Not in the slightest. I certainly wouldn't have swapped places with Jackie."

"What about her children? Did you like them?"

"Babies aren't really my thing. I didn't take much notice of Laura."

"What about the older child? Mrs Winter says you are quite friendly with her; that you are in the habit of taking her for rides on your tractor."

"I think she is quite an enterprising kid, yes. Not a whinger like her mother."

"Would you say you'd formed a close bond with your older niece?"

"I'd say I feel for her the normal affection that any uncle feels for his niece."

"But you didn't feel the same degree of affection for Laura?"

"Laura was a baby. As I've said already, I don't find babies very interesting. I'm sure that as she'd grown older and developed some personality . . ."

"But as it was, she had no personality as far as you were concerned, did she? Did that make her expendable? In your view, was she just an extension of her mother, and therefore a legitimate object on which to vent your fury and jealousy at what you perceived to be the unfair favouritism of your adoptive parents?"

"Objection, your honour! This line of questioning amounts to harassment, and once again has no roots in fact."

"Objection sustained. Sir Ernest, you will please be a little less colourful and considerably more exact in your examination of the defendant." Above the judge's reprimand, the court clerk had added another terse comment in brackets. [Defendant began to speak: 'My niece . . . ']

"Damn! Damn! Damn!"

"What's the matter?" said Katrin, coming in from the hall.

"Sorry, I didn't know I was talking out loud. I'm reading about Arkwright's trial. He was going to say something about Grace when the judge cut him off."

"You can't really think that Arkwright is mixed up in Tina Brackenbury's murder in some way. He's in prison; there's nothing to suggest he knew Tina, is there?"

"Not as far as I know. The common denominator is Grace. That's what interests me. Plus the fact that a woman died with her baby on each occasion."

"But Grace has no contact with Arkwright, does she? And even if she did, she couldn't possibly have killed Tina Brackenbury, though she could have watched her die. And she certainly didn't shoot all those people at Brocklesby Farm."

"You're right, Arkwright won't be allowed to contact her, as he isn't her parent or guardian. I really don't think she's killed four adults, three of them when she was only six years old, but I still think she's mixed up in Tina Brackenbury's death somehow, perhaps as a witness, as you say. And that makes me wonder about the Brocklesby Farm murders, too. The problem with Grace is that she shows no sign of distress. At the same time, I'm sure she's hiding something. But getting her to confide in us is next to impossible, especially when Marie's on the case."

"What about the other girl? Chloe, was that her name?"

"Terrified out of her wits. It's impossible to get any sense out of her. She just collapses into tears."

"Surely that's odd in itself?"

"I'd agree with you, if I didn't think the girl was half-sharp.

And she has good reason to be afraid of the police: her brothers are always getting into trouble."

"And you don't think you'll get anywhere with this Marek Wolansky, either?"

"I haven't met him, but it's unlikely, given what Juliet says about his mental capacity. According to her, he'd have found it impossible to carry out a co-ordinated sequence of actions such as getting access to the house, committing the murders and then leaving again. He barely understands his own name, apparently."

"You seem just to be hitting a series of dead ends. I don't know what else to suggest, but I do think you should pack it in for the evening. See what comes of the interviews with Wolansky and Grace tomorrow. You'll know then whether it's worth talking to Chloe Hebblewhite again."

Chapter 43

TIM LOOKED UP sharply from his desk, sensing that he was being watched. He was surprised to see Superintendent Thornton hovering uneasily in front of him. Diffidence was not one of the Superintendent's more pronounced attributes.

"Ah, Yates!" he said, clearing his throat.

"Yes, sir?" Since Tim was sitting at his own desk during working hours, the Superintendent could hardly have been surprised to see him there. "Would you like a seat?"

Superintendent Thornton sat down on the chair that Tim indicated and looked around him conspiratorially. It was early and apart from the two of them the office was still deserted.

"As you know, Yates," he said, lowering his voice to a mutter, "I'm not an especially politically correct sort of person . . ." Tim raised his eyebrows and suppressed a smile. " . . . but sometimes even I realise that we're in quite a situation and it's up to me to decide when it's time to tread carefully."

"I'm sorry, sir, I think you've lost me."

Superintendent Thornton crossed one leg over the other, placed his elbow on it and rested his chin on the resulting upstretched hand.

"The thing is . . . have you interviewed this Marek Wolansky yet?"

"Not yet, no. PC Tandy is going to visit his mother this morning and explain the situation to her. We'll interview him after that."

"You mean, today?"

"Yes, if we can. Why do you ask?"

"Am I correct in understanding that the man is . . . whatever the term is . . . educationally challenged? Is that it?"

"I haven't met him myself, but according to DS Armstrong he's very severely retarded."

"Exactly. So, do you think it's wise to interview him?"

"He's a suspect in a murder investigation, although, granted, an unlikely one. It's our job to interview him, if only to eliminate him from the enquiry. My own view is that it'll rapidly become apparent that he's incapable of having committed the crime."

"Yes. Quite so. Good."

"You don't want us not to interview him?"

"No, of course not. I'm just saying tread carefully, that's all. We don't want the PCC after us for harassing a vulnerable person, do we?"

"No, sir. I'll bear your advice in mind."

Abruptly the Superintendent unfolded his limbs from the contorted position he'd wrapped them in, stood up and walked away without a further word. Tim grinned, but he was slightly nettled. Superintendent Thornton's 'sensitivities' presented themselves at the most inconvenient times and his message to Tim was clear: "Fuck this one up and you're on your own."

His mobile rang. Juliet's number flashed up on the screen.

"Hello, Juliet. Quiet night in the children's home?"

"Not really . . ."

"You can tell me about it when we meet. I'd like the interview with Grace to wait until we've dealt with Marek Wolansky, so please let Marie know – we'll contact her with a new time. You'll come with me to interview Wolansky, won't you? You've met his mother already, so I think that'll help."

"What am I going to do with Grace?"

"Can't they look after her at the home?"

"She's not enrolled here. And there was an incident last night."

"Involving Grace?"

"No, but they're short-staffed because the warden's ill. The incident's put extra pressure on them. I can't ask them to cope with Grace as well. She can stay in the flat – it's probably the safest place for her – but she'll need someone to look after her. And PC Gilby's going to want relieving soon."

"I've arranged for Giash Chakrabati to come back. Can't you ask Marie to be with Grace?"

"Marie's a child psychologist, not a child minder."

"Point taken, but you're a police officer, also not a child minder."

Juliet sighed.

"I'll ask Tom Tarrant if he can provide suitable care for her. What time do you want to do the interview?"

"As soon as possible. Verity Tandy's visiting Mrs Wolansky at the moment, to pave the way. Provided she doesn't kick up a fuss, I'd hoped to do it this morning."

"I can't promise anything, but I'll do my best. If Tom can't help, I'll have to stay here. If Verity gets on all right with Mrs Wolansky, perhaps she could come with you."

"I guess so. But she doesn't have your insights."

Juliet gave a short laugh.

"I didn't know you appreciated me so much."

"Surely you do know that, Juliet," said Tim, almost succeeding in sounding hurt.

Chapter 44

I'VE LEFT GRACE with Marie. After all my scruples and a prolonged conversation with Tom Tarrant, Tim's solution as to who should look after her was the one they chose. Far from resenting being treated like a childminder, Marie seems to have made it her mission to nurture Grace.

I haven't had an opportunity to talk to Marie yet, but already I know that the stance she's adopted is going to make relations with Grace more difficult. I'm deeply worried about Grace now, though I can't quite put my finger on why. Although I have no evidence, I'm convinced she was involved in the death of Sasha the cat. Finn is clearly a very disturbed child, but I don't believe that his terrifying distress was caused by guilt and remorse, as Jake Fidler seems to think. And I know that there was activity in the flat just before I returned to it, though I'm not even sure what it was I half-glimpsed: did I really see the light go out?

I hardly slept after I returned to the flat once Bill Gilby and I had alerted Jake and I'm weary now. I park on the station forecourt. As I unclip my seat-belt and climb out of the car, I see Verity Tandy approaching. She waits for me at the door. When I catch up with her, I note that she looks as battered as I feel.

"Am I glad to see you!" she exclaims when I'm in earshot. "You'll be able to do the Wolansky interview instead of me now."

I'd almost forgotten why I had to make the minding arrangements for Grace.

"Thanks! That's probably the last thing I need. I take it you've been to prime Mrs Wolansky?"

"Yes; and she can be a lot more difficult than you might think."

"I'm not surprised: the tigress defending her young and all that. I expect she's had to protect Marek from ridicule and other unpleasantness for his whole life. She's probably had to fight to get help from social services as well. What did she say? You must have done a good job, if she says we can go ahead with the interview."

"She'll let us do it, but she'll be there holding Marek's hand and the first sign of panic he shows, she'll make us stop. She's firm about that. I went along with what she said, but I guess you could insist on having him interviewed by experts if she's really obstructive."

"It may come to that. In some ways, perhaps we should, but we have to save as much time as possible. Thanks for paving the way; I know how hard it must have been."

"You're welcome – you've got the worst bit."

"When is she expecting us?"

Verity glances at her watch.

"Any time now. I said you'd be there by about 10.30. He usually attends some kind of day centre today. She's agreed to keep him back this morning – I was lucky to catch her before the bus arrived for him – but she wants him to go there this afternoon. They're coming back for him at twelve, so the sooner you can get there, the better."

"Well, I'm ready. I just need to find Tim. And I'd better pick up my notes from the interview with Grace Winter, as well. If we can get any sense out of Marek, I'll need to know if their two accounts tally."

"You don't seriously think that he was involved, do you? Or that he's likely to say something to incriminate himself?"

"The answer is no, and no – the latter because if he had been there, and even if he'd committed the murders, I don't think he'd have either the power of recollection or the words to describe it. But now that Grace has accused him we have to eliminate him if we can."

"Strange kid. If she's telling lies, what reason can she have?"

"That's a very good question. But I can't answer it."

Verity holds open the door for me. Before I can step through it, Tim comes bounding out.

"Ah, there you are, Juliet. It's time we were going. Are you all set?" He gives Verity a brief nod. "Thanks for talking to the mother. Superintendent Thornton's just told me."

Verity comes the closest to simpering that I've ever seen in her. I like her and I know this is out of character. Why is everyone always so keen to please Tim? I butt in before she can say something sickening like 'Only doing my job, sir!'.

"I'm nearly ready. I just need to fetch my interview notes from yesterday."

"What? Oh, I suppose that's a good idea. I'll bring the car round. I'll meet you here."

Verity continues to hold the door. I go through it, throwing her a conspiratorial grimace as I pass which she doesn't acknowledge. I try not to be annoyed: I focus on the fact that we're both feeling a bit frayed.

I forgive Tim instantly as soon as I get into his car, because all his earlier breeziness has vanished. He gives me a harrowed look.

"I'm sorry this is so tough for you. I can hardly think of anything worse than having to interview someone with profound learning disabilities about the murder of a baby."

"Thanks. I appreciate your concern, but it's as bad for you. Worse, probably, as the parent of a young child yourself. It's not the time to talk about it now – I know we must concentrate on this – but I'm getting more and more concerned about Grace. I'm not convinced she's the miraculously well-adjusted child the psychologists would have us believe."

"I remember you said there was an incident at the children's home last night. But I thought she wasn't involved?"

"I've no proof that she was. It's just a feeling. It was a pretty unpleasant incident, involving the death of a cat. There's a disturbed child there who'd been molesting the cat and he's been blamed for it. On the face of it, he's the most likely culprit, but I've just got an inkling that Grace had something to do with it. She may even have killed the cat herself and framed the other kid."

"Jesus! Do you really think that?"

"I think it's a possibility. Once we're through this interview I want to get in touch with Grace's adoptive mother. And we should insist that we're shown the reports Lenka Astani wrote after the Brocklesby Farm murders, which will probably mean asking for a warrant."

"I thought Dr Astani said she couldn't find anything wrong with Grace? That she'd shown remarkable resilience?"

"That *is* what she said; but I want to see the notes for myself. There may be something – even just something small – that tells a different story."

"Tread carefully, Juliet. If you're trying to build a case to show that a ten-year-old girl is involved in murder, you've got to be damn sure you're right before you tell anyone else."

"I'm not going to tell anyone else. I'm just running a few ideas past you. And I'm well aware that Marie's up to her neck in this, and she's come down heavily in favour of supporting Grace. Marie's a great ally and a formidable enemy . . . and she won't be supporting me if this goes any further."

"As I said, tread carefully; you might like to weigh up the consequences, either way."

"Oh, I've weighed them up, believe me, and I know it would be a lot easier to bury my suspicions, even if the murders are never solved."

"Well, then . . ."

"But what if I'm right, Tim? If Grace Winter is a killer, or fascinated with death because she's witnessed killings, she needs help. Otherwise she'll grow up to commit murder again."

Mrs Wolansky looks haggard when she opens the door. She regards us with suspicion.

"Mrs Wolansky? Do you remember me? I called the other day to ask . . ."

"I know who you are. You'd better come in." She holds the door ajar, creating a narrow space for us to squeeze through whilst she peers down the street.

The kitchen is darker than I remember and, although it's quite a warm day outside, it feels cold. It's not quite as pristine as on the first occasion. The washing-up bowl contains dishes and cups, evidently from breakfast, and there is a stack of newspapers on one of the chairs. She indicates the two chairs that are free, opposite her son. Tim and I take them. Mrs Wolansky remains standing.

Marek is sitting in the same chair that he occupied before. His large head is hunched down into his shoulders. He is squinting dully through half-shut eyelids; it's impossible to gauge the extent to which he registers our presence. He's looking quite smart today; he's wearing a navy-blue polo top and a casual jacket in a lighter shade of blue, perhaps in honour of our visit, but more probably because he's been dressed for his excursion to the day centre.

Mrs Wolansky walks up to him and taps him gently on the shoulder.

"Marek," she says, "there is a gentleman and a lady to see you."

He flinches away from her touch, but his eyes open wider. He's staring directly across at Tim and seems to be focusing on his face.

"Hello, Marek," Tim says. "I've come to ask you a few questions. Nothing to worry about."

"Before you start," Mrs Wolansky cuts in in a low, angry sotto voce, "you understand he has no idea of time? It is no use you talk of last weekend or yesterday or even this morning. He won't know."

Tim nods. "Thank you. I'll try not to confuse him."

She knits her eyebrows, clearly sceptical.

"Marek," Tim continues, "have you ever been in the house next door?"

Marek stares and nods; then immediately afterwards shakes his head.

"He means Tina's house," his mother enunciates slowly. "Tina. You like Tina, don't you?"

Marek smiles and nods more vigorously.

"Have you been to see Tina in her house?" Tim asks. Marek looks puzzled again.

"We have been to see Tina once or twice. Not recently," Mrs Wolansky supplies.

"How recently?"

"I don't think we've been in there since Grace came. Tina thought she might be frightened of him. And then there was the baby. Not many mothers would want Marek hanging round a baby." She gives a short, bitter laugh as Tim tries to show concern. "Oh, it's all right, I understand. People think he's jinxed. It might be catching: he might turn a kid into a half-wit."

"Did you get on with Tina?"

"She was ok. She was like most women round here: not too particular about cleaning her house or the company she kept. But nice enough. She wasn't a difficult neighbour."

"How can I get Marek to respond? Does he know any words at all?"

"He understands quite a lot of words, but speaks not many. Talk very slow to him, maybe show him a picture."

"What sort of a picture?"

"I don't know. A picture of what you want him to help you with. But not one of dead Tina – that would upset him. He's very sensitive."

"I wouldn't dream of doing that, Mrs Wolansky." Tim turns to me. "Do we have a picture of Grace?"

I unclip the photograph that Marie took of Grace from the cover of her file and pass it to Tim. He takes it and stands up. Marek immediately shrinks back in his chair and begins to look agitated. Tim sits down again and passes the photo to Mrs Wolansky.

"Would you show this to him? Ask him if he knows the girl."

Mrs Wolansky kneels down and places the photo on Marek's lap.

"Do you know who that is, darlin'?"

I hardly dare look at him, dreading some kind of anguished outburst; but when I pluck up the courage, I see he is smiling broadly. Incongruously, he starts giggling, making a high-pitched animal noise. He carries on laughing until he is out of control, his head lolling from side to side, his feet drumming the floor.

Mrs Wolansky takes the photograph and places it on the table. She stands up and smooths his brow.

"Calmly, Marek, calmly," she croons. He rests his head against her breast and after a few minutes is sitting still again, though he's still smiling.

"What was so funny?" Tim asks.

"I don't know. We can try to find out." She kneels again so that she is looking up into her son's face. He gazes down at her, his expression less vacant than before. There can be little doubt that the photograph has triggered a pleasant memory.

"You liked the picture of the girl, didn't you, Marek?"

He nods.

"Why did you like it?"

He struggles to speak, spluttering all over her. She seems not to mind. What comes out of his mouth is one very indistinct word. It sounds like a group of consonants strung together without vowels.

"What did you say, darlin'?"

He repeats it again while she puts her ear to his mouth. It's a little clearer this time: "Przzfnt!"

Mrs Wolansky seems to understand.

"She gave you a present?"

He nods, smiling again.

"What sort of a present?"

He sits up straight and starts searching the pockets of his windcheater. He can find nothing in them and is becoming distressed.

"Did you put it in your jacket pocket?"

He nods, his face contorting horribly.

"You'll have been wearing your other jacket, darlin'. Let me fetch it for you. Don't move while I'm gone or you'll upset him," she throws over her shoulder at us as she leaves the room. She's back in a few seconds, carrying the shapeless cotton jacket he'd been wearing when he and I first met.

"Shall I look for you?"

He nods again.

Methodically she works through the pockets, extracting paper tissues and sweets which she lays on the table. She reaches the inside pocket and her fingers close on something. She pulls it out. It lies glinting in her hand.

"What's this? Is this your present?"

"Yes," he says, beaming. He holds out his hand.

Carefully she gathers it up and places it in the middle of his palm. It's an old-fashioned silver locket threaded through a chain of tiny silver beads.

Chapter 45

JENNIFER DOVE FELT a frisson of excitement as the prison doors were opened and she and the other waiting women, together with an assortment of children and the occasional older man, shuffled into the outer perimeter. In her past life, she might have known evil men intimately, but she had never before come face to face with a convicted murderer.

She was relieved to be on the move at last. She and a group of the women had stood outside for almost a quarter of an hour, the wind whipping round the bleak corner where they'd gathered. She was struck by how colourless they were, dressed mainly in drab blacks, greys and browns, their faces on the yellow-to-beige spectrum and drawn with worry and poverty. She herself was wearing a fuchsia mohair jumper over patterned leggings; with gold hoops in her ears and her hair newly coloured in tints of copper, she was now regretting showing off with such exuberance. The other women treated her with suspicion, shunning her at first. Eventually one of the younger ones, a rake-thin woman who'd have been pretty if she'd looked less careworn, spoke to her.

"Haven't seen you here before."

"No. It's the first time I've been."

The woman was sympathetic.

"You'll get used to it. Your old man, is it?"

"No, I'm a prison visitor."

The woman shut down immediately and turned away. An

older woman butted in, addressing no-one in particular in a strident voice.

"Obvious, that was. I don't know why you talked to her. You can see she's a do-gooder. They always dress up like that. In it for the thrills. Or slumming it."

She'd turned away, her face red. The woman was speaking the truth.

They were detained in the outer perimeter for some time before being herded through another door and into a large, bare room. A female prison officer asked each person for their visiting number and ID. Jennifer had written the number on a slip of paper. She handed it over, with her passport. The woman nodded curtly and passed it back to her.

"What's in the parcel?"

"Just a couple of paperback books."

"Show them when you're searched. The queue's over there."

Jennifer looked across to where the warder was pointing and saw a queue had already lined up. A mother with a tiny child clinging to her was removing the baby she was holding from its duvet nest.

"Surely you don't bother to search babies?"

The warder rolled her eyes and gave Jennifer an impatient push.

"Move on, please."

She joined the queue. Several of the women in front of her were accompanied by children. It took a long time for her turn to come. A second female warder was waiting beside the scanning machine.

"Take off your outdoor clothes and put them in the scanner, as well as your handbag. You carrying a mobile?"

"Yes."

"Take it out and put it through separately. Belts and jewellery too. And your shoes. What's in the parcel?"

"Just a couple of paperback books."

"Put them through. Stand there while the dog walks past you."

For the first time, Jennifer noticed a dog-handler walking up and down with a spaniel in tow. The spaniel was moving close in to the people queueing behind her. Children were shying away from it.

"Is it looking for drugs?"

The warder tutted exasperatedly.

"No, it's sussing out who's wearing the best perfume. What do you think?" Then, relenting a little because Jennifer looked so crushed, she added. "You're all right as long as he doesn't sit down next to you. If he does, you're for it."

She was ridiculously relieved when the dog walked past her without pausing.

"Now stand out here and hold your arms wide from your body, feet apart."

She did as she was told. The warder ran a hand-held body-scanner over her arms, legs and torso.

"OK. You can go. Pick up your stuff on the other side."

She put on her belt and shoes and picked up the parcel of books. She couldn't see her handbag, and was panic-stricken for a few seconds until the male official operating the scanning machine stood up and held it out to her.

"A quick word," he said, lowering his voice. "You've got far too much money in there. You know you can only give money to the prisoner with permission, and then not much. And none at all if he's already got £500 in his account here."

"I didn't know that. Thanks for telling me," she said stiffly;

all this officialdom was getting on her nerves. Visiting time would be half over before she'd battled her way through. He gave her a measured look.

"That's all right. And remember, things can walk in here."

"Thanks," she said with more warmth. She realised she had a lot to learn.

She'd expected him to be behind toughened glass, as in the films that she'd seen about prisoners on death row, and wearing something outlandish, perhaps a red or orange boil-er-suit. She'd envisaged herself standing, or sitting on a high stool, staring through the glass at him. Absurdly, she was disappointed when she was taken into another bleak room, this one furnished with small chairs and tables. It was like a very basic café that didn't serve food.

A man was already seated at each of the tables. All were dressed in grey overalls - they looked as if they might have come to fix the plumbing. There were no shocking colours, nothing humiliating. Some managed to look smarter than others: it was a strange thing she'd often noticed about uni-forms - however identical they might be, people always suc-ceeded in wearing them in individual ways.

She recognised him immediately, of course: she'd pored over his photograph in online newspapers and websites so many times that she could have sketched it from memory. Naturally, he was a little older than in the photographs and prison had taken its toll: his face was thinner, his eyes less penetrating, his expression more guarded. But he was very handsome, and he rose to meet her with the dapper self-as-surance that she recognised in his type. Prison could not diminish that.

"Jennifer!" he said, taking her hand. "How nice to meet

you at last. Thank you for coming. Do sit down." From his demeanour, they might have been taking afternoon tea or cocktails at the Ritz. He resumed his own seat and she took the one opposite, as he'd indicated. Over his shoulder, she noted a guard standing against the wall, impassive.

"It's my pleasure. I'm very happy to meet you, too. But how did you know it was me?"

He leaned closer to her and whispered conspiratorially. "It was easy! Most of these women come here all the time, so I've seen them before. And they don't bother to dress up for their men." He was flirting with her already. His next comment almost made her swoon. "I wonder if you'll do something for me."

Chapter 46

MAREK WOLANSKY IS still clutching the silver necklace. An attempt by his mother to take it from him results in the emission of a hideous high-pitched scream, after which he folds the pendant tight within his fingers and lapses into the semi-catatonic state in which I first saw him. Fleetingly, I wonder if he's faking to deflect us from his booty. However, when Mrs Wolansky begins again to talk it's obvious he's quite absent from the conversation.

She's pale, grim-lipped and tearful.

"What will happen now?" she asks.

"I can't tell you that yet," says Tim. "We'll need help from you to clarify a few points. First of all, have you seen that necklace before?"

"Yes, I have. It's Tina's. She nearly always wore it."

"Did Marek ever show any interest in it when he saw her wearing it?"

"I have told you, we haven't been in Tina's house for many months. You can see what Marek is like. He doesn't remember things."

"He seems to have remembered Grace."

"I can't explain that, except perhaps that she gave him something that he likes."

"You think she gave him the necklace? Why would she do that?"

"I don't know, but when you showed him her photograph he started to look for the necklace afterwards."

"Did you know that he knew Grace?"

"No. I told you, Tina didn't want us there after she came."

"You also said that Marek never goes out alone. How could he have met Grace, if she didn't come here? Are you sure he never met her when he was with you? Does anyone else ever take him out?"

I'm watching her closely. She speaks falteringly – she's obviously beside herself with worry – but I can detect no sign that she's lying. She's guarded, even hostile, because she's protecting her son, but I don't think she's being evasive.

"He hasn't met her with me. I don't take him out very much. I rely on the day centre to give us a change. Taking Marek for walks is not easy: he gets distracted by small things and he is frightened by the traffic. And always the children tease him."

"You mean the local children?"

"Any children. But he sees most the ones who live round here."

"Are you quite certain he can't have been in Tina Brackenbury's house without your knowledge? I mean at any time, but particularly last Saturday or Sunday?"

She gives a little gasp and her legs buckle. She throws herself sideways into a chair.

"Mrs Wolansky, are you all right?"

"I have just remembered something." She puts her hand to her forehead. I'm afraid she might faint.

"Would you like me to fetch you some water?" I say.

She glances across at Marek. His eyes are completely closed

now and his chest rises and falls rhythmically. He is sleeping like a baby.

"No, no I will tell you before he wakes up. I don't want him upset. He knows the driver of the minibus – his name is Phil. Phil is very good with the people he picks up for the day centre. He likes Marek. He lives round here – up near Fulney, I think – and sometimes he calls in. He called in on Saturday and sat with Marek for a while. He said he would stay with him while I did a few things upstairs."

"Did he take him out?"

"No, not exactly."

"What do you mean by that, Mrs Wolansky?"

"When I came back downstairs the back door was open and Marek and Phil were not in the kitchen. I went out and found Marek standing outside. Phil came back a few minutes later. He said he'd shouted up the stairs to me that he was just nipping out to buy fags, but I didn't hear him. I began to be very cross with him, but it was upsetting Marek and I thought maybe I was being unfair. He was doing me a favour and nothing bad happened."

"How long was Marek on his own?"

"I don't know. It takes me ten minutes to walk to the shop, but Phil would be more quick. Not more than twenty minutes, I think."

"And when you fetched Marek in, you didn't notice whether Tina's front door was open or closed?"

"I didn't go round the front. You could ask Phil. He might have seen."

"Thank you, we'll do that. I don't want to alarm you, but we'll need to take the clothes that Marek was wearing on Saturday, just for the purpose of eliminating him from the enquiry, you understand. You brought the jacket down just now. It can't have been washed as the pendant was still in the pocket. Have the other clothes been washed since then?"

"His underwear and his shirt. Not trousers."

"Can we have the trousers then, please? And whatever he was wearing on his feet."

"It's the shoes he has on. He doesn't have no others. What will he wear to the centre?"

"Has he got some slippers?"

"He won't wear them. There's some old tennis shoes someone gave him."

"Can you give him those to wear, then? We'll need to take the pendant, as well."

"I will parcel everything up for you. He will be very upset about the shoes and the necklace. It's best I do it when we're alone."

"I'm sorry, Mrs Wolansky, we need to take them now. I'll bring in some evidence bags."

"I'll help you with his shoes," I say. "If we're careful, we can take them off without waking him."

Mrs Wolansky and I kneel down on the floor. Close up, Marek smells of fabric softener and stale urine. I guess he must be wearing an incontinence pad.

We each untie the lace of one of his battered trainers and ease his feet out of them. He barely stirs. Tim returns with the evidence bags and puts the jacket in one of them. I take a bag for each of the trainers.

"Can you get the trousers?" he says to Mrs Wolansky. She nods, goes upstairs, returns with a pair of outsize track-suit bottoms and hands them to Tim, who consigns them to another bag.

"Now the pendant," he says.

Mrs Wolansky takes Marek's hand. In sleep, he has loosened his grip. She extricates the necklace from his fingers and hands it over to Tim as well.

"Thank you very much for co-operating with us, Mrs Wolansky," Tim is whispering so he won't wake Marek up. "I know it's been difficult for you. As I said, I don't know what will happen next. As well as carrying out tests on the clothes, we'll have to take professional advice on how to deal with . . . witnesses like Marek. Until we know how to proceed, I must ask you to ensure that he stays close to home."

"He can go to the day centre?"

"By all means. Under other circumstances, I'd caution him not to discuss Tina Brackenbury or any connection he may have with the murders, even as a bystander. I know it's not necessary in this case, but please make sure nevertheless that no-one tries to talk to him about it. I suppose he has no passport to surrender?"

She bursts out laughing. It is mirth on the cusp of hysteria.

Chapter 47

"Y OU NEED TO interview Grace again quickly," says Tim, as soon as we are in the car. "And we have to talk to this Phil character. And Amy Winter."

"What about the other leads we've got? Tina Brackenbury's ex-husband and the boyfriend?"

"Sorry, I meant to tell you: the husband's got a cast-iron alibi. Opal Smith was right when she said he's working on the North Sea ferries. He was at sea all weekend, returning to Hull on Monday after the murders were reported, so it can't have been him. We haven't tracked down the boyfriend yet. Andy Carstairs is trying to find him. He lives with his mother some of the time, but she says she hasn't seen him for ten days or so."

"That's a bit fishy, isn't it?"

"Maybe, but the bloke's a fly-by-night. Opal Smith was right about that, too. He doesn't have a regular job. No doubt he's involved in all sorts of dodgy enterprises. He's probably got his own reasons for avoiding us."

"Still, you'd think he'd be falling over himself to get dropped from a murder investigation."

"That may not be the way he thinks, but you're right: I'm not discounting him as a suspect. It's just that we need to get to the bottom of exactly what Grace's movements were last Saturday and Sunday, including whether she was in the house at other times than she's admitted and if she somehow enticed Marek Wolansky in there as well. And we need to understand why Amy Winter first adopted her and then got rid of her."

"Lenka Astani said . . ."

"I know what she said, but it sounds feeble to me. Grace is just a little girl, after all."

"I'd have agreed with you one hundred per cent before I met Grace. There's something frightening about that child."

"As you know, I'm a great admirer of your intuition, Juliet, and I have no doubt that you're much more sensitive than I am. But sometimes – just occasionally – I think your imagination runs away with you."

"Very possibly. Talking of which, don't forget that Marie's protectiveness now has to be factored in to all interviews with Grace. That should test my imaginative powers, not to mention your ingenuity. If Marie thinks we're infringing Grace's legal rights or even giving them a slight tweak, she'll leap on us."

"You've just reminded me that we asked the Home Office for permission to interview Lenka Astani to find out more about her assessment of Tristram Arkwright. I'll get Andy to chase them up."

"I really don't see how Tristram Arkwright can be involved. He's in a maximum security jail, for God's sake."

"He wouldn't be the first criminal to exert influence from the inside, but I think it's more probable that if he has a hold on her it's historical. Grace drew a pretty accurate sketch of him yesterday, which as you pointed out is worrying, especially as she can't have seen him for the last four years. Any power he may have over her is most likely

215

to date from the Brocklesby Farm murders, or even before then."

"I've read the police reports. She was carried out of the farmhouse by a policeman. Arkwright was waiting outside. He asked if she was dead and the policeman said no and he thought she was ok. Arkwright took her in his arms briefly before they put her into an ambulance."

"Did he go with her in the ambulance?"

"Yes, I think so. And he could have seen her at any time before he was arrested. It took the police a couple of weeks to bring charges against him. At first, they believed the version of events that he'd suggested, which was that his sister had gone berserk with guns."

"What made them change their minds?"

"Several things didn't quite add up. The pathologist was undecided whether Jacqueline Arkwright died from her single gunshot wound or blunt trauma to the head. Crucially, it hung on which had happened first: if it was the blow to the head, obviously she couldn't have shot herself afterwards. Arkwright's defence lawyer argued that she did shoot herself and hit her head as she fell. The prosecution said that he killed her with a blunt instrument and shot her afterwards to make it look like suicide."

"As evidence that he murdered her, it sounds a bit inconclusive."

"It was, by itself. But there were also rumours circulating that Arkwright had been furious that his parents had been supporting Jacqueline for so long and that when they said they were going to buy her a house locally it was the last straw. Then a witness came forward to say that she'd heard him threaten to kill them."

"To their faces?"

"No, when he was drinking in the local pub."

"Who was the witness? Do you know?"

"Yes, it was Amy Winter."

Chapter 48

TIM HANDED THE bags of clothes and shoes to Andy Carstairs immediately he and Juliet arrived back at the station.

"These are Marek Wolansky's. Can you get Forensics to do some tests on them?"

"Sure. What are they looking for?"

"DNA. Either Tina Brackenbury's or the baby's. Or anything else that can prove that Wolansky was in Tina's house."

"Isn't he the retarded guy?"

"Yes; he's unlikely to be intellectually capable of murder and even less likely to be charged with it. But we still need to know if he can have been involved in any way. When did you ask the Home Office for permission to access Tristram Arkwright's psychiatric reports?"

Andy blinked.

"Sorry, you lost me there for a minute. Swift change of subject! It was yesterday, as soon as you asked me to."

"God, was that only yesterday? How soon do you think we can give them a nudge?"

"I can call them today and ask when we're likely to get an answer. Ten to one they'll be contacting Arkwright's lawyer as well."

"I hadn't thought of that. Call them anyway, will you, and see what you can find out? Say there have been developments in a new case and the information in the reports could be very helpful. I'd rather not spell it out to them, but if they want to ask me some questions, naturally I'll agree to speak to them."

"Yes, boss."

Tim raised an eyebrow. He couldn't decide whether Andy was being ironic or not. Probably not, he decided. Unlike Juliet, if she'd ever called him boss – which as far as he could remember she hadn't.

"When you've done that, I'd like you to help me to interview a bloke called Phil Green. He's the driver who picks up clients and takes them to the disabled day care centre in Priory Road." Tim looked at his watch. "He'll be doing his rounds now. I've asked Verity Tandy to wait at the centre and bring him in for questioning when he's delivered the latest lot. He should have at least a couple of hours to spare before he has to take them all home again."

"Ok. Is he a suspect?"

"I don't think so." As he spoke, it occurred to Tim that Green could very well be a suspect: he'd had as much opportunity as Marek Wolansky to commit the murders and was far more capable. "It's unlikely, at any rate. He was supposed to be looking after Wolansky on Saturday afternoon and left him on his own for a while. I want to find out the exact times he left and came back again, if possible and, if not, to know how long he was gone. And if he noticed anything unusual about Wolansky either before or afterwards."

"Right. Anything else?"

"Not at the moment. I need to know how Ricky's doing with the door-to-door enquiries and whether he's had any luck in tracking down this Frankie Roberts character. But I can ask him that myself."

"I think he has got a lead on Roberts, but I don't know the details."

"Excellent," said Tim. Perhaps they would succeed in making some progress today.

As Andy walked away, Tim became aware of someone standing at his elbow.

"I see you're back, Yates," said Superintendent Thornton. "How did the interview go? With the mentally-challenged man, I mean?"

"It was inconclusive, sir."

"You didn't upset him, I hope?"

"No, sir. Not really."

"Good, good. Well, I must press on. I'd like you to draft a progress report. I want it by 3 p.m. Nothing too specific, but enough to show the media that we're on to it."

"Have you called another press briefing, sir?"

"Yes, Yates, I have; though, if you must know, it was the Chief Constable's idea. He says that people are more likely to be afraid if they're kept in the dark."

"Well, he may have a point, sir; but I don't think we're dealing with a random killer here."

"What makes you say that?"

Tim faltered.

"I don't know, sir – I suppose it's just a hunch."

"Well, leave the hunches to Armstrong, will you? She's better at them than you are. And for God's sake don't start talking about them to the Press. I've just secured extra funding from the Chief Constable to spend on this case – he's determined that 'fear won't be allowed to stalk the streets of Spalding', as he puts it. But we can kiss goodbye to the money if he thinks it's being spent on your hunches."

"I couldn't agree more, sir," said Tim.

After the Superintendent had gone, Tim sat down immediately to write the press release. Juliet was also better at drafting statements intended for the general public than he was, but he'd asked her to go straight back to the children's home to see Grace. He chewed his pen. Needless to say, it was always good to get extra money for murder investigations – and a rarity in his experience. No doubt the Chief Constable's generosity was prompted by outrage that a baby had been murdered and no doubt Superintendent Thornton would put the money to good use. But when Tim looked back over all the murder cases he'd ever been involved in, he suspected this to be among the least-deserving of extra funds. It was another of his unmentionable hunches that the murderer's identity was already staring them in the face.

Chapter 49

I AM SO preoccupied with Grace's next interview and how I'm going to pave the way with Marie that I've forgotten about the dead cat. I'm reminded as soon as I pull up in the grounds of the children's home and see Jake Fidler approaching. He looks serious and sad. His hand is on the car door and he opens it before I can.

"Can I have a word with you? I'd like to ask for your help."

"Yes, of course. Is it about last night?"

He nods.

"Let's talk in my office."

He leads the way. The door is locked, but he opens it by simply punching numbers into the keypad. The elaborate security systems in use last night are relaxed during the day.

His office is a surprisingly formal and imposing room, with a big old-fashioned director's desk and Victorian prints on the wall. Incongruously, a lightweight circular wood table and four chairs with pale blue fabric seats have been shoehorned into the space between the front of the desk and the door. He gestures at them. I remember that he's only the acting warden and guess that the modern furniture is his own choice.

"Please, take a seat. Would you like some tea?"

I'm about to decline when I realise that I'm both thirsty and feeling drained of energy. I didn't eat breakfast with Grace this morning and drank only half of the cup of tea I'd poured myself.

"That would be great, thanks, if it's not too much trouble."

He doesn't answer, but switches on the kettle standing on a trolley beside the desk. It fires up immediately: it must have boiled recently. I see he has already arranged two cups and a teapot on the tray.

"You're well organised!"

"I bring children in here when they're upset or have misbehaved in some way. Talking to them is always the most effective way of dealing with their problems if I can get them to open them up. I tend not to offer them coffee: most are too young and it makes teenagers hyper."

He fills the teapot, raises a small milk-jug.

"Milk?"

"Yes, please. What do you want to talk to me about? Is it Grace?"

"Yes, in a way."

"Has something else happened this morning?"

"No, I don't think so. I saw the policemen do their changeover at ten; the one who's there now is the one who came with you yesterday. I haven't seen Grace. I understand she's still in the flat with the child psychologist. I met her briefly, too. Marie Krakoswka. I know her: she's had several patients here. She said that Grace would need to go out for some exercise at some stage, but she'd make sure I knew when."

"Ideally they should take their walk while the other children are inside. They don't know about her, do they?"

"Obviously several of them saw her arrive. Then you took her straight to the flat so in theory none of them saw her again."

"Why do you say 'in theory'?"

"Because as you know Finn, the young boy whom you found with the dead cat, somehow got into the courtyard. I'm not sure exactly how he managed it, but it occurs to me that if you left the door on the latch he could have reached the handle if he'd found something to stand on. A stool was knocked over just inside the door."

He hands me my tea.

"Oh, God, I'm sorry. I did leave the door on the latch. It was only for a few minutes: I didn't think anyone would be awake at that time."

His face is stern.

"I asked you to take care. The children who live here often get up in the night, because they can't sleep or are having nightmares. Many come from homes where the bedroom represents danger, not safety."

"I'm sorry," I say again.

He gives my arm a light punch.

"Hey, I don't mean to beat you up. I know it was a genuine mistake. Anyway, it was my fault that Finn was roaming about downstairs. I knew he'd gone to bed upset and I should have kept a better watch on him; arranged for him to sleep somewhere other than the dormitory. He was obsessed with Sasha. I won't go into details, but when he first came here he tried to act out on her some of the things that had been done to him. He had an abusive stepfather. Without putting the cat at too much risk – or so I thought – I was trying to teach him to be gentle with her, to treat her with respect. And it was working. He had a bit of a lapse when you arrived, because he was over-excited, and he pulled her tail. But he'd begun to understand what it means to love someone – or something, at any rate. I'm certain that he'd come to love Sasha. He's so traumatised by her death that I've called the doctor out this morning. She's prescribed a sedative."

I'm almost certain I know what Jake will say next. I grip the handle of my cup.

"Are you saying that if I hadn't made it possible for him to get into the courtyard, the cat would still be alive?"

"That would be one way of explaining Sasha's death. We all thought he'd killed her when he was found with her. But it's not Finn's version of events. It took me some time to get him to tell me that. As you saw, he was hysterical."

"What did he say?"

"He said he saw a girl going up the stairs to the flat. Then he found the cat. She was already dead. That was when you found him."

I put down the cup. My hands are sweating. I rub them on my trousers.

"He could just be saying that to get himself out of trouble."

"He could, I agree. But he's not the brightest of children and it's unlikely he understood where Grace was staying. I think it's more than likely that he's telling the truth."

"Even if Grace was in the courtyard, it doesn't prove that she killed the cat."

"I agree, it doesn't."

"You said you wanted me to help. What would you like me to do?"

"I know you've come back to ask Grace some more questions. Without alarming her, can you try to find out if she was in the courtyard last night?"

"I'll do my best. Don't forget she has Marie with her."

"I have nothing but admiration for Marie. She's helped

225

several children that I know of, and undoubtedly dozens of others as well."

He speaks these words as if laying down a challenge. I'm contrite about leaving the door on the latch, but he's beginning to irritate me now. It's as if he's determined to put me in the wrong.

"Quite," I say. "As I've said, I'll do my best; but the questions I need to put to Grace will have to come first. She's a witness in a murder investigation and that must be my priority. If Marie thinks that's all she can cope with today, we'll have to save other questions for another time."

"I understand. But there's one other thing you should know. If Finn did kill the cat, he won't be allowed to stay here. He'll have to go back to a specialised psychiatric unit. We'll have lost all the progress that we thought we'd made with him."

"You say 'go back'. Has he been in a special unit before?"

"Yes, for almost a year. He was released six weeks ago, when his doctors felt he was well enough to come here."

"OK. I'll do my best to get Grace to tell me if she went outside."

"There's also something else. If Grace did kill Sasha, she needs to be in a psychiatric unit herself. I hardly need to tell you how many psychopaths began their careers by being cruel to animals as children."

I shudder inwardly.

"How did the cat die?"

"She was strangled. I'd say a six-year-old would have to be extremely strong to manage that, wouldn't you?"

"Perhaps," I say.

Chapter 50

WHILE TIM AND Andy were still in the interview room talking, Ricky MacFadyen appeared and looked through the window set in the door. Tim beckoned him in.

"Hi, Ricky. Andy says you've found Frankie Roberts."

"Yeah, I've found him, all right. He's in the cells at Lincoln police station, sleeping it off. He was arrested for being drunk and disorderly last night."

"Have you asked them to hold him?"

"Yep, but he isn't going anywhere soon. They think he might be conscious and up to answering questions by this evening. Should I go?"

Tim looked at his watch.

"We can both go. I want to see Amy Winter today, and I think Brocklesby Farm's only about fifteen minutes from Lincoln. She took my call earlier. She was reasonably co-operative, but she said she wanted her husband to be there. Apparently he's out until about six this evening."

"So we question Roberts afterwards?"

"If we can get any sense out of him. Do you know why he was drinking in Lincoln?"

"No. According to his mother, he travels all over the place, so probably knows a lot of pubs around the country, too."

"Does he have previous for getting drunk? If not, that could be significant."

"I don't know. I'll find out. Is Juliet coming with us?"

"No. She needs to stay with Grace Winter."

"What about the door-to-doors?"

"Andy has to wait here for a reply from the Home Office. He can co-ordinate them until you get back."

"Thanks, Andy."

"Don't mention it," said Andy Carstairs, his voice heavy with irony. "I think we'll have to scale them down soon. Although there's some retracing to do, to cover people who were out first time round, the uniforms have gone way beyond the Lady Dymokes now."

"Don't scale it down yet," said Tim. "Superintendent Thornton's just got more money out of the Chief Constable for this case. The sort of thing he'll be expecting to see for it is dozens of coppers combing the streets and questioning people. High profile, in other words."

"There's plenty to do besides that," said Andy.

"Well, you understand the politics as well as I do. Don't look a gift horse in the mouth when it comes from above, even if it causes more work than it pays for."

Chapter 51

PHIL GREEN WAS precisely the type of character Tim had expected him to be. He walked into the station jaunty of step, but his shoulders were hunched apprehensively: he didn't like policemen. He was casually dressed, not quite scruffy – smart enough to do his job without attracting disapproval. He wore an olive-green jerkin over jeans with a short-sleeved shirt and a cotton baseball cap turned back to front. He had a hail-fellow-well-met kind of approach which Tim guessed the passengers he picked up in the day centre's minibus would find reassuring. But his eyes darted everywhere and he seemed to find it hard to look Andy, whom Tim had asked to conduct the interview, straight in the face.

"Thanks for coming in, Mr Green. We appreciate it."

"That's all right. You've got an hour. Have to get back to work then, or my mates will be stuck with a load of clients." Green grinned uneasily.

"It won't take that long," said Andy, taking the chair opposite Green's. "We just want a bit of information from you, that's all."

"Is it about the murders?"

"It's connected with them. Did you know Tina Brackenbury?"

"I wouldn't say I knew her. I said hi to her once or twice, when I was picking up Marek Wolansky. He's a long-termer."

"Yes, we know that. Did you ever go inside Mrs Brackenbury's house?"

"No. Why? Did someone say I had?"

"No, it was just a routine question. Can you tell me what you were doing last Saturday afternoon?"

"Not much, I don't think. Ah yes, I called in on Marek. I do sometimes – he likes me. I had some jam for him. Likes sweet things, he does."

"How long did you stay?"

"Longer than I meant to. His ma asked me if I'd take care of him for a while. She said she had stuff to do upstairs, but I think she wanted a lie-down."

"About how long were you there?"

"Upwards of an hour, I think."

"Did he go out during that time? Or did you?"

Green shook his head. His eyes roamed the room. He fiddled with the zip on his jerkin.

"You're quite sure about that, are you, sir? Because Mrs Wolansky says she came downstairs and you weren't there. She says she found Marek outside, by himself."

"Oh – yes, I did go out for a bit to get some fags. I told Marek to stay put. He usually does what I say."

"But he didn't on this occasion?"

"No, but how was I to know that?" Green spread his hands as if no sane person could have expected Marek to disobey instructions.

"How long were you gone?"

"Ten minutes. Fifteen, tops."

"No longer than that?"

"No, I don't think so."

"You'll appreciate the significance of the question. You

know that Tina Brackenbury and her baby daughter were murdered last weekend."

"I thought it happened on Monday."

"You can't have been paying much attention to the news, sir. We've issued bulletins saying we believe the murders could have happened as long ago as Saturday afternoon. We've asked anyone who was in the area on Saturday or Sunday to contact us to see if they can help with our enquiries. Did you miss that?"

"I suppose so. I didn't see nothing, anyway. I'd have told you if I did."

"Ok. Are you quite sure Marek couldn't have been outside for more than a few minutes? That he wouldn't have had time to go into Tina Brackenbury's house, for example, and come out again?"

Phil Green spluttered out a hoarse yelp of laughter.

"You're barking up the wrong tree now! You're not suggesting that Marek had owt to do with it? He don't have the wit to kill a spider, or at least cover over his traces afterwards."

"Why do you say that? Do you think he could kill if someone else helped him 'cover over his traces'?"

"Look, I don't like the way this is going. If you're going to start . . ."

"It's all right, Mr Green," Tim cut in. "DC Carstairs isn't trying to incriminate either you or Marek. He's just working through the range of events that could possibly have taken place, some of them highly improbable, as you rightly suggest."

"Well, I can tell you for a fact that Marek couldn't have done it."

"Why do you say that, Mr Green?"

"It's obvious. He isn't even half sharp, is he?"

"I agree that he's very severely disabled. And, according to you, he was only on his own for ten or so minutes. So he probably wouldn't have had time to commit the murders even if he was a bit more with it, would he?"

"That's just what I've been saying."

"And I'm agreeing with you. But the thing is, Mr Green, you and Mrs Wolansky both agree that she was upstairs for more than an hour; and you say that normally you would have expected Marek to 'stay put' for quite a while if you told him to. So the question I'm asking myself is, were you really gone for just ten or fifteen minutes, or was it much longer than that – so long, in fact, that Marek formed some hare-brained plan to come and look for you?"

"I don't quite get your drift."

"Well, I'll spell it out for you, shall I? If you left Marek for quite a bit longer than you said, so that he got agitated, you might have been doing more than just picking up a packet of fags. In which case, what were you doing? For all we know, you could have been paying a visit to Tina Brackenbury."

"I told you, I didn't go anywhere near . . . All right, you win. I was gone longer than I said. I nipped into the bookie's as well, and watched a couple of horses I'd backed."

"You can prove that?"

"I've probably still got the betting slips. But if not, Scott who runs the place will tell you I was there."

"So why didn't you tell us this in the first place?"

"I was worried about what Ma Wolansky might do if she thought I'd left Marek for that long. She can be a cow when it comes to her precious son. If she'd told them at the day centre I'd left him for half an hour, I might have got into a row. As

232

it was, she gave me a right bollocking. It took me a while to calm her down."

"So he was actually on his own for half an hour?"

"About that. It could have been a bit longer."

"Thank you, Mr Green. You've been extremely helpful."

"What happens now?"

"Unless there are further developments that link you to the case, nothing, except we'd like a sample of your DNA."

"OK, that's fine by me. Can I go now?"

"Give us the sample first – it's very quick – and then by all means you're free to leave. DC Carstairs will do the test before he shows you out."

"What did you make of him?" Andy asked Tim when he returned.

"Unreliable witness. The second version he gave us was probably more accurate than the first – and we can check at the bookie's – but I wouldn't bank on it. He'll tell us whatever's most convenient for him. I doubt if he's got anything to do with the murders, though. He didn't bat an eyelid over the DNA test, did he?"

"No. But whether he was telling the truth or not, he's given us proof of one thing: Marek Wolansky was on his own long enough to have committed the murders, if he had the wit to do it."

"That's the big imponderable, isn't it? Could he be the killer and, if so, why?"

Chapter 52

I AM TRUDGING up the steps to the flat again.

"Hello, I thought you'd be back soon. Are you ok?" Giash greets me from his perch in the shadows.

"God, you made me jump! How are you today?"

"A damn sight better than last night. I felt like you look now."

"Thanks! That really makes me feel great."

"Tough morning?"

"So-so. I don't want to say too much, particularly here, but Grace identified Marek Wolansky, Tina Brackenbury's disabled neighbour, as a suspect, and now he's succeeded in incriminating himself."

Giash rolls his eyes skywards, nods and points at the door.

"You know Marie Krakowska's in there with her? Apparently, she arrived just before Bill and I switched."

"Yes, I waited for her to get here."

"Means well, I suppose."

I laugh despite myself.

"Don't say any more, Giash. Marie has her detractors but they're far outnumbered by her supporters. And we could do a lot worse."

"You know best. One thing I can tell you is that she's rubbish at making cups of tea."

"That's shameless, but I'll take the hint. I'll bring you a cup next time I make some."

I wonder why my hackles don't rise when Giash casts me in the nice tea lady role. If it had been Tim I'd have been furious.

"I must have a quick word with Marie," I add as I'm about to knock on the door to let her know I'm here. "It'll probably have to be out here; there's not much privacy in there. Would you mind moving a bit? You don't have to go far, just out of earshot."

"I can't go 'far' – I've got strict orders not to leave the flat unguarded. Doubt if I'll be out of earshot in that postage stamp of a yard."

"Well, you can always pretend." I rap on the door.

Marie opens it. She's wreathed in smiles. She's wearing a shalwar kameez in brilliant turquoise. I wonder if Giash minds that she's plundered his national dress.

"Hello! I was just telling Grace you'd be here soon. I'll make some tea."

Giash pulls a face at her retreating back. I close the door on him and follow Marie.

Grace is seated at the table. She's playing with an iPad. She looks up at me and gives me one of her penetrating stares. Then she smiles.

"Hello, Grace."

"Hello, DS Armstrong." She sounds demure and a little plummy, like a prep school girl on her best behaviour.

"I'm afraid Grace is getting a bit bored," Marie gushes. "She's been cooped up in here all morning. We're thinking of going out for a little walk, aren't we, Grace?"

Grace nods, shooting me a swift glance. I sense that she's mocking me, but convince myself I'm imagining it. I tell myself to get a grip.

"Marie – Ms Krakowska – could I speak to you for a couple of minutes? We'll go outside, shall we?"

Marie is bustling about with the kettle in her hand, but she catches my tone and immediately puts it down.

"Of course. Grace, we won't be long. You stay here." She laughs good-naturedly. "As if you can do anything else!" Grace bends her head over the iPad. She doesn't reply.

Marie leads the way back to the outside landing and I follow, shutting both the door to the living room and the outside door firmly behind me. By the time I've joined Marie, Giash has almost made it to the bottom of the flight of steps.

"You've got him well trained," Marie observes.

"Marie, do you think it's a good idea to let Grace have your iPad? You've given her unsupervised access to the Internet."

"Relax; I haven't. I let her play with my iPad yesterday, but I was keeping a close watch on her; and the one she's using now is the one I lend to the teenage boys I'm assessing. It just has games loaded up to it and no browser installed. Surely that isn't what you want to talk to me about?"

"No, it isn't. You remember yesterday Grace both drew a picture and completed a photo-fit. You said the sketch reminded you of Tristram Arkwright, her uncle. I said I thought I recognised the identikit as a likeness of Marek Wolansky, Tina Brackenbury's neighbour. He's acutely mentally disabled. Tim and I both believed it next to impossible that he could have been involved in the murders, but he had to be checked out. We interviewed him this morning. Although he's profoundly challenged – he needs his mother to help him dress and he can speak only a few words – he recognised Grace in a photograph he was shown, despite the fact that his mother says he has no significant power of recall. He produced a silver pendant that

Tina Brackenbury was almost certainly wearing when she died and said that Grace had given it to him as a 'present'."

"Given his intellectual ability, that doesn't mean anything."

"I agree that anything he says would be unlikely to stand up in court, but he's probably incapable of lying. And he got the pendant from somewhere."

"You seem reluctant to consider him as a serious suspect. What if he just helped himself to the pendant after he killed Tina Brackenbury?"

"I'm trying to keep an open mind. The pendant's chain wasn't damaged. That means he would have had to have figured out how to unfasten it. And he certainly recognised Grace in the photo. He wasn't faking that. He linked her to the pendant immediately – and not in an unhappy way. He was pleased that she'd given it to him."

"Just tell me what you want from Grace and I'll try to help you," Marie says in a grim tone that suggests the opposite.

"You know I'll have to interview her again. I'd be grateful if you could let me get through it without interrupting. You can see how important it is. I understand that if she gets upset we'll have to stop."

"My job is to protect her interests."

"I know that, Marie. But neither of us will be acting in her best interests if she's committed a crime and we sweep it under the carpet."

"She's below the age of criminal responsibility."

"That's not the point and actually she isn't. I agree the Crown may decide she's too young to be charged, but even if she's not prosecuted we have to know if she's guilty."

Marie falls silent. She's gripping the iron bannister rail. Her knuckles are white.

"What's wrong, Marie? I'm sorry if we're at odds with each other. We ought to be on the same side."

Marie doesn't answer for several long seconds.

"I know. And you're right. And I know I shouldn't get as involved with my clients as perhaps I sometimes do. But I've got a feeling that child has been through hell, and more than once. I want to try to help her heal now."

"I realise I'm probably oversimplifying things, but isn't to find out the truth and bring it into the open the best way to help her?"

"Perhaps. And perhaps sometimes probing too deeply damages the people concerned even more."

"I'm surprised that you, as a practising cognitive therapist . . ." Suddenly, the penny drops. "Marie, you said you'd come clean about what you found out about Grace when you read Lenka Astani's file after the Brocklesby Farm killings. Is there still something else – something important – that you haven't told us?"

"I've told you as much as I can about Grace's files. And that's the truth."

Still I sense that Marie is holding something back.

"Lenka has other files relating to the Brocklesby killings, doesn't she? Tristram Arkwright was one of her clients, as well as Grace, wasn't he?"

"Yes. But she didn't show me her reports about him. That's the honest truth. If you want to see them, you'll probably have to get permission from the Home Office."

"That's what Lenka herself said. We've already asked for permission."

"In that case, you'll have to wait until you get it. There's nothing else I can tell you."

"Lenka told you something, didn't she? Off the record?"

"For God's sake, Juliet, stop pestering me! I'm doing my best!"

I look at Marie. Her face is as drawn as a plump round face can be, and devoid of colour. I'm smitten with guilt.

"I'm sorry, Marie, really I am. This case is putting a strain on all of us and I seem to have strayed a long way from what we were talking about at first. Will you help me to interview Grace again?"

"I will, but the conditions remain the same. I'm Grace's responsible adult. If I think the interview is distressing her too much, or causing her to incriminate herself unfairly, I shall insist that you stop."

"Understood."

I put my hand on Marie's turquoise sleeve. She leaves it there for a second before gently pushing it away.

I cast a glance in Giash's direction. He's been circling the small courtyard in slow motion, ostentatiously absorbed in scrolling through messages on his phone. Our voices were growing louder as the conversation became more heated; he's bound to have heard most of it. I hope that Grace wasn't listening as well. Giash looks up and catches my eye for a second or two. He gives a sympathetic shrug. I understand what he's saying, but this isn't just about Marie being bloody-minded; the case has touched her personally. I may need to find out why.

Chapter 53

TIM HAD PARKED beyond the boundary wall of Brocklesby Farm, on a track that led to the large barn that stood at right angles to it. Both the farmhouse and the wall were immediately recognisable from the picture he had studied of the 2012 killings. The farm was built of dark grey stone, with a long, sloping slate roof. It was two-storeyed but low-lying: extremely old (he would guess Jacobean), it looked as if it was gradually sinking into the earth. This impression was reinforced by the mullioned windows on the ground floor, the sills of which stood barely two feet from the ground. The windows themselves were small; the house must be dark inside, even in summer. The building would strike even someone who didn't know its history as sinister and unprepossessing. That it was bathed in the glow of late-summer afternoon sunshine served only to emphasise its dour aspect.

Tim rested his arms on the steering wheel while he took in the house and garden. The latter wasn't well-kept. It wasn't exactly overrun, but it contained no trees and the patch of lawn visible beyond the wall was balding and knotted with clumps of weeds. The house itself seemed better cared for: the front door was painted a vivid post-office red. He reflected that this was likely to have been a recent embellishment: Tim doubted if the late Norman Arkwright would have chosen such a colour. There was no sign of life, not even a twitch of the curtains to indicate they had been spotted.

"Are you all right, sir?"

Ricky MacFadyen's voice jolted Tim out of his reverie. He removed his arms from the wheel and turned to face his colleague.

"Sorry, Ricky, I was just trying to get the feel of this place. You know what happened here in 2012, I take it?"

"I know about the Brocklesby Farm murders, but I don't remember the details. Son shot the whole family, wasn't it?"

"Something like that, though there were complications. Tristram Arkwright, the 'son' you mention, was actually adopted, as was his sister. She died along with the parents and her own baby. Her other child, Grace, was the only survivor. None of the adults were Arkwright's blood relations."

"Interesting, that. They say blood's thicker than water."

"They do, don't they? Perhaps that the victims weren't really his relatives at all was what gave him the stomach to do it. But he never admitted to being the killer. Anyway, Norman and Jane Arkwright's will divided their property between their two adopted children. Since one was dead and the other sentenced to life for the murders, Brocklesby Farm passed to Amy Winter and her husband. I can't remember if they are the niece and nephew-in-law, or the other way round."

"Quite an inheritance. You'd need some guts to want to live here, though, wouldn't you?"

"You mean after the killings? That's certainly what the media tried to suggest. Amy Winter went on record as saying that she and her husband weren't superstitious about such things: that over the centuries many people were have bound to have died in the house besides the Arkwrights."

"Sounds a bit hard-boiled."

"A bit too hard-boiled, actually. Amy Winter's apparently suffered a nervous breakdown since then. That's why Grace was being fostered by Tina Brackenbury."

"How much does Amy Winter know of what we know about Grace?"

"I'm not sure. Since she put Grace out for fostering with Tina Brackenbury she must have picked up that Tina and Bluebelle are dead: it's been splashed all over the media for the past three days and the names wouldn't escape her. All I've told her is that we want to speak to her about Grace and that we know she's Grace's adoptive mother."

"Did she make any attempt to find out what had happened to Grace after the Brackenbury killings? Establish that she was all right?"

"Not as far as I know, but if she made enquiries, it would almost certainly have been through Lenka Astani, the psychologist she's been seeing. Astani was Grace's psychologist, too, and, as it happens, also Tristram Arkwright's. She's the woman who's been playing hardball with us since we asked for access to Arkwright's files."

"Wow! The same psychologist for all three. That's a bit unusual, isn't it?"

"It may be; I'm not sure. How many psychologists are there to the square mile in rural areas? It could be quite handy: I think the Astani woman may hold the key to a breakthrough in the Brackenbury murders, but she certainly isn't going to give anything up voluntarily."

"What exactly are you planning to ask Amy Winter?"

"I want to know more about Grace generally: her character, what she likes. Why Amy adopted her. Even more to the point, why she sent her away."

"You say her husband's going to be there? What does he do?"

"Yes, he'll be there. She insisted on it. Understandable, I suppose, if her health's been shaky. They both run the farm. I understand there's a property-letting business, too, also inherited from the Arkwrights. They probably ran that together until Amy had her baby."

"They stood to gain quite a lot from those murders!"

"That's what the cops thought at the time; and Tristram Arkwright did his best to lay the blame at their door. None of it stuck, though. It was pretty clear-cut that Arkwright was the murderer, even if one of the jurors disagreed."

Chapter 54

G RACE IS SITTING at the table, still engrossed in the iPad when Marie and I return. She conceals the device with her hand for a moment before she puts it down. I'm reminded of the way in which she tried to hide the sketch from us yesterday; I'm beginning to suspect that such actions spring from some visceral but otherwise irrational desire for secrecy. What could she have to hide?

She gives Marie a sharp look. Marie is still upset and Grace senses it. I know she'll capitalise on it if she can.

"We'd like to ask you some more questions, Grace," I say.

She turns to Marie as if to ask whether she should agree. Marie nods.

"It won't take very long, Grace. Then we can go out for our walk."

I haven't given the proposed walk much thought until this moment. I'm not sure I should allow it. I'll have to think about it.

"Now for that cup of tea," says Marie.

"Can I have some Coke?" Grace asks.

"I don't think we have any," I say, but Marie produces a can from the fridge. She must have brought a supply with her this morning. She passes it to Grace, as well as a glass.

"Thank you," says Grace, with that characteristic sweet submissiveness that I'm coming to mistrust every time I see it.

"Let's get started," I say. "I'll make the tea a bit later."

Marie and I both seat ourselves at the table. I boot up my laptop.

"Now, Grace," I say, "You remember the identikit picture you made yesterday? Of the man you said you saw leaving Tina's - your Mum's - house?"

"Yes."

"Should I fetch it up on the screen for you?"

"Yes, please."

Grace stares intently at the picture. She shows no emotion.

"Do you have any idea what the name of this person is, Grace?"

She shrugs. "I might do."

I'm suddenly furious.

"Don't try your playground talk on me, Grace. This is serious. Yesterday, you told us you didn't recognise the man in the picture. Are you saying now you do know who it is - or that you think you might know him?" I rap out the words.

Grace's lovely face darkens. She turns to Marie. I shoot Marie an apologetic look, hoping that she won't call time before the interview has properly started. To my surprise, Marie is staring at Grace with an intensity that, if not hostile, certainly isn't calculated to encourage her to try more tricks. Grace realises she is losing ground and changes her attitude immediately. She puts on a tremulous smile, manages to look soulful.

"I'd had a shock. I probably do know who it was. I think it was Marek, from next door."

"You also told us you didn't speak to the man. Was that true? Or are you going to remember that you did speak to him now?"

"No, I didn't speak to him. He brushed past me, like I said. He was in a hurry."

"Where did he go?"

"I don't know. Back next door, I suppose."

"You didn't watch him go?"

She shook her head.

"How well do you know him?"

"Not very. Mum doesn't like him. Says he gives her the creeps."

"Have you been into his house?"

"Not when he was in. Only when his mum was there on her own. Mum used to nip and see her sometimes when he was out. He goes to a school for nutters."

"Who told you that?"

"Chloe did. Or Mavis, I forget which."

"Have you ever spoken to him?"

"Not that I can remember."

"Or given him anything?"

"Why would I give him anything? He's not all there."

"He says you gave him something last Saturday. Do you know what he's talking about?"

"No. He must've made it up."

"Are you sure you didn't go upstairs with him last Saturday?"

"No, I never. I saw him in the hall, like I said. He brushed past me."

"Did you go upstairs by yourself? Or with Chloe?"

"No, I told you. Chloe got panicky 'cos we'd taken the bikes. We'd only just got into the hall when she went home."

"Grace, you made Mrs Hebblewhite believe the man you saw would come after you. You got her so worried that she thought it wasn't safe for you to stay at her house any longer. Why did you do that?"

"It wasn't my idea that I couldn't stay longer. I'd have liked to. I didn't know that she'd go off the deep end like that, did I?"

"No, but you didn't tell her that you thought the man was Marek, your next-door neighbour, either, did you?"

"I was confused."

"You didn't say you were confused; you said you'd had a shock. What was the shock, Grace? What or who was it that shocked you? Was it because you knew something terrible had happened upstairs? Was it because you'd already seen something horrible? Had you done a terrible thing yourself?"

I'm aware that I've raised my voice and Marie is pulling at my sleeve. I try to snatch my arm away, but Marie grabs hold of my wrist. Grace sits quietly, impassive but observant. She sees she won't have to reply.

"I think it's time to take a break now," Marie says.

During the break, Marie keeps a desultory conversation going. She tries to draw Grace in as well and Grace responds with a few words while continuing to play on the iPad. She consumes another can of Coke.

I decide not to pursue the Marek Wolansky angle. It's not just that I know Marie will protest if I put on more pressure: it's also because, although it's unlikely that Grace will incriminate herself except by accident, if she should confess to something with no solicitor present I may be accused of coercion and the evidence disallowed. I'm going to focus instead on the death of the cat. I want to prove that Grace can be cruel . . . and a liar.

"Let's start again, shall we?"

Grace puts down the iPad, then picks it up again. She sighs and stands up slowly, returning to her place at the table, bringing the iPad with her. She rubs both her eyes.

"Are you all right, Grace?" Marie asks.

"When can we go out?"

"Soon, now. In a few minutes. You're not too tired to carry on, are you?" Marie says this briskly, as if Grace's answer must be no. I'm impressed. Grace meets Marie's eye. She drops her gaze first and then turns it on me. I regard her steadily.

"Well, Grace? You'll be all right for another ten minutes, won't you?"

"Yes."

I nod curtly to show her I'm boss, but it's a hollow victory: two adult women pitting their wits against an orphaned child.

"I'm not going to talk to you any more about Marek," I say. "You've answered all the questions I have about him for now."

Grace smiles uncertainly, as if she doesn't know whether she's being let off the hook or not, which is what I intend. She's waiting for what I'm going to say next, her upper body immobile and tense.

"I'd like to talk to you about the cat."

Out of the corner of my eye I see that Marie's puzzled, but I keep my focus on Grace. Her eyes flare wide. She's alarmed. She struggles to compose herself; she takes a long time to answer.

"The cat?"

"Yes, the cat." I say nothing more. The silence hangs heavy in the air. I keep on watching her. She looks trapped. She screws up her eyes in thought, as if she's seeking a way out. She picks up the iPad.

"Put that down, please, Grace. I need you to pay attention. What can you tell me about the cat?"

"Do you mean Mum's cat or the cat that lives here?" Her voice is guileless. I'd forgotten that Tina Brackenbury had a cat. It's a clever answer, but I'm determined to persevere.

"Why do you ask that?"

She shrugs. "I don't know any other cats."

"Why did you think of the cat who lives here?"

"Because I saw it yesterday. Is it all right?"

"Is there any reason why it shouldn't be?"

"That little boy got told off for teasing it. I thought maybe he'd hurt it."

"Do you like animals, Grace?"

"I don't mind them."

"As you said, you saw the cat when we arrived. Did you see it again after that?"

"I don't think so." There is no hesitation.

"Did you sleep well last night?"

"Yes."

"You didn't wake up again after you went to sleep?"

"No."

"I told you I might have to go out briefly to fetch PC Chakrabati's replacement. Do you remember that?"

"Yes. You said you wouldn't be gone long, but not to worry if I woke up and you weren't there."

"Did you wake up?"

"No."

"Did you stay awake until you heard me go?"

"No."

She's sounding more assured now, even defiant.

"Did you get up after you heard me go? Did you get dressed and go outside?"

"No."

"Did you go down the steps by yourself and see the cat in the courtyard? Did you pick her up there?"

"No, I didn't." Her answer is quiet, measured. She's not protesting too much. I'm inclined to believe that she's telling the truth now. At one point, I believe I almost stumbled on what happened, but inadvertently I'm moving away from it. It's like playing Blind Man's Bluff: I was warm, but I'm getting colder now.

"Can I ask a question now?" she says.

"Yes, of course. What do you want to say?"

"I'm just wondering why you're asking me all this. I don't understand how it helps."

She means her words to be challenging, but they fall just short of insolent. I feel my anger rising again and am tempted to wipe the floor with her. I decide to patronise her instead.

"I can quite see that my questions might not make sense to you now. But don't worry, Grace: they will do, eventually."

I expect her to retaliate with scorn or even laughter. In fact, she does manage an odd little snigger, but not before I've seen pure panic etched on her face.

"Is that it?" asks Marie. She sounds relieved that my questions have established no conclusive evidence. In a strange kind of way, so am I.

"That's all for now," I say. "We haven't finished yet, but I don't think we can get any further without a solicitor."

Marie nods. She understands where I'm coming from, but the statement provokes an outburst from Grace.

"What do I need a solicitor for? I haven't done anything!"

She lashes out at the iPad and sends it spinning across the table. I catch and hold it before it can crash to the floor. She gets up quickly and rushes at me, snatching the iPad from my hand.

"Grace!" Marie rebukes her.

"It's all right," I say. "I should have explained more carefully." Grace is standing right beside me, her chest heaving. "You're a minor, Grace," I add. "And you have no parents who can be with you. Depending on the circumstances, we may have to ask a solicitor to look after you. It will be for your sake, not ours."

"What 'circumstances'?"

"I'm going to write a report on what you've just told me. I'm going to ask you to read it and say whether it's true. Then I'll show it to DI Yates and he'll decide what we should do next."

Grace calms down immediately. She holds her head on one side affectedly.

"I think DI Yates really likes me."

"I'm sure he does," says Marie soothingly. "Shall we go for our walk now?"

I revisit my misgivings about the walk and conclude that I was over-reacting. If Marek Wolansky is the man whom Grace saw, there is no mystery murderer stalking the lanes; besides, Giash has instructions not to leave Grace. I'm sure he won't mind following Marie and Grace on a short walk. Marie can't be planning to go far in that get-up.

"Where will you go?" I ask.

"Just down to the river. We'll walk along the bank a little way, perhaps to the next bridge, and come back along the other side."

"All right. I'll ask PC Chakrabati to come with you. I'm going back to the station now. I'll be here again to stay the night before you finish for the day," I say to Marie.

Chapter 55

AMY WINTER TURNED out to be a tall woman, handsome in a masculine sort of way. Her thick dark-blonde hair was fastened at the nape of her neck with a wooden slide. She was raw-boned and a little ungainly: she walked with a slight stoop, as if trying to minimise her height. She was wearing a short-sleeved, round-necked jumper and an A-line skirt, both in a dull shade of blue. Tim guessed she was just the wrong side of forty: old to be a first-time mother.

Her husband had answered Tim's knock at the door and escorted him and Ricky to the sitting-room. Amy had been sitting on a low sofa, part of a huge and elaborate suite that curved around the corner of the inner wall and protruded like a pier into the centre of the room, but she rose to her feet as soon as they entered. She held out her hand and waited for Tim to come close enough to take it.

"Thank you for agreeing to see us, Mrs Winter," he said.

"That's all right," she replied, not smiling. "I realise you have your job to do. And Grace is still our responsibility." She looked at her husband for confirmation. He didn't respond, so she continued in a strained voice, "Norman has already introduced himself, I take it?"

"Mr Winter kindly let us in. I didn't know his name was Norman."

"That's correct," Norman Winter cut in. He'd positioned

himself beside his wife, though a small distance from her. "I was named for my uncle, in case you were wondering."

It had slipped Tim's mind that Tristram Arkwright's adoptive father's name had been Norman. Now he looked more closely at Norman Winter, he could see the family resemblance: Winter had the same hooked nose and dreary expression. He was tall, too, as Norman Arkwright had also been, taller than his wife, although she must have been approaching six foot, and probably a few years older than she was. Amy hadn't been a blood relative of the Arkwrights: perhaps that was why originally she'd been so phlegmatic about moving into the farmhouse.

"Ah, yes. I hadn't made the connection."

"My mother was Norman Arkwright's sister. They were very close."

Tim wasn't sure how to respond to this. Should he offer his condolences for a four-year-old bereavement? Amy Winter came to his rescue.

"DI Yates didn't come here to rake up past history, Norman. He wants to talk about Grace."

Norman Winter assumed a mutinous expression. He didn't reply, but raised his eyebrows. Tim guessed that he was wondering how they would manage to talk about Grace without 'raking up' the past.

"Would you like some tea?" Winter asked.

"That would be very kind," said Tim. The atmosphere in the room could have been cut with a knife. Perhaps tea would help.

"I'll get it," said Amy quickly. She'd been slow to move just a few paces when they'd come in, but she couldn't cross the room quickly enough now. She'd evidently meant it literally when she'd said she didn't want to see them alone.

"Please, sit down," said Norman, after she'd disappeared.

Tim lowered himself on to the sofa. Ricky followed suit, choosing to sit on the pier. It creaked under his weight. Tim took the opportunity to suss out the room. It was large and square, lit by two mullioned windows with no curtains; in their stead were vertical blinds, currently pulled to the side. A narrow steel bar bearing a row of brilliant light bulbs had been suspended from an ornate plaster ceiling rose. Three of the walls were painted pale green; the fourth, the one in which the fireplace was set, was a dark, glossy sage. Tim found both the furnishings and the décor disconcertingly incongruous. Why would anyone choose such décor for a room in a four-hundred-year-old farmhouse? Because they wanted to erase its immediate past?

Norman Winter cleared his throat.

"It's convenient that Amy's stepped out for a few minutes, because I wanted to warn you about her state of health."

"That's helpful. We'd heard that she was ill after she had the baby."

"I think she did have a touch of post-natal depression, yes. But really her illness started when she began to look after Grace. It was Amy's idea to adopt Grace – a very generous impulse – but it didn't work out too well."

"Oh? Why was that?"

"I don't think it was Grace's fault, but although she knew Amy very well from when Jackie . . . from when Amy worked for my uncle . . . they didn't get on after the . . . afterwards. Of course, the whole thing must have been terrible for Grace. And Amy didn't have much experience as a mother. She . . ."

"What are you saying, Norman?" Amy Winter had come back into the room unobserved. Her voice was taut. "Are you implying that I mishandled Grace in some way?"

"No, certainly not. I . . ."

Mrs Winter set down the tray she'd been carrying on a low Japanese-style table and perched on the end of the pier, some feet away from Ricky. She seemed to gain confidence from her husband's discomposure.

"I suggest we start at the beginning, DI Yates. What do you want to know?"

"Starting at the beginning's a good idea. How long had you known Grace when you adopted her?"

"From birth, really. I didn't see her all the time. Jackie – her mother – didn't live with Norman and Jane until after Laura was born. But she came to visit, and brought Grace with her."

"What kind of child would you say she was?"

Amy Winter hesitated.

"I wouldn't say there was anything unusual about her. Except for her looks, which are extraordinary. You've seen her, haven't you? It used to worry Jane that she was so beautiful. She thought Grace was in danger of not being treated like other children because of it."

"Did you see any evidence of that?"

"Norman and Jane were always careful to treat her in a matter-of-fact sort of way. Jane was keen on discipline. Jackie was more inclined to be indulgent, but I think that was just in her nature. She took Grace's looks for granted; she didn't celebrate them in any way."

"You never saw Grace with other children?"

"Not then. Except for Laura. Grace doted on Laura."

"What about her uncle? Did Grace get on with Tristram Arkwright?"

Norman Winter interceded.

"We try not to speak that man's name in this . . ."

"It's all right, Norman. Tristram wasn't keen on most children, but he did like Grace."

"Do you know why that was?"

"Does there have to have been a reason? As I've already said, she was stunningly pretty. People like pretty children."

"Do you know who Grace's father was?"

"No. Jackie didn't even tell her mother that."

"Do you think that Grace and Laura had the same father?"

"I should very much doubt it!" Amy Winter almost shrieked her response, as if the idea was outrageous.

"Why do you say that?"

"Now, Amy . . ."

Amy Winter bit her lip.

"No real reason. Except that there was a big gap between Grace and Laura, and Jackie moved house almost every year. Then she came to live with Norman and Jane just after Laura was born. She wouldn't have done that if she was still seeing Grace's father, would she?"

"I suppose not." Tim tried not to show that he was sceptical. He had often encountered on-off fathers who wouldn't take responsibility for their children. "So once Grace had come to live here, how often did you see her?"

"Most working days. She started going to the primary school in the village, but she was usually home before I left for the day."

"Did you always come here to work?"

"Not always, but mostly. Occasionally I would work from home."

"So you saw Grace most days. Were you and she close?"

Amy Winter stared at him as if she found the question strange.

"You're looking puzzled, Mrs Winter. I'm trying to understand why you adopted Grace. It was a pretty big step to take, wasn't it? Did you and she form some special kind of bond?"

"No, I wouldn't say that."

"Why did you adopt her, then?"

"Oh, for goodness sake, Inspector. The child had lost almost everyone she knew as family in a horrific mass murder. We were just about all she had left. It was an act of simple compassion."

It was Norman Winter speaking. Amy nodded her agreement. Tim tried to assess how fragile she really was. She didn't seem as vulnerable as her husband had suggested, but still he chose his next words carefully.

"I'm sure you tried to act in Grace's best interests, but you had to put her out to foster eventually, didn't you? Was that distressing for her?"

"You have to understand, Inspector, that Grace isn't like other children . . ."

"I'm confused now: you said earlier that there was nothing unusual about her, except her looks."

"That was before the . . . deaths. Afterwards, she . . ."

"What did she do after the deaths, Mrs Winter?"

"She . . . I don't know. She seemed different, that's all."

"And you found her behaviour difficult to bear?"

"I'd wanted . . . Norman and I had wanted . . . our own child for such a long time. When we adopted Grace we'd given up hope. Then, when we discovered that I was pregnant . . . I didn't want my child to grow up in the sort of atmosphere that Grace created."

"What sort of atmosphere was that?"

"It's difficult to explain. Most of the time she wanted to please us – she sought our approval, and that of other adults. But then she would try to . . . play games with us? Outdo us? As I've said, it's difficult to put my finger on it."

"But she was just a child," said Tim, although his limited acquaintance with Grace told him it was likely Amy Winter's concerns were legitimate.

"Yes, just a child," Amy repeated dully. "Anywhere, there it was. Looking after her was making me ill, and I was afraid that would affect my pregnancy. I decided to put Grace out to foster. I didn't abandon her – we haven't abandoned her. I just wanted some space, some time to establish our own family here. We still haven't ruled out bringing her back again one day." The last sentence was unconvincing; it trailed off lamely.

"That's helpful. So how did you choose the foster mother?"

"Excuse me?" Amy Winter seemed to be having difficulty in following him again.

"You asked Tina Brackenbury to be Grace's foster mother. Did you find her through social services?"

"No, I knew her before. And I knew she had experience of fostering."

"How did you know her?"

"Uncle Norman had several businesses. There was a group of service flats in Hull that he let out. Tina worked for him for a while. She cleaned the flats and helped him with some of the other stuff as well – vetting new tenants, getting key money, keeping rent records, that sort of thing. She and her husband lived in one of the flats and she paid for it by taking a reduced wage. He was away a lot – he worked on the ferries."

"Why did she move back to Spalding?"

"She left her husband – he was giving her a hard time. I kept in touch with her. I think he went back to her briefly, even gave up working on the boats, which was always a bone of contention between them. But then he left again – or she kicked him out. I knew she was strapped for cash, so I asked her if she would take Grace. We agreed that Grace and I wouldn't see much of each other for a while – that it would be better for both of us if we took a bit of a break."

"I see. But social services were aware?"

"Yes, it was all done properly."

"Does the name Frankie Roberts mean anything to you?"

"No, I don't think so. Should it?"

"No, I just asked on the off chance. Well, thank you very much for your time, Mrs Winter . . . and Mr Winter."

"Is that all?"

"Yes, unless there is anything else you can think of that would help us with our enquiries into Mrs Brackenbury's murder. And her baby's."

Tim had deliberately left it until the end of their meeting before mentioning the murders. He watched both the Winters closely as they replied.

"Yes, terrible thing that, wasn't it?" said Norman Winter, with a kind of affable awkwardness. "Poor woman! We sympathise with her family. We know what it's like."

"We'll be getting in touch with social services about Grace," Amy Winter added, as if she'd just thought of it.

"I'm sure they'll appreciate that, Mrs Winter," said Tim.

"What did you make of that?" Tim asked Ricky some minutes later, when they'd emerged from the track leading to the farm and reached the road to Lincoln.

"Very odd couple. I'd say they were hiding something, though I don't know what, and I don't see how it could be related to this case. They could have had no reason for wanting to harm Tina and Bluebelle. Tina was doing them a favour - a huge favour - even if she was getting paid for it."

"I agree. I also think you're right when you say they're hiding something. It must be something to do with Grace. What most struck me was that they didn't ask after Grace at all, want to know whether she was all right or even who is now looking after her. And they didn't want to talk about the Brackenbury murders. But I think the key to this whole thing may lie in that relationship."

"Do you mean Tina's relationship with the Winters, or with Grace?"

"Both, probably. And I'm not convinced that Amy Winter doesn't know Frankie Roberts."

"I couldn't gauge her reaction when you asked about Frankie. There's no reason why they should know him, is there, if Tina took up with him after she moved back to Spalding?"

"It's plausible that they don't; on the other hand, they must have been in touch with Tina about Grace after he came on the scene."

"Let's hope he's sober enough to talk to us now. If we're careful, we may be able to find out if he knows the Winters."

"With a bit of luck, he'll be sober, but with a splitting headache. We're more likely to get the truth out of him then."

Chapter 56

"GOD, YOU LOOK rough!" says Andy, as I appear in the office.

"Thanks a lot!" First Giash; now Andy. This case is obviously taking its toll.

"Sorry! I'm just getting some tea. I'll bring you some. There's a message for you: I've stuck it on your computer screen."

"Thanks."

I sit down at my desk and peel the Post-it note off the screen. It's from Nancy Chappell. Andy has scrawled: 'Ask DS Armstrong to call DC Chappell'. It's followed by Nancy's mobile number, which I already have on my phone.

I guess it'll be about the job that Nancy has asked me to give her a reference for. I glance over my shoulder. Andy's still in the kitchen: there's time to give her a quick call now. I pick up the handset, then think again. I'm tired and she'll be disappointed if she didn't get the job; if she wants to speak for longer, Andy will return and make it awkward. I replace the handset as Superintendent Thornton appears at my elbow.

"Good afternoon, Armstrong. How are things going?"

"I'm just back from the children's home, sir. DC Carstairs is looking after the door-to-door enquires. He'll be here in a minute."

"Good, good, but it's the young girl I'm enquiring about. Grace, isn't that her name? You have made sure she's quite safe, haven't you?"

I feel a stab of guilt, but push it away. Marie is out walking along the river bank with Grace as we speak. But what harm can possibly come to her there? No-one knows where she is and we've more or less discounted Mavis Hebblewhite's mystery assassin fears.

"Yes, sir. She's in the flat at the children's home. Marie Krakowska and PC Chakrabati are looking after her. We're being cautious, but we think it's doubtful that anyone is looking for her."

"I couldn't agree more, as far as a possible hit man is concerned. Piece of Gothic nonsense. It's the media I'm worried about. They must not, I repeat NOT under any circumstances know where Grace is, or who she really is. The press are on to the fact that Mrs Brackenbury was fostering a child: that can't be helped; they were bound to talk to anyone they could get hold of in the Dymokes. But we most emphatically don't want them to know that the child is Grace Arkwright. I don't want to be at the centre of sensationalist stories in the gutter press. The Chief Constable wouldn't like it, either. Do I make myself clear?"

"Yes, sir."

"Did the girl that Grace was with know her true identity? Or the girl's mother?"

"I don't think so, sir."

"What about the woman who was murdered? The foster mother?"

"I don't know the answer to that, sir. DI Yates is visiting Amy Winter – the woman who adopted Grace after the

Arkwright killings – today. He'll probably be able to tell you when he returns."

"Adoptive mother AND foster mother; and real mother and foster mother murdered. It's a rum start in life for a child."

"Yes, sir."

"Child's all right, is she? Not in need of a shrink or anything?"

"Not as far as we can tell, sir. She seems to be remarkably resilient."

"Excellent! Well, don't forget what I said. I don't want to see a five-inch headline in the Spalding Guardian shouting 'Three mothers by the age of ten', or some such drivel."

"No, sir."

"Ask Carstairs to come and see me when he shows up again, will you?"

"Yes, sir."

I am sitting motionless, stricken not only with guilt, but also the fear that Grace is going to be pounced on by a gaggle of reporters while she's out for her walk, when Andy returns and puts a mug of tea down beside me. He grins.

"There you go. I thought I heard the Super's voice and decided that discretion was the better part of valour. I just saw him go. What did he want?"

"He wants to make sure that the Press don't get hold of Grace. And he asked to see you, too. I think it's for an update on the door-to-doors."

"Hah! I'll leave my tea here. Otherwise he's bound to ask me to make one for him."

"Ok. Good luck!"

"Thanks." Andy looks at his watch. "I don't know how long Tim's going to be, but someone from the Home Office called about our request to see Tristram Arkwright's psychiatric reports. They wouldn't tell me anything. They want Tim to call them back. I'm not sure what sort of hours they work, but if Tim's going to be late, maybe you should ask him if you can call them? You know more about it than I do."

"Thanks. I don't know if I can reach Tim now, but I can try."

"The guy's number's on my screen."

"On a Post-it note?" I ask, grinning.

"Yes. Am I so predictable?"

"You said it, not me."

I decide to text Tim, rather than call him. He replies almost immediately: 'Please go ahead.'

I peel off the Post-it note, take a swig of my tea and punch in the number. The name Andy's written above it is Jeremy Forster. Someone takes the call immediately.

"Mr Forster's office."

"Hello, this is DS Armstrong calling, on behalf of DI Yates. I believe Mr Forster called a little earlier, when DI Yates and I were both out of the office. I'm returning his call."

"I'll put you through."

I'm actually 'put through' to a loop of canned music: Beethoven's Pastoral Symphony. I find it quite soothing at first, but eventually grow impatient. I'm on the point of hanging up and trying again when the music is cut off suddenly.

"Good afternoon. Forster here. To whom am I speaking?"

"I am Detective Sergeant Juliet Armstrong. I'm calling on

265

behalf of DI Yates. I believe you asked to speak to him earlier. As you'll be aware, we are conducting a murder investigation and DI Yates is unlikely to be back at the police station until late."

"I see. You have DI Yates's permission to call on his behalf? You know what this is about?"

"Yes, sir. I believe it's about our request to see Tristram Arkwright's psychiatric reports."

"Correct. And I'm able to tell you that I have secured permission, both from the minister and from Arkwright's solicitor. I will e-mail a letter of authorisation for you to show Dr Astani. Shall I send it to DI Yates's email address?"

"Yes please. DI Yates will be very grateful. I'm sure he'll want to thank you himself."

"Indeed. Well, kindly tell him that I still need to speak to him. When he reads the psychiatric records, he may find something that surprises him; I don't particularly want to discuss that – it's up to him what he makes of the information. But he does need to know that Arkwright and his solicitor agreed to his seeing the records because they're about to launch another appeal. You probably know that Arkwright spends a great deal of his time appealing against his convictions? And has come up with several different tales relating why he can't possibly be guilty?"

"I've looked at his website."

"An interesting production, isn't it? DI Yates should know that this latest appeal, which Arkwright claims reveals some truths that he's been unable to disclose before, relies in part on information in the psychiatric reports."

"Are you able to give me any details?"

"I'd prefer not to disclose any more. This is highly

confidential. The fewer people who know about it, the better. Please ask DI Yates to arrange to call this number. As soon as he can."

"I'll be sure to pass your message on. Thank you again."

He puts the phone down without replying.

"Supercilious bastard!" I say.

"Now, now," says Andy, returning to his desk. He tests his mug of tea. "Still warm," he says, "so yours should be, too. But you ought to drink it now. Who was that?"

"Our friend from the Home Office. He has some confidential information that he'd 'prefer not to disclose' to me. He'll tell Tim what it is if he calls as soon as he can. What's the betting he'd have told me if I'd been a man?"

Andy grins.

"Steady on," he says. "Did he say we could have the reports?"

"Yes."

"You got further with him than I did. I think he's just a status freak. You need to be careful not to get a feminist chip on your shoulder."

I scowl at him, then laugh despite myself.

We both finish our tea. I decide to go back to my flat for a quick shower before I return to the children's home; I'm not keen on using the flat's bathroom while Grace and I are there alone. I also need some clean clothes. I'm gathering up my things when my mobile rings.

"Juliet? It's Marie." She sounds panicky.

"Marie? Problem?"

"I'm not sure. Perhaps."

"Has something happened to Grace? The Press haven't managed to get hold of her, have they?"

My earlier misgivings about letting Grace go for a walk return in full force. If Grace has been waylaid by reporters and told them some lurid tale, there'll be hell to pay.

"A photographer. As we came back to the home. He just appeared from nowhere and pointed his camera at us."

"What!" The exclamation makes Andy whirl around. Already my mind is leaping forward to the worst possible implications of this, including my own position. I swallow and try to remain calm, signalling to Andy that things are fine.

"Where was Giash?"

"He was walking a little way behind us. He told me he'd do that, so that Grace could chat to me if she wanted to. When I shouted at the photographer, Giash came running up to us and confronted the man. He told him to go, in no uncertain terms."

"And did he?"

"I'd made Grace turn round and walk the other way. Obviously I didn't want any chance of her talking to someone from the Press. When I looked back, he was already at his car. Grace didn't say a thing to him."

Chapter 57

FRANKIE ROBERTS LOOKED rougher than Tim had expected, even allowing for the fact that he was hung over and had been dossing in a police cell for the past eighteen hours. Red-faced and unshaven, he had a bloated body with a sizeable beer gut. The checked shirt he wore was stained in several places and frayed around the collar and cuffs. He didn't seem like the sort of man Tina Brackenbury would have let into her life.

The duty sergeant at Lincoln had had him brought out of the cell and installed him in an interview room. Tim and Ricky were sitting opposite him at a square table. Someone had supplied him with a plastic beaker of water, from which he took frequent minuscule sips, wincing each time. A cardboard vomit bowl had been placed on his side of the table. Tim fervently hoped that he wouldn't need to use it.

"Mr Roberts, thank you for talking to us. This shouldn't take too long."

Roberts regarded him suspiciously with half-closed fishy eyes.

"I didn't have much choice, did I? I don't mind shooting the breeze, but I know my rights. If you're trying to fit me up, I'm entitled to a solicitor."

"We're not trying to 'fit you up', Mr Roberts. DC MacFadyen would just like to ask you a few questions. It's concerning Tina Brackenbury."

"I thought someone would get on to me about Tina sooner or later." He leaned forward, exhaling sour vomit-smelling breath. "All right, then. Get on with it."

Tim pushed his chair back a little to escape the worst of the noxious outflow and turned at right angles so that he could see both Roberts and Ricky. The action wasn't lost on Ricky, who had temporarily covered his nose with his hand. He dropped his hand again, smiling queasily.

"Mr Roberts," he said, "can you confirm that you had a long-standing relationship with Mrs Brackenbury?"

"I've known her for a good while, if that's what you mean."

"How would you describe that relationship?"

"She was my girlfriend. On and off."

"What do you mean by that?"

"She carried on seeing her husband some of the time, even after she'd left him. That was when it was off. She didn't finish with him proper until a year or so back."

"When did you last see her?"

"About free weeks ago."

"That's quite a long time, isn't it, not to see your girlfriend?"

Roberts hesitated. He sized Ricky up as if he were a bull preparing to charge.

"What's it to you?"

Tim felt the muscles of his face go taut: Roberts was beginning to annoy him. Ricky didn't rise to the bait.

"I'm sorry to poke my nose into your private life, Mr Roberts, but you'll understand that because Mrs Brackenbury has been murdered, we're anxious to find out as much as we can about the people she was closest to. Her daughter has told us that you are one of them and the answers you've given us so far seem to confirm that."

"If you mean Opal, she's a poisonous little bitch. She was always putting a spoke in my wheel. Caused a lot of rows with Tina, she did."

"We might come back to that. Can you tell us why it was that you haven't seen Tina for three weeks?"

"We was going through a bad patch. She said I'd nicked some money from her."

"Was she right?"

Again Roberts hesitated.

"I would of paid it back. She knew that. We wouldn't of 'ad a row if Opal hadn't told her not to believe me."

"When did you have this row?"

"It was at least free weeks back, like I said. It must have been, because I've been in digs up here since, working on a building job. I needed the money to pay a week's rent in advance. She was always saying I couldn't 'old a job down, so I didn't think she'd mind 'elping me out."

"Can you remember the exact date?"

"It must have been the first Sunday of the month. The job started next day."

"You mean the first Sunday in August?" Ricky took out his diary and looked at the year planner. "The 7th?"

"Yeah, if you say so."

"And you didn't see Tina again after that?"

"No. I've said, haven't I?"

"Or talk to her on the phone?"

"No. I was sick of her, thought I'd let her stew for a while."

Ricky nodded sympathetically.

"Mr Roberts, do you mind if I ask you a personal question?"

Roberts opened his bloodshot eyes wider and stared back levelly.

"I thought you was already doing that. Go on, then, you can try me."

"We've been told that you were Bluebelle Brackenbury's father. Is that true?"

"Did that come from Opal as well?"

"I think it was generally assumed by Tina's neighbours."

"Oh, 'generally assumed', was it?" Roberts fell silent again and held his head in his hands. When he looked up again, Tim was surprised to see that he was fighting back tears. He took a few more sips from the water and belched ominously.

"It's all right, Mr Roberts, take your time," said Tim.

"I'll tell you one thing," Roberts said, swiping his forearm across his eyes, "She was a lovely little kid. A really bonny lass. If you want to know the trufe, I'm not sure whether she was mine or not. Tina was honest with me about that: said she didn't know, neither. She could of been mine, or she could of 'ad the same dad as Opal. But I'd of been glad to 'ave 'er as mine. That's why I kept on trying to patch things up with Tina."

Tim sensed that they were about to witness the maudlin stage of Roberts's hangover as it set in. He decided to take over, giving Ricky a quick look to warn him.

"Thank you, Mr Roberts, you've been very helpful. Just a couple of other things, and we're done."

Roberts lifted his head and nodded co-operatively. He obviously felt he'd acquitted himself well.

"First of all, where were you last Saturday and Sunday?"

"In the same pub I was in last night."

"And what about Monday?"

"I was working. Here in Lincoln."

"Thank you. You won't mind if I check that with your employer?"

Roberts was visibly flustered.

"I suppose not, no."

"Good. Perhaps you can give DC MacFadyen your boss's name and address. And phone number, if you have it. Then we'll fetch the duty sergeant back in. If he's through with you as well, you'll be free to go."

Chapter 58

WITH MY HEAD in turmoil, I return to the children's home. The gate is closed, so I've had to get out of the car to open it. As I drive through, I see a group of children playing a makeshift game of football on the grass. Jake Fidler is standing on the path watching them. He cuts an austere figure, despite that unruly thatch blowing about his face. He turns when he hears the car engine, smiles and waves. He gestures that he'll come and close the gate, that I should stay in the car, and hurries towards me. When the gate is fastened, he opens the passenger door.

"Ok if I hitch a ride?" he grins.

I don't start driving immediately. I sense he wants to talk to me.

"Sure. How's Finn?"

"He's still upset, but much calmer now. The doctor's given him a mild sedative. But what's really helped him is that I've said that I believe him. It can't magic away his grief for Sasha, but being believed is vital for his self-esteem."

"And do you? Believe him, I mean?"

He stares at the playing children for a long moment before he replies.

"As a matter of fact, I do. He's been cruel to animals in the past, and certainly behaved inappropriately with them, but he's never killed one before. And I'm convinced the therapy has taught him to be kinder to them."

"Is that the same as saying that you think it was Grace who killed the cat?"

"Not quite the same. She had the opportunity, but I don't know enough of her history to understand if she would be capable of it. Did you talk to her about it?"

"Yes, and she was evasive. I think she may have been hiding something, but she likes secrets. Sometimes I almost think she manufactures them. I suppose it's understandable, given her background."

Too late, I realise that I've given away more than I intended to. Jake leaps on my words immediately.

"You haven't told me very much about her. I know she was the foster-daughter of the woman who was murdered. Has she been in foster care for long?"

"A few years, I believe."

"Does she remember her own mother?"

"I think so. Grace was six when her mother died. But I haven't talked to her about it."

"How did her mother die? That can be very important, you know. If the mother's death was violent, children sometimes find it hard to accept - harder than if she'd died of natural causes, say. Some children blame themselves - especially if the mother's death was caused by an abusive partner."

He fixes me with keen brown eyes. I look away.

"I'm sorry, Jake, I'm not allowed to tell you any more about Grace. Her situation's very delicate while the murder enquiry's going on. There is something unpleasant in her past, as you've guessed, but it's important the media don't get hold of it."

"You think I'd talk to the newspapers?" He sounds both hurt and furious, his voice rising as he ends the sentence.

"Of course not. I've been given orders by my boss not to

talk to anyone about Grace. So has Marie. Marie actually knows more about her than I do."

"Marie's far too professional to discuss her cases with anyone not directly involved," Jake says admiringly. I wonder again why what he thinks of as noble in Marie he considers a breach of trust in me.

"Quite. But I'm grateful for your concern. I know you'd like to help Grace, if you could."

"Well, bear that in mind. If social services don't find a new foster home for Grace straight away, she could come here. We have a place free. If she is suffering from a deep-seated grief that she won't share with anyone, the psychologists who support our children are excellent. Marie used to be one of them, as I'm sure you know."

"Thank you. What happens next to Grace won't be my decision. It'll be up to her social workers, but Marie's in touch with them. I'll tell her what you said. I'm curious, though, to know why you're taking such an interest in Grace if you think she killed Sasha. Surely you have enough disturbed children here already?"

"It's precisely because of that that I want to help. It's what I do." He grins again. "Sorry, I don't mean to sound pious. And they're not all disturbed. But, like all children, they are all very inquisitive and capable of putting two and two together and making five," he adds more briskly. "If you don't start the engine up again soon, they'll be talking about us."

He gestures towards the group of children ahead. They've stopped kicking the ball around and have gathered in a knot to stare at us.

I turn on the ignition and drive the few yards to the visitors' parking spaces.

"Damn!" I say, as I straighten up the wheels, "I've forgotten to bring something with me for supper."

"That's all right, I put some more things in the fridge this afternoon."

"Thank you. So you've seen Grace today?"

"No, it was while she was out for a walk with Marie. Marie called me to tell me when they were going, as I asked her to. I didn't want to make a fuss by turning up with the stuff while they were there. I was a bit worried about them going along the river bank on their own – it's very remote there, you know. But they had the policeman with them."

It's on the tip of my tongue to tell him about the encounter with the photographer. I decide not to: although my sense of personal guilt is acute and I could do with a friendly ear, I know if he thinks Grace is compromising security at the home he'll immediately want her to leave, whatever he's just said. I wonder if it's wise not to keep her here anyway, now that the Press are on to her. Just *how* did they find her? Tim will certainly want her to stay somewhere more secure, but the question is, where?

I look at my watch. It's almost 6 p.m.; I hadn't realised it was so late. I haven't given Marie a specific time for my return, but she's been with Grace all day and no doubt is feeling bad about what's happened. Giash is sitting at the top of the flight of steps to the flat. He rises to greet me. I can see he is about to let me have his account.

"I'll come back in a minute, Giash," I say hurriedly. "Sorry – I should have got here earlier."

Marie is waiting just inside the door when I open it, her handbag and the capacious tote bag she always carries already on her arm.

"I'm sorry, Marie," I say, "Have I kept you waiting?"

"Yes. I'm going out tonight," she says breathlessly. I'm surprised. She hasn't mentioned this before.

"I'm sorry," I say again. "Do you have a few minutes, just to talk about what happened?"

"PC Chakrabati can fill you in. If you need a statement from me, I'll give it to you tomorrow. I really must go now."

There's something strange about her behaviour. She's less acerbic than I would have expected, given that she says I've held her up. And although I know that Marie is married, I've never known her put her social life before work: I've often pitied her husband, wondered what sort of life he leads with her. And this morning she didn't mention that she needed to leave at a specific time.

"That's fine. I hope I haven't made you late for something important."

She gives me a strange look and hurries through the door. She hasn't paused to say goodbye to Grace.

I turn into the kitchen area and see Grace standing in the archway that separates it from the sitting area. She's leaning against the wall. She must have been there while I was talking to Marie, silently watching us. The expression she wears is unfathomable, unsettling; but when she catches my eye it vanishes and is replaced by one of her broad, open smiles.

"Hello, Grace."

"Hello."

"Did you have a nice afternoon?"

"Yes. Marie and me went for a walk. Giash came too."

Have they given her permission to use their first names? If she's being deliberately insolent, I won't rise to it.

"That's good. It's a nice day."

"Yes. We met a man just outside. He took my picture and . . ." she stops suddenly.

"I heard about him, Grace. He didn't say anything to you, then?"

"No." She hangs her head. Her guard is up again.

"It's all right, Grace, don't worry about it now. Let's see what we can find to eat, shall we?"

"Jake brought some food. Marie said so."

She gives me a bold look. Again, I don't challenge her.

"Yes, he told me. It was kind of him. We must thank him."

"Marie already did."

"Did she see him? He said he dropped by when you were out."

"She spoke to him on the phone when we came back. And then she 'popped down' to speak to him." She says 'popped down' in a simpering high voice. It's almost certainly the expression Marie herself used.

"That's nice," I say flatly.

I go to the fridge and inspect the shelves. There is more salad, a packet of sesame buns and a wrapped parcel of meat.

"That's burgers," says Grace. "Marie told me."

"Do you like burgers?"

"Yes."

"I'll start cooking them in a few minutes. I just want a word with PC Chakrabati first. If you like, you can help by washing some lettuce."

"All right. I know how to do it. I used to do it for Mum." Her tone is boastful, but her voice wavers on the last word.

"Good," I say again. I curse my ignorance of child psychiatry. Should I allude to her reference to Tina Brackenbury or ignore it? I decide I can't risk getting out of my depth.

"I shan't be long," I say tautly. I leave Grace exploring the kitchen cupboards.

Outside, Giash is leaning over the balcony, looking at the courtyard below.

"I'm back," I say. "Sorry if I was rude earlier. I needed to check on Grace. I also wanted a word with Marie, but she was in a hurry."

He turns to face me.

"Yes. Funny, that, wasn't it?"

"I'm sorry, I'm not with you."

"Funny that Marie had to go dashing off like that. When we went for the walk, you'd think she had all the time in the world. Then there's the photographer and she talks with that Fidler guy and suddenly she can't wait to get out of the place."

"I'm sure the two things aren't connected. She probably just forgot she had to be home by a certain time."

He shrugs.

"If you say so."

"Sorry, Giash, you were here and I wasn't. I'll bear in mind what you're saying. I know Marie gets carried away sometimes. And thank you for dealing with the photographer." I'm not sure what I'm admitting to, any more than I understand what he's trying to suggest about Marie. "Tell me precisely what happened outside."

"Marie was walking with Grace along the Cut. She asked me if I minded walking a few yards behind them, just out of earshot, in case Grace decided to open up and talk to her."

"Talk to her about what?"

"I don't know, but I'm guessing the murders. Anyway, it was fine by me. I quite like the kid, but I find her unnerving. It made more sense for me to stay behind, in any case: if we'd been walking in a row, someone might have crept up on us without noticing."

"Go on."

"Marie only wanted to walk the section of the Cut from the bridge by the road to the next bridge. It's probably less than half a mile. Then she was going to cross the second bridge and come back on the other bank. We were almost back here when I heard her shout and saw the bloke taking a picture of them both.

"She was rooted to the spot for a few seconds, but then she tried to pull Grace away, back towards me. Grace resisted a bit, tried to shake her off. When I got up to them, I told him to leave, which he did."

"How were they both afterwards?"

"Marie looked a bit shaken, but only how you'd expect at the surprise of it. Grace didn't seem bothered at all."

"Thanks. Would you mind giving me all this in a written report? I'm going to need it. By the way, did you tell Grace she could call you 'Giash'?"

"No, did she say I had?"

"No, but that's how she's referring to you. Do you mind?"

He grins.

"Not really. She's just pushing the envelope, like all kids."

"I can ask her to stop, if you like. We don't want her to get the upper hand."

Giash's grin broadens.

"If you ever have kids, you'll realise they always get the upper hand. The trick is to pretend they haven't done. If she starts being rude, we can put her in her place. Right now, I'm thinking it's a good sign. Like I said, it shows she's behaving like a normal kid. I could even take it as a compliment."

Chapter 59

IT WAS NEARLY 9 p.m. by the time Tim had dropped Andy off at his flat and finally pulled into his drive. It was getting dark. He saw that Katrin had turned on the sitting-room light, but had yet to draw the curtains. She was seated on the sofa, bent over her laptop, her head turned towards the window so that he could see her face in three-quarter profile. She was frowning slightly, concentrating on her work. Her hair was drawn back from her face and knotted in a casual chignon at the nape of her neck. Her face was smooth and shadow-free, its classic contours perfectly restored now she'd weathered the debilitating early months of motherhood. He thought her very beautiful. His heart swelled with pride.

She hadn't registered the noise of the car engine, but when he turned off the ignition she noticed the silence, and looked up. Seeing Tim, she smiled at him and, putting down the laptop, rose to meet him. He hurried into the house.

She was already standing in the hall. They embraced and she led him into the kitchen, where the table was laid for two. A bottle of red wine stood, opened, on the kitchen counter, two glasses promisingly placed beside it.

"You've waited supper for me!" he said. "I told you I might not be back until much later."

"I thought it was worth a try. Another half an hour and I've have saved the lasagne for another occasion, got myself some bread and cheese and started making inroads into that wine."

"Thank you," he said, kissing her lightly again. "God, you're wonderful! And I've had a pig of a day."

He washed his hands at the kitchen tap and poured the wine, handing one of the glasses to her.

"Have you made any progress?" she asked sympathetically.

"Some, although most of the information we've gained is making the case harder to solve, rather than the other way round. I told you that Grace Winter identified Marek Wolansky, the mentally-disabled man living next door to Tina Brackenbury, as the person she'd seen leaving the house. We thought she must be mistaken or making it up until we interviewed him. He was virtually incoherent – he certainly didn't understand properly what we were talking about – but he had in his possession a silver pendant belonging to Tina Brackenbury which apparently she always wore. He seemed to associate it with Grace, said she'd given it to him as a 'present' – at least, that's how his mother interpreted the word he was trying to articulate."

"Does that make him a suspect?"

"Not necessarily, but there's a limited number of ways he could have come by the pendant. The most obvious one is that he killed Tina Brackenbury and removed it from her neck."

"Why would he kill her?"

"I don't know the answer to that, but I've yet to discover why anybody would want to kill her. We've also interviewed her boyfriend today. His name's Frankie Roberts. He's got a pretty shaky alibi and he admits the last time he saw her they quarrelled about money, but since she appears either to have given him the money or he helped himself to it anyway, that doesn't add up, either. Then there's a character called Phil Green who was supposed to be looking after Wolansky but left him, probably for longer than he admits, to make a trip to the bookie's. They're all potential suspects, but quite honestly I can't see that either Roberts or Green had a reason for murdering Tina. That leaves Wolansky, who wouldn't have needed a rational reason. He could have killed her because she frightened him, or for some other dimly-perceived delusion."

"Or he could be telling the truth. Perhaps Grace did give him the pendant."

"But why would she do that? And how did she get hold of it?"

"It may not be quite correct that Tina Brackenbury always wore it. She may have taken it off at night."

"True, but we don't think she died at night. We think that she probably took a nap on Saturday or Sunday afternoon, when the baby had her afternoon sleep."

"What was Tina wearing?"

"A T-shirt and underwear."

"If she was wearing her bra, I'd say that your theory is correct. She'd prepared herself for a nap, not for bed for the night. In which case she probably kept the pendant on."

"If you're right, the murderer must have taken the pendant from her neck."

"Either the murderer or someone else who was either in the room at the time or visited the body before it was discovered by the police. But the pendant wasn't snatched from her neck: it had been properly unfastened, the clasp was undamaged. I'd be amazed if Wolansky were capable of undoing it, though."

"Which again suggests he was telling the truth. Have you asked Grace about it?"

"Juliet and Marie have tried. She's evasive. And they don't want to push it because no-one knows how traumatised she is by the deaths."

"If Marek Wolansky didn't enter the house and he was telling the truth when he said that Grace gave him the pendant, either Grace removed it from her foster mother's body herself or someone else removed it and gave it to her."

"Then why would she want to give it to Wolansky? And why would she want to incriminate him by creating the photofit?"

"I think your second question probably answers your first. She gave him the pendant to incriminate him. She probably thought that providing you with his picture wouldn't be enough to brand him a murderer on its own, but she'd also have deduced that you'd be bound to interview him once she'd identified him. You say she's intelligent: she might even have been astute enough to understand that he'd be unlikely to get rid of the pendant and too simple to try to conceal it from you."

"But this is leading us to the conclusion that either Grace is the killer or she knows who the killer is and is protecting them."

"I know. And it's an uneasy thought that's been growing at the back of my mind since I started on the research you asked me to do."

"You mean the murdered children statistics?"

"No. I drew a blank with those. I couldn't find any typical set of circumstances that might indicate why Bluebelle was murdered: she wasn't an abused child; she didn't live with a parent who was violent or dependent on alcohol or drugs; she didn't die as the result of a hit and run. On the face of it, she was too young to have been disliked by another child. But this got me thinking. As I told you, there's a smallish but statistically significant group of murdered children who are killed by other children, and although they're usually not babies, they're often not long out of babyhood. There have been some famous cases. I suppose just about everyone has heard of James Bulger's murder. Although it was longer ago, a lot of people will remember the Mary Bell case, too. James Bulger was a toddler and both the boys Mary Bell killed were under primary school age."

"I'm more familiar with the Bulger case than Mary Bell's. The police thought that one of the boys who murdered James Bulger was much more to blame than the other, didn't they? Based on his home background and the way he behaved in custody?"

"Yes, although their behaviour as adults, once they'd served their time and been released with new identities, suggested that the police might have been wrong about which one was the leader. From what I've read about them, I don't think that at the time there was much to choose between them. They egged each other on and then each tried to say it was mostly the other's fault. Typical of kids the world over when they get into trouble, though thankfully it's not usually for murder. From our point of view, Mary Bell's case is more interesting. She also had a child accomplice, a girl a bit older than she was, but Mary was undoubtedly the driving force behind the murders of the two little boys they killed. Norma Bell, the other girl, who wasn't related to Mary – she just had the same surname – wasn't nearly as bright as Mary."

"I've seen pictures of Mary Bell. She was a very pretty child, wasn't she?"

"Yes, although I'm not sure how immediately relevant that is. She said long afterwards that her mother had exploited her as a child prostitute, which may have had something to do with why she killed, in a convoluted sort of way. You don't think Grace Winter's been forced into prostitution at some point, do you?"

"It's possible, but I think it's unlikely. She's been monitored by social services for most of her life – not that that's fool-proof."

"Well, I hadn't thought of that possibility, but it may be worth hanging onto at the back of your mind. The parallel I found interesting was that, like Mary Bell, Grace has a much dimmer friend, who was with her when she showed up at Tina Brackenbury's house when you were first there, and who Grace now says was with her when she visited the house earlier."

"Chloe Hebblewhite, yes. She was incapable of answering when we questioned her with Grace at the station. The concept of murder seemed to horrify her: she grew quite hysterical, in fact. We had to abandon the interview. We intend to talk to her again, but we thought we'd give her a few days to recover first. She didn't seem to be very material to making progress with the case," Tim added, rather lamely. He had an inkling that Katrin was going to prove him wrong.

"There's a difference between being hysterical because you're sensitive and because you're scared out of your wits."

"Why would Chloe be scared?"

"Could be for several reasons. She might be frightened of Grace, or worried that she's going to be punished for something that she knows she's guilty of."

"Such as committing a murder?"

"Perhaps. I'd keep an open mind about that. I'd say it's

likely she got up to something with Grace, probably something that Grace persuaded her to do, and now she's terrified of being found out."

"If you're right, we need to interview Chloe again, and on her own. But whether or not she's afraid of Grace, she's certainly frightened of her own mother. And I don't see any way round allowing Mavis Hebblewhite to be present at the interview, if she wants to."

"You could try asking her if someone else can accompany Chloe – Tom Tarrant, for example. I think you said he knows Chloe?"

"He knows the whole family. We know some of them, too. Mavis has umpteen children, and they've mostly started breaking the law before they've left primary school. Especially the boys."

"Why don't you give Tom a call tomorrow, see what he says?"

"That's not a bad idea. He's been involved in aspects of this case already. He won't want to do anything to damage Chloe, though."

"It sounds as if she's pretty damaged already. And you might be helping her rather than incriminating her. Perhaps she's got mixed up in something and doesn't know how to extricate herself. You might be doing her a favour."

"That sounds a bit too much like wishful thinking. But I will ask him."

"Good. Now let's try to forget about it and enjoy the rest of the evening. Come and eat."

Tim took a swig of his wine and sat down at the table. He swirled the wine left in his glass around for a few seconds and stood up again. Katrin had had her back to him, removing the lasagne from the oven. She swung round, holding the steaming dish in one oven-gloved hand.

"What's the matter?"

"Nothing," said Tim sheepishly. "That is – would you mind if I called Tom Tarrant now? Before it gets too late?"

Katrin sighed and shoved the dish back into the oven.

Chapter 60

THE EVENING WITH Grace has passed tranquilly enough. She's spent most of her time playing games on the iPad that Marie lent her, breaking off for half an hour to watch a reality TV show. I insist on bed at 10 p.m. again. She doesn't make any specific objection, but drags her feet, taking several minutes to shut down what she's been doing on the iPad and dawdle to the bathroom. Just like a normal kid, as Giash might say.

She's been settled in her room for about half an hour when my mobile rings. I don't recognise the number that's flashed up on the display screen, but when I press the green button the voice that greets me is familiar.

"Nancy!" I say. "It's lovely to hear you. Listen, I'm sorry I haven't written the testimonial yet. I've been busy with a case that's literally been taking up all my time – in a sense, I'm still working now, as I'm looking after a witness. And I want to make a good job of it. When do you need it by?"

"Early next week if you can manage it. But that isn't why I called."

"No? Can I help you in some other way?"

"I'm not sure . . ." Nancy's voice sounds choked. There's a sudden silence.

"Nancy? Are you still there?"

She clears her throat.

"Yes. Look, I'm . . ." she falters again. "I've never asked

this of anyone before. Not like this, anyway." There's another long pause.

I try to sound light-hearted.

"Well, spit it out, Nancy. I can only say no."

"You've no idea how much I don't want you to."

"No pressure there, then. What is it?"

"I was finking you we might get together. You're like me, aren't you?"

It's my turn to pause. I can't think how best to reply to this and I'm acutely conscious that the light is still shining under Grace's door. I know I mustn't say anything that Grace can use against me: I've understood from the start that she is capable of exploiting personal information if she can get hold of it.

I embarrass myself by croaking out a false little laugh. The question has taken me by surprise: nothing if not direct!

"To be honest, Nancy, I don't know myself. I think it's a distinct possibility." I'm brisk now, businesslike.

"Are you being overheard?"

"I don't know the answer to that. It's certainly also possible."

"I'm sorry, Juliet, I fought you'd be on your own at this time in the evening."

"Don't worry about it. I appreciate the distraction! The last few days have been by turns intense and tedious."

She laughs: a raucous, cigarette-tarnished guffaw, but I think it's genuine.

"You're a copper, in uvver words. The fing is, Juliet, although we got off to a bad start, I really like you. Do you want to give it a go?"

I glance again at Grace's door. I think I can see a dip in

the light coming from below it, as if she's standing right up against it and listening.

"I think we could meet to talk about it," I say. "The trouble is, I don't know when I'm going to be able to. This case could drag on for a while yet."

"Don't worry about that. Just tell me when you're ready. It's worf waiting for. And fank you!"

"That's all right. Look, I'd better go now. But I'll keep in touch. And I'll send the testimonial this weekend."

I switch off the phone. I feel as if I'm in shock, appalled and intrigued in about equal measures. My hand is shaking and I could murder a drink. There's no alcohol here, but when I open the fridge I see that Marie has stocked it with yet more cans of Coke. Gratefully I lift one and snap it open.

I've taken only a couple of swigs when the phone rings again. I decide that if it's Nancy again I won't answer, but it is Tim's number that's flashing now.

"Juliet? It's Tim."

"Yes, I know."

"Is everything all right? You sound a bit rough!"

"Thanks a lot." I'm beginning to get a complex about all this. "I'm fine, thank you. I was just going to bed."

"Yes, I know it's late. I'm sorry. I need you to do something for me."

"You do surprise me."

Tim ignores the jibe, probably because he hasn't noticed it, and hurries on.

"I've got to go and see Lenka Astani again tomorrow, now that I've got permission. And there's another urgent interview that needs to be organised, too."

"And you want me to do it? Who's the candidate?"

"Chloe Hebblewhite."

"Well, we've always intended to interview her again, but we said we'd leave it until next week. Why the sudden urgency?"

"Are you alone? I forgot to ask. I assume Grace is in bed?"

"Correct. But I can't guarantee that we're not being overheard."

"Ok, just listen, then. I'll try to answer all the questions you're likely to ask. If you have any others, you can text me."

"Oh, that's great, thank you!" I look at my watch. It's just after 11 p.m. "Just wait a minute while I find my notebook."

Chapter 61

THE NEXT DAY Tim was up very early. He didn't sleep well when he was working on murder cases, so having to get up with the dawn came as something of a relief; but as he emerged from the shower he noticed with a sense of loss that the sun was only just rising. It was possible to ignore that the days were drawing in until the end of August, but after that there was no escaping the signs of the onward march of autumn.

Not wanting to disturb Katrin, he crept to the chest of drawers and fumbled for underwear in the half-light, knocking trinkets to the floor. Katrin stirred and turned over. In the adjacent bedroom, he could hear a small hubbub as Sophia began to wake up. He loved this sound; he had often thought it sounded like the call of the curlews on the salt marshes as they built their cries to crescendo. Reluctantly, he resisted the impulse to look in on her: he didn't have time today. Quickly, he pulled on his clothes and tiptoed out of the house as quietly as he could. As he closed the door, he thought he detected a pause in the curlew-calling sounds. Was Sophia listening to his departure?

Dawn was breaking in earnest as he unlocked his car. Settling himself into the driver's seat, he took a long swig from the bottle of water standing in the console and hoped that Ricky would be sufficiently well-organised to bring coffee. Then he switched on his phone. "Fuck it!" he groaned. Juliet's

294

text was not unexpected, given what he'd said last night, but its content was. A picture of Grace in one of today's papers was the last thing he wanted right now.

Exerting all his self-discipline, he relegated Superintendent Thornton and his likely reaction to the back of his mind. He debated whether to call in at a newsagent's on his way and swiftly decided against it. If he found out a photo had been published, he would be obliged to talk to Thornton about it; and from his perspective, keeping the appointment was more important.

Lenka Astani had offered a very early appointment, at 7.30 a.m., saying she had to attend a hearing at the juvenile court during office hours and needed to prepare for it beforehand. She could spare him half an hour. Tim doubted the truth of this – he thought it unlikely that the court would sit all day, and Lenka didn't strike him as the last-minute type – but he'd neither challenged nor checked up on her. Either she wanted to get the conversation out of the way or she'd hoped that he wouldn't be able to make it. What was certain was that he would be there: he couldn't afford to postpone any longer.

Ricky was waiting at the corner of the Sheep Market, as they'd arranged. Tim noted with approval that he was clutching a cardboard tray bearing two plastic cups. An interesting-looking carrier bag dangled from one finger. He perched the tray on the bonnet of the car while he opened the passenger door, then passed it to Tim, who took the cups and wedged them into the console alongside the water.

"Good man," said Tim. "What's in the carrier bag?"

"Give me a chance to get in," said Ricky good-naturedly. He eased himself into his seat and tossed his briefcase to the back. Tim took note of his girth: he was sure it was increasing.

Ricky peered into the bag and delicately lifted out a solid wedge of something wrapped in a paper napkin, which he handed to Tim.

"What's this?" Tim unfolded it carefully. He found himself holding two generous slices of moist, dark-brown cake cemented together with a thick slather of butter.

"Lincolnshire plum bun," said Ricky with relish. "You can't beat it."

"I've not heard of it before." Tim separated the two slices and examined them.

"You've never lived," said Ricky. "My gran used to make this. I hadn't had any for years, until that little stall in the station yard opened. It's been my breakfast for the last week or two."

"It looks like it," said Tim, as Ricky let out the buckle on the seatbelt.

"No need for that," said Ricky huffily. "If you don't want it, give it back. Sir."

"Point taken," said Tim, grinning. "It's not that I'm not grateful." He took a large bite out of one of the slices. "You're right, it's delicious," he said.

Mollified, Ricky retrieved his own bundle of cake, swiftly whipped away the napkin, and wolfed the plum bun down, eating it like a sandwich. Tim grinned in amusement.

"Feel better for that, do you?"

"As a matter of fact, I do," said Ricky, clearly ready to take offence again.

"Good. Perhaps you'd like to drive? I don't want to get booked for eating at the wheel!"

It was Ricky's turn to grin.

"Sure, but I'll have to heft myself out of this seat again!"

They each got out of the car and changed sides. Ricky moved the driver's chair back a few inches, fastened his seatbelt and took a swig from one of the beakers of coffee. He turned on the ignition.

"Do you know that woman standing over there?" Tim asked, squinting through the windscreen at a slender blonde woman dressed in smart casual clothes who had come to a halt a few yards away from them.

"No. Why?"

"She doesn't seem very anxious for us to see her. She stopped dead in her tracks and now she's turned to go back the way she came."

Ricky sighed.

"How many years have you been working in Spalding, boss?"

"I don't know. About six, is it?"

"At least. And you still think our upright citizens are chuffed when they come across coppers? That they can't wait to socialise?"

"How does she know we're coppers? We're using my car and we don't have uniforms."

"Doesn't take a genius to work out we're coppers, when we're parked right next to the station. Besides, your face has been in the news so much recently that she may have recognised you. Alternatively, she just thinks we look dodgy and doesn't want to walk past us."

Tim laughed and took another bite of his cake.

"I've got something quite interesting to tell you," Ricky added, as they drove round the Sheep Market and the woman disappeared from view.

"This cake is great. Go on."

"Last night when I got back I checked out Normamy Construction. It does exist and it is based in Lincoln."

"Sorry, you've lost me. Should I know something about it?"

"It's the name of the company Frankie Wright said he was working for. He gave me the name so I could corroborate his statement. He wasn't too keen on the idea, though."

"I remember that. I don't think I knew the name of the company. Or didn't register it, anyway."

"Like I said, it's a genuine company. He's probably telling the truth about working for it."

"He seemed to have something to hide, though. Or that he didn't want us to know about."

"You're right, he did. And I think I know what it was."

"Get on with it, Ricky. There's an art to the building up of suspense, but not necessarily one I appreciate, particularly at this time of day."

"Normamy Construction is owned by Norman Winter. Amy Winter's the Company Secretary."

Tim whistled.

"Christ! No wonder he was reluctant to tell us. But that raises the question of exactly who it is who has something to hide. Is it him, or is it the Winters? If it's them, they may have told him to keep his mouth shut."

"They both said they didn't know him."

"That doesn't have to be a lie: Norman Winter probably doesn't hire all the casual labour that works for him. And I doubt if Amy has much to do with temporary brickies. But it's certainly possible they were lying. How are you planning to check out what he said? Are you just going to turn up at this company's depot?"

"Yes. They'll probably start work around the time that we arrive in Lincoln, so I'm taking a chance on it that the foreman'll still be around. Wright gave me his name. If he's already out on a job, there's an office assistant. I thought about e-mailing her to ask him to wait for me, but I decided that it'd be better not to let him prepare himself first."

"Good idea. What's the bloke's name?"

"Reg Jones. No relation to the Winters as far as I can tell, if that's what you're thinking."

Ricky turned briefly to grin again at Tim, but suddenly Tim wasn't listening.

"Fuck!" he said.

"What's the matter?"

"Juliet asked me to call the guy at the Home Office who's given the ok to talk to Lenka Astani about Tristram Arkwright. He said it was important to speak to him before I see Lenka. I forgot all about it."

"Didn't he tell Juliet what it was about?"

"No; she was quite annoyed about that: thought he was talking down to her. Which he probably was, though no doubt he'll do the same to me. It's funny that Juliet forgot to mention it again when I spoke to her yesterday evening, though I now know she had something else on her mind."

"Must be tough, minding that kid."

"It was her own choice. I don't know how we'd have managed if she hadn't offered, though. I'm certain Grace Winter's holding back something she knows she ought to tell us; she definitely needs an adult with her twenty-four-seven. Juliet says we have to appoint a solicitor for her as well."

"Why don't you try the guy from the Home Office now?"

"Are you kidding? He's probably still in bed. I doubt if he shows up for work until ten or so."

"Was it his office number he gave Juliet?"

"No, it's a mobile number. She told him I wouldn't be back at the station during working hours, so he was probably expecting me to call last night. Would have been, if he knows about the appointment with Lenka."

"Worth giving it a whirl, then. Worst he can do is ignore the call. Do you want me to pull over?"

"No, carry on. Neither of us can afford to be late. I just need to hear Juliet's message again."

Tim listened intently to the message and scribbled down a number, which he called. He counted eight rings before the phone went to message. He put his hand over it.

"Told you so!" he said to Ricky in a ferocious whisper. "Bastard isn't up yet. It's gone to message."

"Well, leave a message for him. He'll get back to you."

"Probably not in time, but I guess if he knows I've tried to talk to him it'll let me off the hook a bit if I see Lenka before I know what he wants. Damn, it's cut out now. I'll have to call again."

Tim was about to press the repeat button when the display panel on his phone began to flash. He jabbed at the green button.

"Forster here. Who is that?" said an imperious voice.

"Oh, good morning, sir. Sorry to trouble you this early. It's DI Yates."

"DI Yates, good morning! I'm delighted to speak to you. I thought you'd forgotten about me." Tim decided that Forster sounded more peeved than delighted.

"No, sir, I was just tied up with things connected with

the case until very late and then I didn't want to disturb you."

"That would have been quite all right. I don't give many people this number. When I do, it means they can call when they like. As I believe I made clear to your colleague."

"I see. Thank you, sir."

"I spoke to your colleague yesterday afternoon. DS Strong, wasn't it?"

"DS Armstrong, sir."

"Correct. Did she tell you what it was about?"

"Not exactly. I'm not sure she knew the details."

"Quite. I try to share information on a need-to-know basis. It's simpler that way, don't you think? Anyway, what I wanted to say to you is that it's fine to go ahead with your meeting with Dr Astani and I've instructed her to give you certain facts about Tristram Arkwright she has in her possession, including selected materials from psychiatric reports. But this must all be in the strictest confidence: you may use the information only to further your investigation. You are not, I repeat, NOT, to get involved in Tristram Arkwright's own case or try to reopen it, comment on it or speak to any of the witnesses who appeared at his trial about the case itself."

"Understood, sir. I hadn't intended to discuss the Brocklesby murders with Dr Astani. I just need to know more about his relationship with his niece. I think Dr Astani's psychiatric reports on Arkwright will help."

"Which is why I've authorised her to help you. You should be aware that she's uncomfortable about it: she takes patient confidentiality very seriously, which is laudable."

"Is that why you've instructed us to avoid discussing the Brocklesby murders?"

"It's one of the reasons. But it's mainly because Arkwright is having another push for permission to appeal. He's done it at least half a dozen times before, but apparently – and I don't have the details yet – this time there's an outside chance he will be successful."

Chapter 62

WITHOUT EATING BREAKFAST, Jennifer Dove had checked out of the Lincolnshire Poacher, where the night before she'd registered as Jenny Dalton, and walked through the deserted town. On her back was a small rucksack that contained basic toiletries, the shirt and underclothes she'd had on the previous day and a girl's cotton summer dress. She'd left her car in the car park next to Vine Street, but she'd never visited Spalding before and had managed to get lost trying to find it again. A paper boy had mistakenly directed her to the railway station car park; she'd realised the mistake and was heading back towards Vine Street when she saw the two men in the battered BMW.

Although she had been disappointed yesterday to have found no clue to the girl's whereabouts in the town, having carefully walked the Lady Dymoke streets and asked a couple of people what she'd felt to be innocuous questions, she had too determined a character to abandon the plan that she'd agreed to. She thought she'd give it one more try.

But seeing the two men in the BMW had spooked her. She couldn't be entirely sure that they were policemen, but she thought it likely. One of them seemed vaguely familiar, but that wasn't the reason. It was the way they took in their surroundings, and even more the interest the one she thought she'd seen before showed in her. She turned and headed back towards the railway station, trying to walk briskly without showing panic. When she'd rounded the corner, she looked back over her shoulder. The car didn't appear to be following her, but she knew she'd have to be careful now. She dodged into an alley too narrow for cars to enter and ran until she came to an opening. She found herself in the yard of another pub. Emerging cautiously, she saw that she was back at the top end of the Sheep Market. She could just see the spot where the BMW had been parked; it was no longer there.

She crossed the road and walked sedately back towards the police station, her heart thumping in her chest. She turned left into the Crescent and, resisting the temptation to break into a run again, carried on walking until she reached her car. Apart from another paper boy furiously pedalling past on his bike, she saw no-one else.

She sat in the driver's seat for several minutes, resting her head against the steering wheel until the pounding in her chest subsided. She looked at her watch. It wasn't yet 6.30 a.m. If she set off for Wakefield immediately, she might be able to reach the shop in time to open it as usual. As yesterday the shop had been closed in the afternoon to give her time to put together the corporate orders for the following week, no-one would know that she'd spent the night away from home.

She was slightly afraid of having to tell him she'd had to postpone the plan, but she knew that today she no longer had the courage to carry it through.

Chapter 63

MARIE ARRIVES BEFORE Grace has emerged from her room, just as I'm setting out cereal bowls and mugs for breakfast.

"You're early!" I say. "Grace isn't up yet. I thought you might need a bit longer in bed this morning, too. Did you have a good night out?"

Marie's expression goes blank for a second.

"What? Oh – oh, yes, thank you."

"What did you do?"

"Oh, we were just out with some friends, that's all."

"Great! Well, you're in time for some breakfast, if you'd like some?"

"I'm not worried about the food, but I could kill a cup of tea."

"The kettle's on. I'd like to ask your advice about something. Before Grace gets up. Can we squeeze into the lobby?"

Marie seems apprehensive rather than intrigued. She follows me into the lobby, where we stand facing each other, our backs against the walls. She is neatly dressed in a kind of sailor top and trousers today: it isn't as extravagant on space and oxygen as her usual outfits. Nevertheless, it's a tight fit in the vestibule.

"Tim wants me to interview Chloe Hebblewhite again," I say. "We don't want Mavis with her this time. We think she's more likely to stay calm and tell us whatever she knows if Mavis isn't there. But Mavis is likely to insist that she's present."

"If so, I'm inclined to give her credit for it. I see plenty of kids whose parents don't support them."

"I know that. But you've seen for yourself what sort of effect Mavis has on Chloe. Ideally, Tim would like you to be there instead of her."

"If you're going to do the interviewing, that's impossible: one of us has to stay with Grace."

"I know that, too, and I've pointed it out to Tim. Do you think I could ask Tom Tarrant? He knows the family and Chloe seems to like him."

"You can try, but if Mavis insists don't try to overrule her. Mavis is well tuned-in to her rights, and she'll find a way of making you pay if you break the rules."

"Sure. But there's no legal reason why it shouldn't be Tom? It doesn't matter that he's a man, for example?"

"No, not unless your enquiries take a different turn – sexual abuse, for example."

Marie eyes me beadily.

"We've got absolutely no reason to think that either of those girls has been assaulted."

"Ask Tom, then. But square it with Mavis first."

"Thanks, I will. Do you mind if I go now? I want to get on with this as soon as possible."

"No, that's fine."

I squeeze past her and back into the flat. Marie follows. Grace is seated at the table, scrutinising the iPad. She looks up when she hears us and stares past me at Marie. I turn, hoping to catch Marie's reaction, but she is already moving out of Grace's line of vision.

"Let's get that kettle back on again," she says briskly. "I'm dying for a cuppa."

As it happens, Mavis is distracted by having to deal with the misdemeanours of one of her other children when I call and temporarily indifferent to Chloe's problems. She agrees that Chloe is well enough to be interviewed and raises no objection when I suggest that Tom Tarrant alone should accompany her.

Chapter 64

Dr Lenka Astani stood up as Tim entered her office and smoothed down her immaculate navy-blue pencil skirt. She extended the fingertips of one hand. Tim held them briefly before she pulled away and motioned to the chair she'd positioned in front of her desk, whilst she herself retreated behind it.

He took as long and hard a look at her face as he plausibly could without appearing rude. Her skin was very pale beneath the impeccable make-up and she seemed tired, if serene. Her asymmetrical fringe had been severely fastened back with a tortoise-shell hair slide. She wore a short-sleeved white shirt that looked expensive – silk, he guessed. The navy-blue jacket that matched the skirt was carefully arranged on the back of her chair. She had probably been telling the truth when she said she would be spending the day in court: these were not everyday clothes.

"DI Yates, please have a seat. I'm sorry to have got you up so early. Would you like some tea?"

Tim looked at his watch. It was 7.26 a.m. He didn't want to dissipate the few extra minutes he'd gained by accepting hospitality.

"No, I'm fine, thank you. My DC bought some coffee en route."

A flicker of alarm crossed her face.

"Your DC? I thought you'd come alone."

"I am alone. He has another appointment in the city."

"I see. I understand Mr Jeremy Forster, from the Home Office, has been in touch with you?"

"Yes, we've spoken briefly on the phone."

"So, you understand that there must be strict boundaries to our discussion?"

"Absolutely, but Mr Forster did say that I could ask you any questions that might help me solve the case I'm working on. I've been told not to stray into the detail of the Brocklesby Farm murders, that's all."

"I see," she said again. "How do you wish to proceed?"

For a moment Tim was flummoxed. He'd taken so much trouble merely to secure this interview that he hadn't thought through the details of how to tackle it. There was one vital question for her to answer, but he didn't want to frighten her off by broaching it too soon. He saw that she sensed his embarrassment and was not amused by it. Tim recovered himself quickly.

"Dr Astani, you've been kind enough to tell us about the assessment you made of Grace Winter - Grace Arkwright, as she then was - four years ago. Before we get on to other matters, may I ask if you wish to add anything to what you said the other day?"

"If you mean, am I holding something back about Grace's psychology as she presented during my examinations, the answer is no. As I said, she seemed to be very well-adjusted. Surprisingly so, considering the trauma she'd suffered."

"Did you ask her directly about that night at Brocklesby Farm?"

"To a certain extent. As you can imagine, the police

handling the case were desperate to know if she'd seen anything, even though she was too young to testify."

"What did you ask her?"

"I asked her if she remembered getting into the cupboard where she was found and if she'd herself decided to take refuge there, or whether someone had helped her."

"Was that question suggested by the police?"

"Yes. But her reply wasn't useful to them. She said she couldn't remember getting into the cupboard, or why she'd done so."

"Did you believe her?"

"I had no reason not to. Besides, hers was a very normal reaction. It's common for children who've survived a traumatic incident to block out aspects of it, particularly horrific events they can't come to terms with."

"What else did you ask her?"

"I asked her if she remembered being rescued from the cupboard. She said she did, that a policeman had lifted her out and carried her to her uncle, who was waiting outside."

"That's accurate: it's confirmed by the police reports. Did she show any particular reaction when her uncle was mentioned?"

"No. I thought she seemed quite fond of him. She certainly wasn't repelled by the idea of speaking about him. I couldn't be sure how much she actually knew about the murders. She didn't say that she knew Tristram Arkwright had been accused of them."

"Did she understand he was her only surviving close relative?"

"I certainly didn't put that to her! But the one curious thing about all my talks with her was that she persisted in talking about her little sister, Laura, as if she were still alive. In her own mind, therefore, I don't think she did know that all her relatives were dead. Of course, it's always difficult to gauge how a child of that age processes the concept of death."

"She was told that Laura had died with the others?"

"Yes, as gently as we could. She talked about Laura a great deal. And always in the present tense."

"As a psychologist, what do you make of that?"

"Sometimes when children are faced with an unbearable burden of pain or guilt, they edit it out by pretending that whatever caused it didn't happen. They may come to believe this. It can present in adults, too, though more rarely and usually when they're very disturbed."

"But you said you didn't think Grace was disturbed."

"No, but she was a young child. I wouldn't say this was an unusual copying mechanism in a little girl of six."

"What about Tristram Arkwright?"

Lenka Astani had relaxed visibly as their conversation progressed. She'd abandoned her stiff manner and become more earnest as she grew absorbed in the conversation about Grace, leaning forward in her seat and making eye contact with Tim. But as soon as Arkwright's name was raised, she drew back and immediately assumed her previous hauteur.

"What about him, DI Yates?"

"I'd like to ask you about his relationship with Grace," Tim said, as firmly as he dared. "But firstly, could you tell me what conclusions you drew about him, as a professional psychologist?"

"Are you asking me to summarise my assessment of Tristram Arkwright?"

"Yes, if you could. A summary's fine. I don't need to know all the details."

"It was my opinion that he was – is – suffering from narcissistic personality disorder. He has an inflated idea of his own importance and tends to be melodramatic, continually casting himself in a starring role – as I believe the police statements illustrate."

"Would that make him into a killer?"

"Not necessarily, but if someone to whom he was close did something that he regarded as outrageous, particularly if it threatened his self-esteem, it could goad him to kill. Did goad him to kill. You must remember that he would regard his own interests and concerns as paramount and he'd expect others to do the same. But if you change your mind and decide you are interested in the details, I was examined and cross-examined about this at some length during his trial. I'm sure you can access the relevant reports."

She looked at her watch.

"I can give you another ten minutes or so, DI Yates. Then I really will have to ask you to leave. I've got a considerable amount of work to do before I go to court today."

Tim took a deep breath.

"Of course," he said. "I'm very grateful to you for sparing the time when you're so busy. There's just one other thing . . ."

"What's that?"

"Did Tristram Arkwright ever talk to you about Grace or his relationship with her?"

"Why do you ask?"

Tim shrugged.

"It just seems logical. After all, you were counselling both of them. And, as you're aware, Grace's name and identity was kept out of the murder trial almost entirely, so if he did mention her to you, that information wouldn't have been included in the published evidence."

There was a very long pause.

"He did talk about Grace, yes."

"What did he say about her?"

"He asked me how she was, every time I saw him. Apparently, he'd first asked the police officers who arrested him and then the warders at the prison where he was kept on remand the same question, but he didn't trust their answers."

"Was he talking about who was going to look after her, or her health generally, or her mental state?"

"Mainly the first of those. I did find it odd . . ."

"What did you find odd?"

"He seemed to show a great deal of empathy for Grace during our meetings. More than I would have expected from a narcissist. His behaviour at the trial, when he masked any feelings he might have had for her or alternatively showed that he didn't in fact have any, was much more typical."

"Did he know that Amy Winter had decided to adopt Grace?"

"I believe that he encouraged that idea. Amy went to see him in prison, I understand at his request."

"Do you know if he saw Grace again after the shootings?"

"He took her from the policeman's arms when she was rescued from the farm and went with her in the ambulance. But you know that already. I don't know if she saw him again after that, but she may have done. He wasn't arrested immediately. I'm certain she hasn't seen him since his arrest."

"Did you ever ask him why he seemed so concerned about Grace?"

There was a long pause.

"Not in the way that you suggest. I didn't ask him point-blank what his feelings for her were."

"But you did ask him something to do with her?"

"Inadvertently, yes."

Lenka Astani pushed up her sleeve and glanced at her watch again. Tim suddenly lost patience.

"Dr Astani, I must ask you to be a little more co-operative than by answering my questions either cryptically or briefly, whichever you see fit. I am aware that you're holding back something about Tristram Arkwright, and your behaviour convinces me that if you were to tell me what it is it would help me find Tina Brackenbury's killer, and her daughter's."

Lenka Astani looked crushed. She made a feeble attempt at regaining the upper hand.

"There's no need to shout, DI Yates."

"I'm sorry," said Tim shortly. "But I need to know. What was the question you asked Arkwright that 'inadvertently' led him to tell you something about Grace?"

"I knew that the Arkwrights only adopted Tristram when he was about three years old. I asked him if he could remember his natural parents. He said he couldn't, he'd been told they were both dead and that his first memories were of foster parents who'd given him up to the Arkwrights."

"I don't see . . ."

"Give me a chance, DI Yates," Lenka Astani said coldly. She composed herself, folding her hands neatly on the top of her desk before she continued. "I asked him if he'd ever known any of his blood relatives – whether, for example, he had aunts or uncles, perhaps a grandmother, who might have visited him when he was in foster care."

"And?" snapped Tim. She gave him a look that was could have been stern or stricken.

"He said he'd never known any of his relations as a child, if any existed. That to his knowledge Grace was the only blood relative he had."

"But Grace wasn't a blood relative. Jacqueline Arkwright was also adopted, and from a different family, wasn't she?"

"Precisely." She was staring at him now, waiting for him to understand.

"You mean . . . are you telling me that Arkwright claimed to be Grace's father?"

"Precisely that. He said he wouldn't bring it up at the trial: that he wanted to keep her name out of the papers."

"What was your reaction?"

"I didn't believe him for a minute. I thought it was another attempt at self-aggrandisement, of making himself mysterious and important. What he said threw interesting light on his character, but it wasn't information that could be used to help him in court."

"It's not possible it was true?"

"It's highly unlikely, don't you think, DI Yates? I don't know much about Jacqueline Arkwright – she was dead before I started working on the case – but I know the police discovered that she became estranged from her parents when she was eighteen until Grace was born and then only saw them intermittently before Laura's birth. There was no evidence that Tristram had kept in touch with her; and he seemed quite irritated by her when we spoke of her. As I said, by far the most likely explanation for his claim was to make himself sound interesting. And the reason he didn't want it mentioned in court could have been to protect Grace, as he

315

said, but more probably because he knew it wouldn't bear scrutiny."

"Were any tests carried out to try to establish Grace's paternity?"

"No; no-one asked for any, including Tristram himself."

"So there is a possibility – just a chance – that he was telling the truth?"

"I was afraid you might jump to that conclusion, DI Yates. That's one of the reasons why I was reluctant to tell you. Mr Forster said that I could tell you if pressed, but now you have he will certainly want to speak to you again."

"Why do you say that?"

"Because my other reason for holding back is that Tristram Arkwright is about to launch another appeal against his conviction. And this time, I believe, he is going to try to play the paternity card. And now, DI Yates, you really must excuse me. I've now told you absolutely everything I know that could be of possible relevance to your case, and, frankly, I think you'll be wasting your time if you try to explain the Brackenbury murders by somehow linking them to the ridiculous idea that Grace is Tristram's daughter. I have copied all of the formal psychiatric assessment of Arkwright that Mr Forster has authorised me to disclose. It's in this file, if you wish to take it. Naturally, it contains no reference to his bizarre claim."

Tim rose to his feet. Dr Astani also stood and held out the file. Tim took it.

"Goodbye, DI Yates. I wish you well with your investigation. If I can be of any further help, please let me know."

The irony of her parting offer incensed Tim; nevertheless, she had been helpful, even if the process of getting the information out of her had been worse that drawing hen's teeth. He took the file and then her proffered hand, which again fluttered in his own for seconds before she drew it back.

"Thank you for your time, Dr Astani. I've appreciated it."

She escorted him to the door and closed it firmly behind him. As he walked back to his car he reflected on Arkwright's 'disclosure'. It would certainly have electrified the courtroom if he'd announced that he was Grace's father during his trial. Someone of Arkwright's cast of mind would have revelled in such notoriety. The main reason for concluding that the paternity claim was a lie was that Arkwright had tested it out on his psychologist to see if it would work; her scepticism had persuaded him it wouldn't. She must have been right: it was a red herring and Tim would lose valuable time if he tried to pursue it while investigating the Brackenbury murders.

As he climbed into his car and started the engine, another thought struck him: had Tristram Arkwright persuaded Grace he was her father? The key to understanding Grace's behaviour might not lie in the actual fact of her parentage so much as what Grace herself believed.

Chapter 65

I CAN HARDLY believe my luck when I contact Sunley's, a local firm of solicitors, and am told that Nigel Sunley, who specialises in representing children, is available and willing to support Grace. I ask him when he can come to the station and he says 'immediately'. His offices are in Pinchbeck Road: barely ten minutes' brisk walk away. He'll be with me a good half-hour before Tom Tarrant arrives with Chloe.

From our brief telephone conversation, I imagine Nigel Sunley to be in his fifties, perhaps a portly senior partner who can afford to take on pro bono and legal aid clients. I'm surprised, therefore, to discover that although he's certainly portly, he can barely be out of his twenties. Earnest and idealistic and wearing thick-lensed, round-rimmed spectacles, he looks like a thick-set version of the young W.B. Yeats and speaks like an upper-class character in a 1930s whodunnit.

I outline Grace's story as quickly as I can.

"You're saying she's been involved in two sets of multiple murders?" he asks. "Poor girl."

I nod.

"I know this sounds callous," I say, "but Grace is a very alarming child. It's difficult to warm to her."

He scrutinises me through his bottle-glass lenses.

"Not very surprising, is it?" he says. "You probably wouldn't let people get too close to you if they kept on dying. She may think it's her fault. I take it she's had psychiatric support?"

"Yes. Although both the psychologists who've examined her think that she's weathered her experiences quite resiliently."

"Including these latest deaths?"

"No. We're gradually questioning her, but no psychological assessment has been made yet. We've been advised that it's too soon."

"Really?" He looks sceptical. "So what's my brief? Presumably you think Grace may have committed a crime?"

"We think it's possible. She's changed her story several times, but the more we question her, the closer we think we're getting to the truth. And if she does confess something . . ."

" . . . you need her to have her own solicitor present; otherwise you might be accused of coercion, or, perish the thought, charge her with something that doesn't hold up in court."

"You make us sound very cynical when you put it like that. You may not believe this, but it is Grace's welfare that most interests us. We're aware that she's only just at the age of criminal responsibility, but, if she has committed a crime, she needs help."

"And it would also help you if you had enough evidence against her and/or the disabled man to say your crime was solved and close the case."

I feel my face flush.

"That's true, too. I'm not trying to deny it."

"You say there was another girl with her when she returned to her foster mother's house?"

"Yes. Chloe Hebblewhite. She's coming in for further questioning this morning. She was unwell after the bodies were discovered."

"What do you mean by 'unwell'?"

"Quite hysterical. Unable to face up to the deaths. And, I'd say, troubled about something she won't talk about."

"She's fit for questioning now?"

"Her mother seems to think so."

"Will the mother accompany her?"

"No. She has other children, one of whom has a meeting with his probation officer this morning. Chloe will be accompanied by a responsible adult, Tom Tarrant, a social worker whom she knows and trusts."

"And the mother's happy with this?"

"Yes. As a matter of fact, I'm quite pleased that Mavis Hebblewhite won't be with Chloe. She seems to be afraid of her mother."

"I see. You're going to have to be very careful how you question Chloe, particularly if she does say something that incriminates herself or Grace. I can't represent them both if they should be charged, but I can sit in on the interview with Chloe if you wish; make sure it's conducted appropriately."

I try not to let him see how irritated I am by his judgmental attitude. I know his offer is a generous one and could be of crucial importance. Superintendent Thornton will be furious if we're accused of manipulating child witnesses.

"That's very kind, thank you. I'd like to accept, but first perhaps you'll let me get Chloe settled? As I've said, she's a nervous child and she's not expecting you to be here. And I'll need to explain your presence to Tom Tarrant, as well."

"You can rely on me to treat Chloe sensitively. I'm trained to work with child witnesses and I happen to care a great deal about supporting them properly. Why don't you introduce me to Chloe *and* Tom? Then I can talk to Chloe for a few minutes while you brief him."

"Ok," I say doubtfully. "I'll ask PC Tandy to sit in with you while I'm away. Chloe knows her."

"As you wish."

Tom and Chloe arrive a few minutes later. Chloe is pale but seems quite calm and is neatly dressed in a summer frock with a round collar and smocking on the bodice. Although it fits her, the style is one I'd have expected to appeal to a younger child. Is Mavis trying to make her look more childish than she is?

Nigel Sunley is waiting in the open-plan area.

"Chloe, this is Mr Sunley," I say. "He's going to take you into the room over there talk to you. Tom and I will be with you soon."

Tom bridles immediately.

"What's going on?" he says. "She ought not to be . . ."

At once, Chloe looks alarmed, but Nigel Sunley crouches down and brings his face level with hers.

"Hello, Chloe," he says. "You can call me Nigel. I'm just here to help you, if you need me. Nothing to worry about."

Chloe is reassured. As he straightens up to his full height, she slips her hand in his. Verity Tandy appears at that moment.

"Hello, Chloe," she says. "It's nice to see you again. Let's go and get a drink, shall we?"

Chloe looks at Tom, who has the presence of mind to nod and smile.

"It's all right, Chloe. I'll be there in a couple of minutes."

"What the fuck . . ." Tom says, as soon as they've all disappeared. "Who is Sunley? Another psychiatrist? Why didn't you tell me about him?"

"He's not a psychiatrist; he's a solicitor – one who special-ises in defending juveniles."

"Are you intending to accuse Chloe of something? Because, if so, I've brought her here under false pretences."

"No, and you haven't. I just want to question her. Nigel Sunley's the solicitor we've appointed to represent Grace. I first asked him less than an hour ago, which is why I couldn't tell you he'd be here. He pointed out that if our questioning of the two girls has reached the point where Grace might need a solicitor, Chloe should be offered one, too."

"I understand enough about the law to know that he can't represent both of them, especially if one accuses the other of a crime."

"That's right, he can't, but he can be present today while we question Chloe. After that, if she needs a solicitor, we'll find someone else for her. It was his suggestion that he should stay. I'm certain that he has Chloe's interests at heart: he more or less told me that he doesn't trust the police to handle well the questioning of minors. But he also said that, if we get it wrong, any evidence we obtain from Chloe will be inadmis-sible. Which is correct."

"And if I object?"

"As the responsible adult accompanying Chloe, you're en-titled to do that, and we may have to postpone the interview. I'm not sure how that would help anyone, but if that's what you want to do I can't . . ."

"Just let me think it through for a minute." Tom leans against the wall, his head bowed, pressing the sides of his forehead with both hands. He looks up after a long pause.

"I should have asked this before: what do you think Chloe might have to tell you that merits the presence of a solicitor?"

"I don't know. I'm not even sure she does need the solicitor. One thing I'm certain of is that neither she nor Grace has told us the truth about what they were doing last weekend. Either they've left something out or they've twisted the facts: told lies, in other words. That's what I want to get to the bottom of."

"All right. I agree that Sunley can stay. But if you get anywhere near bringing a charge against Chloe, I insist that you stop. Chloe must have her own solicitor then."

"I think we're both in agreement about that. Making serious charges against minors is a delicate process: we'll have to do it by the book."

Chapter 66

RICKY WAS WAITING when Tim drove past the builders' yard to pick him up, consuming the final morsel of a bacon sandwich.

"Any joy?" said Tim, as Ricky wiped his fingers on a piece of greaseproof and got into the car.

"Doubtful," said Ricky. "Frankie Wright's a bit of a fly-by-night, but he has shown up regularly for work since he was hired on a temporary contract a couple of weeks ago. He was definitely at work on Monday."

"What about last weekend?"

"He was out drinking with a couple of his new mates on Saturday. It seems they went on a right little pub crawl. So his story is backed up there. Neither of them saw him during the day on Sunday, but from what they were saying they probably all had thick heads. He met one of them again on Sunday evening and they had a few more drinks, apparently. To be honest, I can't tell if they're telling the truth or just covering for him. They're a pretty shifty lot. But if they're providing a false alibi, he'd have had to brief them; anyway, we can check with the pubs."

"We'll get the uniforms on to that. Like you, I doubt they'll find anything, but it's worth a try. What about the Winter connection?"

"The foreman says he's responsible for hiring all casuals. If Norman Winter knows Wright, we'd have to find other evidence they were connected."

"It seems an unlikely coincidence that Wright was the boy-friend of Grace's foster-mother. But let's park that for the time being; we might have to return to it later."

"How did you get on with the shrink?"

"She was just about co-operative, but prickly. She dropped one bombshell, though: when she was assessing Tristram Arkwright, he claimed to be Grace's father."

"Wow!" Ricky let out a piercing whistle.

"Ow, do you have to do that? I wouldn't get too excited about it, if I were you. Astani thinks he was making it up and I'm inclined to think she's right. What interests me is whether Grace believed it."

"What about the Winters?"

"If you remember, Amy Winter said no-one knew who Grace's and Laura's fathers were."

"Do you think she knew of Arkwright's claim?"

"It's possible. We both thought she was hiding something from us: it could have been that. I've been trying to work out what else could have influenced her decision to adopt Grace. I thought the reason she gave us was pretty feeble, especially as there seems to be no love lost between her and Grace."

"Do you want to interview her again?"

"Probably, but not yet. Arkwright's claim doesn't incriminate her in any way, particularly as it wasn't taken seriously. And we can't just turn up at Brocklesby Farm on spec: she isn't a suspect in the Brackenbury case. If we see her again, you can bet her husband'll want a solicitor to be there."

"What next, then?"

"Juliet's going to interview Chloe Hebblewhite this morning. She's also looking to appoint a solicitor for Grace. We'll interview Grace today, as well. We need to get the truth from those two girls. Then we'll have a better idea of whether anyone else is involved and, if so, who. We may be over-complicating this case. It may be quite separate from the Brocklesby Farm killings."

"You don't think so, though, do you?"

"I don't like coincidences. I think they're over-rated."

Chapter 67

As TOM AND I enter the interview room, Chloe is chatting happily to Nigel Sunley. She, Nigel and Verity are all seated at the table. Someone's set a glass of milk in front of Chloe. She stops for a moment when she sees us, then carries on with her anecdote. Nigel is giving her his full attention, smiling and nodding and listening intently to her stories.

Verity stands up and comes across to me.

"May I go now? I'm supposed to be helping with the house-to-houses again." She looks weary: it's not surprising. The house-to-house investigations have spread far beyond the Dymokes. Everyone in the force knows that they're just for window-dressing now, the main plank of a manoeuvre designed to convince the public of the thoroughness of the police investigation and the Chief Constable that he's paying for 'proper' policing,

"Sure. Thanks for helping out."

"She's quite a nice kid," Verity whispers. "Not too bright: starved of attention, I'd say."

I nod. Tom walks past me and sits down. I can see he's uneasy about Sunley's presence; I'm myself a bit worried that Sunley will steal the limelight and run the interview the way he wants it to go. As if he understands this, Sunley stands and, taking his chair, moves to the corner of the room.

"That was very interesting, Chloe," he says. "I'm going to

sit over here, as I'm just watching, but we'll talk some more later."

Chloe looks disappointed, but she nods calmly enough. Close up, her face is very pale and there are dark shadows under her eyes. Her lower lip is cracked and sore, as if she's been chewing it.

Tom moves closer in to the table. I set the tape, explaining the procedure to Chloe as I go. It doesn't interest her in the way it fascinated Grace.

"Listen, Chloe," I say, "this is nothing to worry about. Now that you're better, I just want to ask you a few questions about what happened last weekend, and on Monday. Is that all right?"

"Yes," she says tremulously. Already she's getting upset. Her hand is lying on the table. Tom gives it a quick pat.

"It really isn't anything to worry about, Chloe. Just tell the truth. That's all we're asking."

"What if I can't remember?"

"Just say so. We'll understand."

She sips her milk. I give her a few moments, until she puts down the glass.

"Grace came to stay with you last weekend, didn't she, Chloe?"

"Yes."

"Does she often come?"

"Not to stay. She comes round a lot. And I go round to hers."

"Why did she stay this time?"

"Grace thought of it. She said it would be nice. And Mam didn't mind, because she likes Grace."

"Did you want her to come?"

"Yes. No-one plays with me at home."

"What did you and Grace do?"

"We went to Crowland. I know Mam doesn't believe us – she says it's too far for us to have got – but we did go to Crowland, honest we did, and . . ."

"I believe you, Chloe. I'd like to know a bit more about it. What time did you set off?"

"I dunno. Mam says it wasn't that early. It was after we'd had breakfast."

"And that was on Monday?"

Chloe looks blank.

"It was on the same day that you went round to Grace's house later on and saw DI Yates and me there?"

"Yes."

"Did you go out earlier on Monday? Before you went to Crowland?"

"No."

"Did Grace go out earlier on Monday?"

"No."

"And when you came back from Crowland you went straight to your house for sandwiches?"

"Yes."

"OK, I'm reasonably clear about what you and Grace did on Monday. What about Saturday and Sunday?"

Chloe looks blank again.

"What about them?"

"Grace came to stay on Saturday, didn't she?"

"I forget."

"I think she did come on Saturday, as she and your Mum both say so."

Chloe doesn't reply.

"So, what did you do on Saturday? Do you remember?"

Chloe darts a glance at me, then slides her eyes across to the glass of milk, which she grasps again.

"We was just round and about. We didn't do much."

"Did you go out on the bikes on Saturday?"

"No. Grace hasn't got a bike and Jagger wouldn't let her have his."

"But she took Jagger's bike to Crowland on Monday, didn't she?"

"Yes. Mam said she could have it, so Jagger had to let her."

"Was Monday the only day she borrowed Jagger's bike?"

"Yes."

"You're quite sure of that?"

"Yes."

"And you're sure you didn't go out on your bike on Saturday? On your own, maybe?"

"There wouldn't have been no point in that, would there, if Grace hadn't got a bike?"

Chloe has become very tense. I can see she might burst into tears at any time. I know I must ease up on her.

"What about Sunday, Chloe?"

She brightens immediately.

"We was at home all day. Jagger and Donny was in a good mood in the morning. We played ball with them in the garden for a bit. Then me Gran came."

"Did your grandmother come in the afternoon?"

"Before that. She comes to dinner on Sundays. Then it rained. She read me and Grace some stories."

"Ok, thank you. Can you remember what time you got up on Sunday?"

Chloe shrugs. She's a lot happier now.

"Same time as usual, I s'pose. We had breakfast, then Mam was getting ready for Gran. Told us to get out from under her feet. That's when Jagger said we could play ball."

"Did either you or Grace go anywhere on Sunday?"

"No, I've said."

"Did either of you go to Grace's house at all between Grace arriving at your house on Saturday and when you both came to Grace's on Monday afternoon?"

Chloe is silent. She looks stricken.

"Chloe, can you answer DS Armstrong's question?" Tom says gently.

"We never. It wasn't us."

She puts her hand to her mouth as soon as she has spoken.

"What wasn't you, Chloe? What didn't you do?"

"We never went into the house," she says shakily.

"Did you go near the house?"

"Yes. But we didn't go in."

"Why did you go there?"

"Grace said she wanted me to see Bluebelle."

"How did you get there?"

"We walked."

"You say you didn't go in. Did you go through the gate?"

"Yes."

"Did you see anyone?"

"Yes, we saw an old man. He was standing outside."

"Did you speak to him?"

"No."

"Did Grace?"

"No, but she give him . . ."

She falls silent again and bites hard on her sore lip, drawing beads of blood. I sense I don't have much longer before Chloe collapses in tears.

"What did she give him, Chloe?"

"I forget."

"Did you see Tina, Grace's Mum, or Bluebelle?"

"No."

"Did you go into the house?"

"No!"

"Which day was this, Chloe? Was it on Saturday?"

She relaxes a little.

"I suppose so. Or it could have been Sunday."

"But you said you were playing ball with your brothers on Sunday, and then your Gran came."

"It was Saturday, then."

Chloe tries to smile at me.

"Chloe, when did you last see Tina and Bluebelle?"

Chloe grabs hold of the glass of milk again. She holds the base of it in the palm of her left hand, twisting it with her right. Her face, already pale, is ashen.

"Chloe?"

She slams down the glass with such force that it cracks. Milk gushes out of the gash.

"I'm sorry, I didn't mean to . . ."

"It's all right, Chloe, don't worry about the glass," says Tom, mopping at the spillage with a tissue. I repeat my question calmly and slowly, in as friendly a voice as I can.

"Chloe, when did you last see Tina and Bluebelle?"

She raises her head and stares at me; she's like a trapped animal, her eyes so filled with panic and anguish that I'm smitten with pity for her. Nigel Sunley stirs uneasily in his seat. I know if Chloe doesn't answer I won't get away with asking the question again.

She's clutching the edge of the table, her knuckles white with the pressure. She emits an inhuman sound: a roar of pain.

Chloe is sobbing now, tears coursing down her cheeks and making them dirty, a bubble of green snot inflating in one nostril. She's an unprepossessing and terrified little girl, ugly and lost.

"It wasn't meant to be for real," she cried. "I thought it was a game. Grace said it was a game!"

Nigel Sunley stands up.

"I think we need to call a halt there, don't you, DS Armstrong?"

Chapter 68

NIGEL SUNLEY AND I leave the interview room. Tom stays behind to comfort Chloe.

"What now?" I say, when we're out of earshot.

"What's your opinion on what you've just heard?"

"It seems as if Chloe's confessing . . ."

"Let's not jump to any conclusions, even though I know what you were going to say and you may be right. What I meant was, do you think Chloe was telling the truth?"

"Towards the end of the interview, I think she was. She practically had to rip the words out of herself. She didn't want to have to say them. Earlier on I think she was trying to be evasive, but she only succeeded in confusing herself."

"I agree. I think we need to speak to the officer in charge of the investigation."

"DI Yates isn't here yet. He's been to Lincoln to interview another witness. He's probably on his way back to the station now."

"I don't mind waiting for him, provided he arrives soon. You won't be able to keep Chloe here for long without contacting her mother. And she needs a solicitor."

"Won't you represent her?"

"You engaged me to represent Grace Winter. As I explained earlier, they must have separate solicitors. And if what you and I both think Chloe was saying is true, Grace needs me more than she does."

"Do you have a colleague who can represent Chloe?"

"Not at Sunley's, but I'm in touch with various people who specialise like myself. There's someone in Nottingham who might be able to help."

"Mr Sunley! What brings you here?" Superintendent Thornton's voice comes booming over my shoulder. He sounds wary.

Nigel Sunley steps past me and holds out his hand.

"Superintendent Thornton! You're well, I hope? I've just been assisting DS Armstrong. Perhaps we could have a word with you in private?"

Chapter 69

TIM THUNDERED UP the stairs at the station, arriving noisily in the open-plan area. He scanned the row of desks. Andy Carstairs was seated there, alone.

"Where's Juliet?" Tim demanded brusquely.

"She's with Superintendent Thornton. And Nigel Sunley."

"Isn't Sunley the solicitor that Juliet was going to ask to represent Grace Arkwright?"

"Yes, he . . ."

"Fuck! I asked them not to start without me. I want to speak to Sunley, too. Is Grace here as well?"

"No, but . . ."

"I need to speak to them before she gets here."

"Ok, but . . ."

It dawned on Tim that Andy was trying to tell him something with some urgency.

"What is it, Andy? Have you got a lead from the door-to-doors?"

"Not as far as I know, but before you burst in on the Super and Mr Sunley, I think you should know that he's been sitting in on an interview with Chloe Hebblewhite, that's all. They haven't started discussing Grace yet: the conversation up there's about Chloe."

"I'd forgotten that I asked Juliet to interview Chloe again today. Where is she? Is her mother with her?"

"Chloe's in Interview Room 1. I gather that she's quite

upset. No, her mother isn't with her: Tom Tarrant was asked to be the responsible adult."

"So how does Sunley fit in?"

"I think he was here to see Juliet about Grace and he volunteered to help interview Chloe, too."

Tim sighed.

"That's the trouble with people who work with kids. They're busybodies with a cast-iron pretext: that they have the good of the child at heart. Well, I suppose I'd better . . ."

"Ah, Yates, I thought I heard your voice. Could you come up here, please?"

Tim looked up at the staircase and saw Superintendent Thornton peering down at him. An expert on Thornton's state of mind, he saw immediately that currently his boss's disposition was not a sunny one.

"Yes, sir," Tim said. He glanced back at Andy, who had suddenly become engrossed in tapping out something on his keyboard.

"Shut the door, Yates," said the Superintendent when Tim arrived. He had returned to his desk while Tim was clattering up the stairs. Turning from this task, Tim saw Juliet and Nigel Sunley seated on two of the uncomfortable spindly chairs that Thornton kept in a stack in his office. Both were silent, their faces grave. Superintendent Thornton cleared his throat.

"You find us immersed in a bit of a dilemma, Yates. It would seem that those two girls know more about the Brackenbury deaths than they've let on. Chloe Hebblewhite has as good as confessed and she's implicated Grace Arkwright as well."

"Grace Winter," Nigel Sunley corrected him. The Superintendent withered Sunley with a basilisk stare.

"I think we all know whom I'm talking about."

"What has Chloe confessed to, exactly?" asked Tim.

"She hasn't really confessed. She came close to it and Mr Sunley said she shouldn't say any more until she has legal representation. She was getting pretty distraught by that stage, anyway," said Juliet.

It was Tim's turn to feel irritated.

"Ok, I stand corrected. So what do you *think* she was going to confess to?"

"We mustn't speculate," said Sunley, so smugly that Tim wanted to punch his nose. "However, we can tell you that Chloe said she and Grace had played some kind of game that went wrong. And that it took place at the late Tina Brackenbury's house in Lady Margaret Dymoke Street."

"She made it clear that Grace took the lead," added Juliet.

"Well, she would do, wouldn't she? But given what we know of hers and Grace's characters, it's hard to believe she isn't telling the truth. If Mr Sunley's agreed to represent Grace, presumably we have to find another solicitor for Chloe?"

"Yes, indeed," said Sunley. "That's what I was talking to the Superintendent about when you came in. I have a colleague who works in Nottingham who I think would be suitable. He's trained, like myself, in representing child witnesses and defendants. I just need the Superintendent's go-ahead and then I'll call him."

Unexpectedly, Superintendent Thornton closed his eyes for a few moments.

"My God!" he muttered, "I've never known a case like this. Two little girls! We must tread carefully, very carefully indeed. I don't suppose there's any way we can ... just make this disappear?"

Tim could hardly believe his ears.

"Are you suggesting we should try not to bring a prosecution, even if we have evidence that Grace and Chloe are guilty of murder, or assisting in murder?"

"I suppose that wouldn't be very practicable," said the Superintendent, his voice uncharacteristically feeble.

"'Impracticable' is certainly one way of putting it!" said Tim grimly. Juliet twisted round in her chair and caught Tim's eye. Now was not the time to antagonise their boss.

"I understand what you mean, sir," Tim added in a more mollifying tone. "Subjecting those two children to a trial is the last thing anyone wants. But if the evidence is compelling, of course we'll have no choice."

"More than that, if they're guilty, they need help," said Sunley. "There's a long list of hardened criminals who committed serious offences when they were children and for one reason or another got away with it. If Grace and Chloe are put into a rehabilitation programme, there's still a chance they will make useful citizens one day."

Tim thought the conversation was getting more surreal by the minute: on the one hand, Thornton wanted to avoid a trial because he knew if the police made a single mistake, they'd be heaped with vilification; on the other hand, Sunley was behaving like some kind of Victorian Christian tub-thumper, bent on saving their souls – or at least their social usefulness. Tim himself was just an honest copper trying to solve his case – wasn't he? On reflection, that didn't stand up to scrutiny, either. He turned to his moral yardstick for guidance.

"What do you think, Juliet?"

"I think we should bring Grace in for questioning as soon

as possible; and we need to ask Mr Sunley to contact his Nottingham colleague and see if he will represent Chloe."

Superintendent Thornton gave a long, slow nod. He placed his hands on his desk and folded them neatly.

"Quite so," he said. "Quite so. I think we're all agreed."

It was only after Nigel Sunley had been directed to a spare office to phone his colleague in privacy, Tim and Juliet having been less ceremoniously ejected from Thornton's presence, that Tim remembered why he'd been in such a hurry to speak to her.

"There's something else you need to know about Grace," he said. "We'll brief Sunley when he's finished. At a certain point during his interrogation for the Brocklesby Farm murders, Tristram Arkwright claimed he was Grace's father."

"*Is* he Grace's father?" asked Juliet sharply.

"It's unlikely. He didn't pursue the claim after Lenka Astani refused to give it credence."

"But it wasn't checked out? By DNA tests or blood tests or whatever?"

"No. What I find most interesting about it, though, is not whether he *is* her father, but whether she believes he is."

Juliet thought for a moment.

"I see," she said. "Yes, you're right. That could explain a great deal."

Chapter 70

NIGEL SUNLEY'S COLLEAGUE is available and can come straightaway. His name is Graham Sandwell. It's about a ninety-minute drive from Nottingham, so he should be with us early in the afternoon.

Chloe has calmed down. She's been taken to the canteen by Susan Smith, a motherly desk sergeant who's put many young tearaways at ease. Sergeant Smith knows Chloe's brothers – or perhaps I should say Chloe's brothers are known to her – which pleases Chloe. She doesn't seem to reflect on the circumstances in which they might have met.

While Chloe is eating her lunch, I go to find Tom Tarrant. He's still sitting in the interview room. He looks pretty shaken.

"What will happen now?" he asks.

"We've appointed a solicitor to represent Chloe. He'll be here within the next couple of hours. Then we'd like to interview her again, more formally."

"Are you saying that you're going to charge her with . . . with a crime?" I understand why he's faltering. 'Murder' and 'ten-year-old girl' are incongruous partners.

"First, we have to caution her, assuming that we're all agreed that she's not too vulnerable to be formally interviewed."

"She's ten years old!"

"I know that, but her age alone won't prevent us from interviewing her. Ten is the youngest we interview under caution.

Her mental capacity or mental condition are more likely to present obstacles."

"Recently she's shown signs of hysteria."

"I know that, but her mother said she was better."

"Don't you think Mavis should be here?"

"We must give her the opportunity to be here. I'll call her, and ask if she'd like to attend. Otherwise, are you happy to continue acting as responsible adult?"

"'Happy' is hardly the word I'd use. Let's just get this straight: we're going to be inviting Chloe to incriminate herself in a murder case, correct?"

"She's already said too much for us to be able to let it pass. And you of all people understand that if she has committed a serious crime, she needs help. That means getting at the truth."

Tom sighs.

"I suppose so. Christ, why did I have to pick a job where my heart's always at odds with my head?"

"You think it's easier for me? You'd be wrong. Would you like a sandwich?"

"I'm not hungry . . . oh, all right, then. I'll be able to think better if I keep my blood sugar levels up. Do you want me to speak to Mavis?"

"That might be a good idea. Do you know how to reach her?"

"Her number's in my phone. Her kids are in trouble so much she's had to give it to me. She's got a probation appointment with Jagger today – that's why she couldn't come here. I don't know what time it was: she might not be able to answer now."

"Do you want to give it a try while I fetch some sandwiches?

I'll leave it to you how you put it. You know Tim and I would prefer it if she wasn't here, but if you think she should be we'll respect your decision. Chloe's always uptight when she's around, so I'd be grateful if you'd take that into account."

"Sure. What's the solicitor's name? Do you know?"

"Yes, it's Graham Sandwell. He's coming from Nottingham. I don't know him."

"I don't know him very well, either, but I'm pretty convinced he's represented one of the Hebblewhites before. I'll mention his name to Mavis, see what she says. If he's the bloke I'm thinking of, she'll be pleased."

I nod as sympathetically as I can. I'm struggling to see why we should rejoice if Mavis Hebblewhite likes the lawyer we've appointed. Still, if it's enough to keep her out of our hair . . .

Chapter 71

ONE OF THE nonces was being brought in to see him. Like himself, the bloke was a lifer, and studying for an OU degree in History of Art. Jacobs, his name was, a pallid, soft-spoken guy with one of those cheek-high beards the consistency of a child's toothbrush and pink-rimmed, wideawake eyes. Normally he didn't mind Jacobs, who despite being a kiddy-fiddler was quite cultured: they'd even had a conversation about whether 'nonce' was a variation of 'nonse', an old Lincolnshire word meaning 'good-for-nothing'. But Jacobs felt sorry for himself and he had a whiny voice, both of which were irritating. He'd better behave inoffensively today, if he knew what was good for him. Arkwright was in no mood to make allowances.

He glanced at the ugly 1960s clock that hung high on the library wall: 2 p.m. Jacobs wouldn't be here for an hour or so. Arkwright was mired deep in the lethargy of defeat, but he supposed he'd better find something to do, otherwise Jack Rose would do it for him. He'd been disappointed in Jack these past few days: he'd been much less friendly than usual.

He grabbed a roll of J-cloths and began to dust the bookshelves, moving along the metal rows with his customary thoroughness despite a lack of enthusiasm, lifting the books as he went and lining them up with precision after he'd finished. It was a task he'd performed dozens of times: it gave him plenty of time to think.

He should have known he couldn't trust the Dove woman. He'd credited her with more backbone than she possessed, thinking she was a cut above, but he'd been proved wrong. She'd better not show her face here again. If she did, he'd refuse to see her; better still, he'd let her come and then he'd spit in her face. Who did she think she was? Fucking do-good-er, slumming it in prison for kicks. He was too trusting, that was his problem.

He was in the darkest corner of the library now, just out of range of the CCTV cameras. He knew he couldn't loiter there long before Rose or some other officious little twat told him to move back to where he could be seen. He resolved to keep on dusting until it happened. He continued to pick up the books, slamming them down ostentatiously after he'd cleaned the shelves to prove to any eavesdroppers that he was hard at work.

He hadn't been making it up about liking the kid. Well, maybe he had at first: but she'd certainly got under his skin. He'd honestly wanted that Dove woman to save her. Jackie had never had any backbone, but Grace was different. She had something about her, a certain poise, a palpable sense of purpose, even when she was six. There was a logic to her idea of justice; he understood that. He wondered what would happen to her now. He'd have been proud to call her his daughter. In a sense she *was* his daughter: she shared his legacy.

"Move out from behind those shelves, Arkwright, where I can see you. You know better than to skulk about down there."

High volts of rage shot through him. His face felt as if it had been studded with red-hot needles.

"Why don't you f . . ."

"Yes?" said the voice, with an amused sneer. "What was you going to say, Arkwright?"

Chapter 72

MARIE ARRIVES, RED-FACED and angry. She is accompanied by Grace, who is preternaturally calm and very demure. She's wearing the black dress with the white collar in which Mavis had dressed her for her second interview. I wonder whether this was Marie's idea, or whether Grace herself thought it appropriate. Marie is holding Grace's arm and propels her forward slightly as they enter. Grace stands in front of the bank of desks, at once self-possessed and detached from what is happening.

"Where's Tom?" I can see that Marie's at her most truculent: I've already anticipated she'll be on Grace's side in the interview, but I hadn't bargained for such open hostility. I hope she won't compromise her position as responsible adult so much that we must waste time finding someone else to accompany Grace.

"He's in Interview Room 1. He's just having a bite of lunch."

"Can I speak to him?"

"Of course. But he's here to help Chloe. He won't be sitting in on Grace's interview."

Grace snaps out of her good-girl role and is suddenly all ears. Her expression changes. It's no longer bland and circumspect: some powerful emotion crosses her face, but it's difficult to interpret. Rage at Chloe, or fear that Chloe will say something that Grace has forbidden her to reveal? I think back to Tim's glimpsing Grace twisting Chloe's arm in the living room of Tina Brackenbury's house and of her malignant scowl as Chloe stood at her bedroom window watching her leave the Hebblewhites'.

"That's fine," snaps Marie, "but I still want to see him. And you, and DI Yates. If that's all right with you."

Grace quickly looks down at her feet, but not before I catch her smirking. Marie's always been emotional, but it's hard to believe she is behaving as unprofessionally as this. Grace seems to have her completely in her pocket.

"All right. I'll find someone to take care of Grace."

Nigel Sunley appears at that moment. He takes in the situation quickly. I'm not sure if he knows Marie, but I'm guessing their paths will have crossed.

"Can I help?" he says. "Are you Grace?"

Grace nods. He holds out his hand. Grace hesitates for a moment, then takes it, smiling innocently. He gives hers a little squeeze: it's not so much a handshake as a gesture of reassurance.

"My name is Nigel Sunley. I'm a solicitor, and I've been asked to represent you. That means I've come to sit with you in your interview and to help you answer the questions." He bows slightly in Marie's direction. "Ms Krakowska and I have met before. We're colleagues. She'll tell you that you can trust me. You've heard her say she needs to talk to some of the other people here before we start the interview. Perhaps DS Armstrong could offer somewhere we can wait together? I'd like to get to know you a little better."

Marie looks uncertain, then suddenly yields.

"That will be satisfactory," she says stand-offishly, "as long as you don't discuss the case with Grace in my absence."

"You have my word," says Sunley gravely. "DS Armstrong?"

"I've scheduled Room 3 for Grace's interview," I say. "It's bigger than the others. I'll ask DC Carstairs to show you the way."

"Thank you, I think I know where it is. But if DC Carstairs could rustle up some tea, I'm sure we'd be grateful. Would you like tea, Grace?"

"I'd rather have a Coke." It's the first time Grace has spoken since she arrived. Her voice is plaintive and she sounds more childish than usual.

"I'm sure that can be arranged."

I nod. I look across at Andy, who's been sitting quietly at his work-station, and try to convey non-verbal apologies and thanks. He grins and lopes across to join Sunley and Grace.

"You go and talk to Tom," I say to Marie, as cordially as I can manage. "I'll try to find DI Yates."

"I think he's already with Tom," says Andy over his shoulder. "Tom called him back in after his talk with Mrs Hebblewhite."

"Thanks."

I look at Grace to see if this additional information about Mavis has made an impression on her, but her back is to me and she seems to be chatting to Nigel Sunley.

Tim smiles as I enter Interview Room 1.

"Good news," he says. "Mavis Hebblewhite says she can't get away from the other kids today. She's ok with Tom acting as Chloe's responsible adult."

Marie sweeps into the room. Tim's face falls.

"Hello, Marie," he says. "I didn't realise you'd arrived. Where's Grace?"

"She's with Nigel Sunley," I say. "Marie wants to talk to us before we start the interview."

"All of us? Tom'll be looking after Chloe."

"I know that," says Marie grimly. "And before we get on to Grace, have you made it clear to Mavis Hebblewhite that the investigation has taken a new turn? Does she know that Chloe might be charged with a crime?"

"I've made it as clear as I can," Tom says. "Mavis knows we've appointed a solicitor to represent Chloe and that she will be cautioned when the next interview, with her own solicitor present, takes place."

"And she's comfortable with that?"

"Seems to be. It won't be the first time one of Mavis's kids has been cautioned with a solicitor in tow."

"Does she know you might be charging Chloe with . . ."

Tim holds up his hand.

"You have to stop there, Marie. We mustn't jump to conclusions. We just need to explore further some comments Chloe has made that, on the face of it, sounded as if they might be incriminating. If we read more into it than that at this stage, we might jeopardise the interview."

"But I understand that she's incriminated Grace . . ."

"That's a possible interpretation of what she said. Grace will be interviewed separately and Nigel Sunley will support her. As well as you, of course. You're happy with that?"

"I'm happy that I'll be there myself – I think it's essential if Grace is to be fairly treated. And I acknowledge that Sunley's a good choice, if Grace needs a solicitor. My point is that she's suddenly been transformed from a witness to a suspect because of some chance remark of Chloe's. I had no idea until Juliet called me that this was going to happen."

Marie is raising her voice and becoming more breathless as she gets more strident. Tim's manner changes. I can see that he understands what she is going through.

"Take a seat, Marie. Please." His voice is kind.

Marie hesitates. Her truculence has evaporated; now she looks as if she might burst into tears. Tim slides out a chair for her. She sits down beside Tom. Tim and I take the other two chairs. Tom puts his hand on the teapot standing on the tray I've had sent up from the canteen.

"This tea's still warm. Would you like some?"

Marie nods. She contorts her face horribly, trying not to cry, her Dutch-doll features smudging into each other. Tom pours tea with a shaky hand and passes her the cup.

"Marie," Tim says, "You've given a massive commitment to this case. You began as our adviser and at our request you took on the burden of becoming Grace's responsible adult. You've always had a generous heart and it's natural that you feel sympathy for Grace, particularly as we've asked you to look after her. I know you probably don't believe me, but we all sympathise with her. She's a little girl – I was going to say, 'just' a little girl, but she's more than that. She's a child who's had a difficult life, a horrendous life, in fact. We don't know what sort of effect her experiences have had on her, whether they've damaged her or whether they or something else has caused her to commit a crime, but we have to face up to that possibility, horrible as it is, and difficult though it may be for all of us to get to grips with it. Because we have to find out the truth: for Grace's sake, as much as anyone else's. You do see that, don't you?"

The tears are streaming down Marie's cheeks. She takes out a tissue and dabs at her eyes before burying her face in her hands. Her body is shaking, her sobs profound and stricken.

Eventually she raises her head.

"I just don't know if I'm strong enough to do this," she says. "I never thought I'd hear myself say this, but I don't think I've got the bottle."

I get up and go to kneel beside Marie. I give her an awkward hug.

"If you really can't do it, Marie, we'll find someone else to help Grace."

Marie wipes away more tears.

"No," she says, some of her usual resolve returning. "No. It's best if I do it. Grace trusts me. She needs me to be with her."

Chapter 73

NIGEL SUNLEY AND Grace were chatting comfortably in Interview Room 3 when Tim, Juliet and Marie arrived. Sunley was quite at his ease on police premises. He gestured towards a tray on which cups and saucers were stacked. A large teapot and a half-filled cup sat at his elbow.

"Tea?" he enquired. "I took the liberty to order for everyone."

"No, thanks," said Tim shortly.

Grace was sipping Coke through a straw. She raised her large, limpid eyes and stared at Tim, cocking her head slightly to one side. Without quite grasping why, he felt she was putting him at a disadvantage. He motioned to Juliet and Marie to take seats on the opposite side of the table from Sunley and Grace. He positioned himself to one side of the head of the table, so that it wouldn't look as if he was taking too much control.

"I believe we all know each other," Tim said, looking round the table. "Grace, you've been interviewed before this week, so I think you're familiar with how we use the tape?"

"Yes," said Grace in a flat voice. She pushed the Coke away from her.

"Good. I'm turning the tape on now." Tim's voice changed. He was aware that he tended to sound like a news presenter when making statements to the tape, but he'd never managed to tackle it any differently. "This is DI Yates, interviewing

Grace Winter at 2 p.m. on Thursday 25th August 2016. Present in the room are Ms Marie Krakowska, acting as responsible adult, Mr Nigel Sunley, solicitor advising Grace Winter, and DS Juliet Armstrong." Tim turned to Grace and resumed his normal voice. Juliet noticed that this time she wasn't giggling at the procedure with the tape.

"Now, try not to be frightened, Grace. We just need you to answer some questions clearly and truthfully. Ms Krakowska will support you if you get confused or upset. Mr Sunley may wish to give you advice before you answer some of the questions, or even suggest you don't answer at all. You are free to take his advice. Do you understand?"

"Yes."

"Good," said Tim again. "Now, this is a more formal interview than last time. I have to caution you before we start. Do you understand what that means?"

"Yes. Mr Sunley has said. It's a warning."

"Correct. I'm going to give you the caution now. "Grace Winter, I am going to interview you about the deaths of Tina Brackenbury and Bluebelle Brackenbury, which took place on or about Saturday 20th August 2016. You do not have to say anything, but it may harm your defence if you fail to disclose something that you later rely on in court." Now, Grace, do you understand that as well?"

"Let me test you on it," said Nigel Sunley genially. "Grace, could you give us back the statement DI Yates just read out in your own words?"

"I think so," said Grace slowly. "He says he wants to talk about Mum and Bluebelle dying. I can speak about it if I like."

"That's right. And there's another bit, too. Do you remember?"

Grace gives him a sidelong look.

"I'm not sure . . ."

"What might happen if you don't tell us something, Grace?"

"It won't help me later. If I have to go to court."

"Well done. And do you know what 'court' is?"

"It's where Donny and Jagger have to go when they get into trouble."

"Yes." Sunley looked across at Tim and nodded. "I think she understands, DI Yates."

"Now, Grace," said Tim, "I want you to describe to me what you did last weekend."

"I've already told you that."

"I'd like you to tell me again. Let's start with when you set off for Chloe's. When was that?"

"On Saturday morning. Before dinner."

"Did Chloe come to fetch you?"

Grace hesitated.

"Yes, I think so."

"You only think so? Can't you remember clearly?"

"Yes, she did come."

"Was she there when you said goodbye to your Mum?"

"Yes."

"And where was Bluebelle when you were saying goodbye?"

"Mum was holding . . . no, that's wrong. I think Bluebelle was having a sleep."

Grace looked flustered. Tim wondered if she realised she had almost fallen into a trap.

"When you said goodbye to your Mum, did she seem quite normal?"

"Yes."

"And you hadn't fallen out with her? Had an argument or anything like that?"

"No."

"So then you went to Chloe's house. What did you do there?"

"We just hung around. I wanted to borrow Jagger's bike so we could go out, but he wouldn't let me."

"And you hung around the streets for how long? One hour, two hours?"

"I don't know. It was a long time after dinner. It felt like all afternoon."

"But it wasn't all afternoon, was it? Eventually you decided to go back to your house and take Chloe with you, didn't you?"

"Yes. I wanted her to see Bluebelle."

"Did Chloe want to come with you?"

Grace shrugged.

"She couldn't think of anything better to do. She was ok with it."

"You said the other day you took the bikes, even though Jagger wouldn't let you have his. Why was that? It's only a short walk from Chloe's house to yours, isn't it?"

"I suppose we just felt like it," said Grace, with a touch of defiance.

"But because you took Jagger's bike, Chloe got scared and decided to go home before you went into the house. That's what you said when you were first interviewed. Do you stand by that?"

"Pardon?" Grace fixed Tim with luminous eyes.

"DI Yates means, do you still say that Chloe got scared and went home without going into the house?"

"Oh. Yes."

"But you yourself stayed and you did go into the house. How far into the house did you go?"

"Just into the hall. That was when the man – Marek – brushed past me and I came out again. He put the wind up me. So I went back to Chloe's."

"Did you speak to Marek?"

"No."

"Did you give him anything?"

"I've already told you: no."

"Did your Mum wear jewellery, Grace?"

"Sometimes."

"Did she have a particular piece of jewellery that she liked best, something that she wore most of the time?"

"I forget."

"Let me jog your memory. Have you seen this before?"

Tim produced a small clear package. The chased-silver locket could be seen clearly through the polythene, the necklace of silver beads looped behind it. Tim placed it on the table in front of Grace. She smoothed the polythene with one finger.

"Yes. It's Mum's."

"Marek Wolansky says that you gave it to him as a present."

Grace met Tim's eye and held it. She seemed to be thinking, perhaps choosing her words carefully.

"I don't believe you!" she said boldly.

"Oh. Why is that?"

"He can't talk. He doesn't talk."

"You're right, Grace," said Juliet. "He doesn't talk in a way that most people can understand him. But he does say some words, and his mother knows what he means."

Grace gave Nigel Sunley a mute, questioning look. Tim

realised that this child was querying a point of law with him; not only that, but she was sharper on the uptake than the solicitor himself. Sunley, who had appeared mesmerised by the dialogue so far, sprang into action.

"DI Yates, it's very unlikely that Mrs Wolansky's interpretation of her son's incoherent speech could be allowed to stand as evidence in a court of law."

"Ok. Grace, do you know how Marek could have got hold of the locket, if you didn't give it to him?"

"That question is certainly inadmissible, DI Yates; and if you don't mind my saying so, you should know better. Grace can't be expected to conjecture about such a detail."

Grace put her head on one side again, as she had done earlier, and seemed to appraise Tim. It was an oddly assured gesture which unsettled him considerably. Juliet caught his eye and pointed to herself. Tim nodded.

"Grace," said Juliet, "as I think you know, Chloe was here again this morning. She's still here, in fact. We asked her again about the visit you both made to your house, which I think we've now all agreed took place on Saturday. Chloe doesn't like talking about it. It upsets her."

"She's nesh," said Grace contemptuously. "A lot of things upset her."

"She started telling us about the visit, before she got too upset to carry on. She said something about a game that went wrong. Can you tell us what she meant?"

"No, I don't know. Sometimes I think Chloe's not right in the head. No wonder she gets on Mavis's nerves."

"Chloe's also very keen that we know that you and she did manage to bike all the way to Crowland on Monday. Can you explain that?"

"Yes, it was because Jagger . . . ." Grace stopped suddenly.

"Go on, Grace. It was because Jagger did what?"

"It was because Jagger said I couldn't borrow his bike unless we went on a proper run. He said that he wouldn't lend it to me just for messing around the street on." Grace began this explanation lamely, but by the time she'd finished the first sentence she was sounding more convincing.

"I see. Do you get on with Jagger?"

"He's all right. He doesn't like it when Chloe snitches on him to Mavis. Mavis doesn't like it, either: I think Jagger's her favourite."

"Thank you." Juliet paused. She looked at Nigel Sunley and at Marie, who both stared back at her intently. Tim seemed to be deep in his own thoughts. Juliet felt defeated by a sense of isolation, of being entirely alone. Nevertheless, she knew she had to plough on.

"Do you remember the first occasion that you met DI Yates and me?"

"Yes. It was when me and Chloe came back to my house after the bike ride. There were reporters standing outside."

"You came into the house and we talked to you both. You asked us an unusual question: a question that upset Chloe. Can you remember what it was?"

Grace fixed Juliet with her clear green eyes. They seemed to grow darker as she spoke.

"Yes. I asked if we could see them and Chloe didn't want to."

"When you say 'them', you mean your Mum and Bluebelle?"

"Yes."

"Why did you want to see them? You knew they were dead, didn't you?"

Grace's astonishing power of self-possession appeared to be faltering at last. She rubbed her eyes with her knuckles. When she took her hands away from her face her eyes were glassy, her skin pinched and white. She opened her mouth, but no sound came out of it.

"Grace?"

Nigel Sunley was about to intervene when Grace suddenly blurted a string of garbled, panicky words.

"I thought it would be like last time. I thought my Dad would come. He said he'd come one day. He said I'd know the time. I thought it would be him. I thought he would be there."

Grace leaned back in her chair, deathly pale now. Marie took one of her hands and began to chafe it gently.

"DI Yates," said Sunley quietly, "I think you will agree that this interview should be terminated."

"Yes," said Tim. "For the tape, interview concluded at 2.33 p.m. on Thursday 25th August 2016.

While Juliet and Marie were still bending over Grace, Sunley motioned to Tim to follow him out of the room. Once outside, he said, "You may jump to whatever conclusions you like, but you don't have any solid evidence there to charge her. It would seem that she's linked the Brackenbury deaths to the previous traumas in her life, but that's not surprising, and, from what I know of psychology, not uncommon. I suggest you refer her to a psychiatrist now. It's up to you whether you press on with interviewing Chloe under caution – I suppose you might as well when Graham Sandwell arrives, if you do it sensitively – but if it comes to Chloe's word against Grace's there's no way that the CPS would agree to put those two children through a trial. I suggest that you may find it expedient to drop the case."

Chapter 74

TOM TARRANT EMERGED from the interview room, his face ashen, and walked the length of the office. Tim and Juliet were standing by Juliet's work station, a little apart from Nigel Sunley, who was engrossed in texting on his mobile. Tim stepped forward a couple of paces to greet Tom.

"I'd like to apologise, Tom, for all the wasted effort. It doesn't look as if we'll get anywhere near a prosecution now. I'm sorry that it didn't work out."

Tom glared at Tim for long seconds, his eyes bulging, before he brought his hand crashing down on the desk beside him. Juliet flung out one arm involuntarily and knocked over the plastic cup of water sitting on her work unit. Tom's face had flushed a dull brick red. Juliet had rarely seen anyone so convulsed by fury.

"You're sorry 'it didn't work out'!" he shouted, a spray of spit flecking Tim's jacket. "You 'apologise that we won't be getting a prosecution'! Is that all you ever think about? Can't you see that kid in there is very profoundly damaged? And I'd be surprised if the way she's been treated over the last few days hasn't contributed to that."

Nigel Sunley looked up, frowning, and slipped his phone into his pocket. He moved closer to Tom and put his hand on his arm.

"Steady on," he said. "Try to keep calm, Tom. Grace isn't very far away from us: you don't want her to hear you." He glanced over his shoulder at Tim. "Though I have to say I wholeheartedly agree with every word you've just said."

The colour had drained from Tim's face. He opened his mouth to speak, but was still figuring out how to reply when a harsh voice intervened.

"Yates? What is going on down there? This is a police station, not a bear garden."

Tim raised his eyes, knowing he would see Superintendent Thornton peering crossly over the banister from the floor above.

Nigel Sunley had failed to mollify Tom Tarrant, who shook off Sunley's hand and bawled at Thornton.

"I'll tell you what's going on: your officers have just pushed a ten-year-old child to the brink of a breakdown. Your solicitor mate's told them to lay off. And all they're worried about now is that they might not succeed in getting her put away!"

"You'd better come up to my office," said the Superintendent grimly. "All of you."

"Do you want me to come as well, sir?" asked Andy Carstairs, who had been quietly sitting at his work station during the whole outburst.

"Were you involved in this ... this debacle?"

"Not directly, sir."

"Hmn, well, I'm not sure what you mean by 'not directly', but you'd better stay where you are. Keep everything calm down there. Make sure that child is well-cared for and don't let her leave the building. I'm assuming there's someone with her?"

"Marie Krakowska is with Grace," said Juliet quietly.

"Good. What about the other girl?"

"She's in Interview Room 1, with the desk sergeant," said Andy.

"With the *desk sergeant?*" said Thornton testily. "For what reason?"

"We needed someone sympathetic to look after her," said Juliet. "Susan Smith is used to dealing with children. We've only asked her to stay with Chloe until we can go back to her again."

"And then what do you propose to do? Interrogate her within an inch of her wits? I warned you that I wanted you to tread very carefully on this." Superintendent Thornton favoured Tim with one of his most baleful glares.

"If I may intervene," said Sunley, stepping out from behind Tom Tarrant's bulk so that the Superintendent could see him more clearly, "I've asked Graham Sandwell to represent Chloe and he's on his way. He should be here very shortly. I recommend that, since it's too late to ask him to turn back, we go ahead with the interview as planned. And for the record, sir, although, like Mr Tarrant, I deplore DI Yates's enthusiasm for convicting a child, there was nothing inappropriate about the way she was interviewed. The questions were sensitively handled. They happened to strike a nerve in Grace about her past, which was unfortunate."

The Superintendent hesitated.

"All right," he said. "But only because we must try to establish whether these children were mixed up in the Brackenbury murders, regardless of whether we can charge them. And I still want to speak to DI Yates and DS Armstrong. You may wait here for your colleague, Sunley."

Tim and Juliet trudged up the stairs to Thornton's office, each feeling aggrieved. Juliet shot Tim an appraising look and saw he was up for a fight. Once the door was closed, however, Thornton became conciliatory.

"It's frequently struck me, Yates, how like acting this job is," he said as they sat down. "You realise that we have to show compassion where those children are concerned? It will look very bad otherwise."

"If you'll forgive me for saying so, sir, I think we have been compassionate, particularly Juliet, who has spent most of this week trying to care for Grace Winter. And I don't think either of us feels as if we're acting. I can speak only for myself, but I feel as if I've been . . ."

There was an urgent knock at the door. Tim turned and recognised Andy Carstairs' silhouette through the glass. Superintendent Thornton made a swatting motion with his hand.

"Tell him to . . ."

But Andy had already entered the room.

"I'm sorry for interrupting," he said to Tim, "but Professor Salkeld's on the phone. He says he urgently needs to talk to you."

"Ok, thanks. I need to take this," said Tim over his shoulder as he stood up.

Tim was halfway out of the door before the Superintendent registered it and ran down the stairs, overtaking Andy as he went. The phone was lying on Andy's desk, removed from its cradle. Tim seized it.

"Professor? It's Tim Yates."

"DI Yates, good afternoon. You sound breathless."

"Good afternoon, Professor. I've been running downstairs, that's all."

"Well I hope that you'll think my news worth hurrying

for. As promised, I looked for signs of foreign DNA on Tina Brackenbury's neck. And fingerprints. And I've found better samples of both than I would have expected."

"Have you checked them against the databases?"

Professor Salkeld sighed.

"Now why didn't I think of that? Of course I have, Yates. That's why it's taken me four days to get back to you. Now comes the exciting bit."

"You've found a match?"

"I've actually found two matches: for both the DNA and the fingerprints."

"Is it someone known to us? Here in Spalding, I mean."

"I don't know this person from Adam, but I suspect that you might."

"Go on."

"They belong to a youth offender. A young man named Jagger Hebblewhite. The name sounded a bell. Wasn't one of the two girls I met at the crime scene called Hebblewhite?"

Tim was rapt. "You're quite sure of this?"

"No, Tim, I made it up, just to raise your hopes. I worked through the files until I found one belonging to a youth from Spalding. What do you think?"

"I'm sorry," said Tim, "It's just such an amazing stroke of luck, that's all. I can hardly believe it."

"I wouldn't call it luck," said the Professor huffily. "It was bloody hard work!"

Chapter 75

GRAHAM SANDWELL HAS just arrived. Nigel Sunley, having insisted Grace is transferred to the little-used officers' sick-room next to the canteen and asked Marie to call a doctor to check her over, has returned in time to greet him. Chloe is still in Interview Room 1 with Tom Tarrant, who has emerged briefly to ask for more milk and biscuits and to say she's calmer now.

Sandwell is a big bluff man with watery eyes, I'd guess in his late forties. He breathes stertorously as he labours up the stairs, hampered by his bulk and probably a forty-a-day smoking habit. He smells of cigarettes. His clothes are untidy and old-fashioned and his shoes in need of polish. He seems the least likely person to be buddies with Sunley, but the two shake hands enthusiastically. They're obviously at ease in each other's company.

"Are you ready to meet Chloe?" I say.

Sandwell smiles avuncularly.

"I need a bit more of a briefing first," he puffs. "And a chance to get my breath back."

"I'm happy to brief you," Sunley says. And to me, "May we use Interview Room 3 again?"

"I'd rather we both talked to Mr Sandwell here," I say. "No secrets between us, are there?"

"Of course not," says Sunley smoothly, though I can see he doesn't like it. "Is there some tea for Graham?"

"I'll get it," says Andy quickly. It's a good ruse for getting out of an uncomfortable situation, but perhaps I'm being ungrateful.

Sunley's briefing turns out to be succinct and factual, without any frills or spin. His account of the interviews with Chloe and Grace is much the same as my own would have been. I've already told Sunley briefly that Professor Salkeld has found Jagger Hebblewhite's DNA on Tina Brackenbury's body. He has the manners to refer to me when he arrives at this detail.

"Interesting," says Sandwell. "You're going to have to be very careful how you go about this next interview, you know."

"I'm perfectly aware of that."

"Yes, but I mean you need to stay neutral and not try to jump the gun by apportioning blame. You're going to have to stick religiously to the facts. Are they quite clear in your head, or do you need to write them down? You mustn't, for example, allow what you now know about Jagger to suggest to Chloe that she's also guilty. Or Grace, for that matter, though I understand it's unlikely you'll be questioning her again, at least for today."

Although he's speaking in a kindly way, I find his attitude patronising. I'm yet more insulted when Sunley cuts in.

"You're assuming that DS Armstrong will lead the interview, Graham. Is that a foregone conclusion?"

"It certainly is," I say. "It's my decision, and DI Yates's. We'll do it together, like Grace's interview."

"But you see, that's precisely my point. The interview with Grace ended in tears. I certainly don't think it's wise for both you and DI Yates to be present when Chloe's interviewed again. Overkill, you see, and bound to intimidate a very nervous child."

Reluctantly, I concede there could be some truth in this.

"Very well, I'll ask DI Yates if I can interview Chloe on my own, with just Mr Sandwell and Tom Tarrant present. That should do the trick, shouldn't it? Three against one!"

"I hardly think . . ." Sunley's decided to take offence, but Graham Sandwell raises his hand.

"It'll be fine, Nigel," he says. "Your concern for the child does you credit, but you did say that DS Armstrong handled the interview with Grace sensitively. Situations like this are unpredictable. There's no reason to think anyone else would have done better. If DI Yates is comfortable with it, I agree it's a good idea to have only one police officer at Chloe's interview. Now, may I listen to the tape of your first interview with her?"

Graham Sandwell says he's ready as soon as Andy comes back with his tea. I've tracked Tim down and told him Sandwell wants me to be the sole police interviewer. Tim agrees listlessly: I can see he still thinks we'll get no further with this case.

Chloe's pale but calm when we go into the interview room.

"Chloe, this is Mr Sandwell," I say. "I told you he'd be coming, didn't I?"

She gives Sandwell a sideways look.

"Yes. Why can't Nigel be here? I like him."

"He's explained to you why," Tom says gently. "He's really here for Grace. He was just helping out this morning."

"Don't worry, Chloe, I'll be on your side just as much as Nigel," says Sandwell. "You can call me Graham if you prefer. I know your brother, by the way."

"Which one?" asks Chloe suspiciously.

"I know both your brothers, actually. Donovan and Jagger."

"Donny's a good lad. It's Jagger gets him into trouble. I've got other brothers besides them," Chloe adds, as if this is an achievement.

"Really? Well, it's you we're interested in today. You understand about the tape?"

Chloe nods.

"DS Armstrong's going to turn it on now. That means she'll be recording what we all say to each other until she turns it off again."

"I know."

"Good. Now, Chloe, you're going to have to forgive me for going over the same things again. As you know, I wasn't here this morning when DS Armstrong last talked to you."

"Ok."

"Thank you. I understand that everyone got a bit confused then, perhaps because you talked about so many different things, so I'm just going to concentrate on one of them. I want you to cast your mind back again to when you and Grace went round to Grace's house."

"You mean, when we met the police there?"

"No, not that time. The time before that. Can you remember which day it was?"

"She says it must have been Sat'day," Chloe says, pointing at me.

"Why does DS Armstrong say that?"

"Because me Gran comes on Sundays. And on Monday we *did* bike to Crowland."

"Ok, so DS Armstrong's probably right when she says it was Saturday, then?"

Chloe nods.

"Thanks," I say. "I'll take over now. Chloe, did you go into the house?"

"I never!"

"Did you see Grace's Mum?"

"No."

"Did you see anyone?"

"Only the old man."

"Was the old man standing outside?"

"Yes."

"So you went round to Grace's house but you didn't go in and you didn't see anyone except the old man, and then you went home?"

"Yes."

"Why was that? Did something happen to change your mind? Did the old man tell you off?"

"He can't speak right and in any case I wasn't afraid of him. He's not all there."

"When you went home, did Grace come with you?"

"Not at first. She did come, later."

"So at first she decided to stay. Did she go into the house?"

"She said she was going to."

"Did she open the door, or call out to her mother?"

"I don't remember. P'raps I'd gone by then."

"Why didn't Grace come with you? Did she tell you?"

"She would of, but Jag . . ."

"I think you were going to mention Jagger, your brother. Was he there?"

Chloe's hand flies to her mouth.

"Go, on, Chloe. What were you going to say?"

"Nothing."

"Are you afraid of Jagger, Chloe?"

370

She nods.

"Why is that?"

"He beats me up sometimes. He doesn't let Mam see. She likes him best, anyway."

"Are you afraid of Grace?"

"Not always."

"So you have been afraid of Grace on some occasions? Does she beat you up, too?"

"No, not exactly, but she can be that evil . . ."

"If Grace and Jagger ganged up on you, how would you feel?"

"Scared, I suppose."

"Did Grace and Jagger gang up on you, Chloe? Is that what happened last Saturday?"

Chloe's eyes brim with tears, but she's still in control.

"Yes."

"Are you going to tell me what really happened?"

Chloe looks at Sandwell.

"It's ok, Chloe," he says gently. "Just tell us what you remember."

"Grace said it was a game. She said she'd played it before – it was a kind of trick. She showed me what to do."

"What did she show you? Can you show me?" I ask.

Chloe lays her hands on her own throat and squeezes.

"Like that. She said it was just a joke. She said they'd wake up afterwards. She wanted me to do Bluebelle."

"When did she say this? When did she show you what to do?"

"When we was walking there."

"What did you say?"

"Nothing much. But I'd thought about it by the time we

371

got there and I didn't like it. I told Grace I didn't want to. I said I was going."

"What did Grace do?"

"She called after me that I was nesh."

"Did she try to stop you leaving?"

"She might of. She was coming after me when I got to the gate and I see Jagger in the street. She called out to him."

"What did she say to him?"

"She said I'd let her down. She said I'd agreed to play a game with her and now I wouldn't do it. Jagger came and gave me a clip round the ear. He said I would do what Grace wanted if I knew what was good for me."

"Did he know what Grace wanted you to do at that point?"

"No, she didn't say."

"What happened then?"

"I cried. Jagger said I was useless, that I was always crying. He told me to shut up, says I was drawing attention."

"What about Grace?"

"She says if I'm too scared, she dares him to do it instead. And he says, of course he'll do it, he's up for it, as long as she makes it worth his while."

"And he still doesn't know what it is that Grace wants him to do?"

"No. But she says there is something she can give him. He wants to know what it is, but she just walks back into the yard without answering. She tells Jagger they're going into the house, and that they've got to keep quiet."

"What did you do?"

"Jagger tells me to wait by the door, and let them know if anyone comes."

"Is that what you did?"

"Yes. I waited for ages. And then they come out and tell me they want me to go upstairs with them. I don't want to go, but Jagger gives me a thump and then I do. I didn't go into the bedrooms, though. I just looked from the doorways. I could see they was both in bed. It was very quiet."

Chloe's talking as if in a trance. She's unnaturally serene, as if she's describing a film that's being shown to her. I've no doubt that what we're hearing is the exact truth.

"Jagger wanted to push me closer, but Grace said it was time to leave. We went back downstairs and out the door. The old guy was standing outside. Grace said he was watching us. She told Jagger they'd have to give him summat. She said to Jagger 'give it back' and he handed something over. He didn't want to, but he give it her. She went up to the old guy and give it to him. I don't know what it was, but he was pleased. Grace said we should go, quick, before his Mam came out."

Chloe suddenly starts to shiver violently. The spell is broken.

"What's the matter, Chloe?" asks Tom. "You've done really well. There's no need to be afraid now."

She stares at him through a haze of tears.

"You don't know what you're on about. Mam'll kill me when she knows I've told on Jagger."

Chapter 76

TIM PAUSED AT the gate of Brocklesby Farm, waiting for Juliet to catch him up. Juliet's face was drawn; he'd rarely seen her looking so haggard. He'd have preferred to spare her the hassle by asking Ricky MacFadyen to accompany him, but he needed a woman police officer to be with him.

"You ok?" he said as she drew level with him. She nodded. He remembered he'd ask her the same question before she'd entered Bluebelle Brackenbury's bedroom. It seemed to have happened a lifetime's distance in the past, not a mere few days since.

Out of the corner of his eye, he saw Norman Winter approaching, striding along in his gumboots. Even from thirty yards' distance, he could see the farmer's expression was hostile.

"We'd better wait for him to get here. He's big on his wife's 'fragility'," said Tim quietly.

Winter came storming up to them.

"What do you want here?" he demanded. "You did enough damage last time you came."

"This is DS Armstrong," said Tim. "I'm sorry to trouble you again, Mr Winter, but we need to speak to you and your wife."

"Oh? What's it about this time?"

"It's about your responsibilities as Grace Winter's legal guardians."

"Amy isn't well enough for her to come home yet. If it's a matter of paying . . ."

"There's no question of Grace's coming 'home', Mr Winter," said Juliet. "She's been accused of a serious crime and it's emerged she's very disturbed. She's going to need a prolonged period of psychiatric care. You and Mrs Winter must know about it; you have a right to express your views on how she should be cared for and, if you wish, contribute towards supporting her."

"I see." Norman Winter's complexion switched from ruddy to parchment, as if someone had suddenly siphoned away his blood. "You'd better come in."

He led them into his sitting-room too late to obscure his wife as she knelt on the sofa and swiftly hid a wine glass behind the curtain. She scrambled herself back into a sitting position.

"Hello," she said dully, heavy-lidded eyes not quite meeting theirs. "I thought you'd be back."

"Oh? Why was that, Mrs Winter?"

She shrugged bitterly.

"I just knew you wouldn't be letting this go, that's all."

"Now, Amy," said her husband. "Be careful what you say. DI Yates has come to tell us . . ."

"It's all right, Norman: don't bother. It's time we told the truth. We're never going to get any peace otherwise. Besides, I very much doubt that Grace has spared us."

"Amy!" Norman Winter bellowed.

"I've told you to drop it, Norman!" Amy said sharply. "I'm . . ."

A prolonged but muffled wailing caused her to pause. It was coming from a distant part of the house.

"The baby's awake. Go and see to her, Norman. It's better if I do this on my own."

"But . . ."

"Just go," said Amy Winter coldly. Her husband brushed past Juliet and left the room. Amy managed to look Tim in the eye.

"I know the authorities involved in Tristram Arkwright's case think there's something odd about it, something in the recorded facts that doesn't quite hang together. Tristram himself has tried to capitalise on this by saying he's the victim of a miscarriage of justice. He says the police account of what happened on the night they were all murdered doesn't add up. He's even tried to claim that Norman and I committed the murders to inherit his uncle's wealth. That's nonsense, of course. There can be no question that Tristram's a psychopath. He can be very charming; in fact, usually *is* charming on the surface, but once he bears a grudge against someone they're in danger. Tristram never liked Jackie very much – as a child he didn't see why his parents needed to adopt her when they already had him – and he was delighted when Aunt Jane more or less cut her off until after Grace was born. It made him doubly furious when Jackie was not only welcomed back into the family after Laura's birth but was given a lot of financial help.

"I don't know what sort of plan was forming in Tristram's mind, but I doubt he meant everyone to die. I think his main target was Jackie. And possibly Laura – he probably saw Laura as the reason for the softening of his parents' attitude to Jackie."

"What about Grace?"

"I don't understand the exact nature of his relationship

with Grace. Although he'd never liked children, he did show an interest in her. He took her out on his tractor and spent time talking to her. God knows what sorts of ideas he was putting into her head."

"Why do you say that?"

"Grace was devoted to Laura. Jackie could be a pretty slapdash mother and, even though Grace was only six, she spent a lot of time looking after her baby sister. Then something changed. She started resenting the baby and couldn't be trusted on her own with her."

"Did she harm Laura?"

"There were signs that she'd pinched her and pulled her hair. Jackie had always been an indulgent mother, but she clamped down pretty hard on Grace and Grace spent more and more time out of the house, usually with Tristram."

"What do *you* think happened on the night of the murders?"

"Oh, I don't think anything, DI Yates: I know what happened. I was there."

"What did you say?" Since their first meeting Tim had known that Amy Winter was withholding the truth about something, but he hadn't expected this.

"I was there. In the house. I'd been working late with Uncle Norman and they'd persuaded me to stay for supper. It was a long drive home and I'd had a couple of glasses of wine. It wasn't unusual for me to stay: there was a bed made up for me in the attic that I used quite frequently. I told the police this."

"But you didn't tell the police you were in the house that night."

"No. In my defence, they didn't ask."

"If you were there, why didn't Arkwright kill you as well?"

"He would have done if I'd not stayed where I was until later. He didn't know I'd decided to sleep there that night. I heard shouting and I knew it was Tristram. Then I listened to all the shots and waited until everything was quiet before I left the attic. I found the bodies of Uncle and Aunt and Jackie. It was clear they were dead: there was nothing I could do for them. I couldn't see either of the children, so I went downstairs to look for them."

"The baby's body was concealed by Jackie's."

"Yes, but I didn't know that then. I thought either he'd spared them or perhaps Grace had taken Laura and hidden somewhere."

"Was Arkwright still there?"

"Yes, I went into the kitchen and heard voices coming from the scullery beyond it. Tristram was persuading Grace to hide in the big old cupboard in there. I could hear what he was saying quite clearly. He was telling her that she'd done the right thing, that together they would get what they deserved. He was talking to her as if she were an adult."

"What was Grace's reaction?"

"At first, she was afraid of getting into the cupboard, but he told her it wouldn't be for long. She seemed to trust him. He said that he would come back with the police and if they asked her questions she should say she couldn't remember anything."

"Was that all he said?"

"Just a minute, I need a cigarette."

Amy reached for her handbag and took out a packet of Rothmans. She removed a cigarette and lit it shakily, dragging the smoke deep into her lungs.

"No. He made Grace promise never to tell anyone what he had done. He said she knew she could trust him; that he would never . . ." Amy's face twisted . . . "he would never tell anyone that Grace had killed Laura."

"Christ!" said Juliet, sitting down heavily on the outcrop of sofa.

Amy grinned hideously.

"Funny, that's just what I said. That's when Tristram realised I was there."

"What did he do?"

"He shut Grace in the cupboard swiftly and came into the kitchen before I could escape. I was terrified. I didn't know what he'd done with the guns; if he still had one of them, I was in no doubt he'd kill me, too, especially after what I'd just heard. But he was eerily calm, almost friendly, even though we'd never seen eye to eye. He told me to go home and keep my mouth shut, not to tell anyone. He said that if I did he'd say I was his accomplice and Grace would back him up. He said he'd come to see me as soon as he could, to 'sort a few things out'."

"Did you do as he said?"

"Yes. I ran for my car, which was in the barn, in my night-clothes and drove home. I wasn't going to tell anyone, not even Norman, but I collapsed in my own kitchen. Norman came down and found me. I had to tell him then and make him promise to keep it a secret. He wanted to go to the police. We argued about it, but then Tristram was charged with the murders and he agreed there was no point in complicating matters by admitting I'd been there."

"You mean, you realised that you would be the main beneficiaries if he was convicted and you were both worried that if he implicated you that might jeopardise your inheritance?"

"If you want to put it like that. But don't forget there was also Grace to consider."

"Ah, yes, Grace. I'm still quite a long way from understanding why you decided to adopt her."

"She'd lost everyone close to her. Even if it was true that she'd killed Laura, I wanted to give her a chance. She'd had a weird childhood with Jackie, and I was convinced Tristram had corrupted her. I thought perhaps with care and kindness she could turn into a normal child."

"Admirable! But there doesn't seem to have been much actual warmth in your relationship. She always calls you 'Mrs Winter' when she talks about you. Are you sure there was no other reason?"

"What other reason could there have been?"

"Arkwright asked to see you while he was awaiting trial, didn't he? And he'd already had the opportunity to speak to Grace while she was in hospital, being checked over. I've no doubt he talked her into accepting you as her stepmother. I'm more intrigued about how he persuaded you to accept her. I assume he blackmailed you by threatening to tell the police you were an accessory?"

Amy took another drag of her cigarette and nodded.

"Did you know he told Grace that he was her father?"

Amy couldn't have been faking the scorn and revulsion she immediately showed.

"What nonsense! Why would he do that?"

"To keep a hold on Grace. To make her do what he wanted. I think you're right when you say he corrupted her. He persuaded her to kill Laura because he had some half-baked plan of using it as insurance if suspicion fell on him. I think his intention originally had just been to kill Jackie, but he was rather obviously the most likely culprit. If he could sow discord within Jackie's little family, perhaps even engineer an attack by Jackie on Grace, he could throw doubt on his sister's sanity and claim that she'd killed herself. His parents were collateral victims: they simply got in the way. He's still trying to claim that he's innocent, but it's the parents' deaths he can't explain. He's attempting to get the case reviewed again. This time, I think he'll reveal that Grace killed Laura."

"If he does that, will it mean she can't come back here?"

"Ever with an eye to your own situation, aren't you, Mrs Winter? As a matter of fact, I sympathise with you this time. I assume you asked Tina Brackenbury to foster Grace because you were afraid she'd hurt your own child?"

"Yes. Any mother would have done the same."

"Not many mothers have to make that decision, though, do they? And what about Tina herself? As a mother, didn't you feel you owed it to her to warn her of the danger when you found out she was pregnant?"

"Are you saying that Grace killed Bluebelle?"

"Were you ever in any doubt about that?"

"I . . . no, I suppose not. I tried not to admit it to myself. But Grace couldn't have killed Tina: she wouldn't have been strong enough."

"No, but Grace has an excellent memory, and she relied on her experience. She found an accomplice: an older male who could help her."

Amy Winter suddenly clutched her throat and, leaning forward, vomited all over her extraordinary sofa.

Chapter 77

IT IS THE middle of the evening when Tim drops me off at my flat. Since the final interview with Chloe, I've yearned to be alone. I need time to make sense of what's happened.

I'm cold, though the evening is warm. I need a hot drink, but have no energy to fill the kettle. I sit on the edge of my sofa, shivering as if I have 'flu. I'm numb. My feelings have evaporated: I have no more pity or anger left. Only despair.

I rest my head sideways against the arm of the sofa and close my eyes. Grace's extraordinary beauty floats before me. Her lovely face fills my vision, shimmeringly pretty until she scowls and disappears.

I can't cope with the exhaustion. I have to sleep. I open my eyes again. They're stinging. I put my fingers to my cheek and am surprised that it's sticky with tears. I cover my face with my hands and sob.

It's impossible to stop.

I have no recollection of time passing, of how long I'm slumped there. I'm wrenched back to consciousness by the insistent ringing of the telephone. It's on a table right beside me. I decide not to answer, then change my mind. What if it's someone asking for help for Grace?

I lift the receiver. Nancy's no-nonsense Cockney voice comes booming out at me.

"Juliet? 'Ow's your case going? Any chance you might get a couple of hours off over the weekend? I fought I might come to see you on Sunday."

It's not her fault, but her joviality, the sheer ordinariness of her tone, grates.

"Nancy, I'm sorry, but I can't . . . I'm just sorry, that's all."

"Oh, I see." There's an ugly silence. Then the click of the phone as she ends the call.

I stand up, holding on to the arm of the sofa. I'm very shaky. I make it to the tap and fill a glass with water, which I gulp down so fast it hurts my throat. I stare at my face in the speckled little mirror that hangs over the sink. My eyes stare back, bloodshot, my cheeks dirty with tears. My hair is frizzing out in all directions. I am a mess. I'm thirty-five years old and I've never understood less what I'm doing with my life. I'm drained of any sense of purpose.

I realise it's not just because of Grace: it's been happening for a long time. I'd hoped I'd find the DS job inspiring, but it's the same old grind, in the same small town. I need to break out of this, to do something different.

A sharp tinny sound bursts into my thoughts. It's the doorbell. I edge across to the wall and flatten myself against it. It's probably Tim, come back to see how I am because Katrin's berated him for leaving me alone, or perhaps it's Katrin herself. I don't want to see either of them.

The letterbox rattles.

"DS Armstrong? Juliet? Are you there?"

It takes me a couple of seconds to recognise the voice. It's Jake Fidler. He'll know about Grace now: I asked Andy to call him and explain why we wouldn't be returning to the flat at the children's home.

"Juliet?" He persists. He's hammering on the door now. I move closer to it.

"What's the matter? I can't let you in, I'm not well."

"I guessed. That's why I've come. And because I owe you an apology."

"Why aren't you at work?"

"Someone else is doing the night shift. Open the door, Juliet – it's ridiculous talking through it like this."

I try to rub the grime from my face as I'm turning the latch.

"Don't look too closely," I begin, "I'm . . ."

Jake has already enveloped me in a massive hug. I'm afraid I'll cry again.

"Don't," I say, "I can't bear any more tears."

He tightens his grip before, slowly, he releases me. He holds me at arm's length, inspecting my face.

"I don't think you'll cry any more," he says, "but it's ok if you do. What do you expect, after all you've been through this week?"

"I don't want you to feel sorry for me!"

"I'm not. I wanted to make sure you were all right."

"You said you wanted to apologise. You don't have anything to apologise about."

"I do, unfortunately. But first let me make you some tea. Have you had anything to eat lately? Today, even?"

I try to think back to breakfast at the children's home flat, but my memory is blank.

"I'm not sure. But I'm not hungry."

"I'll settle for your drinking tea for now. Later, we'll see."

He leads me to the sofa. I lean back on the cushions and watch him as he negotiates my kitchen as if he's lived here

384

for years. He carries across two mugs of tea, hands me one of them and moves one of the dining chairs so that as he sits down he's facing me.

"Thank you for coming. I thought I didn't want to be alone, but I was wrong."

"I wanted to come. And I promised Marie that I would."

"*Marie?* How have you managed to talk to her? She was going to look after Grace until they found somewhere secure to keep her. Did she come back to the children's home after that?"

"No. She called me. They're holding Grace in the hospital unit at HMP Peterborough, in case you didn't know. It's hardly ideal, but better than putting her in a young offenders' institution. There's a policewoman with her. Someone from the Peterborough force, I think."

"I thought Marie might have wanted to stay with her."

"She may have done, but it has to be a police officer. And Marie's already compromised herself; that's why she gave me your address. Besides that, she's in bits, as you can imagine."

"How has she compromised herself? Do you mean, because she knew more than she let on when we first saw Grace?"

"No, she had a right to claim patient confidentiality there, misguided though it may have been. I'm talking about something much more recent. Something I helped with."

"Go on," I say unsteadily.

"You know I told you I thought Grace had something to do with Sasha's death. Well, Marie went into her bedroom and found blood on the sheets. And some clumps of the cat's hair. She told me about it and we decided to remove the evidence. Marie took the sheets home with her and laundered them. I provided some clean ones."

"That explains why she was in such a hurry to get away yesterday. But I don't understand why you condoned it. You told me yourself you thought Grace needed help."

"She did – does – need help. But Marie and I were both prepared to give her the benefit of the doubt about Sasha. Marie asked her about the blood and she said she'd found the cat injured and tried to look after it, but it had run away from her. She didn't try to imply that Finn was responsible, so in a way that let them both off the hook. We still don't know if it *was* Grace, though it's hard to believe otherwise. And of course we didn't know who had killed Tina and Bluebelle Brackenbury at that time, though I think Marie and I both had a nagging fear Grace was involved."

"I know. I was hoping against hope you were wrong." Unexpectedly a wave of anger consumes me. I have no patience with Jake's mealy-mouthed do-gooding. "Do you know what makes me really annoyed?" I shout. "It's that everyone, ever since the Brocklesby Farm murders, has pussyfooted round Grace, 'giving her the benefit of the doubt', as you say, without having the courage to get to grips with the fact that she was a child who'd been deeply damaged by Tristram Arkwright and in urgent need of help. You're all as bad as one another: Marie, Lenka Astani, Amy Winter and her husband, Tom Tarrant, you, Tim, everyone! I daresay Tina Brackenbury ignored some warning signals, too, though God knows she paid for it."

I expect Jake to capitulate, to admit that he's been weak. Instead, he grabs my wrist.

"Look at me, Juliet." I snatch my wrist away.

"Look at me," he says again.

Reluctantly, my eyes meet his, which are clear and blazing with conviction.

"What about you? You felt uneasy about Grace right from the start. You told me so. Did you try to do anything about that? Did you try to help her?"

"I'm a police officer, not a social worker. I cared for her as best I could. I volunteered to stay in that flat with her. It was my job to keep her safe, not to mess with her mind."

"That's the problem, isn't it? Every one of the people you mention was responsible for her physical or mental safety, or her day-to-day care, or some other fragment of her life, but no-one wanted to take on board what she had become. 'Preternatural', wasn't that how you described her? Not just her name, her identity, but her whole character had changed and everyone chose to ignore it. Grace herself understood. She was clever: she succeeded in ingratiating herself with women like Tina Brackenbury and Mavis Hebblewhite, even with Marie; other children like Chloe and Jagger were no match for her. She was less successful with Amy Winter: they knew too much about each other. I'd guess they were both relieved when Amy decided to ditch her. Only Amy realised that the real Grace Arkwright slipped away years ago, had perhaps been destroyed by her uncle well before her mother and sister died. Grace Winter has replaced her. Until we understand who Grace Winter is, we'll never be able to help her. And we're all guilty of neglecting her and children like her."

Chapter 78

T IM HAD ASKED Juliet, Marie and Tom to meet him early the following day, prior to a formal meeting with Superintendent Thornton to decide what to tell the Press.

"What will happen to Grace now?" Juliet asked.

"And Jagger," said Tom. "Let's not forget him. He's been a tearaway since he was a primary school kid and likely always to have been on the wrong side of the law, but, left to his own devices, I doubt he'd have become a murderer."

"That's certainly what his mother thinks," said Tim, "and she's furious with Chloe for grassing on him, as she puts it. You're going to have to keep a close watch on Chloe, make sure she isn't mistreated."

"We will," said Tom, "but I doubt if Mavis is capable of intentional cruelty. She'll be devastated about Jagger, even so. He's definitely her favourite."

"Will Chloe be strong enough to testify in court?" asked Juliet.

"I don't think anyone will want to put her through that. We've got the tapes and the forensic evidence. If necessary, the judge will question her via videolink."

"Do you think Grace will be tried, then?"

"No. To answer your first question, I'm pretty certain she will be committed to psychiatric care in a secure unit, if somewhere suitable can be found. There aren't many such facilities for children. It's Jagger who'll have to stand trial.

There's nothing to suggest that his mind is disturbed – though I'm sure his defence will try that argument. Or they'll say that Grace was the ringleader – which she almost undoubtedly was, even though she's four or five years younger."

"What about Arkwright? Will anyone challenge him about Grace?"

"Whoever's put in charge of Grace's welfare will probably ask for a paternity test, though no-one seems to think he's really her father. It'll be up to the CPS to decide whether to charge him and/or Amy Winter with perverting the course of justice. If they are charged, I think it's unlikely that she'll get a custodial sentence. But Grace's guardians will have a strong case for demanding her mother's share of the Arkwright estate on her behalf when she reaches maturity."

"What if Grace never recovers?" asked Marie.

"I'm not a lawyer, but I don't think that will make any difference. The money can still be used to maintain her. The Crown could make a claim on it now for that purpose, come to think of it."

"What kind of hold do you think Arkwright had over Grace?"

"Amy Winter says she changed after he started taking an interest in her. And I'm sure she believes he's her father. Whether he found a way of communicating with her after he went inside is unclear. According to Jeremy Forster, he had some convoluted plan of appealing against his conviction yet again and I think he intended it to involve Grace; although why he thought he would be acquitted for the other three Brocklesby murders simply by proving that Grace killed Laura is beyond me."

Superintendent Thornton came bustling into the room.

"Everyone here bright and early, I see. Thank you for that. Now we have to decide what to say to the Press, which could be a little tricky. Never mind: I'm here to tell you that the Chief Constable sends his congratulations. He's really pleased that the case has been solved."

Chapter 79

IT WAS AFTER midnight. He'd been lying weakly in his bunk since lights out. Now he raised himself on one elbow and cautiously lifted the bedclothes. He'd wrapped a wad of J-cloths round the slash in his thigh where Jacobs had stabbed him. He peeled back the makeshift dressing. It was pitch black and he couldn't see, but he could feel the blood still oozing out of him. He clamped the wad back into place and pressed on it as tightly as he could. He'd not reported Jacobs or the injury because he wanted to knife the fucker back tomorrow, but now he could see that he'd have to tell Jack Rose when he showed up in the morning. He lay down again, holding the blankets away from the wound as best he could, and tried to sleep. Grace Arkwright's lovely face floated in and out of his delirium.

Contents

Acknowledgements

YET AGAIN I find it impossible to express how much I owe to Chris and Jen Hamilton-Emery for their unbounded enthusiasm for and faith in the DI Yates novels. Once more, Chris has provided a beautiful jacket; his distinguished typesetting remains the hallmark of my and indeed all Salt novels. I'd also like to thank others who contribute to Salt's successes, including Hannah Corbett, its very distinguished publicist, and Medwyn Hughes and Julian Ball, of PGUK, and their amazing representatives who work with booksellers right across the UK to get the books into the shops.

No writer can claim to be an author without readers. From the bottom of my heart I'd like to thank all of you, including those whom I've actually met, those of you who have taken the trouble to 'meet' me or review my books with such generosity on my blog or on social networks, and everyone who has bought or borrowed my books to read. You are a constant source of inspiration to me.

There are many other people whom I ought to thank here, but as much as I'd like to it's impossible to mention everyone. As always, I'd especially like to single out Sally, who has continually been a staunch supporter and who has provided me with a base in London for many years; and Madelaine and Marc, who are my chief champions in Lincolnshire. Once again, I'd like to record my appreciation for the talented Alison Cassels at Wakefield One and her canny and lively reading groups and Sam Buckley and her reading groups at Bookmark in Spalding, who have followed DI Yates from 'birth'. This year I'd also like to thank Sharman Morriss, who has been promoting my books in Spalding Library and indeed in libraries right across Lincolnshire. Others who have helped me are too numerous to mention, but I can't conclude without expressing my gratitude to Richard Reynolds of Heffer's bookshop in Cambridge, whose knowledge of crime writing and support of crime fiction writers, including myself, is second to none; Tim Walker and Jenny Pugh, of Walker Books in Stamford; and Janet Heneghan, who has several times invited me to speak at the Winchester Literary Festival.

The members of my family continue to provide their unique brand of support. Once again James and Annika have worked meticulously through the final draft, picking up grammatical inaccuracies and other minor inconsistencies with hawk-like precision, and assiduously checking on my behalf the details of such diverse matters as bus timetables, calendars and the properties of electronic devices. Emma continues to teach me what language is all about. And Chris offers the occasional succinct word of praise, appreciated both for its rarity and its perspicacity.

My very sincere thanks to you all.

CHRISTINA JAMES